Bestselling authors
Diana Palmer and Joan Johnston
celebrate the magic of the holidays
with four sparkling tales of forever love in a
special 4-in-1 collection

## LONE STAR CHRISTMAS...
## AND OTHER GIFTS

**CHRISTMAS COWBOY by Diana Palmer**

Ironhearted Corrigan Hart would never admit how much enticing innocent Dorie Wayne meant to him—until a fateful Christmas encounter brought him face-to-face with his long-lost love....

**REDBIRD by Diana Palmer**

It was a case of mistaken identity when hot-tempered Hank Shoeman abducted Poppy O'Brien. Only, his smitten captive wasn't exactly clamoring to get out of his clutches!

**A HAWK'S WAY CHRISTMAS by Joan Johnston**

Over the holidays, sexy single father Gavin Talbot agreed to pose as pregnant Rolleen Whitelaw's doting fiancé. Of course, neither expected their romantic ruse to change both their lives forever....

**TAMING THE LONE WOLF by Joan Johnston**

Everyone thought a lone wolf like Stony Carlton would never, ever be tied down. Trouble was, no one counted on fiery-haired beauty Tess Lowell catching his eye—and taming his elusive heart!

# DIANA PALMER

# JOAN JOHNSTON

## LONE STAR

### *Christmas...*

## AND OTHER GIFTS

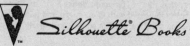

*Silhouette* Books

Published by Silhouette Books
**America's Publisher of Contemporary Romance**

 SILHOUETTE BOOKS

LONE STAR CHRISTMAS...AND OTHER GIFTS

Copyright © 1999 by Harlequin Books S.A.

ISBN 0-373-48386-4

The publisher acknowledges the copyright holders of the individual works as follows:

CHRISTMAS COWBOY
Copyright © 1997 by Diana Palmer

REDBIRD
Copyright © 1995 by Diana Palmer
Text revised for Lone Star Christmas...And Other Gifts.

A HAWK'S WAY CHRISTMAS
Copyright © 1997 by Joan Mertens Johnston, Inc.

TAMING THE LONE WOLF
Copyright © 1995 by Joan Mertens Johnston

Visit us at www.romance.net

**Printed in U.S.A.**

# CONTENTS

## DIANA PALMER:

With over 10 million copies of her books in print, bestselling, award-winning author Diana Palmer is one of North America's most beloved authors. She got her start in writing as a newspaper reporter and published her first romance novel for Silhouette Books in 1982. In 1993 she celebrated the publication of her fiftieth novel for Silhouette Books. *Affaire de Coeur* lists her as one of the top ten romance authors in the country. Diana Palmer is the winner of numerous national Waldenbooks Romance Bestseller awards and national B. Dalton Books Bestseller awards. Her fans the world over treasure her sensual and charming stories.

Diana Palmer's next original novel, *Paper Rose*, will be published in December 1999 by MIRA Books. At the beginning of 2000, look for Diana Palmer's return to Silhouette Special Edition. And in April 2000, this beloved author helps Silhouette celebrate its 20<sup>th</sup> anniversary with *Soldiers of Fortune*, a special collection of three full-length novels, with an original spin-off available from Silhouette Romance in May 2000.

## JOAN JOHNSTON:

Bestselling author Joan Johnston is the celebrated author of more than 35 books and novellas, which have appeared on national bestseller lists more than 50 times and have been translated into 19 languages in 25 countries worldwide. Joan writes historical and contemporary romance, and has won numerous awards for her work from the Romance Writers of America, Georgia Romance Writers and *Romantic Times Magazine*.

# Christmas Cowboy

## by Diana Palmer

Dear Reader,

The Hart boys dropped out of thin air and onto my
computer screen for the first time back in 1996. It was a
special Christmas for us that year because my husband,
James, had just had emergency open heart surgery in February
to replace two failed mechanical valves. When the Harts came
out in "Christmas Cowboy" during Christmas of 1997 in *A
Lone Star Christmas,* a hardcover duet I did with Joan Johnston,
I knew that it wouldn't end with just Corrigan's story. Sure
enough, Simon Hart was featured in a Silhouette Desire novel,
*Beloved,* and Callaghan showed up in a Silhouette Romance
book, *Callaghan's Bride,* both in 1998. I still haven't written
books for Rey and Leo, but they'll be along one day.

"Redbird," which is also featured in this special 4-in-1
collection, was one of my favorites from way back. It was
delightful to get to go back and add a whole new scene to it.
Very rarely do authors get to amend or add to an existing book,
so this was a great pleasure. I hope you like the result.

The thought of Christmas has gotten me through some very
tough times in my life, especially these past two years when I
have faced serious problems not of my making. I am privileged
to have such a broad base of reader support among those of
you who read romance novels. You can't imagine how much
difference you make in my life with your letters and cards, and
your prayers. I treasure each and every one of you. Thank you
for your kindness, and your friendship.

Also, a heartfelt thank-you goes to my wonderful Cornelia (GA)
Police Department, to whom the original "Christmas Cowboy"
story was dedicated. The tree decorated with blue lights in
my yard every Christmas is for them, a brand-new holiday
tradition in my family. They are real heroes, men and women
alike. I treasure them as I treasure my readers, and I remember
them, and you, in my prayers. God bless all of you, and
Merry Christmas!

*Diana Palmer*

To the men and women
of the Cornelia Police Department

OKLAHOMA

ARKANSAS

NEW
MEXICO

Dallas ●

Fort Worth ●

TEXAS

Austin
★

Houston ●

San Antonio ●

<u>Jacobsville</u>

Victoria ●

Gulf of
Mexico

N

MEXICO

All underlined places are fictitious.

# Chapter 1

It was the holiday season in Jacobsville, Texas. Gaily colored strands of lights crisscrossed the main street, and green garlands and wreaths graced each telephone pole along the way. In the center of town, all the small maple trees that grew out of square beds at intervals along the sidewalk were decorated with lights as well.

People were bundled in coats, because even in south Texas it was cold in late November. They rushed along with shopping bags full of festively wrapped presents to go under the tree. And over on East Main Street, the Optimist Club had its yearly Christmas tree lot open already. A family of four was browsing its sawdust-covered grounds, early enough to have the pick of the beautifully shaped fir trees, just after Thanksgiving.

Dorie Wayne gazed at her surroundings the way a child would look through a store window at toys she couldn't afford. Her hand went to the thin scar down an otherwise perfect cheek and she shivered. How long ago it seemed that she stood right here on this street corner in front of the Jacobsville Drugstore, and backed away from Corrigan Hart. It had been an instinctive move; at eighteen, he'd frightened her. He was so very masculine, a mature man with a cold temper and an iron will. He'd set his sights on Dorie, who found him fearful instead of attractive, despite the fact that any single woman hereabouts would have gone to him on her knees.

She recalled his jet black hair and pale, metallic eyes. She'd wondered at first if it wasn't her fairness that attracted him, because he was so dark. Dorie had hair so blond it was almost platinum, and it was cut short, falling into natural thick waves. Her complexion was delicate and fair, and she had big gray eyes, just a shade darker than Corrigan's. He was very handsome—unlike his brothers. At least, that was what people said. Dorie hadn't gotten to meet the others when she left Jacobsville. And only Corrigan and three of his brothers lived in Jacobsville. The fifth Hart male wasn't talked about, ever. His name wasn't even known locally.

Corrigan and three of his four brothers had come down to Jacobsville from San Antonio eight years ago to take over the rich cattle operation their grandfather had left to them in his will.

It had been something of a local joke that the Harts had no hearts, because they seemed immune to women. They kept to themselves and there was no gossip about them with women. But that changed when Dorie attended a local square dance and found herself whirling around the floor in Corrigan Hart's arms.

Never one to pull his punches, he made his intentions obvious right at the start. He found her attractive. He was drawn to her. He wanted her. Just like that.

There was never any mention of marriage, engagement or even some furtive live-in arrangement. Corrigan said often that he wasn't the marrying kind. He didn't want ties. He made that very clear, because there was never any discussions of taking her to meet his brothers. He kept her away from their ranch.

But despite his aversion to relationships, he couldn't seem to see enough of Dorie. He wanted her and with every new kiss Dorie grew weaker and hungrier for him.

Then one spring day, he kissed her into oblivion, picked her up in his arms and carried her right into her own bedroom the minute her father left for his weekly poker game.

Despite the drugging effect of masterful kisses and the poignant trembling his expert hands aroused, Dorie had come to her senses just barely in time and pushed him away. Dazed, he'd looked down at her with stunned, puzzled eyes, only belatedly realizing that she was trying to get away, not closer.

She remembered, red-faced even now, how he'd pulled away and stood up, breathing raggedly, eyes blazing with frustrated desire. He'd treated her to a scalding lecture about girls who teased. She'd treated him to one about confirmed bachelors who wouldn't take no for an answer, especially since she'd told him she wasn't the sleep-around sort.

He didn't buy that, he'd told her coldly. She was just holding out for marriage, and there was no hope in that direction. He wanted to sleep with her, and she sure seemed to want him, too. But he didn't want her for keeps.

Dorie had been in love with him, and his emotional rejection had broken something fragile inside her. But she hadn't been about to let him see her pain.

He'd gone on, in the same vein. One insult had led to another, and once he'd gotten really worked up, he'd stormed out the door. His parting shot had been that she must be nuts if she thought he was going to buy her being a virgin. There was no such thing anymore, even at the young age of eighteen.

His rejection had closed doors between them. Dorie couldn't bear the thought of staying in Jacobsville and having everybody know that Corrigan Hart had thrown her aside because she wouldn't sleep with him. And everybody *would* know, somehow. They always knew the secret things in small towns.

That very night Dorie had made up her mind to take up her cousin Belinda's offer to come to New York and get into modeling. Certainly Dorie had the looks and figure for it. She might be young, but she had poise and grace and an exquisite face framed by short, wavy blond hair. Out of that face, huge gray eyes shone like beacons, mirroring happiness or sorrow.

After that sordid evening, Dorie cut her losses and bought a bus ticket.

She'd been standing right here, on this very corner, waiting for the bus to pick her up in front of this drugstore, when Corrigan had found her.

Her abrupt withdrawal from him had halted him in his tracks. Whatever he'd been going to say, her shamed refusal to look at him, combined with her backward steps, stopped him. She was still smarting from his angry words, as well as from her own uninhibited behavior. She was ashamed that she'd given him such license with her body now that she knew there had only been desire on his part.

He hadn't said a single word before the bus stopped for her. He hadn't said a word as she hurriedly gave her ticket to the driver, got on the bus and waited for it to leave without looking his way again. He'd stood there in the trickling rain, without even a raincoat, with his hands deep in his jean pockets, and watched the bus pull away from the curb. That was how Dorie had remembered him all the long years, a lonely fading figure in the distance.

She'd loved him desperately. But her own self-respect wouldn't let her settle for a furtive affair in the goldfish-bowl atmosphere of Jacobsville. She'd wanted a home, a husband, children, everything.

Corrigan had only wanted to sleep with her.

She'd gone, breathless and sick at heart, all the way to New York City, swearing her father to absolute secrecy about her movements.

There had been a letter, a few weeks after her arrival, from her father. In it, he told her that he'd seen Corrigan only once since her departure, and that he was now hot in pursuit of a rich divorcée with sophistication dripping from her fingers. If Dorie had any parting regrets about her decision to leave town, that was the end of them. Corrigan had made his feelings plain, if he was seeing some woman already.

Dorie wondered if her father hadn't said something unpleasant to Corrigan Hart about his daughter's sudden departure from home. It would have been like him. He was fiercely protective of his only child, especially since the death of her mother from heart disease some years past. And his opinion about philandering men was obvious to everyone.

He believed in the old-fashioned sort of courtship, the kind that ended in marriage. Only a handful of conventional people were left, he told Dorie over and over. Such people were the cornerstones of social order. If they all fell, chaos reigned. A man who loved a woman would want to give her, and his children, his name. And Corrigan, he added, had made it clear to the whole town that he wanted no part of marriage or a family. Dorie would have been asking for heartbreak if she'd given in to Corrigan's selfish demands.

Her father was dead now. Dorie had come home for the funeral as well as to dispose of the house and property and decide her own future. She'd started out with such hopes of becoming a successful model. Her eyes closed and she shivered unconsciously at the memories.

"Dorie?"

She turned at the hesitant sound of her name. The face took a little longer to recognize. "Abby?" she said. "Abby Clark!"

"Abby Ballenger," the other woman corrected with a grin. "I married Calhoun."

"Calhoun!" Dorie was momentarily floored. The younger Ballenger brother had been a rounder and a half, and he was married? And to Abby, of all people, the shy and sweet girl for whom Calhoun and Justin had shared guardianship following the death of their parents.

"Surprising, isn't it?" Abby asked, hugging the other woman. "And there's more. We have three sons."

"I haven't been away that long, have I?" Dorie asked hesitantly.

"Eight years," came the reply. Abby was a little older, but she still had the same pretty gray-blue eyes and dark hair, even if it had silver threads now. "Justin married Shelby Jacobs just after I married Calhoun. They have three sons, too," she added on a sigh. "Not a girl in the bunch."

Dorie shook her head. "For heaven's sake!"

"We heard that you were in modeling…" Her voice trailed away as she saw the obvious long scar on the once-perfect cheek. "What happened?"

Dorie's eyes were all but dead. "Not much. I decided that modeling wasn't for me." She laughed at some private joke. "I went back to school and completed a course in business. Now I work for a group of attorneys. I'm a stenographer." Her gaze fell. "Jacobsville hasn't changed a bit."

"Jacobsville never changes," Abby chuckled. "I find it comforting." The laughter went out of her eyes. "We all heard about your father. I'm sorry. It must have been a blow.''

''He'd been in the nursing home near me for some time, but he always said he wanted to be buried here. That's why I brought him home. I appreciated so many people coming to the funeral. It was kind.''

''I suppose you noticed one missing face in the crowd?'' Abby asked carefully, because she knew how persistent Corrigan Hart had been in his pursuit of Dorie.

''Yes.'' She twisted her purse in her hands. ''Are they still making jokes about the Hart boys?''

''More than ever. There's never been the slightest hint of gossip about any of them and a woman. I guess they're all determined to die single. Especially Corrigan. He's turned into a recluse. He stays out at the ranch all the time now. He's never seen.''

''Why?''

Abby seemed evasive. ''He doesn't mix and nobody knows much about his life. Odd, isn't it, in a town this small, where we mostly know each other's business, that he isn't talked about? But he stays out of sight and none of the other boys ever speak about him. He's become the original local mystery.''

''Well, don't look at me as if I'm the answer. He couldn't get rid of me fast enough,'' she said with a twinge of remaining bitterness.

''That's what you think. He became a holy terror in the weeks after you left town. Nobody would go near him.''

''He only wanted me,'' Dorie said doggedly.

Abby's eyes narrowed. ''And you were terrified of him,'' she recalled. ''Calhoun used to joke about it. You were such an innocent and Corrigan was a rounder. He said it was poetic justice that rakes got caught by innocents.''

''I remember Calhoun being a rake.''

''He was,'' Abby recalled. ''But not now. He's reformed.

He's the greatest family man I could have imagined, a dot-ing father and a wonderful husband.'' She sobered. ''I'm sorry things didn't work out for you and Corrigan. If you hadn't taken off like that, I think he might have decided that he couldn't live without you.''

''God forbid,'' she laughed, her eyes quick and nervous. ''He wasn't a marrying man. He said so, frequently. And I was raised…well, you know how Dad was. Ministers have a decidedly conventional outlook on life.''

''I know.''

''I haven't had such a bad time of it,'' she lied, grateful that her old friend couldn't read minds. She smiled. ''I like New York.''

''Do you have anyone there?''

''You mean a boyfriend, or what do they call it, a sig-nificant other?'' she murmured. ''No. I…don't have much to do with men.''

There was a strangely haunted look about her that Abby quickly dispelled with an offer of coffee and a sandwich in the local café.

''Yes, thanks, I'm not hungry but I'd love some hot chocolate.''

''Great!'' Abby said. ''I've got an hour to kill before I have to pick my two oldest boys up at school and the youn-gest from kindergarten. I'll enjoy your company.''

The café was all but empty. It was a slow day, and except for a disgruntled looking cowboy sitting alone at a corner table, it was deserted.

Barbara, the owner, took their orders with a grin. ''Nice to have pleasant company,'' she said, glaring toward the cowboy in the corner. ''He brought a little black cloud in with him, and it's growing.'' She leaned closer. ''He's one of the Hart employees,'' she whispered. ''Or, he was until this morning. It seems that Corrigan fired him.''

The sound of the man's name was enough to make Dorie's heart race, even after so many years. But she steeled herself not to let it show. She had nothing left to offer Corrigan, even if he was still interested in her. And that was a laugh. If he'd cared even a little, he'd have come to New York looking for her all those years ago.

"Fired him?" Abby glanced at the man and scowled. "But that's Buck Wyley," she protested. "He's the Harts' foreman. He's been with them since they came here."

"He made a remark Corrigan didn't like. He got knocked on his pants for his trouble and summarily fired." Barbara shrugged. "The Harts are all high-tempered, but until now I always thought Corrigan was fair. What sort of boss fires a man with Christmas only three weeks away?"

"Ebenezer Scrooge?" Abby ventured dryly.

"Buck said he cut another cowboy's wages to the bone for leaving a gate open." She shook her head. "Funny, we've heard almost nothing about Corrigan for years, and all of a sudden he comes back into the light like a smoldering madman."

"So I noticed," Abby said.

Barbara wiped her hands on a dishcloth. "I don't know what happened to set him off after so many years. The other brothers have been more visible lately, but not Corrigan. I'd wondered if he'd moved away for a while. Nobody even spoke of him." She glanced at Dorie with curious eyes. "You're Dorothy Wayne, aren't you?" she asked then, smiling. "I thought I recognized you. Sorry about your pa."

"Thanks," Dorie said automatically. She noticed how Barbara's eyes went to the thin scar on her cheek and flitted quickly away.

"I'll get your order."

Barbara went back behind the counter and Abby's puzzled gaze went to the corner.

"Having a bad day, Buck?" she called.

He sipped black coffee. "It couldn't get much worse, Mrs. Ballenger," he replied in a deep, pleasant tone. "I don't suppose Calhoun and Justin are hiring out at the feed-lot?"

"They'd hire you in a minute, and you know it," Abby told him. She smiled. "Why don't you go out there and…"

"Oh, the devil!" Buck muttered, his black eyes flashing. He got to his feet and stood there, vibrating, as a tall, lean figure came through the open door.

Dorie actually caught her breath. The tall man was familiar to her, even after all those years. Dressed in tight jeans, with hand-tooled boots and a chambray shirt and a neat, spotless white Stetson atop his black hair, he looked formidable, even with the cane he was using for support.

He didn't look at the table where Dorie was sitting, which was on the other side of the café from Buck.

"You fired me," Buck snapped at him. "What do you want, another punch at me? This time, you'll get it back in spades, gimpy leg or not!"

Corrigan Hart just stared at the man, his pale eyes like chrome sparkling in sunlight.

"Those purebred Angus we got from Montana are coming in by truck this morning," he said. "You're the only one who knows how to use the master program for the computerized herd records."

"And you need me," Buck agreed with a cold smile. "For how long?"

"Two weeks," came the curt reply. "You'll work that long for your severance pay. If you're still of a mind to quit."

"Quit, hell!" Buck shot back, astonished. "You fired me!"

"I did not!" the older man replied curtly. "I said you could mind your own damned business or get out."

Buck's head turned and he stared at the other man for a

minute. "If I come back, you'd better keep your fists to yourself from now on," he said shortly.

The other man didn't blink. "You know why you got hit."

Buck glanced warily toward Dorie and a ruddy color ran along his high cheekbones. "I never meant it the way you took it," he retorted.

"You'll think twice before you presume to make such remarks to me again, then, won't you?"

Buck made a movement that his employer took for assent.

"And your Christmas bonus is now history!" he added.

Buck let out an angry breath, almost spoke, but crushed his lips together finally in furious submission.

"Go home!" the older man said abruptly.

Buck pulled his hat over his eyes, tossed a dollar bill on the table with his coffee cup and strode out with barely a tip of the hat to the women present, muttering under his breath as he went.

The door closed with a snap. Corrigan Hart didn't move. He stood very still for a moment, as if steeling himself.

Then he turned, and his pale eyes stared right into Dorie's. But the anger in them eclipsed into a look of such shock that Dorie blinked.

"What happened to you?" he asked shortly.

She knew what he meant without asking. She put a hand self-consciously to her cheek. "An accident," she said stiffly.

His chin lifted. The tension in the café was so thick that Abby shifted uncomfortably at the table.

"You don't model now," he continued.

The certainty in the statement made her miserable. "No. Of course I don't."

He leaned heavily on the cane. "Sorry about your father," he said curtly.

She nodded.

His face seemed pinched as he stared at her. Even across the room, the heat in the look was tangible to Dorie. Her hands holding the mug of hot chocolate went white at the knuckles from the pressure of them around it.

He glanced at Abby. "How are things at the feedlot?"

"Much as usual," she replied pleasantly. "Calhoun and Justin are still turning away business. Nice, in the flat cattle market this fall."

"I agree. We've culled as many head as possible and we're venturing into new areas of crossbreeding. Nothing but purebreds now. We're hoping to pioneer a new breed."

"Good for you," Abby replied.

His eyes went back to Dorie. They lingered on her wan face, her lack of spirit. "How long are you going to stay?" he asked.

The question was voiced in such a way it seemed like a challenge. Her shoulders rose and fell. "Until I tie up all the loose ends, I suppose. They've given me two weeks off at the law firm where I work."

"As an attorney?"

She shook her head. "A stenographer."

He scowled. "With your head for figures?" he asked shortly.

Her gaze was puzzled. She hadn't realized that he was aware of her aptitude for math.

"It's a waste," he persisted. "You'd have been a natural at bookkeeping and marketing."

She'd often thought so, too, but she hadn't pursued her interest in that field. Especially after her first attempt at modeling.

He gave her a calculating stare. "Clarisse Marston has opened a boutique in town. She designs women's clothes and has them made up at a local textile plant. She sells all over the state."

"Yes," Abby added. "In fact, she's now doing a lot of designing for Todd Burke's wife, Jane—you know, her signature rodeo line of sportswear."

"I've heard of it, even in New York," Dorie admitted.

"The thing Clarisse doesn't have is someone to help her with marketing and bookkeeping." He shook his head. "It amazes me that she hasn't gone belly-up already."

Abby started to speak, but the look on Corrigan's face silenced her. She only smiled at Dorie.

"This is your home," Corrigan persisted quietly. "You were born and raised in Jacobsville. Surely having a good job here would be preferable to being a stenographer in New York. Unless," he added slowly, "there's some reason you want to stay there."

His eyes were flashing. Dorie looked into the film on her cooling hot chocolate. "I don't have anyone in New York." She shifted her legs. "I don't have anyone here, either, now."

"But you do," Abby protested. "All your friends."

"Of course, she may miss the bright lights and excitement," Corrigan drawled.

She looked at him curiously. He was trying to goad her. Why?

"Is Jacobsville too small for you now, city girl?" he persisted with a mocking smile.

"No, it isn't that at all," she said. She cleared her throat.

"Come home," Abby coaxed.

She didn't answer.

"Still afraid of me?" Corrigan asked with a harsh laugh when her head jerked up. "That's why you left. Is it why you won't come back?"

She colored furiously, the first trace of color that had shown in her face since the strange conversation began.

"I'm not...afraid of you!" she faltered.

But she was, and he knew it. His silver eyes narrowed

and that familiar, mocking smile turned up his thin upper lip. "Prove it."

"Maybe Miss Marston doesn't want a bookkeeper."

"She does," he returned.

She hesitated. "She might not like me."

"She will."

She let out an exasperated sigh. "I can't make a decision that important in a few seconds," she told him. "I have to think about it."

"Take your time," he replied. "Nobody's rushing you."

"It would be lovely if you came back, though," Abby said with a smile. "No matter how many friends we have, we can always use one more."

"Exactly," Corrigan told her. His eyes narrowed. "Of course, you needn't consider me in your decision. I'm not trying to get you to come back for my sake. But I'm sure there are plenty of other bachelors left around here who'd be delighted to give you a whirl, if you needed an incentive."

His lean face was so hard and closed that not one flicker of emotion got away from it.

Abby was eyeing him curiously, but she didn't say a word, not even when her gaze fell to his hand on the silver knob of the cane and saw it go white from the pressure.

He eased up on the handle, just the same. "Well?"

"I'd like to," Dorie said quietly. She didn't look at him. Odd, how his statement had hurt, after all those years. She looked back on the past with desperation these days, wondering how her life would have been if she hadn't resisted him that night he'd tried to carry her to bed.

She hadn't wanted an affair, but he was an honorable man, in his fashion. Perhaps he would have followed up with a proposal, despite his obvious distaste for the married state. Or perhaps he wouldn't have. There might have been a child...

She grimaced and lifted the cup of chocolate to her lips. It was tepid and vaguely distasteful.

"Go see Clarisse, why don't you?" he added. "You've nothing to lose, and a lot to gain. She's a sweet woman. You'll like her."

Did he? She didn't dare wonder about that, or voice her curiosity. "I might do that," she replied.

The tap of the cane seemed unusually loud as he turned back to the door. "Give the brothers my best," Corrigan told Abby. He nodded and was gone.

Only then did Dorie look up, her eyes on his tall, muscular body as he walked carefully back to the big double-cabbed black ranch pickup truck he drove.

"What happened to him?" Dorie asked.

Abby sipped her own hot chocolate before she answered. "It happened the week after you left town. He went on a hunting trip in Montana with some other men. During a heavy, late spring snow, Corrigan and another man went off on their own in a four-wheel-drive utility vehicle to scout another section of the hunting range."

"And?" Dorie prompted.

"The truck went over a steep incline and overturned. The other man was killed outright. Corrigan was pinned and couldn't get free. He lay there most of the night and into the next day before the party came looking for them and found him. By that time, he was unconscious. The impact broke his leg in two places, and he had frostbite as well. He almost died."

Dorie caught her breath. "How horrible!"

"They wanted to amputate the leg, but..." she shrugged. "He refused them permission to operate, so they did the best they could. The leg is usable, just, but it will always be stiff. They said later that it was a miracle he didn't lose any toes. He had just enough sense left to wrap himself in one of those thin thermal sheets the men had carried on the trip. It saved him from a dangerous frostbite.''

''Poor man.''

''Oh, don't make that mistake,'' Abby mused. ''Nobody is allowed to pity Corrigan Hart. Just ask his brothers.''

''All the same, he never seemed the sort of man to lose control of anything, not even a truck.''

''He wasn't himself but he didn't lose control, either.''

''I beg your pardon?''

Abby grimaced. ''He and the other man, the one who was driving, had been drinking. He blamed himself not only for the wreck, but for the other man's death. He knew the man wasn't fit to drive but he didn't try to stop him. They say he's been punishing himself ever since. That's why he never comes into town, or has any social life. He's withdrawn into himself and nobody can drag him back out. He's become a hermit.''

''But, why?''

''Why was he drinking, you mean?'' Abby said, and Dorie nodded. Still, Abby hesitated to put it into words.

''Tell me,'' came the persistent nudge from Dorie.

Abby's eyes were apologetic. ''Nobody knows, really. But the gossip was that he was trying to get over losing you.''

# Chapter 2

"But he wanted to lose me," Dorie exclaimed, shocked. "He couldn't get out of my house fast enough when I refused...refused him," she blurted. She clasped her hands together. "He accused me of being frigid and a tease..."

"Corrigan was a rounder, Dorie," Abby said gently. "In this modern age, even in Jacobsville, a lot of girls are pretty sophisticated at eighteen. He wouldn't have known about your father being a minister, because he'd retired from the church before the Harts came to take over their grandfather's ranch. He was probably surprised to find you less accommodating than other girls."

"Surprised wasn't the word," Dorie said miserably. "He was furious."

"He did go to the bus depot when you left."

"How did you know that?"

"Everybody talked about it," Abby admitted. "It was generally thought that he went there to stop you."

"He didn't say a word," came the quiet reply. "Not one word."

"Maybe he didn't know what to say. He was probably embarrassed and upset about the way he'd treated you. A man like that might not know what to do with an innocent girl."

Dorie laughed bitterly. "Sure he did. You see her off and hope she won't come back. He told me that he had no intention of marrying."

"He could have changed his mind."

Dorie shook her head. "Not a chance. He never talked about us being a couple. He kept reminding me that I was young and that he liked variety. He said that we shouldn't think of each other in any serious way, but just enjoy each other while it lasted."

"That sounds like a Hart, all right," Abby had to admit. "They're all like Corrigan. Apparently they have a collective bad attitude toward women and think of them as minor amusements."

"He picked on the wrong girl," Dorie said. She finished her hot chocolate. "I'd never even had a real boyfriend when he came along. He was so forceful and demanding and inflexible, so devoid of tenderness when he was with me." She huddled closer into her sweater. "He came at me like a rocket. I couldn't run, I couldn't hide, he just kept coming." Her eyes closed on a long sigh. "Oh, Abby, he scared me to death. I'd been raised in a such a way that I couldn't have an affair, and I knew that was all he wanted. I ran, and kept running. Now I can't stop."

"You could, if you wanted to."

"The only way I'd come back is with a written guarantee that he wanted nothing more to do with me," she said with a cold laugh. "Otherwise, I'd never feel safe here."

"He just told you himself that he had no designs on you," Abby reminded her. "He has other interests."

"Does he? Other…women interests?"

Abby clasped her fingers together on the table. "He goes

out with a rich divorcée when he's in need of company,'' she said. ''That's been going on for a long time now. He probably was telling the truth when he said that he wouldn't bother you. After all, it's been eight years.'' She studied the other woman. ''You want to come home, don't you?''

Caught off guard, Dorie nodded. ''I'm so alone,'' she confessed. ''I have bolts and chains on my door and I live like a prisoner when I'm not at work. I rarely ever go outside. I miss trees and green grass.''

''There's always Central Park.''

''You can't plant flowers there,'' she said, ''or have a dog or cat in a tiny apartment like mine. I want to sit out in the rain and watch the stars at night. I've dreamed of coming home.''

''Why haven't you?''

''Because of the way I left,'' she confessed. ''I didn't want any more trouble than I'd already had. It was bad enough that Dad had to come and see me, that I couldn't come home.''

''Because of Corrigan?''

''What?'' For an instant, Dorie's eyes were frightened. Then they seemed to calm. ''No, it was for another reason altogether, those first few years. I couldn't risk coming here, where it's so easy to find people…'' She closed up when she realized what she was saying. ''It was a problem I had, in New York. That's all I can tell you. And it's over now. There's no more danger from that direction. I'm safe.''

''I don't understand.''

''You don't need to know,'' Dorie said gently. ''It wouldn't help matters to talk about it now. But I would like to come back home. I seem to have spent most of my life on the run.''

What an odd turn of phrase, Abby thought, but she didn't

question it. She just smiled. "Well, if you decide to come back, I'll introduce you to Clarisse. Just let me know."

Dorie brightened. "All right. Let me think about it for a day or two, and I'll be in touch with you."

"Good. I'll hold you to that."


For the next two days, Dorie thought about nothing else except coming back to her hometown. While she thought, she wandered around the small yard, looking at the empty bird feeders and the squirrel feeder nearby. She saw the discarded watering pot, the weed-bound flower beds. Her father's long absence had made its mark on the little property. It needed a loving hand to restore it.

She stood very still as an idea formed in her mind. She didn't have to sell the property. She could keep it. She could live here. With her math skills, and the bookkeeping training she'd had in business school, she could open a small bookkeeping service of her own. Clarisse could be a client. She could have others. She could support herself. She could leave New York.

The idea took wing. She was so excited about it that she called Abby the next morning when she was sure that the boys would be in school.

She outlined the idea to her friend. "Well, what do you think?" she asked enthusiastically.

"I think it's a great idea!" Abby exclaimed. "And the perfect solution. When are you going to start?"

"Next week," she said with absolute certainty. "I'll use the Christmas vacation I would have had as my notice. It will only take a couple of days to pack up the few things I have. I'll have to pay the rent, because I signed a lease, but if things work out as I hope they will, that won't be a problem. Oh, Abby, it's like a dream!"

"Now you sound more like the Dorothy I used to

know," Abby told her. "I'm so glad you're coming home."

"So am I," Dorie replied, and even as she said it, she tried not to think of the complications that could arise. Corrigan was still around. But he'd made her a promise of sorts, and perhaps he'd keep it. Anyway, she'd worry about that situation later.

A week later, Dorie was settled into her father's house, with all her bittersweet memories of him to keep her company. She'd shipped her few big things, like her piano, home by a moving service. Boxes still cluttered the den, but she was beginning to get her house into some sort of order.

It needed a new roof, and some paint, as well as some plumbing work on the leaky bathtub faucet. But those were minor inconveniences. She had a good little nest egg in her savings account and it would tide her over, if she was careful, until she could be self-supporting in her business again.

She had some cards and stationery printed and put an ad in the Jacobsville weekly newspaper. Then she settled in and began to work in the yard, despite the cold weather. She was finding that grief had to be worked through. It didn't end at the funeral. And the house was a constant reminder of the old days when she and her father had been happy.

So it was a shock to find Corrigan Hart on her doorstep the first Saturday she was in residence.

She just stared at him at first, as if she'd been stunned. In fact, she was. He was the last person she'd have expected to find on her doorstep.

He had a bouquet of flowers in the hand that wasn't holding the cane and his hat. He proffered them brusquely.

"Housewarming present," he said.

She took the pretty bouquet and belatedly stood aside. "Would you like to come in? I could make coffee."

He accepted the invitation, placing his hat on the rack by the door. He kept the cane and she noticed that he leaned on it heavily as he made his way to the nearest easy chair and sat down in it.

"They say damp weather is hard on injured joints," she remarked.

His pale eyes speared into her face, with an equal mixture of curiosity and irritation. "They're right," he drawled. "Walking hurts. Does it help to have me admit it?"

"I wasn't trying to score points," she replied quietly. "I didn't get to say so in the café, but I'm sorry you got hurt."

His own eyes were pointed on the scar that ran the length of her cheek. "I'm sorry you did," he said gruffly. "You mentioned coffee?"

There it was again, that bluntness that had frightened her so much at eighteen. Despite the eight years in between, he still intimidated her.

She moved into the small kitchen, visible from the living room, and filled the pot with water and a premeasured coffee packet. After she'd started it dripping, and had laid a tray with cups, saucers and the condiments, she rejoined him.

"Are you settling in?" he asked a minute after she'd dropped down onto the sofa.

"Yes," she said. "It's strange, after being away for so many years. And I miss Dad. But I always loved this house. Eventually it will be comforting to live here. Once I get over the worst of the grieving."

He nodded. "We lost both our parents at once, in a flood," he said tersely. "I remember how we felt."

He looked around at the high ceilings and marked walls,

and the open fireplace. He nodded toward it. "That isn't efficient. You need a stove in here."

"I need a lot of things in here, but I have to eat, too," she said with a faint smile. She pushed back her short, wavy platinum hair and curled up on the sofa in her jeans and gray sweatshirt and socks. Her shoes were under the sofa. Even in cold weather, she hated wearing shoes around the house.

He seemed to notice that and found it amusing, judging by the twinkle in his pale eyes.

"I hate shoes," she said.

"I remember."

That was surprising. She hardly remembered the girl she'd been eight years ago. It seemed like a lifetime.

"You had a dog, that damned little spaniel, and you were out in the front yard washing him one day when I drove by," he recalled. "He didn't like a bath, and you were soaked, bare feet, cutoffs, tank top and all." His eyes darkened as he looked at her. "I told you to go in the house, do you remember?"

"Yes." The short command had always puzzled her, because he'd seemed angry, not amused as he did now.

"I never said why," he continued. His face tautened as he looked at her. "You weren't wearing anything under that tank top and it was plastered to you," he added quietly. "You can't imagine what it did to me… And there was that damned Bobby Harris standing on the sidewalk gawking at you."

Bobby had asked her out later that day, and she'd refused, because she didn't like him. He was an older boy; her father never had liked him.

"I didn't realize," she said, amazed that the memory should be so tame now, when his odd behavior had actually hurt in the past. She actually flushed at the thought that he'd seen her that way so early in their relationship.

"I know that, now, eight years too late," he said abruptly.

She cocked her head, studying him curiously.

He saw her gaze and lifted his eyes. "I thought you were displaying your charms brazenly for my benefit, and maybe even for Bobby's," he said with a mocking smile. "That's why I acted the way I did that last night we dated."

Her face thinned with distress. "Oh, no!"

"Oh, yes," he said, his voice deep with bitterness. "I thought you were playing me for a sucker, Dorie. That you were pretending to be innocent because I was rich and you wanted a wedding ring instead of an affair."

The horror she felt showed in her wan face.

"Yes, I know," he said when she started to protest. "I only saw what I wanted to see. But the joke was on me. By the time I realized what a hell of a mistake I'd made about you, you were halfway on a bus out of town. I went after you. But I couldn't manage the right words to stop you. My pride cut my throat. I was never that wrong about anyone before."

She averted her gaze. "It was a long time ago. I was just a kid."

"Yes. Just a kid. And I mistook you for a woman." He studied her through narrow lids. "You don't look much older even now. How did you get that scar?"

Her fingers went to it. The memories poured over her, hot and hurting. She got to her feet. "I'll see about the coffee."

She heard a rough sound behind her, but apparently it wasn't something he wanted to put words to. She escaped into the kitchen, found some cookies to put in a bowl and carried the coffee back to the coffee table on a silver tray.

"Fancy stuff," he mused.

She knew that he had equally fancy stuff at his place. She'd never been there, but she'd certainly heard about the

Hart heirlooms that the four brothers displayed with such pride. Old Spanish silver, five generations old, dating all the way back to Spain graced their side table. There was crystal as well, and dozens of other heirlooms that would probably never be handed down. None of the Harts, it was rumored, had any ambitions of marrying.

"This was my grandmother's," she said. "It's all I had of her. She brought this service over from England, they said."

"Ours came from Spain." He waited for her to pour the coffee. He picked up his cup, waving away cream and sugar. He took a sip, nodded and took another. "You make good coffee. Amazing how many people can't."

"I'm sure it's bad for us. Most things are."

He agreed. He put the cup back into the saucer and studied her over its rim. "Are you planning to stay for good?"

"I guess so," she faltered. "I've had stationery and cards printed, and I've already had two offers of work."

"I'm bringing you a third—our household accounts. We've been sharing them since our mother died. Consequently each of us insists that it's not our turn to do them, so they don't get done."

"You'd bring them to me?" she asked hesitantly.

He studied her broodingly. "Why shouldn't I? Are you afraid to come out to the ranch and do them?"

"Of course not."

"Of course not," he muttered, glaring at her. He sat forward, watching her uneasy movement. "Eight years, and I still frighten you."

She curled up even more. "Don't be absurd. I'm twenty-six."

"You don't look or act it."

"Go ahead," she invited. "Be as blunt as you like."

"Thanks, I will. You're still a virgin."

Coffee went everywhere. She cursed roundly, amusing

him, as she searched for napkins to mop up the spill, which was mostly on her.

"Why are you?" he persisted, baiting her. "Were you waiting for me?"

She stood up, slamming the coffee cup to the floor. It shattered with a pleasantly loud crash, and she thanked goodness that it was an old one. "You son of a...!"

He stood up, too, chuckling. "That's better," he mused, watching her eyes flash, her face burn with color.

She kicked at a pottery shard. "Damn you, Corrigan Hart!"

He moved closer, watching her eyelids flutter. She tried to back up, but she couldn't go far. Her legs were against the sofa. There was no place to run.

He paused a step away from her, close enough that she could actually feel the heat of his body through her clothing and his. He looked down into her eyes without speaking for several long seconds.

"You're not the child you used to be," he said, his voice as smooth as velvet. "You can stand up for yourself, even with me. And everything's going to be all right. You're home. You're safe."

It was almost as if he knew what she'd been through. His eyes were quiet and full of secrets, but he smiled. His hand reached out and touched her short hair.

"You still wear it like a boy's," he murmured. "But it's silky. Just the way I remember it."

He was much too close. He made her nervous. Her hands went out and pressed into his shirtfront, but instead of moving back, he moved forward. She shivered at the feel of his chest under her hands, even with the shirt covering it.

"I don't want a lover," she said, almost choking on the words.

"Neither do I," he replied heavily. "So we'll be friends. That's all."

She nibbled on her lower lip. He smelled of spice and leather. She used to dream about him when she first left home. Over the years, he'd assumed the image of a protector in her mind. Strange, when he'd once frightened her so much.

Impulsively she laid her cheek against his chest with a little sigh and closed her eyes.

He shivered for an instant, before his lean hands pressed her gently to him, in a nonthreatening way. He stared over her head with eyes that blazed, eyes that he was thankful she couldn't see.

"We've lost years," he said half under his breath. "But Christmas brings miracles. Maybe we'll have one of our own."

"A miracle?" she mused, smiling. She felt ever so safe in his arms. "What sort?"

"I don't know," he murmured, absently stroking her hair. "We'll have to wait and see. You aren't going to sleep, are you?"

"Not quite." She lifted her head and looked up at him, a little puzzled at the familiarity she felt with him. "I didn't expect that you'd ever be comfortable to be around."

"How so?"

She shrugged. "I wasn't afraid."

"Why should you be?" he replied. "We're different people now."

"I guess."

He brushed a stray hair from her eyebrow with a lean, sure hand. "I want you to know something," he said quietly. "What happened that night…I wouldn't have forced you. Things got a little out of hand, and I said some things, a lot of things, that I regret. I guess you realize now that I had a different picture of you than the one that was real. But even so, I wouldn't have harmed you."

"I think I knew that," she said. "But thank you for telling me."

His hand lay alongside her soft cheek and his metallic eyes went dark and sad. "I mourned you," he said huskily. "Nothing was the same after you'd gone."

She lowered her eyes to his throat. "I didn't have much fun in New York at first, either."

"Modeling wasn't all it was cracked up to be?"

She hesitated. Then she shook her head. "I did better as a stenographer."

"And you'll do even better as a financial expert, right here," he told her. He smiled, tilting up her chin. "Are you going to take the job I've offered you?"

"Yes," she said at once. Her gaze drew slowly over his face. "Are your brothers like you?"

"Wait and see."

"That sounds ominous."

He chuckled, moving slowly away from her to retrieve his cane from the chair. "They're no worse, at least."

"Are they as outspoken as you?"

"Definitely." He saw her apprehension. "Think of the positive side. At least you'll always know exactly where you stand with us."

"That must be a plus."

"Around here, it is. We're hard cases. We don't make friends easily."

"And you don't marry. I remember."

His face went hard. "You have plenty of reason to remember that I said that. But I'm eight years older, and a lot wiser. I don't have such concrete ideas anymore."

"You mean, you're not still a confirmed bachelor?" She laughed nervously. "They say you're taken with the gay divorcée, just the same."

"How did you hear about her?" he asked curtly.

His level, challenging gaze made her uneasy. "People talk," she said.

"Well, the gay divorcée," he emphasized, his expression becoming even more remote, "is a special case. And we're not a couple. Despite what you may have heard. We're friends."

She turned away. "That's no concern of mine. I'll do your bookkeeping on those household accounts, and thank you for the work. But I have no interest in your private life."

He didn't return the compliment. He reached for his hat and perched it on his black hair. There were threads of gray at his temples now, and new lines in his dark, lean face.

"I'm sorry about your accident," she said abruptly, watching him lean heavily on the cane.

"I'll get by," he said. "My leg is stiff, but I'm not crippled. It hurts right now because I took a toss off a horse, and I need the cane. As a rule, I walk well enough without one."

"I remember the way you used to ride," she recalled. "I thought I'd never seen anything in my life as beautiful as you astride a horse at a fast gallop."

His posture went even more rigid. "You never said so."

She smiled. "You intimidated me. I was afraid of you. And not only because you wanted me." She averted her eyes. "I wanted you, too. But I hadn't been raised to believe in a promiscuous life-style. Which," she added, looking up at his shocked face, "was all you were offering me. You said so."

"God help me, I never knew that your father was a minister and your mother a missionary," he said heavily. "Not until it was far too late to do me any good. I expected that all young women were free with their favors in this age of no-consequences intimacy."

"It wouldn't be of no consequence to me," she said

firmly. "I was never one to go with the crowd. I'm still not."

"Yes, I know," he murmured dryly, giving her a long, meaningful glance. "It's obvious."

"And it's none of your business."

"I wouldn't go that far." He tilted his hat over his eyes. "I haven't changed completely, you know. I still go after the things I want, even if I don't go as fast as I used to."

"I expect you do," she said. "Does the divorcée know?"

"Know what? That I'm persistent? Sure she does."

"Good for her."

"She's a beauty," he added, propping on his stick. "Of an age to be sophisticated and good fun."

Her heart hurt. "I'm sure you enjoy her company."

"I enjoy yours as much," he replied surprisingly. "Thanks for the coffee."

"Don't you like cookies?" she asked, noting that he hadn't touched them.

"No," he said. "I don't care for sweets at all."

"Really?"

He shrugged. "We never had them at home. Our mother wasn't the homey sort."

"What was she like?" she had to ask.

"She couldn't cook, hated housework and spouted contempt for any woman who could sew and knit and crochet," he replied.

She felt cold. "And your father?"

"He was a good man, but he couldn't cope with us alone." His eyes grew dark. "When she took off and deserted him, part of him died. She'd just come back, out of money and all alone, from her latest lover. They were talking about a reconciliation when the flood took the house where she was living right out from under them." His face changed, hardened. He leaned heavily on the cane. "Simon and Cag and I were grown by then. We took care of the other two.''

''No wonder you don't like women,'' she murmured quietly.

He gave her a long, level look and then dropped his gaze. She missed the calculation in his tone when he added, ''Marriage is old-fashioned, anyway. I have a dog, a good horse and a houseful of modern appliances. I even have a housekeeper who can cook. A wife would be redundant.''

''Well, I never,'' she exclaimed, breathless.

''I know,'' he replied, and there was suddenly a wicked glint in his eyes. ''You can't blame that on me,'' he added. ''God knows, I did my best to bring you into the age of enlightenment.''

While she was absorbing that dry remark, he tipped his hat, turned and walked out the door.

She darted onto the porch after him. ''When?'' she called after him. ''You didn't say when you wanted me to start.''

''I'll phone you.'' He didn't look back. He got into his truck laboriously and drove away without even a wave of his hand.

At least she had the promise of a job, she told herself. She shouldn't read hidden messages into what he said. But the past he'd shared with her, about his mother, left her chilled. How could a woman have five sons and leave them?

And what was the secret about the fifth brother, Simon, the one nobody had ever seen? She wondered if he'd done something unspeakable, or if he was in trouble with the law. There had to be a reason why the brothers never spoke of him much. Perhaps she'd find out one day.

# Chapter 3

It was the next day before she realized she hadn't thanked Corrigan for the flowers he'd brought. She sent a note out to the ranch on Monday, and got one back that read, simply, "You're welcome." So much for olive branches, if one had been needed.

She found plenty to keep her busy in the days that followed. It seemed that all her father's friends and the people she'd gone to school with wanted her to come home. Everyone seemed to know a potential client. It wasn't long before she was up to her ears in work.

The biggest surprise came Thursday morning when she heard the sound of many heavy footsteps and looked up from her desk to find three huge, intimidating men standing on her porch just beyond the glass-fronted door. They'd come in that big double-cabbed pickup that Corrigan usually drove, and she wondered if these were his brothers.

She went to open the door and felt like a midget when they came tromping inside her house, their spurs jingling pleasantly on boots that looked as if they'd been kept in a swamp.

"We're the Harts," one of them said. "Corrigan's brothers."

As she'd guessed. She studied them curiously. Corrigan was tall, but these men were giants. Two were dark-haired like Corrigan, and one had blond-streaked brown hair. All were dark-eyed, unlike him. None of them would have made any lists of handsome bachelors. They were rugged-looking, lean and tanned, and they made her nervous. The Hart boys made most people nervous. The only other local family that had come close to their reputations for fiery tempers were the Tremayne boys, who were all married and just a little tamer now. The Harts were relative newcomers in Jacobsville, having only been around eight years or so. But they kept to themselves and seemed to have ties to San Antonio that were hard to break. What little socializing they did was all done there, in the city. They didn't mix much in Jacobsville.

Not only were they too rugged for words, but they also had the most unusual first names Dorie could remember hearing. They introduced themselves abruptly, without even being asked first.

Reynard was the youngest. They called him Rey. He had deep-set black eyes and a thin mouth and, gossip said, the worst temper of the four.

The second youngest was Leopold. He was broader than the other three, although not fat, and the tallest. He never seemed to shave. He had blond-streaked brown hair and brown eyes and a mischievous streak that the others apparently lacked.

Callaghan was the eldest, two years older than Corrigan. He had black eyes like a cobra. He didn't blink. He was taller than all his brothers, with the exception of Leopold, and he did most of the bronc-breaking at the ranch. He looked Spanish, more than the others, and he had the bearing and arrogance of royalty, as if he belonged in another century. They said he had the old-fashioned attitudes of the past, as well.

He gave the broader of the three a push toward Dorie. He glared over his shoulder, but took off his hat and forced a smile as he stood in front of Dorie.

"You must be Dorothy Wayne," Leopold said with a grin. "You work for us."

"Y...yes, I guess I do," she stammered. She felt surrounded. She moved back behind the desk and just stared at them, feeling nervous and inadequate.

"Will you two stop glaring?" Leopold shot at his taciturn brothers. "You're scaring her!"

They seemed to make an effort to relax, although it didn't quite work out.

"Never mind," Leopold muttered. He clutched his hat in his hand. "We'd like you to come out to the ranch," he said. "The household accounts are about to do us in. We can't keep Corrigan still long enough to get him to bring them to you."

"He came over Saturday," she said.

"Yeah, we heard," Leo mused. "Roses, wasn't it?"

The other two almost smiled.

"Roses," she agreed. Her gray eyes were wide and they darted from one giant to another.

"He forgot to bring you the books. The office is in a hel...heck of a mess," Leo continued. "We can't make heads nor tails of it. Corrigan scribbles, and we've volunteered him to do it mostly, but we can't read his writing. He escaped to a herd sale in Montana, so we're stuck." He shrugged and managed to look helpless. "We can't see if we've got enough money in the account to buy groceries." He looked hungry. He sighed loudly. "We'd sure appreciate it if you could come out, maybe in the morning, about nine? If that's not too early."

"Oh, no," she said. "I'm up and making breakfast by six."

"Making breakfast? You can cook, then?" Leopold asked.

"Well, yes." She hesitated, but he looked really interested. "I make biscuits and bacon and eggs."

"Pig meat," the one called Reynard muttered.

"Steak's better," Callaghan agreed.

"If she can make biscuits, the other stuff doesn't matter," Reynard retorted.

"Will you two shut up?" Leopold asked sharply. He turned back to Dorie and gave her a thorough appraisal, although not in the least sexual. "You don't look like a bookkeeper."

"Nice hair," Reynard remarked.

"Bad scar on that cheek," Callaghan remarked. "How did it happen?"

Heavens, he was blunt! She was almost startled enough to tell him. She blurted that it had been in an accident.

"Tough," he said. "But if you can cook, scars don't matter much."

Her mouth was open, and Leopold stomped on his big brother's foot, hard.

Callaghan popped him one on the arm with a fist the size of a ham. "Cut it out!"

"Don't insult her, she won't come!"

"I didn't!"

Reynard moved forward, elbowing the other two out of the way. He had his own hat in his hand. He tried to smile. It looked as if he hadn't had much practice at it.

"We'd like you to come tomorrow. Will you?"

She hesitated.

"Now see what you've done!" Leopold shot at Callaghan. "She's scared of us!"

"We wouldn't hurt you," Reynard said gently. He gave up trying to smile; it was unnatural anyway. "We have old Mrs. Culbertson keeping house for us. She carries a broomstick around with her. You'll be safe."

She bit back a laugh. But her eyes began to twinkle.

"She carries the broomstick because of him," Reynard added, indicating Leopold. "He likes to…"

"Never mind!" Leopold said icily.

"I was only going to say that you…"

"Shut up!"

"If you two don't stop, I'm going to lay you both out right here," Callaghan said, and looked very much as if he meant it. "Apologize."

They both murmured reluctant apologies.

"All right, that's that." He put his hat back on. "If you can come at nine, we'll send one of the boys for you."

"Thank you, I'd rather drive my own car."

"I've seen your car. That's why I'm sending one of the boys for you," Callaghan continued doggedly.

Her mouth fell open again. "It's a…a nice old car! And it runs fine!"

"Everybody knows Turkey Sanders sold it to you," Callaghan said with a disgusted look. "He's a pirate. You'll be lucky if the wheels don't fall off the first time you go around a curve."

"That's right," Rey agreed.

"We'll stop by on our way out of town and talk to him," Leopold said. "He'll bring your car back in and make sure it's perfectly safe to drive. He'll do it first thing tomorrow."

"But…"

They put their hats back on, gave her polite nods and stomped back out the way they'd come.

Callaghan paused at the front door, with the screen open.

"He may talk and act tough, but he's hurt pretty bad, inside where it doesn't show. Don't hurt him again."

"Him?"

"Corrigan."

She moved forward, just a step. "It wasn't like that," she said gently. "He didn't feel anything for me."

"And you didn't, for him?"

She averted her gaze to the floor. "It was a long time ago."

"You shouldn't have left."

She looked back up, her eyes wide and wounded. "I was afraid of him!"

He let out a long breath. "You were just a kid. We tried to tell him. Even though we hadn't seen you, we knew about you from other people. We were pretty sure you weren't the sort of girl to play around. He wouldn't listen." He shrugged. "Maybe we corrupted him. You might ask him sometimes about our parents," he added coldly. "Kids don't grow up hating marriage without reason."

There was a lot of pain in his lean face. He was telling her things she'd never have dared ask Corrigan. She moved forward another step, aware of the other two talking out on the porch in hushed whispers.

"Is he still…like that?"

His eyes were cold, but as they looked into hers, they seemed to soften just a little. "He's not the same man he was. You'll have to find out the rest for yourself. We don't interfere in each other's lives, as a rule." His gaze went over her wan face. "You've been to hell and back, too."

He was as perceptive as his brother. She smiled. "I suppose it's part of becoming an adult. Losing illusions and dreams and hope, I mean." She locked her fingers together and looked up at him quietly. "Growing up is painful."

"Don't let go," he said suddenly. "No matter what he says, what he does, don't let go."

Her surprise widened her eyes. "Why?"

He pulled his hat lower over his forehead. "They don't make women like you anymore."

"Like me?" She frowned.

His dark eyes glittered. He smiled in a way that, if she hadn't been half-crazy about Corrigan, would have curled her toes. "I wish we'd met you before," he said. "You'd never have gotten on that bus." He tilted the hat. "We'll send Joey for you in the morning."

"But…"

The door closed behind him. He motioned to the other two and they followed him down the steps to the four-door pickup truck. It had a big cab. It was streamlined and black, and it had a menacing look not—unlike Corrigan Hart's brothers!

She wondered why they'd all come together to ask her to go out to the ranch, and why they'd done it when Corrigan was gone. She supposed she'd find out. She did wonder again about the fifth brother, the mysterious one that Corrigan had mentioned. None of these men were named Simon.

Later, the telephone rang, and it was Turkey Sanders. "I just wanted you to know that I'm going to have that car I sold you picked up in the morning and put to rights," he said at once. "I guarantee, it's going to be the best used car you've ever driven! If you would, just leave the keys in it, and I'll have it picked up first thing. And if there's anything else I can do for you, little lady, you just ask!"

He sounded much more enthusiastic than he had when he'd sold her the rusty little car. "Why, thank you," she said.

"No problem. None at all. Have a nice day, now."

He hung up and she stared blankly at the receiver. Well, nobody could say that living in Jacobsville wasn't interesting, she told herself. Apparently the brothers had a way with other businessmen, too. She'd never have admitted that the car had worried her from the time Turkey had talked her into buying it, for what seemed like a high price for such a wreck. She had a driver's license, which she had to have renewed. But never having owned a car in New York, it was unique to have one of her own, even if it did look like ten miles of bad road.

It was a cold, blustery morning when a polite young man drove up in a black Mercedes and held the door open for her.

"I'm Joey," he told her. "The brothers sent me to fetch you. I sure am glad you took on this job," he added. "They won't give me any money for gas until that checkbook's balanced. I've been having to syphon it out of their trucks with a hose." He shook his head ruefully as he waited for her to move her long denim skirt completely out of the door frame so that he could close the door. "I hate the taste of gasoline."

He closed the door, got in under the wheel and took off in a cloud of dust.

She smiled to herself. The brothers were strange people.

The ranch was immaculate, from its white wood fences to the ranch house itself, a long elegant brick home with a sprawling manicured lawn and a swimming pool and tennis court. The bunkhouse was brick, too, and the barn was so big that she imagined it could hold an entire herd of horses.

"Big, huh?" Joey grinned at her. "The brothers do things on a big scale, but they're meticulous—especially Cag. He runs the place, mostly."

"Cag?"

"Callaghan. Nobody calls him that in the family." He glanced in her direction, amused. "They said you're the reason Corrigan never married."

Her heart jumped. "No kidding?"

"Oh, yeah. He doesn't even look at women these days. But when he heard that you were coming back, he shaved and bought new clothes." He shook his head. "Shocked us all, seeing him without a beard."

"I can't imagine him with one," she said with some confusion.

"Pity about his leg, but he's elegant on a horse, just the same."

"I think he gets around very well."

"Better than he used to." He pulled up in front of the house, turned off the engine and went around to help her out.

"It's right in here."

He led her in through the front door and down a carpeted hall to a pine-paneled office. "Mrs. Culbertson will be along any minute to get you some coffee or tea or a soft drink. The brothers had to get to work or they'd have been here to meet you. No worry, though, Corrigan's home. He'll be here shortly and show you the books. He's trying to doctor a colt, down in the barn."

"Thank you, Joey."

He tipped his hat. "My pleasure, ma'am." He gave her a cursory appraisal, nodded and went back out again.

He'd no sooner gone than a short, plump little woman with twinkling blue eyes and gray hair came in, rubbing her hands dry on her apron. "You'd be Miss Wayne. I'm Betty Culbertson," she introduced herself. "Can I get you a cup of coffee?"

"Oh, yes, please."

"Cream, sugar?"

"I like it black," she said.

The older woman grinned. "So do the boys. They don't like sweets, either. Hard to get fat around here, except on gravy and biscuits. They'd have those every meal if I'd cook them.''

The questions the brothers had asked about her cooking came back to haunt her.

"None of them believe in marriage, do they?" she asked.

Mrs. Culbertson shook her head. "They've been bachelors too long now. They're set in their ways and none of them have much to do with women. Not that they aren't targeted by local belles," she added with a chuckle. "But nobody has much luck. Corrigan, now, he's mellowed. I hear it's because of you.''

While Dorie flushed and tried to find the right words to answer her, a deep voice did it for her.

"Yes, it is," Corrigan said from the doorway. "But she isn't supposed to know it.''

"Oops," Mrs. Culbertson said with a wicked chuckle. "Sorry.''

He shrugged. "No harm done. I'll have coffee. So will she. And if you see Leopold…''

"I'll smash his skull for him, if I do," the elderly woman said abruptly, and her whole demeanor changed. Her blue eyes let off sparks. "That devil!''

"He did it again, I guess?"

She made an angry noise through her nose. "I've told him and told him…''

"You'd think he'd get tired of having that broomstick thrown at him, wouldn't you?" Corrigan asked pleasantly.

"One of these days he won't be quick enough," Mrs. Culbertson said with an evil smile.

"I'll talk to him.''

"Everybody's already talked to him. It does no good.''

"What does he do?" Dorie asked curiously.

Mrs. Culbertson looked at Corrigan, who'd started to answer, with eyes that promised culinary retribution.

"Sorry," he said abruptly. "I can't say.''

Mrs. Culbertson nodded curtly and smiled at Dorie. "I'll just get that coffee. Be back in a jiffy."

She left and Corrigan's dark eyes slid over Dorie's pretty figure.

"You look very nice," he said. His eyes lifted to her wavy hair and he smiled appreciatively. "I always loved your hair. That was a first for me. Usually I like a woman's hair long. Yours suits you just as it is."

Her slender hand went to the platinum waves self-consciously. "It's easy to keep like this." She shifted to the other foot. "Your brothers came to the house yesterday and asked me to come out here and look at the household accounts. They say they're starving."

"They look like it, too, don't they?" he asked disgust-edly. "Good God, starving!"

"They were very nice," she continued. "They talked to Turkey Sanders and he's repairing my car."

"His *mechanic's* repairing your car," he told her. "Tur-key's having a tooth fixed."

She knew she shouldn't ask. But she had to. "Why?"

"He made a remark that Cag didn't like."

"Cag. Oh, yes, he's the eldest."

He brightened when he realized that she remembered that. "He's thirty-eight, if you call that old." Anticipating her next question, he added blithely, "Leo's thirty-four. I'm thirty-six. Rey's thirty-two."

"So Cag hit Turkey Sanders?"

He shook his head.

"Then who broke his tooth?"

"Leo."

"Cag got mad, but Leo hit Turkey Sanders?" she asked, fascinated.

He nodded. "He did that to save him from Cag."

"I don't understand."

"Cag was in the Special Forces," he explained. "He was

a captain when they sent him to the Middle East some years back." He shrugged. "He knows too much about hand-to-hand combat to be let loose in a temper. So we try to shield people from him." He grinned. "Leo figured that if he hit Turkey first, Cag wouldn't. And he didn't."

She just shook her head. "Your brothers are…unique," she said finally, having failed to find a good word to describe them.

He chuckled. "You don't know the half of it."

"Do they really hate women?"

"Sometimes," he said.

"I'll bet they're sought after," she mentioned, "especially when people get a good look at this ranch."

"The ranch is only a part of the properties we own," he replied. "Our people are fourth-generation Texans, and we inherited thousands of acres of land and five ranches. They were almost bankrupt when the old man died, though," he mused. "He didn't really have a head for figures. Broke Grandad's heart. He saw the end of his empire. But we pulled it out of the fire."

"So I see," she agreed.

"The only problem is, none of us are married. So if we don't have descendants, who's going to keep the empire going?"

She thought of the most terrible answer to that question, and then got the giggles.

He raised an eyebrow.

She put a hand over her mouth until she got herself back under control. "Sorry. I was only thinking of that movie about the man who got pregnant…!"

He gave her a level look, unsmiling.

She cleared her throat. "Where are the accounts?"

He hesitated for a minute, and then opened the desk drawer and took out a set of ledgers, placing them on the spotless cherry wood desk.

"This is beautiful," she remarked, stroking the silky, high-polished surface.

"It was our grandfather's," he told her. "We didn't want to change things around too much. The old gentleman was fond of the office just the way it is."

She looked around, puzzled by the plain wood paneling. There were no deer heads or weapons anywhere. She said so.

"He didn't like trophies," he told her. "Neither do we. If we hunt, we use every part of the deer, but we don't have the heads mounted. It doesn't seem quite sporting."

She turned as she pulled out the desk chair, and looked at him with open curiosity.

"None of your brothers are like I pictured them."

"In what way?"

She smiled. "You're very handsome," she said, averting her eyes when his began to glitter. "They aren't. And they all have very dark eyes. Yours are gray, like mine."

"They favor our mother," he said. "I favor him." He nodded toward the one portrait, on the wall behind the desk. It looked early twentieth century and featured a man very like Corrigan, except with silver hair.

"So that's what you'll look like," she remarked absently.

"Eventually. Not for a few years, I hope."

She glanced at him, because he'd come to stand beside her. "You're going gray, just at the temples."

He looked down into her soft face. His eyes narrowed as he searched every inch of her above the neck. "Gray won't show in that beautiful mop on your head," he said quietly. "It'll blend in and make it even prettier."

The comment was softly spoken, and so poetic that it embarrassed her. She smiled self-consciously and her gaze fell to his shirt. It was open at the collar, because it was warm in the house. Thick black hair peered over the button, and unwanted memories of that last night they'd been together came flooding back. He'd taken his shirt off, to give her hands total access to his broad, hair-roughened chest. He liked her lips on it...

She cleared her throat and looked away, her color high. "I'd better get to work."

His lean hand caught her arm, very gently, and he pulled her back around. His free hand went to the snaps that held the shirt together. He looked into her startled eyes and slowly, one by one, he flicked the snaps apart.

"What...are you...doing?" she faltered. She couldn't breathe. He was weaving spells around her. She felt weak-kneed already, and the sight of that broad chest completely bare drew a faint gasp from her lips.

He had her by the elbows. He drew her to him, so that her lips were on a level with his collarbone. She could hear his heartbeat, actually hear it.

"It was like this," he said in a raw, ragged tone. "But I had your blouse off, your breasts bare. I drew you to me, like this," he whispered unsteadily, drawing her against the length of him, "and I bent, and took your open mouth under my own...like this..."

It was happening all over again. She was eight years older, but apparently not one day less vulnerable. He put her cold hands into the thick hair on his chest and moved them while his hard mouth took slow, sweet possession of her lips.

He nudged her lips apart and hesitated for just a second, long enough to look into her eyes and see the submission and faint hunger in them. There was just the hint of a smile on his lips before he parted them against her soft mouth.

# *Chapter 4*

She had no pride at all, she decided in the hectic seconds that followed the first touch of his hard mouth. She was a total washout as a liberated woman.

His hands had gone to her waist and then moved up to her rib cage, to the soft underside of her breasts. He stroked just under them until she shivered and moaned, and then his hands lifted and took possession; blatant possession.

He felt her mouth open. His own answered it while he touched her, searched over her breasts and found the hard nipples that pushed against his palms.

His mouth grew rougher. She felt his hands move around her, felt the catch give. Her blouse was pushed up with a shivering urgency, and seconds later, her bare breasts were buried in the thick hair that covered his chest and abdomen.

She cried out, dragging her mouth from his.

He looked into her eyes, but he wouldn't let her go. His hard face was expressionless. Only his eyes were alive, glittering like gray fires. He deliberately moved her from side to side and watched her face as he did it, enjoying, with a completely masculine delight, the pleasure she couldn't hide.

"Your nipples are like rocks against me." He bit off the words, holding her even closer. "I took your breasts inside my mouth the night we made love, and you arched up right off the bed to give them to me. Do you remember what you did next?"

She couldn't speak. She looked at him with mingled desire and fear.

"You slid your hands inside my jeans," he whispered roughly. "And you touched me. That's when I lost control."

Her moan was one of shame, not pleasure. She found his chest with her cheek and pressed close to him, shivering. "I'm sorry," she whispered brokenly. "I'm so sorry...!"

His mouth found her eyes and kissed them shut. "Don't," he whispered roughly. "I'm not saying it to shame you. I only want you to remember why it ended the way it did. You were grass green and I didn't know it. I encouraged you to be uninhibited, but I'd never have done it if I'd known what an innocent you were." His mouth slid over her forehead with breathless tenderness while his hands slid to her lower back and pulled her even closer. "I was going to take you," he whispered. His hands contracted and his body went rigid with a surge of arousal that she could feel. His legs trembled. "I still want to, God help me," he breathed at her temple. "I've never had the sort of arousal I feel with you. I don't even have to undress you first." His hands began to tremble as he moved her sensually against his hips. His mouth slid down to hers and softly covered it, lifting and touching and probing until she shivered again with pleasure.

"I thought you knew," she whimpered.

"I didn't." His hands moved to the very base of her

spine and lifted her gently into the hard thrust of his body.
He caught his breath at the wave of pleasure that washed
over him immediately. "Dorie," he breathed.

She couldn't think at all. When he took one of her hands
and pressed it to his lower body, she didn't even have the
will to protest. Her hand opened and she let him move it
gently against him, on fire with the need to touch him.

"Eight years," she said shakily.

"And we're still starving for each other," he whispered
at her mouth. His hand became insistent. "Harder," he said
and his breath caught.

"This...isn't wise," she said against his chest.

"No, but it's sweet. Dorie...!" He cried out hoarsely,
his whole body shuddering.

Her hand stilled at once. "I'm sorry," she whispered
frantically. "Did I hurt you?"

He wasn't breathing normally at all. His face was buried
in her throat and he was shaking like a leaf. She brushed
her mouth over his cheek, his chin, his lips, his nose, whis-
pering his name as she clung to him.

His hand gripped her upper thigh, and it was so bruising
that she was afraid she was going to have to protest. He
fought for sanity, embarrassed by his weakness.

She was still kissing him. He felt her breasts moving
against his chest, intensifying the throbbing, hellish ache
below his belt.

He held her firmly in place with hands that shook.

She subsided and stood quietly against him. She knew
now, as she hadn't eight years ago, what was wrong with
him. She felt guilty and ashamed for pushing him so far
out of control.

Her fingers touched his thick, cool hair lovingly. Her lips
found his eyelids and brushed softly against them. He was
vulnerable and she wanted to protect him, cherish him.

The tenderness was doing strange things to him. He still

wanted her to the point of madness, but those comforting little kisses made his heart warm. He'd never been touched in such a way by a woman; he'd never felt so cherished.

She drew back, and he pulled her close again.

"Don't stop," he whispered, calmer now. His hands had moved up to the silken skin of her back, and he smiled under the whisper of her lips on his skin.

"I'm so sorry," she whispered.

His fingers slid under the blouse again and up to explore the softness of her breasts. "Why?" he asked.

"You were hurting," she said. "I shouldn't have touched you…"

He chuckled wickedly. "I made you."

"I still can't go to bed with you," she said miserably. "I don't care if the whole world does it, I just can't!"

His hands opened and enfolded her breasts tenderly. "You want to," he murmured as he caressed them.

"Of course I want to!" Her eyes closed and she swayed closer to his hands. "Oh, glory," she managed to say tightly, shivering.

"Your breasts are very sensitive," he said at her lips. "And soft like warm silk under my hands. I'd like to lay you down on my grandfather's desk and take your blouse off and put my lips on you there. But Mrs. Culbertson is making coffee." He lifted his head and looked into her dazed, soft gray eyes. "Thank God," he whispered absently as he searched them.

"Thank God for what?" she asked huskily.

"Miracles, maybe," he replied. He smoothed the blouse up again and his eyes sketched her pretty pink breasts with their hard dark pink crowns. "I could eat you like taffy right now," he said in a rough tone.

The office was so quiet that not a sound could be heard above the shiver of her breath as she looked up at him.

His pale eyes were almost apologetic. "I think I have a death wish," he began huskily as he bent.

She watched his mouth hover over her breast with a sense of shocked wonder. Her eyes wide, her breath stopped in her throat, she waited, trembling.

He looked up, then, and saw her eyes. He made a sound in the back of his throat and his mouth opened as he propelled her closer, so that he had her almost completely in that warm, moist recess.

She wept. The pleasure grew to unbearable heights. Her fingers tangled in his hair and she pulled him closer. She growled sharply at the sensations she felt. Her hips moved involuntarily, searching for his body.

The suction became so sweet that she suddenly arched backward, and would have fallen if it hadn't been for his supporting arm. She caught her breath and convulsed, her body frozen in an arc of pure ecstasy.

He felt the deep contractions of her body under his mouth with raging pride. His mouth grew a little rough, and the convulsions deepened.

Only when he felt her begin to relax did he lift his head and bring her back into a standing position, so that he could look at her face.

She couldn't breathe. She sobbed as she looked up into his pale eyes. The tears came, hot and quick, when she realized what had happened. And he'd seen it!

"Don't," he chided tenderly. He reached for a handkerchief and dried her red eyes and wiped her nose. "Don't be embarrassed."

"I could die of shame," she wept.

"For what?" he asked softly. "For letting me watch you?"

Her face went red. "I never, never...!"

He put a long forefinger against her lips. "I've never seen a woman like that," he whispered. "I've never known one who could be satisfied by a man's mouth suckling at her breast. It was the most beautiful experience I've ever had.''

She wasn't crying now. She was staring at him, her eyes wide and soft and curious.

He brushed back her wild hair. ''It was worth what I felt earlier,'' he murmured dryly.

She colored even more. ''I can't stay here,'' she told him wildly. ''I have to go away…''

''Hell, no, you don't,'' he said tersely. ''You're not getting away from me a second time. Don't even think about running.''

''But,'' she began urgently.

''But what?'' he asked curtly. ''But you can't give yourself to me outside marriage? I know that. I'm not asking you to sleep with me.''

''It's like torture for you.''

''Yes,'' he said simply. ''But the alternative is to never touch you.'' His hand slid over her blouse and he smiled gently at the immediate response of her body. ''I love this,'' he said gruffly. ''And so do you.''

She grimaced. ''Of course I do,'' she muttered. ''I've never let anyone else touch me like that. It's been eight years since I've even been kissed!''

''Same here,'' he said bluntly.

''Ha! You've been going around with a divorcée!'' she flung at him out of frustration and embarrassment.

''I don't have sex with her,'' he said.

''They say she's very pretty.''

He smiled. ''She is. Pretty and elegant and kind. But I don't feel desire for her, any more than she feels it for me. I told you we were friends. We are. And that's all we are.''

''But…but…''

''But what, Dorie?''

"Men don't stop kissing women just because they get turned down once."

"It was much worse than just getting turned down," he told her. "I ran you out of town. It was rough living with that, especially when your father took a few strips off me and told me all about your past. I felt two inches high." His eyes darkened with the pain of the memory. "I hated having made an enemy of him. He was a good man. But I'd never had much interest in marriage or let anyone get as close to me as you did. If you were afraid, so was I."

"Cag said your parents weren't a happy couple."

His eyebrow lifted. "He never talks about them. That's a first."

"He told me to ask you about them."

"I see." He sighed. "Well, I told you a little about that, but we're going to have to talk more about them sooner or later, and about some other things." He lifted his head and listened and then looked down at her with a wicked grin. "But for the present, you'd better fasten your bra and tuck your blouse back in and try to look as if you haven't just made love with me."

"Why?"

"Mrs. Culbertson's coming down the hall."

"Oh, my gosh!"

She fumbled with catches and buttons, her face red, her hair wild as she raced to put herself back together. He snapped his shirt up lazily, his silvery eyes full of mischief as he watched her frantic efforts to improve her appearance.

"Lucky I didn't lay you down on the desk, isn't it?" he said, chuckling.

There was a tap on the half-closed door and Mrs. Culbertson came in with a tray. She was so intent on getting it to the desk intact that she didn't even look at Dorie.

"Here it is. Sorry I took so long, but I couldn't find the cream pitcher."

"Who drinks cream?" Corrigan asked curiously.

"It was the only excuse I could think of," she told him seriously.

He looked uneasy. "Thanks."

She grinned at him and then looked at Dorie. Her eyes were twinkling as she went back out. And this time she closed the door.

Dorie's face was still flushed. Her gray eyes were wide and turbulent. Her mouth was swollen and when she folded her arms over her chest, she flinched.

His eyes went to her blouse and back up again. "When I felt you going over the edge, it excited me, and I got a little rough. Did I hurt you?"

The question was matter-of-fact, and strangely tender.

She shook her head, averting her eyes. It was embarrassing to remember what had happened.

He caught her hand and led her to the chairs in front of the desk. "Sit down and I'll pour you a cup of coffee."

She looked up at him a little uneasily. "Is something wrong with me, do you think?" she asked with honest concern. "I mean, it's unnatural...isn't it?"

His fingers touched her soft cheek. He shook his head. "People can't be pigeonholed. You might not be that responsive to any other man. Maybe it's waiting so long. Maybe it's that you're perfectly attuned to me. I might be able to accomplish the same thing by kissing your thighs, or your belly."

She flushed. "You wouldn't!"

"Why not?"

The thought of it made her vibrate all over. She knew that men kissed women in intimate places, but she hadn't quite connected it until then.

"The inside of your thighs is very vulnerable to being caressed," he said simply. "Not to mention your back, your hips, your feet,'' he added with a gentle smile. ''Love-making is an art. There are no set rules.''

She watched him turn and pour coffee into a ceramic cup. He handed it to her and watched the way her fingers deliberately touched his as he drew them away.

He wanted her so much that he could barely stand up straight, but it was early days yet. He had to go slowly this time and not push her too hard. She had a fear not only of him, but of real intimacy. He couldn't afford to let things go too far.

''What sort of things are we going to talk about later?'' she asked after she'd finished half her coffee.

''Cabbages and kings,'' he mused. He sat across from her, his long legs crossed, his eyes possessive and caressing on her face.

''I don't like cabbage and I don't know any kings.''

''Then suppose we lie down together on the sofa?''

Her eyes flashed up to see the amusement in his and back down to her cup. ''Don't tease. I'm not sophisticated enough for it.''

''I'm not teasing.''

She sighed and took another sip of coffee. ''There's no future in it. You know that.''

He didn't know it. She was living in the past, convinced that he had nothing more than an affair in mind for them. He smiled secretively to himself as he thought about the future. Fate had given him a second chance; he wasn't going to waste it.

''About these books,'' he said in a businesslike tone. ''I've made an effort with them, but although I can do math, my penmanship isn't what it should be. If you can't read any of the numbers, circle them and I'll tell you what they are. I have to meet a prospective buyer down at the barn in a few minutes, but I'll be somewhere close by all day.''

"All right."

He finished his coffee and put the cup back on the tray, checking his watch. "I'd better go." He looked down at her with covetous eyes and leaned against the arms of her chair to study her. "Let's go dancing tomorrow night."

Her heart jumped. She was remembering how it was when they were close together and her face flushed.

His eyebrow lifted and he grinned. "Don't look so apprehensive. The time to worry is when nothing happens when I hold you."

"It always did," she replied.

He nodded. "Every time," he agreed. "I only had to touch you." He smiled softly. "And vice versa," he added with a wicked glance.

"I was green," she reminded him.

"You still are," he reminded her.

"Not so much," she ventured shyly.

"We both learned something today," he said quietly. "Dorie, if you can be satisfied by so small a caress, try to imagine how it would feel if we went all the way."

Her eyelids flickered. Her breath came like rustling leaves.

He bent and drew his mouth with exquisite tenderness over her parted lips. "Or is that the real problem?" he asked at her mouth. "Are you afraid of the actual penetration?"

Her heart stopped dead and then ran away. "Corrigan!" She ground out his name.

He drew back a breath so that he could see her eyes. He wasn't smiling. It was no joke.

"You'd better tell me," he said quietly.

She drew her lower lip in with her teeth, looking worried.

"I won't tell anyone."

"I know that." She took a long breath. "When my cousin Mary was married, she came to visit us after the

honeymoon was over. She'd been so happy and excited.''
She grimaced. "She said that it hurt awfully bad, that she
bled and bled, and he made fun of her because she cried.
She said that he didn't even kiss her. He just…pushed into
her…!''

He cursed under his breath. "Didn't you talk to anyone
else about sex?''

"It wasn't something I could discuss with my father, and
Mary was the only friend I had," she told him. "She said
that all the things they write about are just fiction, and that
the reality is just like her mother once said—a woman deals
with it for the pleasure of children.''

He leaned forward on his hands, shaking his head. "I
wish you'd told me this eight years ago.''

"You'd have laughed," she replied. "You didn't believe
I was innocent anyway.''

He looked up into her eyes. "I'm sorry," he said heavily.
"Life teaches hard lessons.''

She thought about her own experience with modeling.
"Yes, it does.''

He got to his feet and looked down at her with a worried
scowl. "Don't you watch hot movies?''

"Those women aren't virgins," she returned.

"No. I don't guess they are." His eyes narrowed as he
searched her face. "And I don't know what to tell you. I've
never touched an innocent woman until you came along.
Maybe it does hurt. But I promise you, it would only be
one time. I know enough to make it good for you. And I
would.''

"It isn't going to be that way," she reminded him
tersely, denying herself the dreams of marriage and children
that she'd always connected with him. "We're going to be
friends.''

He didn't speak. His gaze didn't falter. "I'll check back
with you later about the books," he said quietly.

"Okay."

He started to turn, thought better of it and leaned down again with his weight balanced on the chair arms. "Do you remember what happened when I started to suckle you?"

She went scarlet. "Please…"

"It will be like that," he said evenly. "Just like that. You won't think about pain. You may not even notice any. You go in headfirst when I touch you. And I wasn't even taking my time with you today. Think about that. It might help."

He pushed away from her again and went to the desk to pick up his hat. He placed it on his head and smiled at her without mockery.

"Don't let my brothers walk over you," he said. "If one of them gives you any trouble, lay into him with the first hard object you can get your hands on."

"They seem very nice," she said.

"They like you," he replied. "But they have plans."

"Plans?"

"Not to hurt you," he assured her. "You should never have told them you could cook."

"I don't understand."

"Mrs. Culbertson wants to quit. They can't make biscuits. It's what they live for, a plateful of homemade buttered biscuits with half a dozen jars of jam and jelly."

"How does that concern me?"

"Don't you know?" He perched himself against the desk. "They've decided that we should marry you."

*"We?"*

"We're a family. Mostly we share things. Not women, but we do share cooks." He cocked his head and grinned at her shocked face. "If I marry you, they don't have to worry about where their next fresh biscuit is coming from."

"You don't want to marry me."

"Well, they'll probably find some way around that," he said pointedly.

"They can't force you to marry me."

"I wouldn't make any bets on that," he said. "You don't know them yet."

"You're their brother. They'd want you to be happy."

"They think you'll make me happy."

She lowered her eyes. "You should talk to them."

"And say what? That I don't want you? I don't think they'd believe me."

"I meant, you should tell them that you don't want to get married."

"They've already had a meeting and decided that I do. They've picked out a minister and a dress that they think you'll look lovely in. They've done a rough draft of a wedding invitation…"

"You're out of your mind!"

"No, I'm not." He went to the middle desk drawer, fumbled through it, pulled it further out and reached for something pushed to the very back of the desk. He produced it, scanned it, nodded and handed it to her. "Read that."

It was a wedding invitation. Her middle name was misspelled. "It's Ellen, not Ellis."

He reached behind him for a pen, took the invitation back, made the change and handed it back to her.

"Why did you do that?" she asked curiously.

"Oh, they like everything neat and correct."

"Don't correct it! Tear it up!"

"They'll just do another one. The papers will print what's on there, too. You don't want your middle name misspelled several thousand times, do you?"

She was all but gasping for breath. "I don't understand."

"I know. Don't worry about it right now. There's plenty of time. They haven't decided on a definite date yet, anyway."

She stood up, wild-eyed. "You can't let your brothers decide when and who you're going to marry!"

"Well, you go stop them, then," he said easily. "But don't say I didn't tell you so."

He pulled his hat over his eyes and walked out the door, whistling softly to himself.

## *Chapter 5*

First she did the accounts. Her mind was still reeling from Corrigan's ardor, and she had to be collected when she spoke to his brothers. She deciphered his scribbled numbers, balanced the books, checked her figures and put down a total.

They certainly weren't broke, and there was enough money in the account to feed Patton's Third Army. She left them a note saying so, amused at the pathetic picture they'd painted of their finances. Probably, the reason for that was part of their master plan.

She went outside to look for them after she'd done the books. They were all four in the barn, standing close together. They stopped talking the minute she came into view, and she knew for certain that they'd been talking about her.

"I'm not marrying him," she told them clearly, and pointed at Corrigan.

"Okay," Leo said easily.

"The thought never crossed my mind," Rey remarked.

Cag just shrugged.

Corrigan grinned.

"I'm through with the books," she said uneasily. "I want to go home now."

"You haven't eaten lunch," Rey said.

"It's only eleven o'clock," she said pointedly.

"We have an early lunch, because we work until dark," Cag volunteered.

"Mrs. Culbertson just left," Rey said. He sighed. "She put some beef and gravy in the oven to warm. But she didn't make us any biscuits."

"We don't have anything to put gravy on," Leo agreed.

"Can't work all afternoon without a biscuit," Cag said, nodding.

Corrigan grinned.

Dorie had thought that Corrigan was making up that story about the brothers' mania for biscuits. Apparently it was the gospel truth.

"Just one pan full," Leo coaxed. "It wouldn't take five minutes." He eyed her warily. "If you can really make them. Maybe you can't. Maybe you were just saying you could, to impress us."

"That's right," Rey added.

"I can make biscuits," she said, needled. "You just point me to the kitchen and I'll show you."

Leo grinned. "Right this way!"

Half an hour later, the pan of biscuits were gone so fast that they might have disintegrated. Leo and Corrigan were actually fighting over the last one, pulled it apart in their rush, and ended up splitting it while the other two sat there gloating. They'd had more than their share because they had faster hands.

"Next time, you've got to make two pans," Corrigan told her. "One doesn't fill Leo's hollow tooth."

"I noticed," she said, surprisingly touched by the way they'd eaten her biscuits with such enjoyment. "I'll make you a pan of rolls to go with them next time."

*"Rolls?"* Leo looked faint. *"You can make homemade rolls?"*

"I'll see about the wedding rings right now," Rey said, wiping his mouth and pushing away from the table.

"I've got the corrected invitation in my pocket," Cag murmured as he got up, too.

Leo joined the other two at the door. "They said they can get the dress here from Paris in two weeks," Leo said.

Dorie gaped at them. But before she could open her mouth, all three of them had rushed out the door and closed it, talking animatedly among themselves.

"But, I didn't say…!" she exclaimed.

"There, there," Corrigan said, deftly adding another spoonful of gravy to his own remaining half of a biscuit. "It's all right. They forgot to call the minister and book him."

Just at that moment, the door opened and Leo stuck his head in. "Are you Methodist, Baptist or Presbyterian?" he asked her.

"I'm…Presbyterian," she faltered.

He scowled. "Nearest Presbyterian minister is in Victoria," he murmured thoughtfully, "but don't worry, I'll get him here." He closed the door.

"Just a minute!" she called.

The doors of the pickup closed three times. The engine roared. "Too late," Corrigan said imperturbably.

"But didn't you hear him?" she burst out. "For heaven's sake, they're going to get a minister!"

"Hard to get married in church without one," he insisted. He gestured toward her plate with a fork to the remaining chunk of beef. "Don't waste that. It's one of our own steers. Corn fed, no hormones, no antibiotics, no insecticides. We run a clean, environmentally safe operation here."

She was diverted. "Really?"

"We're renegades," he told her. "They groan when they see us coming at cattle conventions. Usually we go with Donavan. He's just like us about cattle. He and the Ballenger brothers have gone several rounds over cattle prods and feed additives. He's mellowed a bit since his nephew came to live with him and he got married. But he likes the way we do things."

"I guess so." She savored the last of the beef. "It's really good."

"Beats eating pigs," he remarked, and grinned.

She burst out laughing. "Your brother Cag had plenty to say on that subject."

"He only eats beef or fish. He won't touch anything that comes from a pig. He says it's because he doesn't like the taste." He leaned forward conspiratorially. "But I say it's because of that movie he went to see. He used to love a nice ham."

"What movie?"

"The one with the talking pig."

"Cag went to see *that?*"

"He likes cartoons and sentimental movies." He shrugged. "Odd, isn't it? He's the most staid of us. To look at him, you'd never know he had a sense of humor or that he was sentimental. He's like the others in his lack of conventional good looks, though. Most women can't get past that big nose and those eyes."

"A cobra with a rabbit," she said without thinking.

He chuckled. "Exactly."

"Does he hate women as much as the rest of you?"

"Hard to tell. You haven't seen him in a tuxedo at a

social bash. Women, really beautiful women, followed him around all night dropping their room keys at his feet.''

''What did he do?''

''Kept walking.''

She put down her fork. ''What do you do?''

He smiled mockingly. ''They don't drop room keys at my feet anymore. The limp puts them off.''

''Baloney,'' she said. ''You're the handsomest of the four, and it isn't just looks.''

He leaned back in his chair to look at her. His eyes narrowed thoughtfully. ''Does the limp bother you?''

''Don't be ridiculous,'' she said, lifting her gaze. ''Why should it?''

''I can't dance very well anymore.''

She smiled. ''I don't ever go to dances.''

''Why not?''

She sipped coffee. ''I don't like men touching me.''

His eyes changed. ''You like me touching you.''

''You aren't a stranger,'' she said simply.

''Maybe I am,'' he murmured quietly. ''What do you know about me?''

She stared at him. ''Well, you're thirty-six, you're a rancher, you've never married, you come from San Antonio.''

''And?''

''I don't know any more than that,'' she said slowly.

''We were a couple for several weeks before you left town. Is that all you learned?''

''You were always such a private person,'' she reminded him. ''You never talked about yourself or your brothers. And we never really talked that much when we were together.''

''We spent more time kissing,'' he recalled. ''I was too wrapped up in trying to get you into bed to care how well we knew each other," he said with self-contempt. "I wasted a lot of time."

"You said that we shouldn't look back."

"I'm trying not to. It's hard, sometimes." He moved forward to take her hands under his on the table. "I like classical music, but I'm just as happy with country or pop. I like a good chess game. I enjoy science fiction movies and old Westerns, the silent kind. I'm an early riser, I work hard and I don't cheat on my tax returns. I went to college to learn animal husbandry, but I never graduated."

She smiled. "Do you like fried liver?"

He made a horrible face. "Do you?"

She made the same face. "But I don't like sweets very much, either," she said, remembering that he didn't.

"Good thing. Nobody around here eats them."

"I remember." She looked around at the comfortably big kitchen. There was a new electric stove and a huge refrigerator, flanked by an upright freezer. The sink was a double stainless-steel one, with a window above it overlooking the pasture where the colts were kept. Next to that was a dishwasher. There was plenty of cabinet space, too.

"Like it?" he asked.

She smiled. "It's a dream of a kitchen. I'll bet Mrs. Culbertson loves working in here."

"Would you?"

She met his eyes and felt her own flickering at the intensity of his stare.

"If you can make homemade bread, you have to be an accomplished cook," he continued. "There's a high-tech mixer in the cabinet, and every gourmet tool known to man. Or woman."

"It's very modern."

"It's going to be very deserted in about three weeks," he informed.

"Why is Mrs. Culbertson quitting?"

"Her husband has cancer, and she wants to retire and stay at home with him, for as long as he's got," he said abruptly. He toyed with his coffee cup. "They've been married for fifty years." He took a sharp breath, and his eyes were very dark as they met hers. "I've believed all my life that no marriage could possibly last longer than a few years. People change. Situations change. Jobs conflict." He shrugged. "Then Mrs. Culbertson came here to work, with her husband. And I had to eat my words." He lowered his eyes back to the cup. "They were forever holding hands, helping each other, walking in the early morning together and talking. She smiled at him, and she was beautiful. He smiled back. Nobody had to say that they loved each other. It was obvious."

"My parents were like that," she recalled. "Dad and Mom loved each other terribly. When she died, I almost lost him, too. He lived for me. But the last thing he said on his deathbed—" she swallowed, fighting tears "—was her name."

He got up from the table abruptly and went to the window over the sink. He leaned against it, breathing heavily, as if what she'd said had affected him powerfully. And, in fact, it had.

She watched him through tears. "You don't like hearing about happy marriages. Why?"

"Because I had that same chance once," he said in a low, dull tone. "And I threw it away."

She wondered who the woman had been. Nobody had said that any of the Hart brothers had ever been engaged. But there could have been someone she hadn't heard about.

"You're the one who keeps saying we can't look back," she remarked, dabbing her eyes with her napkin.

"It's impossible not to. The past makes us the people we are." He sighed wearily. "My parents had five of us in ten years. My mother hadn't wanted the first child. She didn't have a choice. He took away her checkbook and kept her pregnant. She hated him and us in equal measure. When she left it was almost a relief.'' He turned and looked across the room at her. ''I've never been held with tenderness. None of us have. It's why we're the way we are, it's why we don't have women around. The only thing we know about women is that they're treacherous and cold and cruel.''

''Oh, Corrigan,'' she said softly, wincing.

His eyes narrowed. ''Desire is a hot and unmanageable thing. Sex can be pleasant enough. But I'd gladly be impotent to have a woman hold me the way you did in my office and kiss my eyes.'' His face went as hard as stone. ''You can't imagine how it felt.''

''But I can,'' she replied. She smiled. ''You kissed my eyes.''

''Yes.''

He looked so lost, so lonely. She got up from the table and went to him, paused in front of him. Her hands pressed gently against his broad chest as she looked up into his eyes.

''You know more about me than I've ever told anyone else,'' he said quietly. ''Now don't you think it's time you told me what happened to you in New York?''

She sighed worriedly. She'd been ashamed to tell him how stupid she'd been. But now there was a bigger reason. It was going to hurt him. She didn't understand how she knew it, but she did. He was going to blame himself all over again for the way they'd separated.

''Not now,'' she said.

''You're holding back. Don't let's have secrets between us,'' he said solemnly.

''It will hurt,'' she said.

''Most everything does, these days,'' he murmured, and rubbed his thigh.

She took his hand and held it warmly. "Come and sit down."

"Not in here."

He drew her into the living room. It was warm and dim and quiet. He led her to his big armchair, dropped into it and pulled her down into his arms.

"Now, tell me," he said, when her cheek was pillowed on his hard chest.

"It's not a nice story."

"Tell me."

She rubbed her hand against his shirt and closed her eyes. "I found an ad in the paper. It was one of those big ads that promise the stars, just the thing to appeal to a naive country girl who thinks she can just walk into a modeling career. I cut out the ad and called the number."

"And?"

She grimaced. "It was a scam, but I didn't know it at first. The man seemed very nice, and he had a studio in a good part of town. Belinda had gone to Europe for the week on an assignment for the magazine where she worked, and I didn't know anyone else to ask about it. I assumed that it was legitimate." Her eyes closed and she pressed closer, feeling his arm come around her tightly, as if he knew she was seeking comfort.

"Go ahead," he coaxed gently.

"He gave me a few things to try on and he took pictures of me wearing them. But then I was sitting there, just in a two-piece bathing suit, and he told me to take it off." His breathing stilled under her ear. "I couldn't," she snapped. "I just couldn't let him look at me like that, no matter how good a job I could get, and I said so. Then he got ugly. He told me that he was in the business of producing nude calendars and that if I didn't do the assignment, he'd take me to court and sue me for not fulfilling the contract I'd signed. No, I didn't read it," she said when he asked. "The fine print did say that I agreed to pose in any manner the photographer said for me to. I knew that I couldn't afford a lawsuit."

"And?" He sounded as cold as ice.

She bit her lower lip. "While I was thinking about alternatives, he laughed and came toward me. I could forget the contract, he said, if I was that prudish. But he'd have a return for the time he'd wasted on me. He said that he was going to make me sleep with him."

"Good God!"

She smoothed his shirt, trying to calm him. Tears stung her eyes. "I fought him, but I wasn't strong enough. He had me undressed before I knew it. We struggled there on the floor and he started hitting me." Her voice broke and she felt Corrigan stiffen against her. "He had a diamond ring on his right hand. That's how he cut my cheek. I didn't even feel it until much later. He wore me down to the point that I couldn't kick or bite or scream. I would never have been able to get away. But one of his girls, one of the ones who didn't mind posing nude, came into the studio. She was his lover and she was furious when she saw him with me…like that. She started screaming and throwing things at him. I grabbed my clothes and ran."

She shivered even then with the remembered humiliation, the fear that he was going to come after her. "I managed to get enough on to look halfway decent, and I walked all the way back to Belinda's apartment." She swallowed. "When I was rational enough to talk, I called the police. They arrested him and charged him with attempted rape. But he said that I'd signed a contract and I wasn't happy with the money he offered me, and that I'd only yelled rape because I wanted to back out of the deal."

He bit off a curse. "And then what?"

"He won," she said in a flat, defeated tone. "He had friends and influence. But the story was a big deal locally for two or three days, and he was furious. His brother had a nasty temper and he started making obscene phone calls to me and making threats as well. I didn't want to put Belinda in any danger, so I moved out while she was still in Europe and never told her a thing about what had happened. I got a job in New Jersey and worked there for two years. Then Belinda moved out to Long Island and asked me to come back. There was a good job going with a law firm that had an office pretty close to her house. I had good typing skills by then, so I took it.''

"What about the brother?" he asked.

"He didn't know where to find me. I learned later that he and the photographer were having trouble with the police about some pornography ring they were involved in. Ironically they both went to prison soon after I left Manhattan. But for a long time, I was even afraid to come home, in case they had anyone watching me. I was afraid for my father.''

"You poor kid," he said heavily. "Good God! And after what had happened here…" His teeth ground together as he remembered what he'd done to her.

"Don't," she said gently, smoothing out the frown between his heavy eyebrows. "I never blamed you. Never!''

He caught her hand and brought it to his mouth. "I wanted to come after you," he said. "Your father stopped me. He said that you hated the very mention of my name.''

"I did, at first, but only because I was so hurt by the way things had worked out." She looked at his firm chin. "But I would have been glad to see you, just the same.''

"I wasn't sure of that." He traced her mouth. "I thought that it might be as well to leave things the way they were. You were so young, and I was wary of complications in my life just then." He sighed softly. "There's one other thing you don't know about me.''

"Can't you tell me?''

He smiled softly. "We're sharing our deepest secrets. I suppose I might as well. We have a fifth brother. His name is Simon."

"You mentioned him the first time you came over, with that bouquet."

He nodded. "He's in San Antonio. Just after you left town, he was in a wreck and afterward, in a coma. We couldn't all go back, and leave the ranch to itself. So I went. It was several weeks before I could leave him. By the time I got back, you weren't living with Belinda anymore and I couldn't make her tell me where you were. Soon after that, your father came down on my head like a brick and I lost heart."

"You called Belinda?"

"Yes."

"You wanted to find me?"

He searched her eyes quietly. "I wanted to know that you were safe, that I hadn't hurt you too badly. At least I found that much out. I didn't hope for more."

She traced his eyebrows, lost in the sudden intimacy. "I dreamed about you," she said. "But every time, you'd come toward me and I'd wake up."

He traced the artery in her throat down to her collarbone. "My dreams were a bit more erotic." His eyes darkened. "I had you in ways and places you can't imagine, each more heated than the one before. I couldn't wait to go to bed, so that I could have you again."

She blushed. "At first, you mean, just after I left."

His hand smoothed onto her throat. "For eight years. Every night of my life."

She caught her breath. She could hardly get it at all. His eyes were glittering with feeling. "All that time?"

He nodded. He looked at her soft throat where the blouse had parted, and his face hardened. His fingers trailed lightly down onto her bodice, onto her breast. "I haven't touched a woman since you left Jacobsville," he said huskily. "I haven't been a man since then."

Her wide eyes filled with tears. She had a good idea of what it would be like for a man like Corrigan to be incapable with a woman. "Was it because we fought, at the last?"

"It was because we made love," he whispered. "Have you forgotten what we did?"

She averted her eyes, hiding them in embarrassment.

"You left a virgin," he said quietly, "but only technically. We had each other in your bed," he reminded her, "naked in each other's arms. We did everything except go those last few aching inches. Your body was almost open to me, I was against you, we were moving together…and you cried out when you felt me there. You squirmed out from under me and ran."

"I was so afraid," she whispered shamefully. "It hurt, and I kept remembering what I'd been told…"

"It wouldn't have hurt for long," he said gently. "And it wouldn't have been traumatic, not for you. But you didn't know that, and I was too excited to coax you. I lost my temper instead of reassuring you. And we spent so many years apart, suffering for it."

She laid her hot cheek against his chest and closed her eyes. "I didn't want to remember how far we went," she said through a mist. "I hurt you terribly when I drew back…"

"Not that much," he said. "We'd made love in so many ways already that I wasn't that hungry." He smoothed her soft hair. "I wanted an excuse to make you leave."

"Why?"

His lips touched her hair. "Because I wanted to make you pregnant," he whispered, feeling her body jump as he said it. "And it scared me to death. You see, modern women don't want babies, because they're a trap. My mother taught me that."

# Chapter 6

"That's not true!" She pressed closer. "I would have loved having a baby, and I'd never have felt trapped!" she said, her voice husky with feeling. Especially your baby, she added silently. "I didn't know any of your background, especially anything about your mother. You never told me."

His chest rose and fell abruptly. "I couldn't. You scared me to death. Maybe I deliberately upset you, to make you run. But when I got what I thought I wanted, I didn't want it. It hurt when you wouldn't even look at me, at the bus stop. I guess I'd shamed you so badly that you couldn't." He sighed. "I thought you were modern, that we'd enjoy each other and that would be the end of it. I got the shock of my life that last night. I couldn't even deal with it. I lost my head."

She lifted her face and looked into his eyes. "You were honest about it. You'd already said that you wanted no part of marriage or a family, that all you could offer me was a night in your arms with no strings attached. But I couldn't manage to stop, or stop you, until the very last. I was raised to think of sleeping around as a sin.''

His face contorted. He averted his eyes to keep her from seeing the pain in them. ''I didn't know that until it was much too late. Sometimes, you don't realize how much things mean to you until you lose them.''

His fingers moved gently in her hair while she stood quietly, breathing uneasily. ''It wasn't just our mother who soured us on women. Simon was married,'' he said after a minute. ''He was the only one of us who ever was. His wife got pregnant the first time they were together, but she didn't want a child. She didn't really want Simon, she just wanted to be rich. He was crazy about her.'' He sighed painfully. ''She had an abortion and he found out later, accidentally. They had a fight on the way home from one of her incessant parties. He wrecked the car, she died and he lost an arm. That's why he doesn't live on the ranch. He can't do the things he used to do. He's embittered and he's withdrawn from the rest of us.'' He laughed a little. ''You think the four of us hate women. You should see Simon.''

She stirred in his arms. ''Poor man. He must have loved her very much.''

''Too much. That's another common problem we seem to have. We love irrationally and obsessively.''

''And reluctantly,'' she guessed.

He laughed. ''And that.''

He let her go with a long sigh and stared down at her warmly. ''I suppose I'd better take you home. If you're still here when the boys get back, they'll tie you to the stove.''

She smiled. ''I like your brothers.'' She hesitated. ''Corrigan, they aren't really going to try to force you to marry me, are they?''

''Of course not,'' he scoffed. ''They're only teasing.''

"Okay."

It was a good thing, he thought, that she couldn't see his fingers crossed behind his back.

He took her home, pausing to kiss her gently at the front door.

"I'll be along tomorrow night," he said softly. "We'll go to a movie. There's a new one every Saturday night at the Roxy downtown."

She searched his eyes and tried to decide if he was doing this because he wanted to or because his brothers were pestering him.

He smiled. "Don't worry so much. You're home, it's going to be Christmas, you have a job and plenty of friends. It's going to be the best Christmas you've ever had."

She smiled back. "Maybe it will be," she said, catching some of his own excitement. Her gaze caressed his face. They were much more like friends, with all the dark secrets out in the open. But his kisses had made her too hungry for him. She needed time to get her emotions under control. Perhaps a day would do it. He was throwing out broad hints of some sort, but he hadn't spoken one word of love. In that respect, nothing had changed.

"Good night, then," he said.

"Good night."

She closed the door and turned on the lights. It had been a strange and wonderful day. Somehow, the future looked unusually bright, despite all her worries.

The next morning, Dorie had to go into town to Clarisse's shop to help her with the bookkeeping. It was unfortunate that when she walked in, a beautiful woman in designer clothes should be standing at the counter, discussing Corrigan.

"It's going to be the most glorious Christmas ever!" she was telling the other woman, pushing back her red-gold hair and laughing. "Corrigan is taking me to the Christmas party at the Coltrains' house, and afterward we're going to Christmas Eve services at the Methodist Church." She sighed. "I'm glad to be home. You know, there's been some talk about Corrigan and a woman from his past who just came back recently. I asked him about it, if he was serious about her." She laughed gaily. "He said that he was just buttering her up so that she'd do some bookkeeping for him and the brothers, that she'd run out on him once and he didn't have any intention of letting her get close enough to do it again. I told him that I could find it in my heart to feel sorry for her, and he said that he didn't feel sorry for her at all, that he had plans for her…"

Clarisse spotted Dorie and caught her breath. "Why, Dorothy, I wasn't expecting you…quite so soon!"

"I thought I'd say hello," Dorie said, frozen in the doorway. She managed a pasty smile. "I'll come back Monday. Have a nice weekend."

"Who was that?" she heard the other woman say as she went quickly back out the door and down the street to where she'd parked the car Turkey Sanders had returned early in the morning, very nicely fixed.

She got behind the wheel, her fingers turning white as she gripped it. She could barely see for the tears. She started the engine with shaking fingers and backed out into the street. She heard someone call to her and saw the redhead standing on the sidewalk, with an odd expression on her face, trying to get Dorie's attention.

She didn't look again. She put the car into gear and sped out of town.

She didn't go straight home. She went to a small park inside the city and sat down among the gay lights and decorations with a crowd that had gathered for a Christmas concert performed by the local high school band and chorus. There were so many people that one more didn't matter, and her tears weren't as noticeable in the crush of voices.

The lovely, familiar carols were oddly soothing. But her Christmas spirit was absent. How could she have trusted Corrigan? She was falling in love all over again, and he was setting her up for a fall. She'd never believe a word he said, ever again. And now that she'd had a look at his beautiful divorcée, she knew she wouldn't have a chance with him. That woman was exquisite, from her creamy skin to her perfect figure and face. The only surprising thing was that he hadn't married her years ago. Surely a woman like that wouldn't hang around waiting, when she could have any man she wanted.

Someone offered her a cup of hot apple cider, and she managed a smile and thanked the child who held it out to her. It was spicy and sweet and tasted good against the chill. She sipped it, thinking how horrible it was going to be from now on, living in Jacobsville with Corrigan only a few miles away and that woman hanging on his arm. He hadn't mentioned anything about Christmas to Dorie, but apparently he had his plans all mapped out if he was taking the merry divorcée to a party. When had he been going to tell her the truth? Or had he been going to let her find it out all for herself?

She couldn't remember ever feeling quite so bad. She finished the cider, listened to one more song and then got up and walked through the crowd, down the long sidewalk to where she'd parked her car. She sat in it for a moment, trying to decide what to do. It was Saturday and she had nothing planned for today. She wasn't going to go home. She couldn't bear the thought of going home.

She turned the car and headed up to the interstate, on the road to Victoria.

Corrigan paced up and down Dorie's front porch for an hour until he realized that she wasn't coming home. He drove back to town and pulled up in front of Tira Beck's brick house.

She came out onto the porch, in jeans and a sweatshirt, her glorious hair around her shoulders. Her arms were folded and she looked concerned. Her frantic phone call had sent him flying over to Dorie's house hours before he was due to pick her up for the movie. Now it looked as if the movie, and anything else, was off.

"Well?" she asked.

He shook his head, with his hands deep in his jacket pockets. "She wasn't there. I waited for an hour. There's no note on the door, no nothing."

Tira sighed miserably. "It's all my fault. Me and my big mouth. I had no idea who she was, and I didn't know that what I was telling Clarisse was just a bunch of bull that you'd handed me to keep me from seeing how much you cared for the woman." She looked up accusingly. "See what happens when you lie to your friends?"

"You didn't have to tell her that!"

"I didn't know she was there! And we had agreed to go to the Coltrains' party together, you and me and Charles Percy."

"You didn't mention that you had a date for it, I guess?" he asked irritably.

"No. I didn't realize anyone except Clarisse was listening, and she already knew I was going with Charles."

He tilted his hat further over his tired eyes. "God, the webs we weave," he said heavily. "She's gone and I don't know where to look for her. She might have gone back to New York for all I know, especially after yesterday. She had every reason to think I was dead serious about her until this morning."

Tira folded her arms closer against the cold look he shot her. "I said I'm sorry," she muttered. "I tried to stop her and tell her that she'd misunderstood me about the party, that I wasn't your date. But she wouldn't even look at me. I'm not sure she saw me. She was crying."

He groaned aloud.

"Oh, Corrigan, I'm sorry," she said gently. "Simon always says you do everything the hard way. I guess he knows you better than the others."

He glanced at her curiously. "When have you seen Simon?"

"At the cattle convention in San Antonio last week. I sold a lot of my Montana herd there."

"And he actually spoke to you?"

She smiled wistfully. "He always speaks to me," she said. "I don't treat him like an invalid. He feels comfortable with me."

He gave her an intent look. "He wouldn't if he knew how you felt about him."

Her eyes narrowed angrily. "I'm not telling him. And neither are you! If he wants me to be just a friend, I can settle for that. It isn't as if I'm shopping for a new husband. One was enough," she added curtly.

"Simon was always protective about you," he recalled. "Even before you married."

"He pushed me at John," she reminded him.

"Simon was married when he met you."

Her expression closed. She didn't say a word, but it was there, in her face. She'd hated Simon's wife, and the feeling had been mutual. Simon had hated her husband, too. But despite all the turbulence between Tira and Simon, there had never been a hint of infidelity while they were both married. Now, it was as if they couldn't get past their respective bad marriages to really look at each other romantically. Tira loved Simon, although no one except Corrigan knew it. But Simon kept secrets. No one was privy to them anymore, not even his own brothers. He kept to himself in San Antonio. Too much, sometimes.

Tira was watching him brood. "Why don't you file a missing persons report?" she suggested suddenly.

"I have to wait twenty-four hours. She could be in Alaska by then." He muttered under his breath. "I guess I could hire a private detective to look for her."

She gave him a thoughtful look and her eyes twinkled. "I've got a better idea. Why not tell your brothers she's gone missing?"

His eyebrows lifted, and hope returned. "Now that's a constructive suggestion," he agreed, nodding, and he began to grin. "They were already looking forward to homemade biscuits every morning. They'll be horrified!"

And they were. It was amazing, the looks that he got from his own kinfolk when he mentioned that their prized biscuit maker had gone missing.

"It's your fault," Rey said angrily. "You should have proposed to her."

"I thought you guys had all that taken care of," Corrigan said reasonably. "The rings, the minister, the gown, the invitations…"

"Everything except the most important part," Cag told him coldly.

"Oh, that. Did we forget to tell her that he loved her?" Leo asked sharply. "Good Lord, we did! No wonder she left!" He glared at his brother. "You could have told her yourself if you hadn't been chewing on your hurt pride. And speaking of pride, why didn't you tell Tira the truth instead of hedging your bets with a bunch of lies?"

"Because Tira has a big mouth and I didn't want the whole town to know I was dying of unrequited love for Dorie!" he raged. "She doesn't want to marry me. She said so! A man has to have a little pride to cling to!"

"Pride and those sort of biscuits don't mix," Rey stressed. "We've got to get her back. Okay, boys, who do we know in the highway patrol? Better yet, don't we know at least one Texas Ranger? Those boys can track anybody! Let's pool resources here…"

Watching them work, Corrigan felt relieved for himself and just a little sorry for Dorie. She wouldn't stand a chance.

She didn't, either. A tall, good-looking man with black hair wearing a white Stetson and a Texas Ranger's star on his uniform knocked at the door of her motel room in Victoria. When she answered it, he tipped his hat politely, smiled and put her in handcuffs.

They were halfway back to Jacobsville, her hastily packed suitcase and her purse beside her, before she got enough breath back to protest.

"But why have you arrested me?" she demanded.

"Why?" He thought for a minute and she saw him scowl in the rearview mirror. "Oh, I remember. Cattle rustling." He nodded. "Yep, that's it. Cattle rustling." He glanced at her in the rearview mirror. "You see, rustling is a crime that cuts across county lines, which gave me the authority to arrest you."

"Whose cattle have I rustled?" she demanded impertinently.

"The Hart Brothers filed the charges."

"Hart…Corrigan Hart?" She made a furious sound under her breath. "No. Not Corrigan. Them. It was them! Them and their damned biscuits! It's a put-up job," she exclaimed. "They've falsely accused me so that they can get me back into their kitchen!"

He chuckled at the way she phrased it. The Hart brothers and their mania for biscuits was known far and wide. "No, ma'am, I can swear to that," he told her. His twinkling black eyes shone out of a lean, darkly tanned face. His hair was black, too, straight and thick under that wide-brimmed white hat. "They showed me where it was."

"It?"

"The bull you rustled. His stall was empty, all right."

Her eyes bulged. "Didn't you look for him on the ranch?"

"Yes, ma'am," he assured her with a wide smile. "I looked. But the stall was empty, and they said he'd be in it if he hadn't been rustled. That was a million-dollar bull, ma'am." He shook his head. "They could shoot you for that. This is Texas, you know. Cattle rustling is a very serious charge."

"How could I rustle a bull? Do you have any idea how much a bull weighs?" She was sounding hysterical. She calmed down. "All right. If I took that bull, where was he?"

"Probably hidden in your room, ma'am. I plan to phone back when we get to the Hart place and have the manager search it," he assured her. His rakish grin widened. "Of course, if he doesn't find a bull in your room, that will probably mean that I can drop the charges."

"Drop them, the devil!" she flared, blowing a wisp of platinum hair out of her eyes. "I'll sue the whole damned state for false arrest!"

He chuckled at her fury. "Sorry. You can't. I had probable cause."

"What probable cause?"

He glanced at her in the rearview mirror with a rakish grin. "You had a hamburger for lunch, didn't you, ma'am?"

She was openly gasping by now. The man was a lunatic. He must be a friend of the brothers, that was the only possible explanation. She gave up arguing, because she couldn't win. But she was going to do some serious damage to four ugly men when she got back to Jacobsville.

The ranger pulled up in front of the Harts' ranch house and all four of them came tumbling out of the living room and down to the driveway. Every one of them was smiling except Corrigan.

"Thanks, Colton," Leo said, shaking the ranger's hand. "I don't know what we'd have done without you."

The man called Colton got out and opened the back seat to extricate a fuming, muttering Dorie. She glared at the brothers with eyes that promised retribution as her hand-cuffs were removed and her suitcase and purse handed to her.

"We found the bull," Cag told the ranger. "He'd strayed just out behind the barn. Sorry to have put you to this trouble. We'll make our own apologies to Miss Wayne, here."

Colton stared at the fuming ex-prisoner with pursed lips. "Good luck," he told them.

Dorie didn't know where to start. She looked up at Colton and wondered how many years she could get for kicking a Texas Ranger's shin.

Reading that intent in her eyes, he chuckled and climbed back into his car. "Tell Simon I said hello," he called to them. "We miss seeing him around the state capital now that he's given up public office."

"I'll tell him," Cag promised.

That barely registered as he drove away with a wave of his hand, leaving Dorie alone with the men.

"Nice to see you again, Miss Wayne," Cag said, tipping his hat. "Excuse me. Cows to feed."

"Fences to mend," Leo added, grinning as he followed Cag's example.

"Right. Me, too." Rey tipped his own hat and lit out after his brothers.

Which left Corrigan to face the music, and it was all furious discord and bass.

She folded her arms over her breasts and glared at him.

"It was their idea," he said pointedly.

"Arrested for rustling. Me! He…that man…that Texas Ranger tried to infer that I had a bull hidden in my motel room, for God's sake! He handcuffed me!" She held up her wrists to show them to him.

"He probably felt safer that way," he remarked, observing her high color and furious face.

"I want to go home! Right now!"

He could see that it would be useless to try to talk to her. He only made one small effort. "Tira's sorry," he said quietly. "She wanted to tell you that she's going to the Coltrains' party with Charles Percy. I was going to drive, that's all. I'd planned to take you with me."

"I heard all about your 'plan.'"

The pain in her eyes was hard to bear. He averted his gaze. "You'd said repeatedly that you wanted no part of me," he said curtly. "I wasn't about to let people think I was dying of love for you."

"Wouldn't that be one for the record books?" she said furiously.

His gaze met hers evenly. "I'll get Joey to drive you home."

He turned and walked away, favoring his leg a little. She watched him with tears in her eyes. It was just too much for one weekend.

Joey drove her home and she stayed away from the ranch. Corrigan was back to doing the books himself, because she wouldn't. Her pride was raw, and so was his. It looked like a complete stalemate.

"We've got to do something," Cag said on Christmas Eve, as Corrigan sat in the study all by himself in the dark. "It's killing him. He won't even talk about going to the Coltrains' party."

"I'm not missing it," Leo said. "They've got five sets of Lionel electric trains up and running on one of the most impressive layouts in Texas."

"Your brother is more important than trains," Rey said grimly. "What are we going to do?"

Cag's dark eyes began to twinkle. "I think we should bring him a Christmas present."

"What sort of present?" Rey asked.

"A biscuit maker," Cag said.

Leo chuckled. "I'll get a bow."

"I'll get out the truck," Rey said, shooting out the front door.

"Shhh!" Cag called to them. "It wouldn't do to let him know what we're up to. We've already made one monumental mistake."

They nodded and moved more stealthily.

Corrigan was nursing a glass of whiskey. He heard the truck leave and come back about an hour later, but he wasn't really interested in what his brothers were doing. They'd probably gone to the Christmas party over at Coltrain's ranch.

He was still sitting in the dark when he heard curious muffled sounds and a door closing.

He got up and went out into the hall. His brothers looked flushed and flustered and a little mussed. They looked at him, wide-eyed. Leo was breathing hard, leaning against the living-room door.

"What are you three up to now?" he demanded.

"We put your Christmas present in there," Leo said,

indicating the living room. "We're going to let you open it early."

"It's something nice," Cag told him.

"And very useful," Leo agreed.

Rey heard muffled noises getting louder. "Better let him get in there. I don't want to have to run it down again."

"Run it down?" Corrigan cocked his head. "What the hell have you got in there? Not another rattler...!"

"Oh, it's not that dangerous," Cag assured him. He frowned. "Well, not quite that dangerous." He moved forward, extricated Leo from the door and opened it, pushing Corrigan inside. "Merry Christmas," he added, and locked the door.

Corrigan noticed two things at once—that the door was locked, and that a gunnysack tied with a ribbon was sitting in a chair struggling like crazy.

Outside the door, there were muffled voices.

"Oh, God," he said apprehensively.

He untied the red ribbon that had the top securely tied, and out popped a raging mad Dorothy Wayne.

"I'll kill them!" she yelled.

Big booted feet ran for safety out in the hall.

Corrigan started laughing and couldn't stop. Honest to God, his well-meaning brothers were going to be the death of him.

"I hate them, I hate this ranch, I hate Jacobsville, I hate you...*mmmfff!*"

He stopped the furious tirade with his mouth. Amazing how quickly she calmed down when his arms went around her and he eased her gently out of the chair and down onto the long leather couch.

She couldn't get enough breath to continue. His mouth was open and hungry on her lips and his body was as hard as hers was soft as it moved restlessly against her.

She felt his hands on her hips and, an instant later, he

was lying between her thighs, moving in a tender, achingly soft rhythm that made her moan.

"I love you," he whispered before she could get a word out.

And then she didn't want to get a word out.

His hands were inside her blouse and he was fighting his way under her skirt when they dimly heard a key turn in the lock.

The door opened and three pair of shocked, delighted eyes peered in.

"You monsters!" she said with the last breath she had. She was in such a state of disarray that she couldn't manage anything else. Their position was so blatant that there was little use in pretending that they were just talking.

"That's no way to talk to your brothers-in-law," Leo stated. "The wedding's next Saturday, by the way." He smiled apologetically. "We couldn't get the San Antonio symphony orchestra to come, because they have engagements, but we did get the governor to give you away. He'll be along just before the ceremony." He waved a hand at them and grinned. "Carry on, don't mind us."

Corrigan fumbled for a cushion and flung it with all his might at the door. It closed. Outside, deep chuckles could be heard.

Dorie looked up into Corrigan's steely gray eyes with wonder. "Did he say the governor's going to give me away? Our governor? The governor of Texas?"

"The very one."

"But, how?"

"The governor's a friend of ours. Simon worked with him until the wreck, when he retired from public office. Don't you ever read a newspaper?"

"I guess not."

"Never mind. Just forget about all the details." He bent to her mouth. "Now, where were we…?"

The wedding was the social event of the year. The governor did give her away; along with all four brothers, including the tall, darkly distinguished Simon, who wore an artificial arm just for the occasion. Dorie was exquisite in a Paris gown designed especially for her by a well-known couturier. Newspapers sent representatives. The whole world seemed to form outside the little Presbyterian church in Victoria.

"I can't believe this," she whispered to Corrigan as they were leaving on their Jamaica honeymoon. "Corrigan, that's the vice president over there, standing beside the governor and Simon!"

"Well, they sort of want Simon for a cabinet position. He doesn't want to leave Texas. They're coaxing him."

She just shook her head. The Hart family was just too much altogether!

That night, lying in her new husband's arms with the sound of the ocean right outside the window, she gazed up at him with wonder as he made the softest, sweetest love to her in the dimly lit room.

His body rose and fell like the tide, and he smiled at her, watching her excited eyes with sparks in his own as her body hesitated only briefly and then accepted him completely on a gasp of shocked pleasure.

"And you were afraid that it was going to hurt," he chided as he moved tenderly against her.

"Yes." She was gasping for air, clinging, lifting to him in shivering arcs of involuntary rigor. "It's…killing me…!"

"Already?" he chided, bending to brush his lips over her swollen mouth. "Darlin', we've barely started!"

"Barely…? Oh!"

He was laughing. She could hear him as she washed up and down on waves of ecstasy that brought unbelievable noises out of her. She died half a dozen times, almost lost consciousness, and still he laughed, deep in his throat, as he went from one side of the bed to the other with her in a tangle of glorious abandon that never seemed to end. Eventually they ended up on the carpet with the sheet trailing behind them as she cried out, sobbing, one last time and heard him groan as he finally shuddered to completion.

They were both covered with sweat. Her hair was wet. She was trembling and couldn't stop. Beside her, he lay on his back with one leg bent at the knee. Incredibly he was still as aroused as he'd been when they started. She sat up gingerly and stared at him, awed.

He chuckled up at her. "Come down here," he dared her.

"I can't!" She was gasping. "And you can't...you couldn't...!"

"If you weren't the walking wounded, I sure as hell could," he said. "I've saved it all up for eight years, and I'm still starving for you."

She just looked at him, fascinated. "I read a book."

"I'm not in it," he assured her. He tugged her down on top of him and brushed her breasts with his lips. "I guess you're sore."

She blushed. "You *guess?*"

He chuckled. "All right. Come here, my new best friend, and we'll go to sleep, since we can't do anything else."

"We're on the floor," she noted.

"At least we won't fall off next time."

She laughed because he was outrageous. She'd never thought that intimacy would be fun as well as pleasurable. She traced his nose and bent to kiss his lips. "Where are we going to live?"

"At the ranch."

"Only if your brothers live in the barn," she said. "I'm not having them outside the door every night listening to us."

"They won't have to stand outside the door. Judging from what I just heard, they could hear you with the windows closed if they stood on the town squa... Ouch!"

"Let that be a lesson to you," she told him dryly, watching him rub the nip she'd given his thigh. "Naked men are vulnerable."

"And you aren't?"

"Now, Corrigan...!"

She screeched and he laughed and they fell down again in a tangle, close together, and the laughter gave way to soft conversation. Eventually they even slept.

When they got back to the ranch, the three brothers were gone and there was a hastily scrawled note on the door.

"We're sleeping in the bunkhouse until we can build you a house of your own. Congratulations. Champagne is in the fridge." It was signed with love, all three brothers—and the name of the fourth was penciled in.

"On second thought," she said, with her arm around her husband, "maybe those boys aren't so bad after all!"

He tried to stop her from opening the door, but it was too late. The bucket of water left her wavy hair straight and her navy blue coat dripping. She looked at Corrigan with eyes the size of plates, her arms outstretched, her mouth open.

Corrigan looked around her. On the floor of the hall were two towels and two new bathrobes, and an assortment of unmentionable items.

He knew that if he laughed, he'd be sleeping in the barn for the next month. But he couldn't help it. And after a glance at the floor—neither could she.

\*    \*    \*    \*    \*

# Redbird

## by Diana Palmer

# *Chapter One*

She was there again. Hank Shoeman glared out the window at the figure on the balcony of the ski lodge below. His cabin was on a ridge overlooking the facility, just far enough away to give him the privacy he needed when he was composing. But it wasn't far enough away from the binoculars the slender young woman at the ski lodge was directing toward his living room window.

He shoved his hands into his jeans pockets and glowered at the distant figure. He was used to attention. Leader of the rock group Desperado, and a former linebacker for the Dallas Cowboys, Hank had had his share of adulation from women. In the old days, before his marriage and divorce, it had been flattering and heady to a Texas ranch boy. Now, it was nothing more than a nuisance. He'd had all he wanted of love. And he'd had more than he wanted of starstruck young girls looking for it.

He sighed, the action pulling his silk shirt taut over a hard, impressively muscular chest, and tautening the jeans that outlined powerful long legs and narrow hips. He was

thirty-eight, but physically he looked no more than thirty.
He had a good body, still fit and athletic. It was his face
that frightened people.

He wore a thick beard and a mustache and his dark hair,
while scrupulously clean, was unruly and thick around his
collar. He wasn't bad-looking, but it was impossible to see
that. He liked the camouflage, because it kept all but the
most enthusiastic young groupies at bay.

None of the rock group looked much better than Hank
with his growth of beard, except for Amanda, of course.
The other three male members of the band—Deke and Jack
and Johnson—looked as disreputable as Hank did. But Desperado's music won awards, and they were much in de-
mand for public appearances.

The problem with that right now was that Amanda was
pregnant. It would be the first child for Amanda and her
husband, Quinn Sutton, who lived in Wyoming with his
son Elliot. The whole family was anxious because
Amanda's pregnancy had been fraught with problems and
she'd been forced to take to her bed to prevent a miscar-
riage. That meant canceled public appearances and vicious
rumors that the band was about to break up. It was let
people think that, or admit that Amanda was in fierce dif-
ficulties with her pregnancy. No one wanted that tidbit of
information to get out, and have reporters hounding her.
For the moment, they didn't know exactly where in Wyoming she lived. And Hank was here in Colorado, far away
from the group's studios—both the one down the hill from
Quinn Sutton's ranch in the Tetons, and the one in New
York City.

Reporters had hounded him so much that he'd had to
escape from the New York studio where the group did
some of their recording. It had been impossible to go near
Amanda's house, for fear of leading reporters right to her
doorstep.

So, this cabin in Colorado was Hank's last resort. He'd
come here to work on a new song which he hoped might

be a contender for another award. The music had been written, now it was up to Hank to complete the lyrics, but it was slow going. Worrying about Amanda and the future of the group was not conducive to creative effort.

Perhaps he was working too hard, he thought. He needed a break. That woman at the ski lodge was getting on his nerves. If she was a reporter spying on him, he wanted to know it. There had to be some way to get her off his trail and spare Amanda any further media blitz.

He shrugged into his parka and drove to the ski lodge in his white Bronco. The chains made a metallic rhythm on the thick-packed snow covering the road that led to the lodge. Bad weather had plagued the area this January, and there had just been a long period of subzero temperatures and blinding snow, which had made it impossible to ski for the past several days.

When he got to the lodge, it wasn't crowded at all. People who could get out had already gone. Only a handful of hearty, optimistic souls were left in residence, hoping for slightly less arctic temperatures and better skiing when conditions improved.

He walked into the lodge, towering over everyone and attracting a lot of unwanted attention. He went straight to the owner's office.

Mark Jennings got up from his desk and walked around it to shake hands with the visitor.

"What brings you down here, Hank?" he asked with a grin. "Lonesome, are you?"

"I should be so lucky," Hank murmured dryly. "I came down to see which one of your guests is auditioning for the KGB."

Mark's smile faded. "What?"

"You've got a guest with binoculars who spends a lot of time looking in through my living room window," he replied. "I want to know who she is and what she's looking for."

Mark whistled. "I had no idea."

"It's not your job to watch the guests," the other man said, clapping him on the shoulder with a big hand. "Maybe she's a groupie. I'd like to know, in case she's trying to gather material for the wire services. I've had enough publicity just lately."

"I understand. What can I do to help?"

"I thought I'd hang out in the café for a while and see if she turns up for lunch. I'd recognize her. She's wearing a bright blue parka and a matching cap."

Mark frowned. "Doesn't sound familiar, but I don't get out of this office much lately. We don't have a lot of people staying here, though, so she shouldn't be too hard to spot."

"If you don't mind, I'll have a look around."

Mark nodded. "Help yourself. Any chance that you and the group might sign on next season for entertainment?" he added hopefully.

Hank chuckled. "Ask me again in a few months."

"Don't think I won't!"

Hank shook hands with him and went on into the café, shucking his parka as he walked. It was a bad time to have to hunt down a spy. He was already upset enough about Amanda and the relentless press. Lately his career was playing a bad second to complications of every sort.

He glanced around as he walked into the small café. There were only three women in it. Two of them were drinking coffee at a table overlooking the ski lift. The other was clearing tables. She saw Hank and grinned.

"Hi, Hank," she greeted him, tossing back her blond hair. "Long time no see!"

"I've been busy, Carol," he said with an affectionate smile. She'd been a waitress at Mark's place for several years. There was nothing romantic between them; she was just a friend.

She moved closer, so that they wouldn't be overheard. "Better watch your step down here today," she said confidentially. "One of the women at the side table is a reporter for *Rolling Stone*. I heard her telling the other woman that she'd gotten some juicy gossip about Amanda and that you were in hiding up here. She said she was going to file a really big story with her magazine over her computer modem tonight.''

He caught his breath in muted anger and stared at the table intently. One of the women was very petite with short dark hair. The other was a redhead, attractive and full figured. He scowled. "Which is which?" he asked impatiently.

She grimaced. "That's the thing, I couldn't tell. I dropped a plate and I wasn't looking at them when I overheard her. Sorry, Hank. You know most of their reporters, don't you?''

He nodded. "But I don't recognize either of those women. She could be a stringer or even a free-lancer, hoping to find something worth selling to them on a tentative go-ahead.''

"I'll bet it's the redhead," she whispered. "She looks like a reporter.''

"And I'd bet on the brunette," he remarked as he suddenly registered the color of her jacket. Royal blue. She was the one who'd been spying on him with the binoculars.

"Could be," Carol replied. "I wish I could be more help. Heard from the rest of the group?''

He shook his head. "We're all taking a rest from public appearances.''

"I guess you need one! Give everyone my best, won't you?''

"Sure.''

He watched the women from the next room, staying out of sight for a minute, before leaving the lodge. He was easily recognizable these days, with all the media attention, and he couldn't afford to give that reporter a shot at him.

He was going to have to do something, but what? If she filed that story, reporters were going to swarm Amanda like ducks on bugs. He couldn't have that. Her pregnancy had been one big secret so far, ever since she started to show and the band cut short their tour. They were still recording, but no one knew why they'd left the road so quickly. Where Amanda was, on Quinn Sutton's ranch, no one was likely to be able to get near her. Quinn was a formidable bodyguard, and he loved his pretty blond wife to distraction even if they'd gotten off to one of the world's worst starts.

He leaned against the hood of the Bronco, ignoring the sudden snow flurries and folded his arms over his chest while he tried to decide on a course of action. How was he going to prevent the reporter from filing her story? All sorts of wild ideas occurred to him, the first being that he could cut the telephone wires.

"Great solution," he murmured to himself. "You should try writing fiction."

As he turned over possible solutions to his problem, lo and behold, the brunette came walking out the front door of the ski lodge with a camera and binoculars around her neck and a backpack over one shoulder. She came down the steps and started around the Bronco and Hank when the perfect solution presented itself to him on a silver platter.

Without thinking about consequences, jail terms or FBI intervention, he suddenly walked behind her, picked her up bodily and slid her into the Bronco past the steering wheel. Before she could get over the shock, he had the vehicle headed up the mountain.

Poppy O'Brien stared at him with wide dark eyes full of shock. "Either I'm still asleep and dreaming or I'm being kidnapped by a grizzly bear," she said suddenly.

"I'm not a grizzly bear."

"You look like a grizzly bear."

He didn't look at her. "Insults won't do you any good."

"Listen, I have terrible diseases..." she began, using a ploy she'd heard on a television talk show.

"Don't flatter yourself," he remarked with a speaking glance. "I don't seduce midgets."

"Midgets?" Her dark eyes widened. "I'm five foot five!"

He shrugged. "Okay. So you're a tall midget. You're still too small for a man my size."

She looked at him fully then. His head almost touched the roof of the Bronco. He was huge; not fat, but well built and powerful looking. "Are you one of those wild-eyed mountain men who kidnap hikers?"

He shook his head.

"Hopelessly lonely and desperate for companionship?"

He smiled reluctantly. "Not a chance."

"Then would you like to tell me why you've kidnapped me?"

"No."

She leaned back against the seat. He looked sane, but one could never tell. She studied him with curiosity and just a little apprehension. "What are you going to do with me?" she asked again.

"I don't know."

"That's reassuring."

"I won't hurt you."

"That's even more reassuring." She frowned as she studied him. "You look familiar."

"Everyone says that."

"Have you ever worn a wide-brimmed hat and asked people not to start forest fires?"

He did chuckle then. "Not lately."

"I'm on my way to look for a lost dog. I promised."

"He'll come home."

She glared at him. "After I've found the dog, I have to pack. I'm leaving tomorrow," she informed him.

"Fat chance."

She took in a sharp breath. "Now you listen here, Tarzan of the Snow Country, what you're doing is a federal offense. You could be arrested. You could go to jail."

"Why?"

"Because you're kidnapping me!"

"I'm doing no such thing," he returned, pulling up into the driveway of the cabin. "I'm extending my hospitality to a ski lodge guest who was lost in the mountains."

"I am not lost!" she stormed. "I was at the ski lodge, right in front of the ski lodge…!"

"You looked lost to me. It's snowing. Very hard, too," he remarked as he got out of the truck. In fact, it was worse than snow. It looked like the beginnings of a blizzard. "Come on. Let's get inside."

She folded her arms. "I am not leaving the truck," she informed him bluntly.

"It isn't a truck. It's a four-wheel-drive vehicle."

She lifted her chin. "Oh, details, details! I am not… ohh!"

In the middle of her impassioned resistance, he picked her up and carried her to the cabin.

She was too shocked to resist. She'd been independent most of her life, and at twenty-six she was used to being on her own. She was attractive, and she knew it, but she was also intelligent and studious, traits that didn't endear her to suitors. Her choice of career had made it impossible for her to carry on any sort of affair. She'd spent years in school with midterms and final exams always hanging over her head, with lab after lab eating up her free time. The only people she spent time with were fellow students. The curriculum required for a science degree was so much more difficult than that required for a liberal arts degree that it often seemed she did nothing but study.

And then after graduation, there was the apprenticeship, and that required all sorts of odd hours that none of the other partners wanted. She was the one who spent weekends and holidays and nights at work. Two boyfriends had quickly given her up for women who had nine-to-five day jobs and were geared to nights on the town.

None of that had prepared her for being swept off her feet, literally, by a blue-eyed grizzly bear.

The sheer power and size of his body had her as spellbound as a young girl. She lay in his huge arms like a statue, gaping up at him as he balanced her easily on one knee while he unlocked the cabin door.

He caught that rapt stare and laughed mirthlessly. He was used to the look. His ex-wife had found him fascinating at first. Afterward, it was his best friend and the man's bank account that fascinated her. The divorce was inevitable, with all the time Hank spent on the road. His best friend had probably been inevitable, too. Hank was powerful and talented, but he wasn't handsome. His best friend was. He'd given in to the divorce without a protest, and the parting had been amicable—on the surface, at least. He'd settled a nice amount of money on her. She was grateful. He was alone, as usual. He'd gone home afterward to the Texas ranch that his father and five brothers still owned. It had been comforting there, but he never had fit in. The only horse big enough for him to ride was a Percheron and he'd never been able to spin a rope. He often thought that his brothers despaired of him.

He put the woman down and closed the door, locking it and pocketing the key. Then he took a good, long look at her. She was attractive, pert and pretty and a little irritated. Her dark eyes glared up at him fearlessly.

"You can't keep me here," she informed him.

"Why not?"

"Because I have responsibilities. I have a job. I need a telephone right now, as a matter of fact, so that I can tell someone I'm not looking for that dog."

"Dream on," he said pleasantly. "Can you cook?"

Her eyebrows lifted. "Cook what?"

"Anything."

He was stripping off his parka as he spoke. Her eyes drifted over a magnificent body in jeans and a well-fitting, long-sleeved red shirt. He could have graced a magazine cover. He was perfectly proportioned and huge. He made her feel like a child as he towered over her.

"I can cook toast," she said absently. "How tall are you?"

"Six foot five," he said.

"You must eat like a horse."

He shrugged. "I use up a lot of calories."

She was still staring at him, fascinated. "Who are you?"

He laughed without humor and his blue eyes began to glitter. "Pull the other one."

"I beg your pardon?"

"You might as well get comfortable," he informed her. "You're going to be here for several days."

"I am not. I'll walk back to the lodge."

"Not in that you won't," he said, gesturing toward the window, where snow was coming down outside at a frightening rate.

She gnawed on her lower lip, a nervous habit that often resulted in a sore mouth. "Oh dear," she said uneasily, more worried about the possibility of losing her job than of being sequestered here with a madman.

"You'll be perfectly safe here," he said, mistaking her apprehension. "I won't attack you."

"Oh dear, oh dear," she repeated again. "They'll think I'm having too good a time to come back. They'll think I'm not serious about my job. They didn't really want me in the beginning because they thought I was too young. They'll use this as an excuse to find someone to replace me."

"No doubt," he said irritably. "But what does it matter? You'll find another job."

She glared at him. "Not like this one, I won't!"

"Pays good, does it?" he asked, thinking that reporters always seemed to get a high rate of pay for selling out people's private lives for public consumption.

"Very good," she retorted, "with excellent chances for advancement."

"Too bad."

"You have no right to keep me here," she informed him.

"You had no right to spy on me," he returned.

Her face stiffened. "I beg your pardon?"

"You've had those damned binoculars trained up here for the past few days," he said shortly. "Spying on me."

"Spying...and why, pray tell, would I want to spy on you? Do you think I'm so desperate for a man that I have to peek through windows to get a glimpse of one?"

"You don't need to play games with me," he said coolly. "I'm not likely to be taken in by you. I'm an old hand at fending off groupies."

"This is unreal," she snapped. "Things like this don't happen except in books and movies! Men don't go around kidnapping women unless it's a desert and they're wearing long sheets!"

"Sorry," he said. "I didn't have a sheet handy."

"And what do you mean, calling me a groupie?" She put her hands on her slim hips and glowered up at him with flashing dark eyes.

"Why were you spying on me?"

"Spying...!" She threw up her hands. "I was watching a bald eagle," she said shortly. "They've just released a pair of them ten miles north of the ski lodge, as part of a federal repopulation program. I'd come to see them."

"Oh, my God, tell me you're not one of those animal-loving fanatics!"

"If there were more of us in the world, it wouldn't be in such a mess."

He looked angry as he studied her. "They tried re-populating wolves up north. The damned things are eating lambs and calves all over the mountains, and the people who released them went back home to their apartment buildings."

He said it with such sarcasm and contempt that she almost took a step backward. But she was made of sterner stuff. "Nature exists largely on a system of checks and balances. You've overlooked the fact that without preda-tors, prey multiplies. If you don't believe that, look at Aus-

tralia where the rabbits hadn't enough natural enemies and
overran the country.''

"Well then, why don't we ship them some of our leftover wolves?" he asked smugly.

"Show me a wolf who can survive in the desert and it
might be a good idea."

"You hotshot animal lovers might consider crossbreeding a wolf with a camel. I hear they're doing some fantastic
genetic experiments in labs all over the country."

"To produce healthier animals and disease-resistant
strains of plants."

"Hybrids," he scoffed. "Hybrids are sterile, aren't
they?"

"I don't deal in experiments," she informed him hotly.
"I wouldn't know."

"They turned loose two eagles. Isn't that an experi-
ment?"

She was losing ground. "Why have you brought me
here?" She tried again for an answer.

"I'm a lonely man," he said sarcastically. "I don't have
any company up here, and I can't get girls. So periodically,
I stake out the ski lodge and appropriate their overflow."
He lifted an expressive hand. "Think of it as repopulating
my bachelor environment with healthy new specimens.
That should appeal to someone like you. And think of all
the juicy material you can use later."

"Material? Use? For what?"

"Cut it out," he said carelessly. "We both know what
you do for a living. I heard it all from Carol at the lodge."

"Carol? Oh, the blond waitress." She sighed. "Well, I
guess it doesn't matter if you know, does it? I mean, I
wasn't exactly hiding it from anyone."

"Just as I thought. Now. How about something to eat?"
He indicated the window. "It's highly doubtful that you
could go anywhere right now even if I was willing to let
you leave. Which I'm not."

She pursed her full lips and stared up at him curiously.

"When the snow clears, I'm heading out," she informed him sweetly. "Or you'll find yourself in jail the minute I can get to a telephone."

"Threats are only useful when you can enforce them."

"And you think I can't?"

"I think that by the time you leave, you won't need any." He was hopeful that he could convince her not to bother Amanda. He was persuasive when he tried to be, and if she liked animals, she had to have a soft center. Knowing the enemy was half the battle. He didn't think he was in for any surprises with her.

# Chapter Two

"What's your name?" he asked as he fried bacon.

"Poppy O'Brien," she replied. "And yours?"

He chuckled. She was a game player, all right. "Call me Hank."

"Hank what?"

He glanced toward her with an insolent smile. "Just Hank," he said with faint challenge.

She joined him in the kitchen. "Have it your way. I suppose if I'd kidnapped someone I wouldn't want to give them my real name, either." She started opening cabinets.

"What are you doing?" he demanded. It irritated him that she felt free to rifle through his kitchen.

"I'm going to make biscuits. Unless you think you can."

"I can make biscuits," he said defensively.

"A lot of people can. But can you eat them?" she asked.

He hesitated. After a minute, he paused in his own chore and produced vegetable shortening, flour, milk and a big bowl. "Go for it."

She rolled up the sleeves of her blue sweater and proceeded to make drop biscuits. He'd finished with the bacon and was working on beating eggs in a bowl.

"They'll be cold by the time the biscuits get done if you cook them now," she said pointedly.

He didn't argue. He finished beating the eggs, covered the bowl and put them in the refrigerator. Then he perched himself on the edge of the big table and watched her pat the biscuits into a pan and dab milk onto the tops.

"You do that as if it's a regular thing with you," he commented.

"It is," she said. "I've been feeding myself for a long time. Eating out is expensive. I cook a lot."

"Do you cook for someone?" he probed.

She smiled as she put the biscuits into the oven she'd already had him preheat. "Yes. For myself."

He stuck his hands into his pockets and stared her down.

She lifted a shoulder. "I don't have time for that sort of thing," she said. "I work nights and weekends and holidays. Before I got this job, I was in school."

High school, he figured, by the look of her. She seemed very young. She wasn't hard on the eyes at all, with that trim figure and her big dark eyes and soft oval face. She had a vulnerable manner that appealed to his masculinity. His wife had been a take-charge sort of woman, very businesslike and intelligent, but with hard edges that he could never smooth. She liked being a real estate executive and she had no thoughts of being a housewife and mother. She didn't like children. She did enjoy pretty clothes and parties, though. His best friend was taking her to a lot of those, he heard.

Poppy glanced at him and saw the expression that narrowed his deep blue eyes. "Do you have someone to cook for?" she asked bluntly. If he could ask questions, so could she.

"I was married," he said flatly. "She took up with my best friend and divorced me. I wasn't home enough to suit her."

"I'm sorry."

"Don't be. It was a friendly divorce. We weren't compatible." He looked down at his hand-tooled leather boots. "I wanted kids. I have a bunch of brothers back home."

She leaned back against the pine counter and folded her arms across her chest. "I don't have any family left. My mother died when I was born and my father was killed in an airplane crash four years ago."

"Are you an only child?"

She nodded. "It's a good thing I was goal-oriented and self-sufficient, I guess," she confessed. "I threw myself into studying and got over it in time."

"How did you manage to support yourself while you got through high school?" he asked curiously.

"High school?" Her eyes widened. "I was in college." She laughed. "How old do you think I am?"

"Eighteen. Maybe nineteen."

She grinned. "Thanks. I'm twenty-six."

His heavy brows drew together. "Hell!"

"I am. I have a degree."

"In what—"

The thunderous, crashing sound outside cut him off. He rushed to the window and looked out. Snow had come off the mountain above the lodge in a small avalanche, taking down telephone lines and power lines.

"Good thing Mark's got emergency generators," he murmured. "So have I. But those telephone lines are well and truly out until this weather clears a little."

"Do you have a phone?" she asked from beside him.

He looked at her. "No. I've been using the phone at the lodge. I hate telephones. Unlisted numbers are a farce—there's no such thing. You ought to know that."

She wondered how he did know that her private line was flooded with calls from people at two in the morning whose problems couldn't wait until the office opened.

She laughed. "Well, yes, I do know."

He glanced back out the window. "The lodge is okay,

at least. I met a guy in the ski patrol this morning when I went out for supplies. He said they'd checked the slopes earlier and there was no threat. I wonder what caused the avalanche?''

"People skiing outside the safe boundary, a gunshot from an irresponsible hunter, God knows." She grimaced. "I hope that poor dog got found."

"Marshmallow heart," he accused. "The only dog I know of around here is a stray who hangs around the lodge for handouts. He belongs to a retired Austrian skier who lives about a half mile over the hill. That dog knows these mountains better than any human being, and he doesn't get lost. Somebody was pulling your leg." One eye narrowed. "Who sent you out?"

She frowned. "It was one of the younger ski instructors, the one they call Eric. He said that he'd start from the other end of the trail and we'd meet in the middle at some little cabin…" She stopped. "Why are you laughing?"

"Eric Bayer," he said, nodding. "They call him St. Bernard, because he's pulled that lost-dog stunt so many times with pretty young tourists. That cabin is almost a shrine to his prowess as a lover."

She flushed to her hairline. He watched, smiling.

"Where do you come from?" he asked lazily.

"Sioux City, Iowa," she said. "Why?"

"It figures." He moved back into the kitchen just in time to remove the biscuits before they burned. They looked light and fluffy and they were just tanned enough to be tempting. "Nice," he pronounced.

"Thanks." She got butter from the refrigerator while he scrambled the eggs. She made coffee and when the eggs were ready, she poured it into two thick mugs and put them on the small, square kitchen table.

"Forks," he said, handing her one. "I don't fuss with table settings when I'm alone here."

"Ah," she said. "So you're not usually alone?"

"Only when I'm working." He raised his fork and took

a mouthful of scrambled egg. "And you should know," he added mockingly, "because *Rolling Stone* prints something about every visit I make here."

Her eyebrows arched. "Rolling Stone? They're a rock group, aren't they? I thought they were in England. Do they have a newsletter?"

"You do that amazingly well," he remarked.

"Do what?"

"The innocent look," he replied, finishing his eggs before he started on the biscuits. "I wish I had some jam. I ate the last of it yesterday and forgot to get more."

"Too bad. What was that about looking innocent?"

"Eat your lunch before it gets cold. These are great biscuits!"

They must have been, he was on his fourth one. She smiled. "Breakfast for lunch," she remarked. "I can't wait to see what you eat for the evening meal."

"Cereal, usually," he remarked. "Or sandwiches. I don't cook much when I'm working. If I get a yen for breakfast in the middle of the day, I have it," he added firmly.

She smiled. "I wasn't complaining. I love breakfast."

Her easy acceptance of the odd meal put him at ease. He finished eating and sat back with the coffee mug in one huge hand and looked at her. She was small. Not tiny, but small, and beautifully proportioned. He liked her soft complexion and those big brown eyes. She had a pretty mouth, too, very full and sweet-looking.

"I feel I should tell you that I know karate."

His eyebrows lifted. "Do you, really?"

She nodded.

He smiled lazily. "Do you really think it would do you any good against someone my size?" he asked gently.

She looked him over. "You ruined it."

"Ruined what?"

"I was going to tell you that I knew karate and several *other* Japanese words."

It took a minute to sink in. When it did, he began to laugh.

She smiled, too. "And to answer that, no, I don't think it would do me a bit of good against someone your size. Even if I knew how to use it." She finished her coffee and put the mug down. "Why did you think I was spying on you?"

"You kept looking in my living room window."

"The eagle was sitting on the top limb of one of those aspen trees behind your house."

He let out a soft whistle. "There really was an eagle?"

"Two of them," she amended. "Beautiful eagles. They're huge birds. I'd never seen any up close before. I thought they were small, but they aren't, and they have pale golden eyes."

"I've seen eagles," he replied. "I spend a lot of time here and in Wyoming."

"I'd love to see Wyoming," she remarked. "I've always wanted to go to Cheyenne during the rodeo season."

"Don't you animal lovers consider rodeo a cruel sport?" he taunted.

"I'm not a fanatic," she said pointedly. "And I know better than some people how well treated most rodeo stock is. My dad used to handle bulls for the bull-riding events, back in Oklahoma."

"I thought you said you were from Sioux City."

"I live there now. I grew up outside Oklahoma City." She touched the rim of the coffee cup. "Where are you from?"

She was laying it on thick, but he was too tired to question her. He'd been up late for the better part of a week trying to write lyrics that just wouldn't come. "I'm from Texas, up near Dallas."

"Around the cross-timbers country?" She smiled at his surprise. "I've been through there a time or two with Dad, when he went to rodeos."

"It's pretty country. So is this."

The portable generator made a noise and he glared toward the back of the house. "Damn that thing," he muttered. "I knew I should have replaced it. If it goes out, we'll freeze and starve to death in here."

"Hardly," she said. "There's plenty of cut wood out front and you have a fireplace. I know how to cook on a fireplace."

"Good thing," he muttered. "I sure as hell don't."

"I gather that there's no way out of here except down the mountain we just came up?"

He nodded.

She looked out at the blinding snow and rubbed her arms. "You still haven't told me why you brought me up here."

"Does it matter now?" he asked. "You can't leave, anyway. From the looks of that snow, we're going to be cabin-bound for a few days until they can get the snowplows in."

"Well, yes, I think it does matter," she replied. "After all, nobody's ever tried to kidnap me before. I'd like to know what I've done."

"Why do you insist on playing games with me?" he muttered. "I know who you are!"

"Yes, you've already said so."

"Then you know what you've done," he said. "You threatened to call in a story that would damage several careers and possibly cost a woman her child."

"Call in a story." She repeated it again, staring blankly at him. "Call it in to whom? And how would I, since the only things I know how to fill out are medical reports?"

"Medical reports?"

She glowered at him. "Yes, medical reports, prescriptions, medicines, that sort of thing. I have a degree. I'm in practice. That's why I need to be back home, before I lose the partnership I've worked so hard to get!"

"You're a doctor?" he bellowed.

"Yes. Dr. O'Brien!"

He slapped his hand over his forehead. "Oh, God, I got the wrong one!"

"Wrong one. Am I to gather that you meant to kidnap some other poor woman?"

"Yes!" he said impatiently. He ran his hand through his bushy, thick hair. "Damn! Damn, damn, damn, she's probably halfway to New York by now with a heaving bosom full of unsubstantiated facts!"

"She, who?" Poppy demanded.

"That damn reporter!"

"The girl I was sitting with when you came in? But she isn't due to leave for two more days. She's meeting her fiancé in Salt Lake City and then they're going on to Los Angeles."

"She is?"

"That's what she said."

He leaned forward. "This is important. Did she say anything to you about Amanda Sutton?"

"I don't remember any names," she said. "She was talking about a singer who'd vanished from sight and the breakup of a big rock group."

"Which rock group?" he asked.

She grimaced. "Sorry," she said apologetically. "I don't keep up with pop music. I like classical and opera."

He stared at her, long and hard.

"You needn't look like that," she muttered, sweeping back the fall of hair that dropped onto her brow. "There isn't one thing wrong with symphonies and opera!"

"I didn't know that anyone in the world still listened to them." From his perspective, rock music was all that existed. He spent all his time with people who composed it or played it.

"I see," she returned. "You're one of those MTV fanatics who think that music without a volcanic beat isn't worth listening to."

"I didn't say that."

"I am so *tired* of skeletal men in sprayed-on leather

pants wearing guitars for jockey shorts, with their hairy chests hanging out!''

He couldn't hold back the laughter. It overflowed like the avalanche that had brought half a ridge down a few minutes before. ''You're priceless.''

''Well, aren't you tired of it, really?'' she persisted. ''Don't you think that there's a place in the world for historical music, beautiful music?''

He sobered quickly. He didn't know how to answer that. It had been a long time since he'd listened to anything classical, and he'd certainly never thought of it in that way. ''Historical music?'' he asked.

''Yes.'' She began to smile. ''It's like talking to someone who lived a century, two centuries ago. You play the notes they wrote and hear them, just as they heard them. History comes alive in that moment, when you reproduce sounds that were heard in another time.''

His heart leapt in his chest. He thought about the history she'd mentioned. Then her wording came back to him.

''You said you play the notes...do you play?''

''Piano,'' she said. ''A little. I only had lessons for five years, and I'm not gifted. But I do love music.''

His face softened under its thick covering of hair. ''But not rock music,'' he persisted.

''So much of it is noise,'' she said. ''After you listen to it for a while, it all blurs into steel guitars. But, once in a while, another sort of song sticks its head out and a few people find magic in it.'' She mentioned one of his songs, one of Desperado's songs. ''There were a lot of flutes in it,'' she recalled, closing her eyes and smiling as she remembered it. ''Beyond it was a high, sweet voice that enunciated every word. And the words were poetry.'' Her eyes opened, dark and soft with memory. ''It was exceptional. But it wasn't their usual sort of music, either. The announcer said so. He said the composer did the song on a dare and didn't even want it included on the album, but the other members of the group insisted.''

That was true. Hank had been certain that no one would like the soft, folksy song he'd written. And to his amazement, it had won a Grammy. He'd let Amanda accept it for him, he recalled, because he was too embarrassed to take credit for it publicly. "Did you see the video?"

She shook her head. "I've never had time to watch videos. I just listen to the radio when I'm driving."

Incredible. She loved his music and she didn't even know who he was. He wasn't sure if he was insulted or amused. It was the only song of that sort that he'd ever written and he'd sworn that he'd never do another one. A lot of the music critics hadn't liked it. He was trying to break out of the mold and they didn't want to let him. It was a kind of musical typecasting.

"Do you remember the group the reporter was talking about?" he asked, returning to his earlier question.

"She told me, but I was watching the eagle out the window," she confessed sheepishly, and with a grin. "I'm afraid I wasn't listening. She was alone and wanted to talk, and I was the only other person handy when she came in. She was friendly and I didn't mind sharing the table. It was just that the eagle came pretty close to the window..."

"You really do like animals." He chuckled.

"I guess so. I was forever bringing home birds with broken wings and once I found a little snake with its tail cut off by a lawnmower. I couldn't stand to watch things suffer and not try to help."

His blue eyes searched her dark ones for longer than he meant to. She stared back, and he saw the color flood her cheeks. That amused him deep inside and he began to smile.

Poppy felt her heart race. He didn't seem to be dangerous or a threat to her in any physical way, but that smile made her feel warm all over. She hadn't been at a disadvantage, except when he'd carried her inside the cabin. Now she wondered if she shouldn't have fought a little harder for her freedom. He was very big and powerful, and if he wanted to, he could...

"You're amazingly easy to read," he remarked gently. "There's nothing to be nervous about. I don't force women. It's the other way around."

She didn't quite believe him. He had a fantastic physique, but he looked like a grizzly bear. She couldn't imagine him being beset by women.

"Are you rich?" she asked.

His eyes narrowed and the smile faded. "Meaning that I'd have to be rich to attract a woman?" he drawled with muted anger.

He hadn't moved or threatened, but the look in his eyes made her uncomfortable. "I didn't say that."

"Yes, you did."

"I didn't mean to insult you. It's just that you're, well, you're...bushy."

His lips compressed. "Bushy?"

"You look like a grizzly bear!"

"A lot of men wear beards and mustaches!"

"Most of them have some skin on their faces that shows, too!"

He moved away from the window and took a step toward her. She took a step back.

"There's no need to start stalking me," she protested, looking him right in the eye. She stopped. "I won't run. You can't make me run. I'm not afraid of you."

She acted like a woman confronting an attack dog. It would have amused him if he'd been a little less insulted.

"I haven't had to chase women in ten years," he said through his teeth, and kept coming. "They chase me. They hound me. I can't even check into a hotel without having someone search the room. I could have a woman twice a day if I felt like it, and I wouldn't have to pay them for it. I turn down more proposals in a week than you've probably had in your lifetime. But you think I look like a grizzly bear and no woman would want me unless I was rich."

She held up a hand, nervous of him now. "I didn't say that at all," she began soothingly. She came up against something hard, and realized that he'd edged her back against a wall. "Now, see here," she said firmly, "this isn't any way to win an argument, with sheer brute force."

"Isn't that what you think I'd need to get a woman?"

"I didn't mean it," she assured him. She tried to edge past him, but he put an arm that was like a small tree trunk past her on one side and another on the other side and trapped her.

"What makes you think you're qualified to judge?" he continued irritably. "You're almost thin. There's nothing to you. You act as if you've spent your life buried in books. What do you know about men?"

"I date," she said shortly. "In fact, I can go out anytime I like!" And she could, with one of her partner's sons, who seemed to have six hands and used every one of them the time she'd been crazy enough to go to a movie with him. He'd have taken her out again if she liked, but she wouldn't go to the front door with him!

"How much do you have to pay him?" he mocked.

When that sank in, she drew in an angry breath, forgot her embarrassment and fear and raised her hand sharply toward his hairy cheek.

He caught it with depressing ease and pressed it against the side of his face. The hair that grew on it was surprisingly soft, when it looked like steel wool.

"You don't know much about men's egos, do you?" he asked, bending. "If you don't learn one other thing, you'd better learn right now that insults have consequences. And I'm just the man to show you how many!"

She started to defend herself, and before she could get a single word out, his lips had opened and fitted themselves exactly to the shape of her soft, shocked mouth.

# Chapter Three

It hadn't occurred to her that a human grizzly bear would be so good at kissing. He wasn't clumsy or brutal. He was slow and almost tender. Even the huge hands that slid around her waist and brought her lazily against him were all but comforting.

He nibbled at her upper lip where it clung stubbornly to her lower one. "It won't hurt," he breathed softly. "Give in."

"I won't..."

The parting of her lips gave him the advantage he'd been looking for. He eased them open under his with a pressure that was so slow and arousing that she stood, stunned, in his embrace.

He towered over her. At close range, he was even larger than he'd seemed at first. His big hands spread over her back, almost covering both her shoulder blades, and he smiled against her shocked gasp. His teeth gently worried her lower lip while his tongue trailed over it, and she thought dizzily that she'd never known such an experienced caress from the few, the *very* few, men she'd dated.

He felt her stiffen and lifted his head. The blue eyes that searched her dark ones were wise and perceptive. His hand came up and traced the soft color that overlaid one high cheekbone.

"You taste of coffee," he murmured.

It was beginning to dawn on her that he might not be lying about his success with women. And she didn't think it was because he was rich. Not anymore.

He didn't see fear in her face, or experience. He saw a charming lack of it. His big thumb smoothed over her lips and her body seemed to leap into his at the sensation he produced.

"Nothing to say, Poppy?" he asked.

She shook her head, her eyes unblinking as they sought his for reassurance.

"You're perfectly safe," he replied, answering the look. "I'm not a rake, even if I do fit the picture of a kidnapper. But I had noble motives."

"You're...very big, aren't you?" she faltered.

"Compared to you," he agreed. His eyes narrowed as he studied her. She did look very small in his arms. He looked down to her breasts, pressed against his shirt. She barely came up to his chin and she had a fragile build. If he made love to her, it would be touch and go, because she was so much smaller. He scowled.

"What's wrong?" she asked curiously.

He met her eyes. "I was thinking about how careful I'd have to be with you in bed," he said absently.

She flushed and pushed at him. "You'd be lucky!" she raged.

He smiled at her ruffled fury and let her go. "Wouldn't I, though?" he agreed lazily. Her red face told him things she wouldn't. "You're very delicately built. I've deliberately limited myself to tall, buxom women because I'm so big. Do you know, I can't even let myself get into fistfights unless I can find another man my size?''

She studied him, under the spell of a hateful attraction. Her heart was still racing. His shirt was open at the neck and there was a dark, thick nest of hair in it. She wondered what he looked like under his clothes and could have choked on her own curiosity.

"You never told me what you do," she said, diverting her eyes to his face.

"I used to play professional football," he volunteered.

She frowned, searching his features. "I'm sorry. I don't watch it. I'm not much of a sports fan."

"It figures. It was a long time ago."

That explained how he could afford this nice cabin in such a luxury area of the state. He'd probably made a fortune in professional sports and saved a lot of it. It would explain the women, too. All at once, it bothered her to think of him with women.

She wrapped her arms over her breasts. "How long will that last, do you think?" she asked, nodding toward the snowstorm.

"A couple of days," he said. "I'll get you back to the lodge as soon as I can, I promise." He sighed heavily, wondering where that reporter was, and if she'd managed to get out. "I fouled this up really good," he muttered. "Poor Amanda. She'll never forgive me if they get to her."

Amanda? She frowned. "Have I missed something?"

"Probably." He turned away. "I'll check on that generator. I don't have a television here, but there's a piano and plenty of books. You ought to be able to amuse yourself."

"Thanks."

He paused as he shouldered into his parka and looked at her. "If you don't get back to your job, they won't really fire you, will they?"

"I don't know." It worried her. She interpreted his expression and smiled ruefully. "Don't worry. I'd be stuck at the lodge anyway, even if you hadn't kidnapped me, wouldn't I?''

That seemed to lessen the guilt she read on his face. ''Maybe. Maybe not. I'm sorry. I'll make it up to you, if I can. I should have made sure before I acted.''

''What were you going to do with that reporter?'' she asked.

''I was going to keep her here until I could warn Amanda,'' he said. ''She's not having an easy time of it and all the wire services are after the story. I thought I was safe here, but they can track you down anywhere.''

Amanda must be his girlfriend, because he was trying so hard to protect her from the press. She wondered why. ''Is she married?'' she asked involuntarily.

''Yes,'' he said solemnly. ''I'll be back in a minute.''

So that was it, she thought as he left the cabin. He was in love with a married woman and the newspapers were after him. He must be somebody very famous in sports to attract so much media attention even if he didn't play football anymore. She wished she'd paid more attention to sports. He was probably very famous and she'd go home without even knowing his name. She thought whimsically of selling her story to the tabloids—''I was kidnapped by a football star...'' But of course she couldn't do that, because she didn't even know his full name.

She wandered out of the huge living room and down the hall. There were two bedrooms, one with a huge, king-size bed and the other with a normal bed. They were nicely decorated and furnished, and each had its own bathroom. Farther down was a room with all sorts of electronic equipment, including speakers and recorders and wires and microphones, a huge keyboard, an electric guitar and a piano. She stood in the doorway, fascinated.

After a minute, she approached the piano, drawn by the name on it. She knew that name very well; it was the sort of instrument even a minor pianist dreamed of being able to afford. It must be his hobby, playing, and he must be very rich to be able to buy something so astronomically expensive to indulge that hobby on.

Her fingers touched the keys and trembled. It was in perfect tune. She sat down on the bench, remembering when she was a child how she'd dreamed night after night of owning a piano. But there had been no money for that sort of luxury. She'd played on other people's pianos when she was invited, and along the way she'd picked up some instruction. Eventually, when her father died, she was left with a huge insurance policy that she hadn't even wanted; she'd wanted her parent back. But the money had put her through college, bought her a small, inexpensive piano and lessons to go with it. And it had made it possible for her to make her own way in the world. She didn't earn a lot just now, but if she could continue in the partnership—if they didn't fire her—she had prospects.

She put her trembling hands on the keyboard, thinking that if she'd had the opportunity to study as a child, she might have made music her life.

She closed her eyes and began to play the *Moonlight Sonata,* softly at first, and then with more power and pleasure and emotion than she'd ever felt before. This magnificent instrument was all hers to enjoy, and enjoy it she did. When the last chord died into the stillness, she came back to her surroundings with a jolt as she realized that she wasn't alone in the room.

She turned around. Hank was there, leaning against the doorway, something in his eyes that she couldn't grasp. He wasn't smiling. His face was somber and oddly drawn.

"I'm sorry!" she stammered, rising quickly to her feet. "I didn't mean to presume…"

"Why aren't you playing professionally?" he asked surprisingly.

She stared at him blankly. "I chose medicine instead of music."

"A noble choice, but you have a gift. Didn't you know?"

She looked around her, embarrassed. "You play, too, I guess? Is it a hobby?"

He smiled to himself. "You might say that."

"I've never thought of a football player as a musician," she said quietly. "It's...surprising."

"Some people think so. I'm too damned big for most hobbies. At least music fits me."

She smiled gently and turned her attention back to the piano. She touched it with loving fingers. "She's lovely, isn't she?" The wonder in her voice was evident. "A real lady."

He was touched and delighted by her unconscious reverence. "That's what I call her," he remarked. "Odd that you'd think the same way, isn't it?"

"I guess a lot of people love music."

"Yes. Even football players."

She laughed self-consciously, because he sounded bitter. "Did that sting? I'm sorry. I didn't mean to sound disparaging. I've never known anybody in sports before. I know a little about baseball, and once I met a minor-league baseball player."

"The thrill of your life?"

"Oh, no, getting my degree was that." She glanced at him uneasily. Some people were immediately hostile when she mentioned her extensive education.

He lifted a bushy eyebrow. "Fitting me for a mold?" he mused. "Will you faint if I tell you that I have a degree of my own?"

Her eyes brightened. "Really?"

"I'm a music major," he said.

"I'll bet that gave the sports announcers something to talk about during games—" She stopped dead. Things she'd read and heard on television, bits and pieces were coming back to her. She didn't follow sports, but there was one sports figure who'd confounded the critics and the fans when he suddenly dropped out of professional football to found of all things a rock group. He'd only had a mustache then, not a full beard and long hair besides. She'd seen his photograph in the paper, and she'd seen an interview on television.

"Oh, my God," she said in a whisper.

"Put it together, did we?" he mused, smiling. "Go ahead."

"Desperado," she said. "You played for the Dallas Cowboys and quit after the best season you'd ever had to go into music. Everybody thought you were crazy. Then you won a Grammy..."

"Several Grammies," he said, correcting her.

"Several. Amanda is your lead singer," she added, remembering that tidbit. "She's beautiful. But...didn't she marry?"

He chuckled. "Yes. She married a poor Wyoming rancher and she's very, very pregnant and Quinn Sutton is beside himself with worry. She's not having an easy time. We're trying to protect her from the press and it hasn't been easy. We're all afraid that word is going to get out about her problems with the pregnancy and she's going to be covered up by the press."

"We?"

"The group," he said. "She's very special to all of us, although she and Quinn are deeply in love."

"Are you in love with her?" she asked bluntly.

"I was, in the old days," he said easily. "We all were. She's beautiful and talented. But now she's kind of like a kid sister that we try to take care of. I'd do anything to protect her. Even," he added ruefully, "kidnap a reporter."

"That would have been terribly intelligent," she said sarcastically. "What a story it would make!"

"I didn't say I was thinking clearly," he muttered darkly. "I had to act fast, before she could file that story. And look what a great job I did!"

"Anybody can make a mistake. But she doesn't know about Amanda, you know," she added. "She knew that you were here and she was going to tell her office that a man at the lodge said you were about to get engaged to someone you met here. *That's* the hot scoop she had.''

He leaned back against the door and laughed delightedly. ''Good God!''

''So it doesn't really matter if she gets to a phone, does it?''

''No.'' He groaned and ran a hand through his thick hair. ''Hell, I could have saved myself all this trouble!''

''Not to mention saving me a little,'' she said irritably.

He looked surprised. ''I saved you from St. Bernard.''

Her lips protruded. ''I don't need saving from a man like that. He had lips like a lizard.''

He chuckled. ''Did he?''

She closed the lid on the piano. ''He wasn't my type at all.''

He moved closer and raised the lid. ''What is your type?'' he asked as he ran his elegant fingers over the keyboard.

''I'll know the minute I find him,'' she assured him.

He lifted his head and looked into her dark eyes. ''You don't like rock music, you said.''

''I don't listen to it,'' she confessed. ''Except that one song that I told you about.''

''Yes. This one.''

He sat down at the piano and began to play it, softly, smoothly, his eyes seeking hers.

''It was you,'' she said slowly.

He nodded. ''Amanda sang it. I don't have a lead voice, only one good enough to second the rest of them. But I can write music. None of them can.''

She came to stand just behind him, with a soft hand on his shoulder as he increased the tempo.

''I meant it to be a rock song. Amanda made me slow it down. They ganged up on me and made me put it on the album. I didn't want to.''

''Why?''

''Because it's intimate,'' he said shortly. ''It's part of

me, when I do something like this. There are things I don't
want to share with the world."

"You should share music like this, though," she replied.
"It's exquisite."

He smiled at her. "But you like opera. And historical
music."

Her fingers became unconsciously caressing on his
shoulder. "Yes. But this is beautiful."

He finished the piece and lifted his hands from the keyboard. She hadn't moved.

He reached up and smoothed his fingers over her hand
before he lifted it to his mouth.

He swiveled around and caught her by the hips, his eyes
darkening, narrowing as they looked up at her.

She felt him move before she saw him. He drew her to
him and eased her to her knees between his outstretched
legs. Then he framed her face in his big hands and bent to
kiss her with slow, tender hunger. She started to protest,
but he stayed the instinctive backward movement of her
head and kept kissing her, until she gave in to him and slid
her arms around his neck.

It wasn't until his hand trespassed onto her soft breast
that she stiffened and caught his fingers.

He lifted his head and looked at her flushed face as she
fought with his invading hand. There was something very
calculating about his expression.

"You're…analyzing me," she accused.

"You aren't used to a man's hand on your breast," he
commented, watching her gasp. "You're twenty-six, right?
Then why haven't you had a man, Poppy?"

"For heaven's sake!" She pushed at him and he let her
go. She scrambled to her feet, pushing back her hair, and
stared unseeing out the window while she fought for composure.

He joined her at the window, leaning idly against the
window frame with his big hands in his pockets. "Are you
physically or emotionally scarred in some way?"

She shook her head.

"Then, why?"

She frowned. "What do you mean, why?"

"Why haven't you slept with anyone yet?"

He seemed to think it was a matter of course, that women had the same freedom that men did and should enjoy it.

"Well, I don't respect men who sleep around just because they want to satisfy a fleeting physical hunger. Why should I want to be that way myself?"

He frowned. "Everyone sleeps around."

"Bull," she said, raising her hand when he started to speak. "And don't quote me statistics. Statistics depend on whom you interview. If you ask two hundred people in New York City what they think of a free sexual life-style, and then you ask the same question of two hundred people in a small town in Iowa, you're going to get a heck of a different set of statistics!"

His big shoulders moved. "I hadn't thought about it that way. But the times are changing."

She only smiled.

"Don't tell me," he chided gently. "You're going to save yourself for the man you marry."

"Of course I am," she said matter-of-factly.

He threw up his hands. "Lunacy," he muttered. "You don't know what you're missing."

"Sure I do. I'm missing all those exciting risks, including the one that can kill you." She pursed her lips as she studied him. "And if we're going to get so personal, how much of a swinger are you?"

"I'm not," he replied, shocked. "Only an idiot sleeps around these days!"

She burst out laughing.

He liked the way she laughed, even the way she lost her temper. "Want to draw straws to see who gets to cook supper?"

She traced his face with soft eyes. "I'll do it, if you'll tell me what you like. Not cereal," she added.

"Steak and baked potatoes and salad, then," he said.

"I like steak, too."

"Two of each for me," he added. "I have to get enough protein."

"I'll bet you're expensive to feed," she remarked.

"Yes. But I'm rich," he added with a meaningful glance.

"I take it all back, what I said about buying women for yourself," she told him pertly.

"Oh?"

The expression on his face was only faintly threatening, but she left him with the piano, just the same.

They shared meals and conversation for two days. He didn't come near her in any sexual way, although she caught his gaze on her. He wasn't feeling well. His skin was flushed and he had a terrible cough. He'd been out working on that generator her first day at the cabin, and he hadn't really been dressed properly for the cold and the vicious snow. He'd caught a cold and it had gone into his chest. She was worried now, because he was obviously feverish and there was no telephone, no way to get him to a hospital. When he went to bed, he refused to take even an aspirin.

She went to bed in the guest room, reluctantly, hoping that he'd be better the next day even when she knew in her gut that he wouldn't.

The third morning, he didn't get up. If only she had access to her supplies back at the clinic in Sioux City, she could have used enough antibiotic to do him some good. As it was, she could only hope that he had a virus or the flu and not pneumonia. If it was a bacterial pneumonia, he could die if help didn't come in time.

She went into his bedroom to check on him, and had to force her legs to carry her the rest of the way. He'd thrashed his way out of the covers and he was lying there totally nude on top of the sheet and blanket. Her embarrassed eyes couldn't leave him. She'd never seen a man in such a condition before. He was beautiful without his clothing, tanned all over, with just enough body hair to make him attractive to the sight and not enough to make him repulsive. It was all on his chest and flat stomach, black and curling hair that ran over his broad chest in a wedge and down over the ripple of powerful muscles to his flat stomach and powerful thighs. Her eyes lingered there with curiosity and fascination and a little fear. She didn't need anyone to tell her that this man was physically exceptional.

He groaned and his eyes opened. He was flushed with fever, his lips dry, his body lifting as he coughed and grimaced from the pain.

"I've picked up that damned bug my band had," he said hoarsely. "Getting chilled working on the generator must have pushed me over the edge." He sat up, realized his condition and with a rueful smile, jerked the sheet over his hips. "Sorry. I must have kicked off the covers. But then, you're a doctor. I don't suppose you're easily shocked by a man's body."

She wasn't about to answer that.

He lay back and coughed again. She moved a little closer, grimacing. "We're going to have a problem if you get worse. Your medicine cabinet is inadequate and I don't have my bag. I don't even have the right medicines or enough of them. The best I'm going to be able to do is mix up a folk remedy for cough and give you aspirin for fever."

"I don't need nursing," he told her.

"Of course not," she agreed. "Oh dear, oh dear."

He closed his eyes, too weary to talk anymore, and fell asleep. She spent the rest of the day sitting by his bedside in a chair, trying to keep his fever down with aspirin and his cough at bay with a mixture of honey, lemon and whiskey. Amazingly the cough remedy seemed to do some good. But the fever didn't go down, despite the aspirin.

The generator was holding, thank God, so it was warm in the cabin. She had to get that fever down. He did at least have a thermometer, but what it registered was hardly reassuring. A high fever could burn up the very cells of the body. She had to stop it.

She got a basin of warm water and a washcloth and towel. With a deep breath as she gathered her nerve, she turned the covers back.

He lay quietly until she began to bathe him, then he groaned harshly and opened his eyes. "What are you doing?" he asked in a weak, raspy tone.

"Trying to get the fever down," she said. "I'm sorry, really I am. But this is the only way I know. The aspirin is only holding it at bay. It's very high. I'll try not to let you get chilled·in the process."

"Stroke of luck, kidnapping you," he said with wan humor. "And they say you can't find a doctor when you need one."

She winced, but his eyes had closed again and he didn't see it. She kept on sponging him down, drying him with the towel as she went and feeling his skin slowly begin to cool.

It wouldn't have been so complicated if his body hadn't started reacting to the motion of the washcloth against areas that were normally hidden to the eyes.

He groaned again when she reached his flat stomach and his eyes opened as his powerful body suddenly reacted helplessly—and visibly—to her touch.

She drew her hand back at once and blushed to the roots of her hair. The terrible thing was that she couldn't drag her eyes away. She was paralyzed by the forbidden sight, fascinated and shocked.

"It's all right, Poppy," he said huskily. "Don't be embarrassed. It's a natural reaction, even if it seems shocking to you."

Her wide eyes sought his for reassurance.

"Go ahead," he said gently. "Don't worry about it. We'll both ignore it. Okay?"

She hesitated for a minute, but as the shock wore off, she began to weigh her embarrassment against his state of health. "Sorry," she said as she continued, working her way down his powerful legs.

"You're a doctor," he murmured, but he was watching her narrowly. "Aren't you?"

"Well, yes. Sort of."

His eyebrows lifted. "Sort of?"

She cleared her throat as she finished sponging him down and gently pulled the cover up to his waist, averting her eyes as she did so. "Yes. I am a doctor. I have a degree and a diploma to prove it. But…"

"But?"

"Well…I'm not exactly the sort of doctor you think I am." She put the basin and cloth on the floor by the bed.

"What sort are you?" he persisted.

She bit her lower lip and looked at him guiltily. "I'm a veterinarian," she confessed.

# Chapter Four

"You're a what!"

"Please lie down, and don't get excited," she pleaded, pushing him gently back against the pillows. "And it's all right, really, I did have two years of premed, so I'm not a dunce about human anatomy."

"I don't believe this," he groaned, throwing a big arm across his eyes. "My God, I'm being treated by a vet!"

"I'm a good vet," she muttered. "I haven't lost a patient yet. And you shouldn't complain about being treated by a vet, if you insist on looking like a grizzly bear!"

She got up from the bed and walked out with the basin and cloth and towel, fuming. He acted as if she were guilty of malpractice, and she'd been nursing him all night long!

He must have thought about that, because when she went back into the bedroom, he was more subdued.

"I'm sorry," he said shortly. "It was a shock, that's all. I don't guess you slept all night, did you?"

"I slept in the chair there," she said. "I was nervous about leaving you with such a high fever."

"Thanks."

"I'd have done the same for any sick animal," she replied.

"Rub it in," he said with a wan smile.

She smiled at him. "I'd love to."

He was barely strong enough to glower at her. "What if you catch this stuff?"

"Then I guess you'll have to look after me, if the blizzard doesn't stop," she informed him.

He lifted an eyebrow and let his eyes work their way up and down her slender body with a speaking glance. "I'd get to sponge you down, then, huh?" He smiled wickedly. "What a thrill."

She flushed. "You stop that! I didn't enjoy it!"

"Didn't you? I thought you were familiar with a man's anatomy until I saw that scarlet blush. I wondered if you were going to faint." His blue eyes narrowed. "You haven't seen a naked male like this before, have you?"

She moved restlessly. "I've seen lots of naked male dogs," she said defiantly.

He chuckled, stifling a cough. "It's not quite the same thing."

She could have agreed wholeheartedly with that, but she wasn't going to. She pushed back her hair with a weary hand. "If you'll be all right for a few minutes, I'll heat up some soup."

"You're tired. Why don't we both sleep for a little while, and then you can worry about food."

"Are you sure?"

"I'm sure. I don't feel half as bad as I did last night. Go on. Grab a couple of hours' sleep. I'll wake you if I need you."

"How will I hear you?" she asked worriedly. "The guest room is down the hall...."

"Curl up beside me, if you're concerned about that. It's a big bed."

She wasn't sure, and it showed.

"Don't be silly," he said gently. "I'm too sick to be a threat."

He was. She gave in, smiling shyly as she went around to the other side of the bed and lay down, all too aware of the expanse of his hair-roughened chest, the length of his powerful body. He was really huge this close and she'd never been more aware of her lack of stature. Of course, beside him, a six-foot woman would seem small. She curled up under the covers and stifled a yawn.

"Don't you want to put on something less constraining?" he said. "I won't look."

She smiled. "I'm too tired even to do that. I could sleep for…a week…." Her voice trailed off. She was out like a light.

It was dark when she woke up. A night-light was on and Hank was snoring gently beside her. He'd knocked the covers off again, but it was chilly now. She got up and went around the bed to replace them, pulling them up over his chest and tucking them over him. He looked younger when he was asleep, relaxed and unstressed. She wondered what he was like when he wasn't upset or sick. She'd probably never have the chance to find out, because he was famous and she was a nobody in the veterinary practice back home. It would be something to remember, though, that she'd known someone like him, even briefly. Under normal circumstances, she was certain that they'd never have met at all.

She went into the kitchen and heated some soup. He must be hungry. He was a huge man. He needed nourishment.

She carried the bowl of soup back into the bedroom and put it on the bedside table before she shook him awake.

"Let me take your temperature first, then I'll feed you," she said, sitting beside him on the bed. She put the thermometer under his tongue and he watched her while she timed it. It beeped just as she'd counted off a minute.

"It's down!" she said, delighted.

"Of course it's down, it was only a virus," he muttered.

"How can you be so sure?"

"Damned if I know. I'm not a vet," he said, drawling out the word.

"I still know more about medicine than you do," she said curtly, reaching for the soup.

"The hell you do. I've had more operations and been in more emergency rooms than you'll ever see over the years."

With all sorts of football injuries, no doubt, she thought, but she didn't argue. He was obviously feeling better and spoiling for a fight.

"Eat," she demanded, holding a spoon of chicken noodle soup to his firm lips.

"I hate chicken soup."

"It's made with real chickens," she said coaxingly.

"Prove it."

She put the spoonful back into the bowl and searched until she found a tiny cube and produced it for him to see. "There!"

"Right. A square chicken. A microscopic square chicken."

"You really must feel better," she said pointedly. "You're being very unpleasant."

"I have a reputation for being very unpleasant," he informed her. "Ask the group."

"You're one of them. They wouldn't admit it. They'd lie for you. They wouldn't want your adoring public to know what a bad man you really were."

"Point taken." He laid back against the propped pillows with a sigh. "Okay. Go ahead. Feed me."

She did, liking the power it gave her. She smiled, enjoying herself. She'd never had anyone to take care of, because her father had never been sick. She took care of animals but it really wasn't the same.

He was enjoying her tender ministrations, too, and hating to admit it. "I'll be back on my feet by tomorrow," he said. "So don't get too fond of this routine."

"God forbid," she agreed.

But he let her feed him the entire bowl of soup, and the warm feeling it gave him wasn't just from the temperature of the liquid. Afterward, he stretched and then relaxed with a long sigh. "God, I'm weak. I feel as if I don't have enough strength to get up." He smiled grimly. "But I've got to, for a minute." He threw back the cover, ignoring her flush, and got to his feet. He staggered a little, and she forgot her discomfort in the rush of concern she felt.

She got under his powerful arm and helped support him.

"Thanks," he said, starting toward the bathroom. "I feel like I've been clotheslined."

"I guess you do. I'm sorry you're sick."

His arm tightened. "You'd better be glad of it," he said grimly as he noticed her shyly appreciative eyes on his body. "I like having you look at me like this. I like it too damn much."

She felt pulsing heat run through her body, and quickly averted her eyes. "I'm not looking," she said at once.

"Of course you're looking. You can't help it. I fascinate you, don't I?"

She glared up at him. "I'll find you some shorts."

"I won't wear them," he returned with a cool smile. "I'm not changing the habit of a lifetime to satisfy some prudish animal doctor."

"I am not a prude!"

"Right."

She refused to notice his amused expression. She helped him to the bathroom door, waited until he called her and then helped him back to bed, averting her eyes while she tugged the sheet up to his waist.

He sighed, his chest rattling a little. He propped himself up on the pillows and coughed, reaching for a tissue.

"It's a productive cough, at least," she said to herself. "That's a blessing. And if the fever's dropping, hopefully, it's a viral bronchitis and not pneumonia."

He lifted an eyebrow. "Well, you sound professional enough."

"Medicine is medicine," she said pointedly. "Of course, the anatomical structure is a bit different and the pharmacology certainly is, but ways to treat illnesses are basically the same."

He didn't feel like arguing. He yawned widely. "I'm so tired," he said softly. "So tired. I feel as if I haven't had any rest in years."

"From what you've said, I wonder if you've had any rest at all," she remarked. "Perhaps being stuck up here is a godsend."

"I wouldn't say that," he murmured. "The only good thing about it is that reporter doesn't know about Amanda. God forbid that she should cause trouble. Most of that magazine's reporters are top-notch."

"She doesn't work for a magazine," she recalled. "She said she was trying to sell a story that would get her foot in the door. But she was also on the trail of some sports star who was supposed to be hiding out in the Tetons up in Wyoming."

"A hopeful," he said, relieved.

"She was pretty optimistic. And very ambitious."

He fingered the sheet. "Something you should know about."

"I only want to work in a partnership and not have to do all the rough jobs and odd hours," she said wistfully. "I was lucky to get the partnership at all. There are four of us in the practice, but I'm the junior one. So until I prove myself, I can't really expect much free time."

"It sounds to me as if they're the lucky ones," he muttered. "Are they all men?"

She nodded. "All older than me, too. I'm just out of college and full of new ideas, new theories and treatments and they think I'm a hotshot so they won't listen."

"You probably make them feel threatened," he said pointedly. "And as to who's the lucky one, I think it's the other partners, not you. They're getting all the benefits and none of the unpleasant work."

"I could hardly open my own practice fresh out of school," she began.

"Why not? Plenty of people do!"

"I'm not rich," she said. She went to the window and looked out. The snow was still coming down without a break in sight in the sky. "I barely had enough money in the bank to finish school, and part of it was done on government student loans. I have a lot to pay back. That doesn't leave much over for furnishing an office."

"I see."

She shrugged and turned back with a smile. "I don't mind working my way up from the bottom. Everybody has to start somewhere. You did."

It was a nicely disguised question. He adjusted the pillows and leaned back again. "I started as a second guitarist for a group that got lost at the bottom of the pop charts. Eventually I worked up to helping do backup work for some of the better musicians. That's how I met Amanda Sutton—she was Amanda Corrie Callaway back then," he added with a smile. "She and I started working together on a project, along with another guy in the band, and we discovered that Amanda had a voice like an angel. It didn't take us long to put an act together, add a drummer and a second guitarist, and audition for a record company." He shook his head remembering. "We made it on the first try. Amazing, that, when some people take years just to get a record company executive to listen to them."

"Didn't it help that you'd been a football star?"

"Not in music," he replied with a rueful smile. "I was a nobody like the rest of the group until our first hit."

"Why the name Desperado?" she asked.

"You've never seen a group shot of us, I gather?"

She smiled apologetically. "Sorry."

"Look in the top drawer of the desk over there against the wall." He pointed toward it.

She opened it and there was a photograph of four men and a woman.

"Now do you need to ask why?" He chuckled.

"Not really." They were a frightening bunch, the men, all heavily bearded and mustached with unruly hair and they looked really tough. Amanda was a striking contrast, with her long blond hair and dark eyes and beautiful face.

"We've been lucky. Now, of course, we may really have to stop performing. It all depends on how Amanda is doing." He looked briefly worried. "I hope she's all right. I can't even telephone to ask how she is. At least I know Quinn won't let anything happen to her. He's a wild man where Amanda is concerned."

She thought about having someone that concerned for her welfare and wondered how it would feel. Her father had cared about her, but no one else had since he died. She'd been very much alone in the world.

She picked up the soup bowl, but her mind not at all on what she was doing.

He didn't understand the sadness in her face. He reached out and caught her wrist. "What's wrong?" he asked softly.

She shrugged. "I was wondering what it would be like to have someone worry that much about me," she said, and then laughed.

He let go of her wrist. He'd been wondering the same thing. His lean hand smoothed over the bedcover. "I want a bath. Do you suppose you could run some water for me?"

"You're very weak," she cautioned. "And what if you get chilled?"

"It's warm in here. Come on. I can't stand being grungy."

"Grungy?"

He chuckled. "Maybe there's a better word for it some-where."

"If you get stuck in the tub, how will I ever get you out?" she asked worriedly, measuring him with her eyes. "Heavens, I couldn't begin to lift you!"

"That's a fact. But I wouldn't risk it if I didn't think I could cope. Humor me."

"All right. But if you drown," she advised, "I'm not taking the rap for it."

She went into the bathroom and filled the tub with warm water. It was a Jacuzzi, luxurious and spotless, and she envied him. Her guest bedroom had a nice shower, which she'd used the night before, but nothing like this. She put soap and lotions and towels close to hand and went to help him out of bed and across the tub.

"It's big," he declared as he lowered himself into it. "Why don't you strip off and come in with me?"

She chuckled, trying not to let her faint, remaining em-barrassment show. She'd grown used to the sight of his body, although it still intimidated her a bit. "I might fall and break my leg. Where would we be then?"

He stretched his big arms over the sides. "Just as well, I suppose." He sighed, letting his gaze wash over her like warm water. "You aren't the type, are you?"

"What type?"

"For brief interludes," he said seriously. "You're a for-ever-after girl, despite the fact that forever-after doesn't ex-ist anymore."

"It could, if two people loved each other enough," she said.

"My wife and I loved each other, when we married," he said. "We thought it would last forever." He smiled cynically. "It lasted for a while, then we burned out."

She chewed on her lower lip and frowned a little. "Oh."

"I learned one thing from it. Marriage requires more than a mutual fever. You need common interests, backgrounds, and you need to be friends as well as lovers. That's trite, but it's true.''

"It's a hard combination to find," she said.

"People don't have time to look for it anymore." He picked up the cloth and soap and lathered his arms and chest slowly.

"I'd better go…"

"Don't be silly. Sit down."

She perched herself on a chair by the bench that contained a hair blower and electric razor, along with a rack of lotions and powders. She folded her hands together on her jean-clad legs and tried not to look uncomfortable.

"In the old days, people lived in small communities and everyone knew everyone," he said while he bathed. "Now we're all so busy trying to support ourselves that we move around like migrating birds. We don't stay in one place long enough to get to know people."

"Your singer, Amanda. How did she meet her husband?''

He chuckled. "They got snowbound together up in Wyoming," he said. "And he was the ultimate misogynist. He hated Amanda on sight. But she's feisty and she has a kind heart. It was only a matter of time until they fell in love. Unfortunately that happened before he found out who she really was. He went all noble, because he was poor and she was famous. So for her own good, he threw her out. She left and her plane crashed on the way to L.A.''

She caught her breath. "He must have been devastated."

"Half out of his mind," Hank replied, remembering the band's nightmare trip back to Wyoming. They'd all left on the bus because Hank and the boys didn't like airplanes. But Amanda had insisted on flying. Hank had felt responsible because he hadn't pushed harder to get her to come with them. "Quinn skied down an unpatrolled ridge into the valley to get her—only a handful of men in the country could have made that run, but he was an Olympic contender in downhill in his younger days. Hell of a trip it was. He

found her badly concussed, damn near dead, and he had to
have another man ski down to help tow her out of the valley
on a litter to a waiting helicopter. There was too much wind
for the chopper to land where the crash occurred. As it was,
they barely made it in time. Three days after the doctor
pronounced her on the mend, they got married, right there
in the hospital.''

"My goodness!''

"They'd been married for two years when she got pregnant,'' he recalled. "They were both over the moon about
it, but she's a lot more fragile than she looks. It's been a
rough pregnancy and she's had to have constant medical
care. We'd more or less given up touring when she first
married, but we had one commitment we couldn't break,
for a charity in New York. She barely got through it and
Quinn put his foot down, hard. He's kept her home since
then. He won't even let her do recording sessions now. The
rumor is that we're breaking up the group.''

"Are you?''

He finished bathing his legs. "I don't know.'' He looked
at her. "The band wouldn't be the same without Amanda.
No singer could replace her.''

"I don't suppose so,'' she agreed gently. "But I'm sure
the baby is the most important thing to her right now.''

He nodded. There was a bitter look on his face that she
didn't miss.

"Why didn't your wife want a child?''

He glared at her. "That's none of your business.''

He sounded fierce, but she overlooked the bad temper
because of the sadness in his blue eyes. "I'm sorry. I didn't
mean to pry.''

He paused long enough to wash his hair and rinse it
before he said anything else. "She said that I wasn't cut
out to be a parent,'' he said shortly. "That I wasn't home
enough or patient enough. And besides that, she didn't want
a child who might grow up to look like me.''

Her eyes lingered on his broad shoulders and chest, on

the power and strength of his tanned, hair-roughed skin. "What's wrong with you?" she asked dreamily.

He caught his breath as the surge of desire shot through him like a bolt of lightning.

She saw the tautness of his face and grimaced. "I keep putting my foot in it, don't I?" she said miserably. "Honestly, you make me feel like a babbling adolescent!"

"That isn't how you make me feel," he said with grim humor. "What she meant," he explained, "was that I've got a thick neck and an oversize body and a face that only a mother could love. She said with her luck, she'd have a little girl with a big nose and feet like a duck."

"What a cruel thing to say," she replied, wounded for him. "I expect you'd have a very pretty little girl with blue eyes and brown hair. Except that if you have four brothers, it's a lot more likely that you'd have a little boy."

"So I've heard." He let his narrowed eyes sweep over her. "You're very delicately built," he said quietly. "Slender hips, small breasts, almost a foot shorter than I am. We'd have a hard time just making love, much less having a child together."

She couldn't believe he'd said that. She just looked at him, flustered.

"You know everything there is to know about me, physically." He continued in that same quiet, gentle voice. "But it's one thing to look, and another to consider the problem of intimacy." His eyes narrowed more. "I'll bet you're as small as I am big," he said insinuatingly.

She jumped up from the chair, red faced and shocked. "How dare you!"

"Tell me you haven't thought about how we'd fit together in my bed," he challenged, and he wasn't smiling.

Her fists clenched at her sides. "You can't talk to me like this!"

He searched her outraged eyes with curiosity and faint tenderness. "Another first, hmm?" he mused. "And you're a vet. How did you survive labs?"

"Half the people in my class were women," she informed him. "We forced the men to respect us enough not to make sexist remarks."

"I'm not making sexist remarks," he argued. "I'm indulging in a little sexual logic." He pursed his lips and held her eyes relentlessly. "If I'm very careful, we might try," he said gently.

"Try what?"

"And I can use something. There won't be any risk."

She clenched both fists tighter. "You can stop right there. I'm not sleeping with you!"

He smiled without malice. "You will," he replied. "Eventually."

"I won't be here eventually. The minute the snow lets up and the snowplow clears the roads, I'm getting out of here!"

"I've never been to Sioux City," he remarked conversationally. "But you're an old-fashioned girl, so I guess I'll have to chase you for a while, won't I?"

"You don't need to start thinking that you'll wear me down. You won't. I have no inclination whatsoever, at all, to…to…"

He stood up slowly in the middle of her tirade, turned off the Jacuzzi and stepped out onto the mat. She couldn't take her eyes off him. It must be some deep-seated weakness, she decided, some character flaw that made her into a blatant Peeping Tom.

And it was worse than ever when he reacted to her appreciative eyes and laughed about it.

She groaned as she pulled a huge bath sheet from the heated towel bar and handed it to him.

He ignored the bath sheet. His hand shot around her wrist and jerked, pulling her completely against his wet body. Even in his weakened condition, he was alarmingly strong.

She started to struggle, the sheet dropping to the floor, but he clamped a big hand around her waist and held her firmly to him, groaning in pleasure as her hips moved sharply in her efforts to escape.

She subsided at once, made breathless by the huge body so intimately close to her. He was so tall that she felt the insistent pressure of him, not against her hips but against her midriff. She caught onto him to keep from reeling, and the feel of that thick mat of hair under her hands paralyzed her with curious pleasure.

''Shrimp,'' he accused at her temple.

''Giant,'' she taunted.

His hands swept over her back, burning hot through her thin cotton blouse, flattening her breasts against his diaphragm.

''We don't even fit together like a normal man and woman,'' he remarked as he looked down at her. ''We're like Mutt and Jeff.''

But it felt right. It felt as natural as breathing to stand close against his aroused body and be at home. She laid her cheek against his damp chest and just stood there, letting him hold her close, while she tried to deal with the unfamiliar feelings that were overwhelming her. It felt like more than physical attraction. It felt like…love.

# *Chapter Five*

"**I**'m out of my mind," he said pleasantly. "I must be, even to consider such a thing with a midget like you. We'd be totally incompatible in bed."

She closed her eyes and relaxed against him, feeling him tauten in response. "No, we wouldn't. I studied anatomy. I'd have to be a foot shorter than I am to be worried. A woman's body is very elastic."

"Is yours elastic enough to accommodate mine?" he asked quietly.

She lifted her head and looked up into his blue, blue eyes. She felt the hunger all through her, burning and hot. "I think so," she said involuntarily.

His jaw clenched as he searched her face. "Then, let me."

She swallowed. Her fingers went up to touch his hair-roughened face. His lips were the only bit of skin visible below his cheekbones and his blue eyes. "I can't."

He scowled. "Those damned old-fashioned ideas again! This is the nineties, for God's sake!"

"I know." She traced his hard mouth and wanted so much to lie in his arms and learn what it was to love. But it wasn't what she wanted. "I'm not emotionally strong enough for brief affairs. That's why I don't have them. I really do want a home and children, Hank. I want my husband to be the first. If that's outdated, I'm sorry. I don't feel inferior or out of step just because I put a high value on my chastity. I hope the man I marry will feel the same way about his body."

His hands loosened. "In other words, you don't want a permissive man for a husband."

She lowered her eyes to his broad chest. "I suppose a lot of women think a man like that can reform, that he can be faithful. But if he's had a hundred women, he's already proven that he can't. He sees sex as an itch to scratch. He'll probably always consider it that casual, so he'll feel free to sleep around after he marries. And it will probably surprise him if his wife objects."

His big hands smoothed up and down her arms. "I guess I've given you the impression that I'm that way with women."

She looked up. "Yes."

He took a slow breath and smiled tenderly. "You don't think I might one day value a woman enough to become faithful rather than risk losing her?"

"I don't know you," she said solemnly.

"No. You really don't." He hesitated for another minute, but then he let her go and bent to pick up the bath sheet she'd dropped.

She moved away while he dried himself, finding a robe hanging behind the door that she handed to him when he was through. He put it on without a protest and let her help him back to the bedroom.

"Your hair is still damp," she said.

"It dries fast. Don't bother about the blower." He started toward the bed, but she diverted him into the chair.

"I want to change the sheets first. You'll be more comfortable."

He smiled. "Thanks."

"Where are they?"

He told her where to look and sat like a lamb while she remade the bed and then helped him out of his robe and into the bed.

"Are you all right?" she asked, because he looked so tired.

"I'm just weak. I think I may sleep for a while."

"That would be the best thing for you. Do you need anything?"

He shook his head. He studied her blouse for a long time, and she wondered why until she looked down and flushed. It had gotten so damp while she was standing against him that it had become see-through, and she wasn't wearing anything under it because her bra and the clothes she'd put on yesterday were in the load of laundry she'd started earlier.

Her arms came up over her body and she looked at him defensively.

"They're very pretty," he said with quiet reverence, and no mockery.

"Marshmallows," she muttered with self-contempt.

"Stop that," he said sharply. "I don't like big women."

Her eyebrows lifted. "All men do…"

"Not me," he repeated. "You're perfect just the way you are."

He eased her inferiority complex quite a lot, because he obviously wasn't lying about the way he felt. She managed a self-conscious smile. "Thanks."

He arched his arms behind his head and shifted with an oddly sensuous movement of his body. His eyes cut into hers, faintly glittering. "Open your blouse and come down beside me. I'll put my mouth on them and show you ten different ways to moan."

She flushed, jumping to her feet. "No doubt you could.

I'm grass green that way. But I wouldn't thank you for reducing me to that condition, even if a dozen other women have.''

She walked toward the door and heard him mutter under his breath.

''I haven't had a hundred women,'' he said angrily.

''Oh, sure.'' She laughed as she put her hand on the doorknob.

''I've had one. My wife. And she left me impotent.''

The shock that tore through her spun her around to face him. He wasn't joking. It was all there, in his drawn face, his bitter eyes, even in the taut line of his mouth.

''But you're not impotent!'' she blurted.

''Not with you,'' he said, chuckling softly. ''You can't imagine what a shock it was to find out. I've been putting off women for years because I was sure that I couldn't perform in bed.''

She leaned back against the door. Her legs felt weak. ''You weren't married for very long, though, were you?''

''Six years,'' he told her. ''Before that, I gave everything in me to football. I lived in the gym. I had no interest in seducing scores of women, however prudish that sounds. I was like you, bristling with idealism and romance. I saved myself for the right woman. Except she wasn't the right woman,'' he said shortly. ''We burned each other up in bed, but we had nothing to talk about in broad daylight.''

''Did she...know?''

''No,'' he replied. ''Because by the time we decided to get married, I discovered that I was one in a line. She'd had one lover after another until I came along, and never wanted to marry any of them. She said that she didn't think she could ever be faithful to one man, but I was certain that she could. More fool me,'' he added bitterly. ''Amusing, isn't it, that you know already that permissive people find it difficult to be faithful, and I had to learn it the hard way.''

''I wasn't in love,'' she reminded him. ''You were.''

"I should have known. Permissive people don't seem to make faithful lovers."

"But if she was like that," she began, moving closer to the bed, "experienced, I mean...how did you become impotent?"

"I stopped being able to want her after she had her third extramarital affair," he said honestly. "And without a lifetime of experience behind me, I thought that meant that I was permanently demanned. So I didn't try."

She saw him quite suddenly in a different light. Not as a playboy of the music world, but as an intense, deeply emotional man who felt things right down to his soul.

"Feeling sorry for me, Poppy?" he taunted as she paused by the bed.

"Oh, no. I'm feeling sorry for her," she said. "How sad to have someone love you so much and to be able to feel nothing in return."

"She's happy. She has a husband who doesn't require faithfulness, and plenty of money to spend."

"That wouldn't make me happy."

He smiled. "What would?"

"Being loved. Having a home. Having children. I'd still practice, of course. I guess I'd have to marry a man who was willing to sacrifice a little so that I could, but I'd make sure he never regretted it."

"Do you have hang-ups about sex?" he asked curiously.

"Just about having it before I get married," she replied, and grinned at him. "Deep-seated principles aren't easily uprooted."

"People shouldn't try to uproot them," he replied. "I'm sorry about that. It was a delicious surprise to find myself so quickly capable with you. I wanted to explore it." He shrugged. "But I shouldn't have put pressure on you."

"I want to," she said sincerely. "I'll bet you're a wonderful lover. But I want it all, the white wedding gown, the wedding night, the honeymoon...I'm greedy."

He smiled. "Don't sound as if you're apologizing for it.

You're a breath of fresh air to a cynic like me." He frowned quizzically at her. "Has it occurred to you that in a few days we've become as intimate as a married couple except in one respect?"

"We still don't know each other."

"You'd be surprised at what I know about you," he remarked gently. "You like to go barefoot on the carpet. You're neat, but not fanatical about it. You like to cook, but you don't like to clean up. You're intellectual so no situation comedies for you. You like nature specials and news and politics and music. You have a kind heart and you like animals and children, but underneath all that is a passionate nature held under very tight control." His eyes narrowed on her body. "You'll be a demanding lover, little Poppy, and some lucky man will probably find you next to insatiable in bed."

She lifted both eyebrows. "Stop that."

"I wish it was going to be me," he replied. "But I've already messed up one marriage by leaping in with my eyes closed after a one-week courtship. I'm not going to do it twice in one lifetime."

"Neither would I, although you didn't ask."

"Sit down." He pulled her down on the bed and drew her hand to his chest, holding it there. "I'm on the road six months out of the year, recording and making business deals, doing interviews and talk shows and working with underprivileged inner-city kids. It's a project of mine, finding volunteers to work with them once a week to help keep them out of trouble," he added with a grin. "When I'm home, and home is Texas, I compose to the exclusion of everything else. Sometimes I go for a whole day without eating, because I'm so wrapped up in my work that I forget to cook." He smoothed his thumb over the back of her hand. "I'd make a lousy husband. In fact, I did. I can't really blame her—"

"I can." She interrupted him. "If you love someone,

you accept it all, the separations, the good times, the bad times, the illnesses. It's all part of marriage.''

"You've already had the illness part," he mused.

"I'd have done that for anyone," she protested.

"You did it for me, though," he replied. "Blushing all the way. You don't do it so much anymore, though," he added amusedly. "You're getting used to me, aren't you?''

"You're very nice, when you forget to grumble.''

"I have my faults. A quick temper is the worst of them. But I don't drink or gamble, and when I'm not working, I'm fairly easy to get along with." He searched her eyes. "Why are you called Poppy?''

"My father told me that my mother loved flowers," she recalled. "But he added that when I was born, the first thing she thought of was a poem about poppies growing in Flanders Fields where the veterans of World War I were buried. She went into the hospital to have me on Veterans Day and they were selling Buddy Poppies...." She smiled.

"Muddled, but I get the idea," he said. "My name is Henry, but everyone called me Hank from the time I was in grammar school.''

"It's a nice name.''

"So is yours." He drew her hand to his lips and kissed it softly. "Thank you for taking care of me.''

The gentle caress was thrilling. She smiled. "It was very educational.''

One blue eye narrowed. "Just don't start experimenting with men who aren't sick," he said.

Her eyebrows went up.

He laughed and let go of her hand. "Now I know I must be delirious with fever.''

"I guess so," she murmured dryly. "I'll finish the wash then clean up the kitchen while you nap.''

"You don't have to do that," he said gently.

"We both need some clean clothes. It's no trouble.''

"Thanks, then.''

She shrugged, smiled and went back to her chores. All

the while she was thinking about Hank and how easily they seemed to fall into living together. Not that it was the normal sort of living together, she reminded herself.

But it was exciting all the same, and there was a closeness here that she'd never known. She liked just being with Hank, listening to his deep voice as he talked. He was intelligent and kind, and not at all the unprincipled rounder she'd thought he was. She thought of him in a totally different light now, and she knew that she was going to miss him terribly when the weather broke enough to let them out of this cabin.

She tried to put it out of her mind while she did the chores. She was beginning to feel very much at home here. The views were spectacular and she enjoyed the solitude. It would have been the ideal place to live, with the right man.

It occurred to her that Hank was the right man, the one she'd been looking for all her life. But it was impossible. You couldn't fall in love in four days, not the sort of love you needed to get married. Besides, Hank had a failed marriage behind him and he didn't want to risk a second. All that would have been left for them was an affair, which she couldn't accept.

She finished the washing and put the clothes into the dryer, wondering how it was going to be when she got back home. Probably she'd put this adventure into perspective and forget about it in a few months. Of course she would.

Hank slept for the rest of the afternoon, while Poppy amused herself with the piano, lowering the volume to keep from disturbing the man in the master bedroom. The song he was working on was lying on the table beside the piano. She glanced over the tune and began to pick it out, slowly, smiling as the beautiful melody met her ears.

He didn't have more than a few words on paper, rhyming words mostly and not in any sort of order. Love, he'd writ-

ten, when the feeling stirred fluttered like a…and he'd
crossed out two words that didn't quite rhyme with it.

"A bright redbird," she mumbled, "playing in the
snow."

"That's it!"

She jumped and caught her breath. Hank was leaning
against the doorframe in his bathrobe. His blue eyes were
glimmering, and he was laughing.

"I couldn't get the rhyme or any sort of reason to go
with those words," he explained. "But that's it, that's exactly it…!"

He moved to the piano and slid onto the bench beside
her. He played the song with a deep bass beat that emphasized the sweetness of the high melody.

"Love when the feeling stirred, fluttered like a redbird,
playing in the snow," he sang in his deep, soft voice, looking at her and grinning. "Flew like an arrow through the
sky, higher than a redbird flies, left me all aglow."

Only words, she thought, but when the music was put
with them, major and minor chords intermixing, when he
sang the words, when the deep, throbbing counterrhythm
caught her up—it was going to be a hit. She knew it and
felt goose bumps rise on her arms at the power and beauty
of it.

"You feel it, too, don't you?" he asked, stopping. "It's
good, isn't it? Really good."

"The best yet," she had to agree. "Who did the music?"

One corner of his mouth tugged up just a fraction of an
inch and she laughed. "Silly question," she murmured.
"Sorry."

"It will take some more work, but that's the melody."
He chuckled. "Imagine that, I'd been sitting in here for a
solid week trying to come up with something, anything…and all I needed was a veterinarian to point me in
the right direction." He grinned at her. "I suppose you treat
birds, too, don't you?"

She nodded. "Parrots and canaries and parakeets, for

lung infections. Birds are mostly lung, you know." She searched his face. "You shouldn't be up. It's too soon."

"I heard you playing my song," he explained. "I had to come and see what you thought of it."

"I think it's great."

He smiled. "Thanks." She was slowly touching the keys again and some soft sadness in her face touched him. "What's wrong?" he asked.

She looked up. "The snow's stopped."

He looked out the window. He hadn't noticed. He got up from the bench and walked to stare out the other window down at the road. It had stopped, and the sun had come out. "Great skiing weather now," he murmured. "The snowplows will dig us out by tomorrow." He stuck his hands into the pockets of his robe. "You'll be free."

What an odd way to put it. "I don't plan to rush out and file kidnapping charges against you," she said pointedly.

He turned. "That wasn't how I meant it, although I will apologize handsomely for kidnapping you by mistake." His eyes swept over her very slowly, almost possessively. "I suppose you'll be rushing back to your practice."

"I need to."

"What if you don't have a job to go back to?" he persisted seriously.

She blew out a soft breath. "Well, I suppose they'll repossess my car and my apartment first..."

"Is there somewhere else you could work, if you had to?"

"Of course!" she said, laughing. "Sioux City isn't that small. There are other practices. I could find something, but it wouldn't be as a partner. I'd have to start at the bottom again."

"Honey, I don't think you've realized that you're at the bottom right now."

The endearment made her heart race. She dropped her eyes before he could read the pleasure it gave her.

"Sorry. That slipped out," he said, teasing.

"Oh, I liked it," she replied. "Nobody ever called me honey except the mailman, and he was seventy."

He burst out laughing. "I'll have to make up for that. You can't leave until morning, anyway, not unless they get those roads cleared early."

"I wouldn't leave until you were well, regardless," she said, surprised at his assumption that she couldn't wait to get out.

His face smoothed. All expression went out of it. "I see."

"You needn't look shocked," she said. "You'd do it for me."

"Yes, I would." He began to realize how much he'd do for her. Under different circumstances, they might have had a real beginning. But it was the wrong time, the wrong place, and he was still afraid of the risk.

"It's been an experience I'll never forget," she said absently. "I'll listen to your tapes from now on. I suppose I was a bit of a musical snob."

"Maybe I was, too. I think I'll buy an opera tape or two."

She smiled. "That's nice. You might try Puccini."

"Is he that Italian singer?" he asked.

"He's the composer. He's dead. But Domingo and Pavorotti sing the operas he wrote. My favorite opera is *Turandot*."

"*Turandot*." He smiled back. "I'll remember."

She got up from the piano. "How about something to eat?"

"You took the words right out of my mouth!"

She went into the kitchen and made potato pancakes and steak and biscuits with a side salad. When she went to call Hank, he was out of bed and dressed in jeans and a green pullover shirt. Despite that overshadowing growth of hair that covered his face, concealing its shape, he looked wonderful to Poppy.

"Are you sure you feel like eating at the table?" she asked worriedly.

"Yes. I'm still a little weak, but I'm on the mend." He smiled. "Doesn't it show?"

She nodded. "I guess it does."

They ate at the small table in the kitchen. His appetite was much better, and he was only coughing occasionally now. He ate heartily. Considering the speed of his recovery, it didn't take much guesswork to tell that overall, he was in great shape.

"How did you learn to cook like this?" he asked.

"From my dad. He was a chef. He really was good at it, too. He taught me how to make pastries and sauces. I enjoy cooking."

"It shows. This is delicious."

"Thank you!"

They were silent until they finished eating. They drank their second cup of coffee at the kitchen table, and Hank stared into his mug pensively.

"You're brooding, aren't you?" she asked.

He nodded. He looked up into her eyes and held them for a long, static moment. "I haven't had anyone around me, close like this, for a long time. You've grown on me, Poppy," he mused half-humorously. "I'm going to miss you."

She smiled back, a little sadly. "I'm going to miss you, too. I haven't had anyone to look after or care about since my dad died. It's been lonely for me."

He turned the coffee mug idly on the table's glossy surface. "Then suppose we keep in touch," he suggested without looking at her.

Her heart leapt. "Oh, that would..." She calmed her tone. "That would be nice. I'd like that."

He smiled at her. "So would I. I'll give you the address here and in Texas. Write to me when you get back."

"Are you terrible about answering letters?" she asked.

He shook his head. "I'm very good about it, in fact. I

answer most of my own fan mail with the help of a secretary.''

''I see.''

''No, you don't.'' He corrected her, interpreting her expression accurately. ''I don't leave her to do the answering,
I dictate the replies. And I won't let anyone answer your
letters. I'll do it myself.''

Her stiff posture relaxed. ''Then I'll write.''

''And don't assume that if you don't hear back immediately that I've forgotten you or that I'm ignoring you,''
he added. ''I'm on the road a lot, I told you. It may take a
week or two, sometimes longer, for my mail to catch up
with me.''

''I'll remember,'' she promised.

He reached out and covered her soft hand with his big
one. ''One more thing,'' he said gently, coaxing her eyes
up to meet his. ''Find another job.''

She gaped at him. ''My job is my business.''

''Your job is a joke,'' he returned. ''They're using you,
sweetheart, dangling the idea of a partnership so that they
can get someone to take over the jobs they don't want.
There won't be any partnership. One day they'll find someone more useful and you'll be out on your ear, perhaps at
the most inconvenient time.''

''You're very cynical,'' she remarked.

He nodded. ''I'm an expert on people who use other
people,'' he told her. ''I've been used a time or two myself.''

She wiggled her eyebrows. ''Can I have three guesses
about how they did it?''

He glowered at her. ''I'm serious.''

She finished her coffee. ''Okay. I'll think about it.''

''You do that.''

She got up and put the dishes in the dishwasher. ''Is
there anything else that needs doing?''

''Yes.'' He came up behind her and slipped his lean arms

around her, hugging her back against him. "I need to be ravished."

She laughed with pure delight. "I'm not up to your weight," she reminded him, looking up over her shoulder with sparkling dark eyes. "And besides, I'd never be able to overpower you."

"I'll help."

She shook her head. "No. I expect that you're as addictive as caffeine. One taste of you wouldn't be enough. I'd get withdrawal symptoms."

He chuckled and hugged her closer for a minute. "So would I. And I'm probably still a little contagious," he added with a sheepish grin as he let her go. "No matter," he mused, watching her. "When I'm well and truly back on my feet, I'll come calling. Then, look out."

The soft warning kept her going, all through the rest of the day, and through the anguish of the parting the next morning, when he had to take her to the ski lodge and leave her with barely more than an affectionate hug.

She worried about him all the way to the airport on the lodge's shuttle bus, because even though the snowplows had been along, the roads were still treacherous. But as the shuttle passed the road to his cabin, she saw that his Bronco was safely parked at the door and smoke was coming out of the fireplace. He'd made it home, and hopefully, he'd be fine. She settled back into her seat, trying not to cry. It was amazing, she thought, how five days in Colorado had altered the rest of her life. Her last thought as they left the snow-covered valley behind was how would she survive until she saw Hank again?

# Chapter Six

Poppy began to realize very quickly after her return to Sioux City, Iowa, that Hank had been right about her supposed partnership. The vets with whom she worked seemed to have plenty of free time and yet they made three times her salary. She was always the one to work nights and weekends and holidays, and whenever the weather was particularly bad, it was Poppy who had to go out on large-animal calls. That could be very difficult indeed when she was asked to deliver a calf or a foal, or treat a mean-tempered bull for a cut.

She had bruises all over her, a bad cold and there was no mention of an increased salary or a partnership two months later. She was getting fed up. And not only with the veterinary practice.

She'd written twice to Hank. So far, there hadn't been even a postcard in reply. On one of the music talk shows, which she'd started watching, there had been one tidbit about Amanda Sutton being in a hospital in Wyoming awaiting the birth of her first child and some more rumors about the breakup of her group, Desperado. But that was all the news there had been. Remembering how fond Hank was of Amanda, Poppy hoped she was all right and that her child had been born healthy.

She tried very hard to remember what Hank had said about not being upset if she didn't hear from him right away. But when two months rolled into three, she began to put the past in perspective. The time she'd spent with Hank had been a five-day interlude and nothing serious had really happened, except for a few kisses. He'd told her he wanted nothing less than another marriage, so what had she expected? Perhaps he'd decided that even friendship with her was too much of a risk, and he'd withdrawn.

She couldn't blame him. He hadn't had an easy time of it where women were concerned. But the last thing on her mind had been trapping him into a relationship he didn't want. When she thought about it, it seemed likely that he'd had his share of ambitious women stalking him because he was rich and famous. She wasn't like that, but he wouldn't know. He didn't know her at all. Apparently he didn't want to.

Poppy tried to put him out of her mind, but his new song, ''Redbird,'' had just been released on an album along with several other newly recorded tracks. It meant that Amanda had to be working again, because her sweet, clear soprano could be heard above the deep bass voices of her group. The song that Poppy had given him the inspiration for was as beautiful as it had sounded in the cabin, and it was a surprise to find that her first name was mentioned in the dedication of the album, jointly to Carlton Wayne Sutton— very obviously the new baby—and herself. She tingled all over at the thought that Hank had remembered her even that well. She was a nobody, after all, hardly his sort of woman. The terrible thing was that she had no close girlfriends, no one to share the thrill with. She mentioned it to a clerk in the nearby record shop, but he only smiled and agreed that it was a great honor. She was sure that he didn't believe her.

Her stamina was giving out. Despite her youth, the practice was really getting her down. Eventually she couldn't take it anymore and she went looking for another job.

She found it in a very small practice in a town twenty miles outside Sioux City, in a farming community. The elderly veterinarian there had one young partner but needed someone to take care of the office while the two of them were out on large animal calls. Poppy wasn't overly eager, but she was pleasant and had qualifications that they liked.

"What about experience?" Dr. Joiner, the elder partner, asked gently.

"I'm working for a group practice in Sioux City," she explained, "but I have to do all the large animal calls and work nights and holidays and weekends." She smiled sheepishly. "I'm sorry. I suppose that sounds as if I'm lazy. I'm not, and it is a great opportunity to learn how a practice works. But I'm so tired," she concluded helplessly.

Dr. Joiner exchanged a speaking glance with his young partner, Dr. Helman. "It isn't quite so busy here," he explained. "But we have enough work for three people. The thing is, I can't offer you a partnership. You'd be a salaried employee and nothing more."

"Oh, that's all right," Poppy said, relieved. "I don't think I've got enough stamina for another partnership."

Dr. Joiner chuckled. "Dr. O'Brien, you're a peach. I'll be happy to have you aboard. When can you start?"

She explained that she'd have to give two weeks' notice, and that she'd make sure she got a reference from her partners. She thanked Dr. Joiner again, smiled at Dr. Helman and set off to her office with a lighter heart.

The partners weren't surprised when she announced her resignation, and they gave her a good recommendation as well. They apparently expected that no junior partner was going to last very long with what was expected of her or him. But they were interviewing other new graduates the last few days Poppy worked for them. She couldn't even warn the excited prospective employees. They'd have to find out the truth the same harsh way she had. But it would teach them a good lesson. Heaven knew, she'd learned hers.

She kept her apartment. It was only a twenty-five-minute drive to the new office, and she'd have to have time to look for a new place to live that was closer, if her new job worked out.

The job itself, after the long, strenuous practice she'd left, was wonderfully uncomplicated and enjoyable. She didn't have to work every weekend. The other vets alternated with her. Each one was on call a different night, so she didn't have to work every night, either. Holidays were shared. It was heavenly and the odd thing was that she made just as much money as she'd made in the practice. She felt at home after just one week on the job. She decided that moving closer was a pretty safe bet, considering how well they all worked together.

She found a room in a nice, comfortable boarding house and paid a week's rent in advance. Then she went to pack up her things and have them moved to her new home.

It didn't take long, because she didn't have much. She made two trips in her car and was just packing it for the third time when the telephone rang inside. It was supposed to be disconnected already, so she ignored it. The last few calls had been salespeople doing promotions. She couldn't imagine who might be looking for her, short of her old partners. Certainly, she knew, it wouldn't be Hank Shoeman. It had been over four and a half months and he'd surely forgotten all about her by now. She'd faced that fact, without much enthusiasm, because her memories of him were sweet.

She settled in her new apartment in the boarding house and got more comfortable in her job over the next week. She'd just finished examining and inoculating a three-month-old poodle puppy when she heard the waiting-room door open. She was alone in the office, because it was just after hours and the receptionist had gone home. Drs. Joiner and Helman were out on calls.

"I'll only be a minute!" she called out. She finished with the poodle, assured the owner that he was in excellent health and that he'd be automatically notified when to bring the dog back for his next round of shots.

He thanked her and she smiled happily as she watched him leave. She finished writing up the chart and went out into the waiting room, hoping that it was going to be something uncomplicated so that she could go home and eat.

She opened the outer office door with her professional smile, and stopped there, frozen in place.

The man looked familiar, and not familiar. He was wearing a gray suit. His hair was conventionally cut. He had a mustache, nothing more. The rest of his lean, handsome face was clean-shaven, and except for a couple of thin scars and a crooked nose, it was an appealing face. Blue eyes twinkled out of it as he studied her in her neat white lab coat.

"Nice," he said pleasantly. "You haven't lost a pound, have you? And I gather that this new job doesn't require your life's blood."

"Hank?" she asked uncertainly.

He nodded.

"Your hair...your beard," she began.

"I'm changing my image," he explained. "I'm tired of looking like a refugee from a cave."

"You look very nice," she said.

"So do you. How about supper?"

"There aren't any restaurants around here," she told him. Her heart was beating madly. "You didn't answer my letters."

"It's a long story," he said. "I'll tell you everything you want to know. But for now, I'd enjoy a good meal. I've spent two days tracking you down and except for breakfast at the hotel and a couple of sandwiches, I'm running on empty.''

"There are lots of restaurants in Sioux City," she said.

"Then we'll go there. Do you need to stop by your apartment first?''

She shook her head, bemused by the sight of him. He looked unspeakably elegant and sexy. She wanted to throw herself into his arms and tell him to forget about explanations, it was enough that he was here. But she couldn't do it. He was probably on his way to or from Texas and had only stopped in because he wondered what had happened to her. It wasn't a proposal or a proposition; it was just a visit. She had to remember that and not let her imagination run away with her.

She took off her lab coat and slid her arms into the deep pink cotton jacket she wore over her pale pink blouse. She took time to run a brush through her hair and refreshen her makeup before she rejoined Hank in the outer office.

"I have to lock up," she explained, and took time to do that, too. When the lock was secure and checked, and the burglar alarm set, she walked with Hank to his car. But she stopped short when she saw it, and her uplifted face was wary and a little scared.

He reached down and took her hand, holding it tightly in his. "It's all right," he said gently.

The driver came around, smiling, and opened the door of the big white stretch limousine for them. Hank helped Poppy inside and slid in next to her. The driver closed them in and went around to get behind the wheel.

Hank had already told him where to go. He took off without a word, and Hank closed the curtains between front and back and turned on the interior light.

Poppy's expression fascinated him. She looked at everything, explored the CD deck, the television, the well-stocked bar, the telephone...

"Six people could ride in here," she remarked, smoothing her hand over the burgundy leather seat.

"Six people usually do," he replied, stretching out lazily to study her. "Like it?"

She grinned. "I love it. I only wish I had a friend that I could brag about it to."

"Surely you have one or two."

She shook her head. "I don't make long-lasting friends that easily. Only casual ones. My best friend married years ago, and we lost touch."

He crossed one long leg over the other. "Did you see the song on the charts?"

"Yes! It was great! Thank you for the dedication."

He waved her thanks away. "Thanks for the help. Everyone loved it, especially Amanda."

"How is she?"

"Blooming," he said with a smile. "She and Quinn and Eliott are all moonstruck over that baby. They take him everywhere, even to recording sessions with the group." His eyes were sad and faintly wistful. "I've always envied them that closeness. Now I envy them the baby."

"The album was dedicated to him, too," she recalled.

"He's a good-looking kid," he said. "Even cries with rhythm. We're all going to buy him a set of drums when he's two."

"Do they still hang people in Wyoming?" she asked meaningfully.

He got the joke at once and chuckled. "Quinn might just do that to me." He locked his hands behind his head, pulling his suit coat pleasantly taut over the powerful muscles of his chest and arms while he looked at her. "I've been tying up loose ends, settling business affairs, getting recording contracts and publicity tours finalized. I'm free for the next two months."

"You're not in town on business, then?" she asked conversationally.

His blue eyes narrowed. "You know why I'm in town, Poppy."

Her heart jumped but her face gave nothing away. "Actually I don't. I wrote you two letters, neither of which was ever answered. There wasn't a telephone call or any communication for months. You don't ignore people for almost half a year and then just drop by as if you saw them yesterday.''

"You're mad." He sighed. "Yes, I was afraid you would be. I kept trying to put down what I felt on paper, and failing miserably. I couldn't boil it down to a telephone call, either. Just when I thought I'd fly out here, something kept coming up. It's been a long five months, honey. The longest five months of my life. But I'm here now, and you're going to have hell getting rid of me.''

"Don't you have contractual obligations to fulfill?" she asked.

He shook his head, slowly. "That's why it took me so long to come after you. I didn't want any interruptions."

She shifted back against the leather seat. "I won't have an affair with you, so if that's why you came, I'll save you the time."

He began to smile. "Have you forgotten what a low boiling point you have with me?"

"Yes," she said uncomfortably. "And that should bother you. One more groupie might be more than you could take."

"Not if she was you," he said pointedly. "I'd love having you throw yourself at me and hang on for dear life."

"Why?"

"That's something we'll talk about for the next few days." He stretched again and yawned. "I haven't slept. You're a hard woman to track down. Eventually I phoned every single veterinarian's office in the city. Do you know how many there are?"

"I have a fairly good idea," she replied, shocked. "Couldn't you have had your secretary or someone do that for you?"

"Why, no," he said, surprised at the question. "It

wouldn't have occurred to me to trust something so important to another person.''

She flushed. ''You'd forgotten all about me, surely? I've seen some of the photos on your other albums. You attract beautiful women.''

''Beauty isn't everything,'' he replied. ''And sometimes it isn't anything at all. You're beautiful to me, Poppy, because you have the kindest heart of any woman I've ever known. I've never had anyone want to take care of me when I was sick until you came along. And under those circumstances, too, when I'd practically kidnapped you. You'd have been perfectly justified in walking out and leaving me there to cough myself to death.''

''I couldn't have done that,'' she protested.

''Not even if you'd hated me. Yes, I know. But I don't think you hated me, Poppy,'' he mused, watching her like a hawk. ''In fact, I think you felt something quite different on that last day we spent together.''

''Compassion,'' she said abruptly.

''Compassion.'' He smiled. ''Is that all I get?''

''What do you want?''

He leaned forward with his hands clasped loosely over his long legs. ''I want you to love me, Poppy,'' he drawled deeply. ''I want you to become so obsessed with me that you grow pale if I'm out of your sight for an hour. I want you to hate women who look at me or touch me. I want you to ache for me in your bed at night, and go hungry for the feel of me in your arms.''

She already felt that way. She wasn't telling him so, however. She cleared her throat. ''Well!''

''And before you start raging at me about indecent proposals before dinner,'' he added slowly, ''I want a hell of a lot more than one night with you.''

Her eyebrows levered up. ''An affair is still...''

''I want a baby, Poppy,'' he said in a deep, soft whisper. ''I want a son of my own, so that I don't have to stand over Amanda and Quinn and covet theirs.''

Her body reacted to the statement in an unexpected way, so that she had to fold her arms over her breasts to keep him from noticing.

He noticed anyway, and his eyes gleamed with feeling. "You want it, too, don't you?" he said coaxingly. "A home, a husband, a family of your own. Maybe a few pets to look after, too."

"My job…"

"Whatever," he said easily. "If you want to keep on practicing, that's all right with me. It will give you and the kids something to do when I'm out of town."

Her heart was racing wildly in her chest. He looked sane. Perhaps he had a fever again.

"I'm not crazy," he explained. "I'm just lonely. So are you. So if we get married and make a family together, neither of us will ever have to be lonely again."

"There are plenty of women who would be willing…"

"I want you," he said simply. "You can't imagine how empty my cabin has been since you left." He laughed, but without mirth. "All my life I've been self-sufficient, independent. Women have chased me for years, before and after my marriage. But here you come, spend less than a week in residence, and you're living with me still, here and here." He touched his head and his heart. "I can't get rid of you. And believe me, I tried. I tried for five months."

She glared at him. "Maybe I had more success at it than you did," she taunted.

"Maybe you didn't."

He reached across the space that separated them and lifted her body right into his arms.

"Now, you see here…!"

His mouth hit hers while she was getting the last word out. He wasn't brutal or rough, but the action was amazingly effective. She went under without a protest. Her arms went around his neck and she lifted to the slow, soft caress of his hands even as her mouth opened to accept the deep, hard thrust of his tongue inside it.

Her legs trembled where they lay over his. He drew her closer and deepened the kiss even more, held it until he felt her begin to shudder. His hand smoothed up over her thighs, her flat stomach, her breasts. She moaned.

"You got over me, right?" he whispered against her mouth. "It's really noticeable, how completely you've gotten over me. Open your mouth again…"

She barely heard him above the wild throb of her heart. She clung to him while one kiss led to another, each more arousing than the one before. He turned her so that her hips pressed deeply into his own, so that his arousal was suddenly blatantly threatening. But she wasn't afraid.

"You're so small," he groaned as he let his mouth slide onto her throat. "Too small!"

She kissed his cheek, his temple, his closed eyelids with quick, warm lips. "I'll fit you," she promised. "I'll fit you like a glove."

"Poppy," he groaned again in anguish.

"Do stop worrying," she whispered as she found his mouth. "I love you."

"No more than I love you," he whispered back, holding her closer. "Are you going to marry me, complications and all?"

"I don't seem to have any choice. How else can I protect you from scores of sex-crazed beautiful women?"

He chuckled and kissed her again, murmuring his agreement against her soft, welcoming mouth.

And they were married, six months to the day after Hank had abducted Poppy to his mountain cabin. The whole group of Desperado was there as witnesses in the small Wyoming church where Amanda had married Quinn Sutton several years before. They spoke their vows and exchanged rings. The look Hank gave his new bride would have melted snow, but fortunately it was summer.

"Where are you going for your honeymoon?" Amanda

asked them when they'd changed and were ready to get into the limousine.

"That's our secret." Hank chuckled. He kissed Amanda's cheek, and the baby's, and shook hands with Quinn Sutton and Elliot.

"Well, write when you get time," Quinn asked. "Let us know you're okay."

"I'll do that. Take care of each other. We'll be in touch."

The Suttons all stood close together, waving until Poppy and Hank were out of sight.

"They're a very special couple, aren't they?" Poppy asked, sliding as close to Hank as she could get.

"A very special family," he agreed. "We're going to be one, too. I'll prove that to you tonight," he said, his voice deepening, lowering. There had been nothing more than kisses all during the time they waited for their wedding day. Now the time had come for all the secrets to be unveiled for Poppy and she was as excited as she was apprehensive. She loved him. That had to be enough, she reminded herself. She slid her small hand into his big one and snuggled close.

But she was less comfortable after they ate a leisurely supper and cleared away the dishes. Her disquiet showed on her face, too.

He tossed aside the dishcloth and pulled her gently in front of him. "Weddings are traumatic at best," he said quietly. "We can wait until you're rested and feel more like a new experience."

She nibbled at the skin on her lower lip. "I'm not usually so cowardly," she began.

He took her face in his big hands and tilted it up to his tender eyes. "I don't have anything that you haven't already seen," he reminded her.

"But I do," she said miserably. She plucked at his shirt. "And I'm grass green and inhibited...!"

"And five minutes from now, you won't know your own name," he whispered as his mouth searched for her lips and opened on them.

Actually it took less time than that for him to reduce her to insensibility. Her desire for him matched his for her, and by the time he carried her into the bedroom, she was fighting her way to his bare chest through the confining shirts that separated them.

"Slowly," he whispered as he put her down and slid onto the bed beside her. "Slowly, darling, we have all the time in the world. Nice and easy, now. Let's not rush."

She was shivering with new sensations, new expectations, but he gentled her until she lay drowsily in his big arms and let him undress them. She didn't have the will to protest or the sense to be embarrassed as he studied her pink nudity with covetous, possessive eyes. His hands were slow and thorough, like his warm mouth. He aroused her and excited her, and when she was whimpering softly with the overwhelming pleasure of his ardor, he moved into total possession.

She stiffened a little and gasped, but his mouth savored hers, and pressed reassuring kisses over her closed eyelids as he coaxed her into accepting the raw intimacy of his body.

"You are...very much a virgin," he whispered against her trembling lips, and he smiled. "Is it all right? Am I hurting you?"

"No," she managed to say. Her nails dug into his shoulders as he moved again, very tenderly.

"It stings, doesn't it?"

"Yes."

"Only a little further," he said half to himself, and his mouth crushed down hard on hers, his tongue shooting deeply into her mouth. The action shocked her so much that she relaxed and allowed him complete and total access to the soft warmth of her body.

She cried out, surprised, because it was the most profound experience of her entire life. Her eyes opened wide and she looked straight into his.

"Yes," he whispered huskily. "It's a miracle, isn't it? Man and woman, fitting together so closely, so completely, that they form one person." He kissed her damp face gently as he began to move, each tender shift of his body bringing a sudden, sharp pleasure that lifted her to him in delight. "Feel the rhythm and move with me," he coaxed, smiling as she began to match him. "Think of it as composing a symphony, making music...that's it. Hard now, baby. Cut loose and move to the beat. Move hard. Real hard...!"

She lost control of herself completely then and although she heard his urgent whispers, she seemed outside her body, watching it dance to his tune, contort and convulse with pleasure that seemed to feed on itself. Finally there was a hot burst of it that made her cry out against the unbearable sensations deep within her body. She buried her face against his throat and moaned endlessly as it went through her in waves. Somewhere in the heat of it, she heard him, felt him, as he joined her in that surreal existence with a hard shudder that arched his powerful body down roughly against hers.

Minutes later, the dazzling heat and color began to fade away and she found tears falling down her cheeks.

"It stopped," she whispered miserably.

He rolled onto his side and gathered her very close. "We'll get it back again when we've rested." He kissed her gently. "For a first time, it was fairly volcanic, wasn't it?" he mused. He laughed delightedly. "And we fit, don't we?"

"Oh, yes." She nuzzled closer, shivering with pleasure and love. "Hank..."

His mouth slid over hers. "We've just said all there is to say, and we never spoke a word," he whispered into her mouth. "I'm glad you waited for me, Poppy. I wish that I'd been able to wait for you, all my life."

She hugged him closer. "I'll settle for the rest of our

lives,'' she said gently, ''and everything that's ahead of us.''

His big arms folded her close. ''Love, then. Years and years of it.''

She smiled against his chest. ''And children to share it with.''

''Yes.'' He tugged the cover over them, because it was chilly at night this high up in the mountains. ''I'm glad I didn't apologize for abducting you,'' he murmured. ''It was the only sensible thing I've done in the past few years.''

''All the same, you can't abduct anyone else, ever.''

''Oh, I'm reformed,'' he promised her with a grin. ''The only thing I expect to abduct in the future is a piano now and again, so that I can compose an occasional song.''

Her eyes fell to his mouth. ''I particularly like the way you compose in bed. Would you like to try a new theme? Something on the order of a blues tune?''

He rolled over, smoothing her body against his in the growing darkness. ''I think I can manage that.'' He chuckled. ''How about you?''

She whispered that she had no doubts at all; about that, or about the future with him. It was going to be wonderful. And she told him that, too.

# Epilogue

As their first Christmas together approached, Hank worried over what sort of present to give his bride. She was enjoying her brand-new veterinary hospital, which took up a lot of her time. Hank had been in Wyoming, working on a new album with the group Desperado, his own band, for two weeks. The time had stretched painfully, although he'd phoned Poppy every night. She sounded cheerful, but very tired, and when he got home, he noticed that she had dark circles under her pretty eyes.

"You have to take on a partner," he told her as they lay together curled up I the big king-size bed, "you can't keep on at this pace. You'll drop in your tracks."

"I know." She snuggled closer, smiling. "It's nice to have you back home. How did the recording session go?"

"Very well," he murmured drowsily. "We did fourteen tracks in all, and ten of them are new. I think it's going to work out better than anything we've done before." He rolled over and looked down at her with pure possession.

"I'm glad we've stopped doing live concerts. I don't like being away from you, even long enough to record albums."

"I don't like it, either." She pulled him down to her and kissed him softly. "I missed you."

"I missed you, too." She frowned a little as he touched her. She was always thin, even if well-made, but she seemed to be putting on some weight. "Girl, you're getting wider," he teased. "I like it."

She chuckled. "Too many doughnuts at the café on my way to the office," she confided. "But I've always been thin. I gain and then I lose it right back, usually." She nuzzled against his broad chest. "I'm so sleepy!"

"Then go to sleep," he said softly, kissing her forehead. He brushed an enormous hand over her soft hair and frowned. "Poppy, where's Bean?" he asked suddenly,. Haning noticed the absence of a huge stray tomcat she'd taken in just before he left for Wyoming.

"The little girl next door adoped him," she said, smiling to herself. "We have visiting rights, but he gets to sleep with her."

His hand had stilled. "But you love pets. I don't mind if you have a cat or a dog, or whatever else suits your fancy. You're a vet. You wouldn't be if you didn't love animals."

"Oh, that's not why I gave up Bean," she confided.

"Then why did you?"

"Because I'm not supposed to be exposed litter boxes for a while."

"Why not?" He lifted his head and looked down at her. "You're not sick or anything?"

She grinned, reaching up to him again with a light in her ehes that made his heart ship. "No I'm not sick. I have a special Christmas present for you."

"Christmas is still tow weeks away," he reminded her, "even if you do have the tree already set up in the living room."

She laughed. "I had to have a tree. You can help me decorate the rest of it in the morning."

"Lucky me," he mused. He searched her eyes. "Are you trying to tell me something?"

She nodded. She drew one of his big hands to her soft belly and pressed it there. "Guess what, Hank?" she whispered.

"She felt his whole body go rigid, saw the curiosity in his dark eyes turn to certainty. She felt the very moment when he realized what she was saying without words.

"A baby!" he exclaimed, breathless.

"A baby," she whispered, joy almost shooting from every nerve beneath her skin. "Our baby. Merry Christmas, my darling."

He was speechless. He gathered her close to him, bent over her with closed eyes and thanked God mentally for all he was worth. He'd never dreamed of a baby. Poppy was the best luck he'd ever had, but a child of his own was an incredible surprise. He hugged her gently and kissed her temples. "A boy, maybe," he said huskily. "I have five brothers."

She chuckled. "My father was one of three boys and my mother was the only girl among three children. We have excellent chances for a son."

"A little girl would suit me just as well," he murmured contentedly. "She'll have to like football, though," he added. He'd once been a linebacker for the Dallas Cowboys and he still followed the team on television.

"We'll take what we get, and be happy with it," she said.

"Indeed we will." He looked down into her soft eyes and shook his head. "I'll never know what I did to deserve you, cupcake," he said sincerely.

"That goes for me, too, Hank." She hugged him tight. "I never dreamed that we'd be so happy, that we'd have so much."

"And we've barely begun, together. I feel exactly the

same way, Poppy. It's definitely a time for counting our blessings.'' He curled her into his arms and smiled with pure joy. It was going to be, he decided, the very best Christmas of his entire life.

And it was.

*     *     *     *     *

From the bestselling author
who launched the Montana Mavericks saga....

## DIANA PALMER

In December 1999,
Mira Books presents

# PAPER ROSE

Tate had come to her rescue in her teens, a bold and strong hero. Now Cecily was a woman on her way to a brilliant career, but Tate still thought of her as a girl who needed protecting. Her love for him was a paper rose, which longed for the magic to make it real.

Now a political scandal has an unknowing Tate caught in the middle, and it is Cecily who must come, secretly, to *his* rescue and protect him from a secret which could destroy his life. And in the process, her paper rose has a chance to become real....

Just turn the page for an exciting preview of PAPER ROSE.

# Chapter One

In the crowded airport in Tulsa, Cecily Peterson juggled her carry-on bag with a duffel bag full of equipment, scanning the milling rush around her for Tate Winthrop. She was wearing her usual field gear: boots, a khaki suit with a safari jacket. Her natural platinum blond hair was in a neat braided bun atop her head, and through her glasses with large lenses, her pale-green eyes twinkled with anticipation. It wasn't often that Tate Winthrop asked her to help him on a case. It was an occasion.

Suddenly, there he was, towering over the people around him. He was Lakota Sioux, and looked it. He had high cheekbones and big black, deep-set eyes under a jutting brow. His mouth was wide and sexy, with a thin upper lip and a chiseled lower one, with perfect teeth. His hair was straight and jet-black. He was lean and striking, muscular without being obvious. And he'd once worked for a very secret government agency. Of course, Cecily wasn't supposed to know that—or that he was consulting with them on the sly right now in a hush-hush murder case in Oklahoma.

"Where's your luggage?" Tate asked in his deep, crisp voice.

She gave him a pert look, taking in the elegance of his vested suit. "Where's your field gear?" she countered with the ease of long acquaintance.

Tate had saved her from the unsavory advances of a drunken stepfather when she was just seventeen. He'd been her guardian angel through four years of college and the master's program she was beginning now—doing forensic archaeology. She was already earning respect for her work. She was an honors student all the way, not surprising since she had eyes for no man in the world except Tate.

"I'm security chief of the Hutton corporation," he reminded her. "This is a freelance favor I'm doing for a couple of old friends. So this *is* my working gear."

"You'll get all dusty."

He made a deep sound in his throat. "You can brush me off."

Her eyes lit up and she grinned wickedly. "Now that's what I call incentive!"

"Cut it out. We've got a serious and sensitive situation here."

"So you intimated on the phone. What do you want me to do out here?" she asked, sounding like the professional she was. "You mentioned something about skeletal remains."

He looked around her stealthily. "We had a tip that a murder could be solved if we looked in a certain place. About twenty years ago, a foreign double agent went missing near Tulsa. He was carrying a piece of microfilm that identified a mole in the CIA. It would be embarrassing for everybody if this is him and the microfilm surfaced now."

"I gather that your mole has moved up in the world?"

"Don't even ask," he told her. "All you have to do is tell me if this DB is the one we're looking for."

"Dead body," she translated, then frowned. "I thought you had an expert out here."

"You can't imagine what sort of expert these guys brought with them. Besides," he added with a quick glance, "you're a clam. I know from experience that you don't tell everything you know."

"What did your expert tell you about the body?"

"That it's very old," he said with exaggerated awe. "Probably thousands of years old!"

"Why do you think it isn't?"

"For one thing, there's a .32 caliber bullet in the skull."

"Well, that rather lets out a Paleo-Indian hunter," she agreed.

"Sure it does. But I need an expert to say so, or the case will be summarily dropped."

"You do realize that somebody could have been out to the site and used the skull for target practice?"

He nodded. "Can you date the remains?"

"I'll do the best I can."

"That's good enough for me. You're the only person I could think of to call."

"I'm flattered."

"You're good," he said. "That's not flattery."

"When do we leave for the site?" she asked.

"Right now."

After they retrieved her luggage from the baggage claim, he led the way to a big black sport utility vehicle. He put her bags in the back and opened the door for her. She wasn't beautiful, but she had a way about her. She was intelligent, lively, outrageous and she made him feel good inside. She could have become his world, if he'd allowed her to. But he was a full-blooded Lakota, and she was not. If he ever married, something his profession made unlikely, he didn't like the idea of mixed blood.

He got in beside her and impatiently reached for her seat

belt, snapping it in place. "You always forget," he murmured, meeting her eyes.

Her breath came uneasily through her lips as she met the
level stare and responded helplessly to it. He was handsome
and sexy and she loved him more than her own life. She
had for years. But it was a hopeless, unreturned adoration
that left her unfulfilled. He'd never touched her, not even
in the most innocent way. He only looked.

"I should close my door to you," she said huskily. "Refuse to speak to you, refuse to see you, and get on with my
life. You're a constant torment."

Unexpectedly, he reached out and touched her soft cheek
with just his fingertips. They smoothed down to her full,
soft mouth and teased the lower lip away from the upper
one. "I'm Lakota," he said quietly. "You're white."

"There is," she said unsteadily, "such a thing as birth
control."

His face was very solemn and his eyes were narrow and
intent on hers. "And sex is all you want from me, Cecily?"
he said mockingly. "No kids, ever?"

She couldn't look away from his dark eyes. She wanted
him. But she wanted children, too, eventually. Her expression told him so.

"Cecily, what you really want I can't give you. We have
no future together. If I marry one day, it's important to me
that I marry a woman with the same background as my
own. I don't want to live with a young, and all too innocent,
white woman."

"I wouldn't be innocent if you'd cooperate for an hour,"
she muttered outrageously.

He chuckled. "Under different circumstances, I would,"
he said, and there was suddenly something hot and dangerous in the way he looked at her as the smile faded from
his lips, something that made her heart race even faster.
"You tempt me too often. This teasing is more dangerous
than you realize."

She didn't reply. She couldn't. She was throbbing,

aroused, sick with desire. In all her life, there had been only this man who made her feel alive, who made her feel passion. Despite the traumatic experience of her teens, she had a fierce connection to Tate that she was incapable of feeling with anyone else....

# A Hawk's Way Christmas

## by Joan Johnston

Dear Cherished Readers,

Those of you who have enjoyed the HAWK'S WAY series will be delighted to know that "A Hawk's Way Christmas," in which another Whitelaw daughter finds true love during the holiday season, is included in this collection. This is the tenth story of a total of twelve I've written about the Texas Whitelaws. It's the only novel I've ever written in which the relationship is never consummated during the course of the book. You'll discover why when you read this tender and enchanting love story.

"Taming the Lone Wolf," the other story of mine included in this 4-in-1 collection, incorporates a pervasive theme in my writing—how a man who believes he doesn't need anyone can become not only a loving partner, but an immediate father, as well. In this case, my hero wants nothing to do with mother or daughter, until love "tames the lone wolf."

I hope you'll find as much enjoyment reading these stories of love and hope as I did in writing them.

Best wishes of the holiday season,

Joan Johnston

For my mom,
who taught me the true meaning of Christmas.

And for my children,
who light up my life all year round.

# Hawk's Way Family Tree

Key:

**Hawk's Way**
1. Honey and the Hired Hand
2. The Rancher and the Runaway Bride
3. The Cowboy and the Princess
4. The Wrangler and the Rich Girl
5. The Cowboy Takes a Wife
6. The Unforgiving Bride

**Children of Hawk's Way**
7. The Headstrong Bride
8. The Disobedient Bride
9. The Temporary Groom
10. The Virgin Groom
11. A Hawk's Way Christmas
12. The Substitute Groom

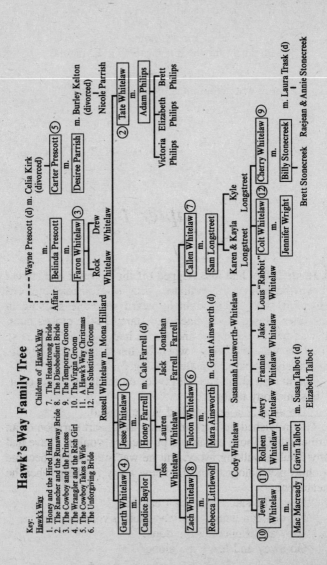

# Chapter 1

Gavin Talbot had just stepped off the elevator and started down the hall of the pediatric wing of Houston Regional Hospital, when he thought he heard someone sobbing in the linen closet. He stopped and stared at the closed door. It was nearly midnight, and Gavin had decided he was so tired he was delusional, when he heard the sound again. Definitely sobbing. Female sobbing.

Gavin rapped his knuckles twice on the linen closet door. "Is somebody in there?"

"Go away," a tear-choked voice replied.

Gavin wished he were interning as a heart surgeon or an orthopedist. Those exhausted physicians wouldn't have had any trouble walking away. But he was studying to become a child psychologist, and he knew a cry for help when he heard one.

"Hey," he said. "Maybe I can help."

"No one can help," the tear-choked voice replied.

"How about opening the door?"

"Go away and leave me alone."

"I can't do that. Look, it's late. Why not have a cup of coffee with me in the cafeteria? Maybe we can work things out."

"You don't even know what the problem is!" an exasperated voice replied.

"I'm a good listener," he said. "Why don't you tell me?"

Absolute silence. He figured she was thinking about it. Gavin said nothing, just waited patiently and was rewarded when the door inched open and a swollen-eyed, tearstained face peeked out.

"How do I know you're not a serial killer?"

He held his hands wide, letting her get a good look at the wrinkled blue oxford-cloth shirt, the sleeves casually folded up to reveal muscular forearms, and the frayed, belt-less Levi's he wore to make the kids he worked with feel more comfortable. "No gun, no knife, not even a needle. My name's Gavin Talbot. I'm working at the hospital on a research grant."

She opened the linen closet door wider, but hesitated on the threshold. He noticed her shoulder-length blond hair was cut in a fringe around her face, and she had pale, red-rimmed gray eyes that looked as desolate as any of the dying children he had ever counseled at the hospital.

Her shapeless dress was topped by a white hospital lab coat, identifying her as a medical student, and Gavin made an informed—and intuitive—guess about her situation.

Medical students were notoriously overworked and under tremendous stress to perform at high levels, and fatigue and depression were common. She fit the profile. Dark circles played under her eyes, and her short frame was so delicate she looked fragile, like she would break if he were to hold her in his strong arms.

"I'm R. J. Whitelaw," she said, extending her hand. It held a wadded-up Kleenex. She quickly stuffed the tissue into her lab coat pocket and extended the hand again.

Gavin swallowed her small hand in his and was startled by her firm grip. It conveyed confidence and self-assurance; there was nothing the least bit fragile about it. "It's nice to meet you, R.J.," he said. "I know some Whitelaws, Zach and Rebecca. They own a ranch in northwest Texas called Hawk's Pride. Any relation?"

Her lips curved in a wobbly smile that cracked as she broke down and sobbed, "My par-hents."

"I don't recognize R.J. as one of their kids' names," he said.

"I'm Ro-hol-le-heen."

She groped for her Kleenex, and he handed her the hanky from his back Levi's pocket. "Try this."

"Tha-hanks," she said, then blew her nose noisily.

"You don't remember me, do you?"

Her brow wrinkled as she rubbed at her reddened nose. "Should I?"

"We spoke on the phone. Your sister Jewel asked me to get in touch with you after I spent last summer as a counselor at Camp LittleHawk."

"Oh, no!" Her gray eyes filled to the brim with tears that quickly spilled over. "You ca-han't tell her you saw me li-hike this."

"I promise not to do that," Gavin said, taking Rolleen's arm and heading her toward the cafeteria. "Let's go get that coffee and find a quiet place to talk."

Camp LittleHawk, a camp for kids with cancer located on the Whitelaws' northwest Texas ranch, had been started by Rolleen's mother Rebecca and was now run by Rolleen's sister Jewel. Gavin had met most of the Whitelaw clan over the summer, when he'd worked at the camp, and had promised Jewel he would look up her sister Rolleen when he got back to Houston.

And he had. He and Rolleen had traded phone messages several times, but they'd both been so busy, he'd given up trying to get together with her. Now he'd met her, and

Gavin was suddenly a lot more than a detached observer of someone in trouble.

He knew Rolleen was the eldest of the eight Whitelaw kids. And smart. "Rolleen's away at medical school," Rebecca had told him proudly. "She's been at the top of her class during each of the past two years."

Obviously something had gone very wrong. He wondered if she was having trouble keeping up her grades, and if so, why.

When they reached the cafeteria, the door was locked and all the lights were out. Gavin looked at his watch and made a disgusted sound. "I forgot the cafeteria closes at midnight over the holidays."

"I wasn't thinking, either." Rolleen disengaged her arm from his and said, "Thanks anyway for the offer."

She had already turned to leave when Gavin caught her by the shoulder. "Wait. Why don't we go across the street to the Coffee Caper? They're open twenty-four hours a day."

She wiped at the tears on her cheeks with the heel of her hand, shook her head, then looked up at him with those desolate gray eyes. "I don't want anyone to see me looking like this."

"There must be someplace we can go to talk," he said. "Your place? Or mine?"

She looked at him askance. "I'm not in the habit of inviting strangers home with me—or going home with them."

He smiled his most trustworthy smile and said, "I'm not a stranger. I spent the entire summer working for your sister. I'm sure if you gave Jewel a call, she'd be willing to vouch for me."

Rolleen visibly shuddered. "No. I don't want to speak to her—to any of them—right now. They'd know...they'd know..."

When tears began to spill from her eyes again, he simply

pulled her toward him—tugging when she at first resisted—
put his arms around her and hugged her gently, aware of
his much greater size and strength.

She gripped him tightly around the waist while she cried,
as though if she didn't, she would fly away into pieces. The
strength of her hold on him once again contradicted his
fragile image of her. There was nothing delicate about her
crying, either. Her whole body heaved with sobs so painful
they made his throat ache—and he didn't even know what
her problem was.

Yet she hadn't collapsed entirely. She was still standing
on her own two feet. There was plainly more to R. J. Whitelaw than met the eye.

When the sobbing had resolved into hiccups, Gavin kept
one arm around Rolleen and began walking her down the
deserted hall toward his mentor's office, where he'd been
headed in the first place. He got out his key and unlocked
the door and eased her inside. When he reached for the
light, her hand was there to stop him.

"Don't. I look awful."

If she was able to think about how she looked, she was
feeling better, Gavin thought. The light streaming in from
the hall through the old-fashioned, half-shuttered venetian
blinds was enough for them to see each other's faces, and
she was right about her appearance. Her eyes and nose were
puffy and swollen and red.

"All right," he conceded. "No light. Why don't you sit
down and take it easy?" He eased her onto the well-used
black leather couch and felt her tense as he sat down beside
her. He put more distance between them and heard her
exhale in a relieved sigh.

She rested her elbows on her knees and dropped her face
into her hands. He didn't resist the urge to put a comforting
hand on her shoulder and rub at what turned out to be very
tense muscles on her shoulders and neck.

"That feels wonderful," she said.

"Let's get rid of this," he said, easing off her lab coat. He angled her slightly away, so he could use both hands effectively, and said, "You want to tell me about it?"

"There's nothing you can do to help," she said resignedly.

"What have you got to lose by telling me?"

She sighed again. "Nothing, I suppose."

Between the softness of her skin, the small, enticing curls on her nape and the little sounds of pleasure she was making, Gavin realized he was becoming aroused in the seductive darkness. He stopped what he was doing and slid back across the couch.

He leaned forward, draping his arms on his widespread thighs, and said, "I'm listening, Rolleen, if you'd like to talk."

"I've been using R.J. at school," she said. "I think it sounds more—never mind."

More what? Gavin wondered. But he didn't ask. He was merely providing a friendly shoulder for the sister of a friend. "Rolleen's what I've heard you called all summer," he said. "It's unusual and pretty—like you."

She started to speak, stopped herself, then said, "Rolleen's fine."

He had a feeling it wasn't really fine, but he didn't want to get sidetracked talking about her name when something much more important was bothering her. "All right, Rolleen," he said. "Shoot."

She hesitated as though on a high diving board, her face thoughtful, then dove in. "If you've met my parents you know they think I'm the perfect daughter."

"I don't think I heard a disparaging word about you all summer," he admitted with a smile. "And praise was heaped on your head."

She made a face. "That's the problem. I've always been the 'good little girl.'"

"Really? How come?"

"Because by the time Zach and Rebecca adopted me from the Good Souls Orphanage I'd made a promise to God that if He sent somebody to take me out of that place, I'd repay Him by being the best daughter any parents could ever have."

Gavin realized he was hearing the truth and was humbled by it. "It sounds like you kept your promise."

Her mouth shifted in a crooked smile. "Pretty much. I stole some gum once from the five-and-dime in town—to see if I could get away with it." Her lips quirked as she admitted, "I didn't. And I got caught smoking once in the high school bathroom. But I was a straight-A student and president of the student council and a soloist with the church choir and helpful around the house. And a devoted daughter."

She looked up at him, and the grief and despair were back in her eyes. "That's why what's happened is so awful. Momma and Daddy are going to be so disappointed in me when they find out what I've done."

Her eyes began misting again, and he reminded her, "You still haven't told me what it is you've done that's so bad you don't want your family finding out about it."

She stood slowly and turned in profile, then pressed her hands along the front of her dress from the waist downward. He saw the slight outward curve of her belly, and felt his stomach turn over. *She's pregnant.*

"I'm pregnant," she said.

He stood, crossed away from her to the desk and settled his hip on the corner, trying to be nonchalant. But he knew the Whitelaws well enough to know they *would* be disappointed in their daughter, of whom they were so proud. "Who's the father?" he asked. "And where is he?"

"One of my professors," she replied. "He's spending the next year at the Centers for Disease Control in Atlanta, completing a study on viruses."

"Does he know about the baby?"

"Yes."

"And?"

"He said the problem is mine, and that I should solve it. Meaning, I should get an abortion," she said bitterly. "Or give up the baby for adoption."

"Those are available options," he said neutrally.

"Not for me! I'm going to have this baby and keep it and love it enough for both parents!"

She slumped back onto the couch. "But I'm going to have to quit medical school to do it. I can't ask my parents to support me and a child, too. That wouldn't be fair to them."

"Don't you think that ought to be their decision?"

"I know they wouldn't begrudge me the money," she said. "But I can't take advantage of them like that. After everything they've done for me, look how I've repaid them—by getting pregnant without a husband, without even a fiancé!"

She took a hitching breath and blew it out. "I'm sorry. I shouldn't be burdening you with my problems." She walked past him to stare out through the half-open venetian blinds, her arms crossed protectively over her small bosom. "I dread spoiling everyone's Christmas when I go home next Tuesday. I'd stay here, but then they'd know something was wrong and come after me."

She turned to face him. "Christmas has always been a special time of year for my family. On Christmas Eve, Momma always tells the story of how she met and married Daddy, and how together they picked each one of us to be the family Momma could never bear in her womb…"

Her face was crumpling again, and he quickly asked, "How will they know you're pregnant, if you don't tell them?"

"The eight of us kids have always shared bedrooms. It's hard to keep secrets when you share a double bed," she said, managing a brittle smile. "I'll be four months pregnant by Christmas, and I'll be dressing and undressing in front of my sisters. They'll surely notice my figure has changed.''

''I see.''

''Even if I could hide in the bathroom to dress, I've never worn blousy clothes, so that would be a tip-off. And if I tried wearing jeans...'' She turned and held her dress tight against her slim figure—slim except for the bulge in the middle. ''They'll see the truth for themselves. And my family is so physical—rambunctious, playful, ripping and tearing around the house, horseback riding at a full gallop, flag football that ends up being full tackle—they'd know the instant I excused myself from any of those activities that something was up.''

''You do seem to have a problem,'' Gavin murmured.

Her chin began to quiver. ''Momma will cry when she finds out. And Daddy...he'll get quiet as a sunset on the prairie. But I'll know he's feeling bad, because it'll be right there in his eyes. He's no poker player, my dad.''

She swallowed hard before she said, ''They'll be so unhappy, it'll spoil Christmas for the whole family. And that'll be one more thing I'll have to feel guilty about.''

Her chin was still quivering, but she had her teeth clenched to keep from losing control. He was pretty sure an iron rod ran down Ms. Whitelaw's slender back.

''I don't know what I'm going to do,'' she said unhappily.

Respecting that inner core of strength—and the pride that had put it there—Gavin resisted the urge to offer platitudes. He wanted to help her, but he wasn't sure what he could do. He had little personal experience to draw on. The rollicking Christmas she had described was nothing like what Christmas had been for him in the past, or was going to be like for him this year.

He had come from a small family, an only child of parents who had died in a private plane crash when he was eleven, and he had a small family of his own—himself, his four-year-old daughter Beth and his grandmother Hester. This was the first Christmas since his wife, Susan, had died. Or, more precisely, since Susan had committed suicide, scrawling a note that said nothing about why she had taken her own life, but telling him that Beth was not his child.

Gavin had spent the past year tortured by thoughts of the woman he'd loved in another man's arms. Wondering endlessly why Susan had killed herself. Wondering what he had done to make his wife betray him. And furious at the thought that his precious daughter, whom he had adored, was not his own flesh and blood. He had become a distant parent to his child, unable to hug her and love her the way he had before Susan's revelation.

Gavin was certain his grandmother was planning to manipulate things so he ended up spending a lot of time over the Christmas holiday with Beth. Hester firmly believed that time and proximity would wear down his reserve.

But she was wrong. Ever since he had read Susan's note, he hadn't been able to look at his daughter without feeling physically ill. He couldn't bear to disappoint Hester by staying away at Christmas—he wasn't sure how many Christmases his grandmother had left—but he had been desperately searching for a way to avoid being alone with Beth.

Gavin looked up and met Rolleen's grim, gray-eyed gaze. "I may have a solution to your problem," he said tentatively.

Her brows rose in question.

"This may sound a bit farfetched, but hear me out before you say no," he said.

"All right."

"I think we should get engaged."

Rolleen backed up against the door and stared at him wide-eyed. "What?"

He rose and came toward her, but when she reached for

the doorknob, he stopped and held out his hands placatingly. "Don't leave. Please just listen."

"I'm listening."

"What I'm suggesting is a temporary, make-believe engagement," Gavin said, warming up to his subject as he realized what a good idea it was. "When you go home for Christmas, I'll go with you. You'll still be pregnant and unmarried, of course, but you'll have a doting fiancé on your arm. We'll tell your parents there are practical reasons why we can't marry now, but we plan to marry before the baby's born."

"What reasons?" Rolleen said. When he frowned she explained, "They'll want to know why we aren't married."

"I'm sure we can come up with some good excuses," he said. "What do you think?"

"It's not a bad idea," she said, "but I couldn't let you—"

"I'm not doing this only as a favor to you. I want something in return."

Her eyes narrowed. "I'm listening."

"We can spend the holiday until Christmas Eve at your family's ranch, but I want you to come to my house on Christmas Day and spend the rest of the holiday there."

A pinched V appeared at the bridge of her nose. "Why?"

"It's a long story, and I've got two weeks before Christmas to tell you all about it. Suffice it to say, I'll play your fiancé and you'll play mine for the duration of the holidays."

"We don't even know each other!"

"But we have an excuse for knowing each other. It was your sister Jewel who arranged the introduction by asking me to look you up in August—about four months ago," he pointed out, letting her see how easy it would be to carry out the deception.

"I don't know anything about you," Rolleen said.

"We'd never be able to fool my family. They'd know right away we were strangers."

"Not if we spend the next ten days getting to know each other," Gavin argued.

Rolleen pursed her lips. "I still won't have solved the problem of telling my parents I'm going to be a single mother."

"No, but you'll have saved Christmas for everybody. After you've been back at school for a while, you can call or write your parents and say we've broken up."

Rolleen folded her hands together behind her back and wandered past him to the other side of the room, examined an autographed Cal Ripken, Jr. baseball in a hermetically sealed case on the credenza, then meandered back to the door. She turned to face him and said, "I suppose it might work."

"It'll work, all right," Gavin said, thinking how agreeable his grandmother would be when he asked her to keep Beth while he had some grown-up time with his fiancée. Hester would be glad to see him happy again and downright ecstatic at the thought he might marry and provide her with more grandchildren. Rolleen's presence would provide a welcome distraction on all counts.

"How do you propose we get to know each other?" Rolleen asked.

"We're going to have to spend some time together, at my place, at yours, kissing, touching—"

"Whoa, there! Hold your horses!" Rolleen said. "Kissing and touching?"

Gavin shrugged. "I don't know any engaged couples who don't kiss and touch. Do you?"

He watched as Rolleen scratched the back of her neck, and recalled the enticing curls on her nape. He might be kissing her there sometime soon, he realized in amazement.

"I hadn't figured on getting intimate with another man," she said thoughtfully.

"I'm not suggesting we go to bed together," Gavin said, "although, if you have any birthmarks I should know about—"

"I see your point," she interrupted. "And my family *will* expect us to kiss and hold hands."

"And touch," Gavin said. "Don't forget I've met them."

She wrinkled her nose like a kid facing a plateful of lima beans and spinach and brussels sprouts. "Within reason," she conceded.

"All right, then. We're agreed?"

"Agreed," Rolleen said, extending her hand.

Her hand and wrist were fragile, he realized, but the woman extending them wasn't. He was glad she had a strong backbone. She was going to need it to stand up to the interrogation his grandmother was certain to give her. All in all, Gavin was satisfied with the bargain he'd made. Rolleen seemed like a pretty levelheaded young woman. They should both be able to accomplish their goals with a minimum of fuss and bother.

"Can I give you a ride home?" he asked.

She started to shake her head, then said, "I suppose we might as well start getting acquainted. I can show you how to get to my apartment."

Gavin rolled down his sleeves and buttoned them, then retrieved a navy blue wool sport coat from a hook and slipped it on. He picked up Rolleen's lab coat from the couch and said, "Have you got a jacket somewhere?"

"In my hospital locker," she said.

"Let's go get it." He slipped his arm around her waist, and she immediately stiffened.

He kept his arm where it was and looked down at her until she looked back up at him. "You okay?" She managed a smile, and he felt her relax slightly.

"I guess this is going to take some getting used to," she said. "Bear with me, will you?"

"Sure." He opened the office door and ushered her through it, noticing how soft and feminine her hip felt pressed against his. She was so small tucked in beside him, his protective instincts rose, and he tightened his hold on her waist.

She made a sound of protest in her throat, then made a face and shook her head. "I'm sorry. It's just... Never mind."

"What?" he asked. When she kept her face forward, he said, "You might as well tell me. We need to learn everything there is to know about each other in the next ten days. As you said yourself, we might as well start now."

She took a deep breath, let it out and admitted, "I'm not used to being around men—I mean, this close. I never dated much in high school." She shot him a quick, shy smile. "Too busy being the perfect daughter," she explained. "And I was too busy studying in college so I would be sure to get into medical school. So Jim... He was my first... Jim was my first lover," she managed to get out.

Gavin stopped and stared down at her. "You've got to be kidding."

"I'm afraid not."

"So your parents are going to be *shocked* and pleased that you're bringing a man—me—home for Christmas."

She nodded. "I never told my family about my relationship with Jim, because he was one of my professors. As far as they're concerned, you'll be the first man I've shown a serious interest in dating."

"I'm going to get grilled like a hamburger."

Her gray eyes focused intently on his face. "I'll let you out of the bargain, if you don't think you can handle it."

Gavin's lips flattened. Her lack of experience with men might make the situation a bit more difficult, but not impossible. "I can handle it. I can handle anything."

*Except a four-year-old who isn't your daughter after all.*

"Let's get going," he said, urging Rolleen down the hall. "The sooner we get started, the sooner this'll all be over."

# Chapter 2

Rolleen rolled over in bed and groaned. She had invited Gavin Talbot to return to her apartment for lunch at noon today to begin their "courtship."

*What was I thinking last night? How could I have agreed to such a bizarre plan? We're never going to get away with it. My family will know right away that we're not really lovers.*

Not if she and Gavin Talbot knew everything there was to know about each other. Not if she could successfully pretend she felt affection and admiration for him.

That wasn't going to be too difficult, Rolleen admitted. At least the admiration part. The man was gorgeous. Tall, dark and handsome. The proverbial knight in shining armor riding to the rescue. Intelligent, kind, considerate, compassionate…and sexy.

Yesterday, when Gavin had rubbed her shoulders, she'd felt the strength of his hands, and the tenderness, and wished she'd tried harder to meet him in August when he'd first called her. She'd been too busy buying books, getting into the routine of classes and catching up with friends she hadn't seen over the summer. Jim Harkness had made his move the first week of classes, and by the time Gavin called the third and fourth times, she was already secretly seeing her professor.

Rolleen swallowed down the acid that rose in the back of her throat. It wasn't the baby making her feel so sick. It was bitterness over Jim's behavior. Just in case, she reached for one of the saltines she kept beside the bed, bit off a corner and began chewing.

She was determined not to let her feelings toward Jim make her ill. Her inexperience with men had led her to misjudge Jim's intentions. She had thought his emotions were as much engaged as hers; he had thought she knew he always had an affair with one of his students. She had been naive. *And in love for the first time.*

Her nose stung and ready tears came to her eyes. Rolleen felt her stomach turn and ran, hand over mouth, for the bathroom. She barely made it in time.

*Forget about Jim,* she admonished herself a few minutes later, as she rinsed her mouth and pressed a cold, wet washcloth to her face. Rolleen groaned again as she examined herself in the mirror. Her eyes looked less puffy, but they were still bloodshot, and her nose was raw and tender where it had been wiped so many times. She had to stop crying over spilt milk. *Jim's gone from your life forever. You were a fool and an idiot.*

Once. She'd been a fool once. Never again. She would never again give her heart so quickly or completely. Which was why Gavin's offer of a pretend engagement had been so appealing. Her parents would find solace in the fact she was happy and in love with the baby's father, even if she wasn't married. If she went home looking like she looked now, they would feel her pain and suffer along with her.

Rolleen wondered if she would be able to fake with Gavin the same euphoric feelings she'd felt when she'd given herself to Jim—to the man she'd loved—for the first time. Perhaps. But she would have to put a smile on her face to do it. Which meant no more tears.

She dabbed at her eyes with the cool washcloth one more time, then set it aside, looked in the mirror and said, "No looking back, Miss Whitelaw. Think about the wonderful life growing inside you and the joy and happiness ahead of you." That thought brought a smile to Rolleen's face and, amazingly, she felt better.

When Rolleen heard Gavin's knock at the door shortly before noon, she met him wearing a boat-necked, short-sleeved red silk blouse, black designer jeans with a silver-buckled belt, polished-up-but-worn-out black cowboy boots and a practiced smile, looking very much like her old, stylish self.

"Hi, Gavin," she said cheerfully. "Come on in."

He didn't budge. "Rolleen? Is that you?"

She laughed, grabbed his hand and pulled him inside. "Don't tell me I looked so bad last night you don't recognize me."

"You look…different."

"It's the smile," she said, beaming at him. "It was missing last night."

He finally returned her smile with one of his own that nearly took her breath away, revealing a single dimple in his left cheek. "I had no idea you were so beautiful," he said. "It shouldn't be too difficult to convince your folks I fell in love with you."

Rolleen felt something shift inside. The experience was disturbing, because she'd felt something similar the first time she'd laid eyes on Jim. She quelled the feeling. She wasn't interested in getting involved with another man. And unlike Jim, Gavin had made his position clear from the start. This was all *pretend*.

"Come on in and make yourself comfortable," she said, gesturing him inside her one-bedroom apartment. A ceramic, cowboy-dressed Santa, a table-size pine Christmas tree with winking lights and a fragile crystal nativity evidenced her love of everything to do with Christmas.

"Can I get you something to drink?" she asked.

"Nothing right now," Gavin said, searching for a place to sit that wasn't already occupied by something else.

"Let me clear a place for you," she said with a laugh that acknowledged the clutter. "Growing up in a house with so many kids, I always had to put my things away or lose them. Since I've had a place of my own, I guess I've gone a bit overboard in the other direction."

"I never had to be neat, so I'm not," he admitted with a grin that made her heart take an extra thump.

Rolleen quickly turned away from all that powerful sex appeal, moving a stuffed kangaroo she'd bought for the baby the day she'd learned she was pregnant, a book on childbirth and a red-and-green ruffled Christmas pillow from the secondhand sofa to make space for Gavin. "I thought we could talk for a little while before we eat," she said.

By the time she turned around, Gavin had already claimed her favorite overstuffed corduroy chair by shifting copies of *Vogue* and *Elle* and *The New England Journal of Medicine* to the wooden coffee table.

"Are you sure I can't get you something to drink?" she asked, her nerves getting the better of her as she dropped what she'd picked up back onto the couch.

"Nothing for me."

She waffled about where she ought to sit, then settled on the end of the couch closest to him, reminding herself she was a pregnant woman and that letting herself fall for a handsome face was how she'd gotten that way. She pulled off her boots, tucked her red-Christmas-stocking-clad feet under her and leaned on the broad arm, her attention focused on Gavin. She noticed he was sitting on the front edge of the chair, rather than settling into it and looked as uncomfortable as she felt.

"Where should we start?" she asked.

He rose immediately and paced across the sea green carpet, making a detour around her wooden coffee table, which was littered with as many life-style and fashion magazines as medical journals. Rolleen made most of her own clothes and had once upon a time dreamed of becoming a fashion designer—before she realized her parents expected her to pursue one of the professions more commonly chosen by someone of her extraordinary intelligence.

Gavin abruptly stopped pacing and turned to face her, his hands behind his back. "Have you had any second thoughts since last night?"

"Second, third and fourth thoughts," she admitted. "But I haven't changed my mind."

He hesitated, then crossed and settled more comfortably into the chair, this time leaning forward with his forearms braced on his knees. "I've been thinking about it, too. But I couldn't come up with any better plan to solve your dilemma—or mine—so we might as well go for it. What does the J in R.J. stand for?" he asked.

"Jane."

"Rolleen Jane," he said. "I like it."

The hairs stood up on her arms when he said her name. Rolleen rubbed them down and countered, "It's a better name for a doll than a doctor. Rolleen Jane: she speaks, she sits, she wets! R.J. sounds more like somebody you'd want to have deliver your baby."

Gavin chuckled. "How about plain Rolleen."

"*Plain* Rolleen?"

"Make that just Rolleen."

"*Just* Rolleen?"

He laughed and said, "I'm sticking with Rolleen. I like it. By the way, is that what you want to be, an obstetrician?"

"A pediatrician," she corrected.

"Why?"

"Because I love children."

"Then you're glad about the baby?"

She looked down and placed her hand on the gentle curve where her child was growing inside her, then looked up at Gavin. "I was at first. And I am now."

He nodded with understanding.

She liked that about Gavin, Rolleen decided. He understood so much without her having to explain it. "What kind of doctor are you?" she asked.

He smiled, and the dimple reappeared.

She told herself she wasn't charmed, as he explained, "I'm not a medical student. I'm studying for my Ph.D. in child psychology. Eventually I plan to counsel dying kids."

Rolleen picked a tuft of stuffing from the couch. "To be honest, that sounds like distressing work."

"Difficult," Gavin conceded. "But ultimately quite uplifting." She raised a questioning brow, and he continued, "We're all going to die. Kids with cancer or other debilitating diseases have time to think about it in advance. I help them through denial and bargaining and anger, and from depression to acceptance, before they actually have to face dying."

"I imagine it must be hard to work with someone—to become intimately acquainted with someone—you know is going to die." *Isn't it hard to share their pain?*

She dared a glance at him, looking for an answer to her unasked question, and found it in the eloquent sorrow reflected back to her from his dark eyes.

"They don't all die," he said. "A few of them miraculously recover. I always hope that will happen."

"You're an optimist," she said, suddenly finding it easier to smile. "That's good. My parents would expect me to choose a spouse who believes the glass is half-full, rather than half-empty."

"Tell me about your life growing up," Gavin said. "The kind of anecdotes you might have shared with me when we were getting to know each other."

"I've already told you about my nefarious activities in school," she said with a smile. "As far as my family goes...it's been an adventure growing up on a cattle and cutting horse ranch, especially as one of the Whitelaw Brats."

*"Whitelaw Brats?"*

She grinned and said, "Playful pranks and high-spirited, harmless mischief are a time-honored Whitelaw tradition. My brothers and sisters and I—even though all eight of us were adopted—felt compelled to uphold it."

"For instance?"

"Jewel and I tied a big red bow to the tail of old Mr. Cooper's bull—which wasn't easy, believe me," she said, smiling as she remembered how Jewel had held on tight to the bull's tail through the fence while she tied the bow. "Another time we used a curling iron on Hardy Carmichael's golden retriever, Butch. He was the cutest thing you ever saw when we were done."

Gavin laughed and said, "I'm envious. It sounds like you had a lot of fun together."

Gavin's laughter warmed someplace deep inside Rolleen. The sensation was pleasant, without being threatening, so she didn't fight it.

"It was fun," she agreed. "Especially with so many of us so close to the same age. I'm the eldest at 24, Jewel's 22, Cherry's 21, Avery's 20, Jake's 19, Frannie's 16, Rabbit's 15—Rabbit's real name is Louis. We call him Rabbit because—"

"He liked vegetables when he was a kid, especially carrots," Gavin finished for her.

She straightened her legs and relaxed into a sprawl on the sofa. "I'm telling you things you already know."

Gavin cleared his throat and said, "I didn't know exactly

how old everybody was, although I'd pretty much guessed. By the way, you forgot Colt.''

"I saved the best for last,'' she corrected. "Colt's fourteen and the rebel in the family. He's also the only one of us who was adopted as a newborn, so he's the only one who hasn't known any parents except Zach and Rebecca. All of us kids had a hand in raising him—which is probably why he's such a maverick. Too many cooks spoiling the broth, or something like that.''

"I got the impression your father intends for Colt to take over the ranch.''

"It wouldn't surprise me if Colt ends up running Hawk's Pride. He's always had an affinity for the land, he rides like he was born on a horse and Dad's been teaching him the business since he was old enough to walk.''

"What plans did your parents have for you?'' Gavin asked.

"I'm fulfilling them,'' she said with a smile. The smile faded. "At least I was until…'' Rolleen found another imperfection in the secondhand couch and tried to repair it.

"You said last night you plan to leave school and try to support yourself. What kind of work will you do?''

Rolleen bit her lower lip anxiously. "I'd rather not say.''

"I need to know everything—all about the real Rolleen Jane Whitelaw—or this isn't going to work,'' Gavin said.

She looked at him and found she couldn't look away. His dark eyes compelled her to share all her secrets. *That's what he does for a living,* a cautionary voice reminded her. *It has nothing to do with you personally.*

"If we start hedging with each other this early in the game, we might as well call it quits,'' he said.

Rolleen lowered her eyes to avoid his scrutiny. Her hands knotted in her lap. Being a sympathetic listener might be his job, but he was good at it, Rolleen conceded. No one knew what she was about to tell Gavin Talbot. Not any of her family, not her friends, not anyone. It had been her deep, dark secret.

She took a deep breath and said, "There's a salon in Houston called The Elegant Lady that features designer clothing. They've been wanting me to work with them for some time."

Gavin picked up one of the fashion magazines from the coffee table and thumbed through it. "What would you do for them?"

"Design clothing."

Gavin shut the magazine and stared at her. "Don't you have to go to design school for that? Or have some kind of training and experience?"

Rolleen pulled her knees up to her chest and wrapped her arms around her legs. "For the past three years I've been selling my designs—that is, fashions I've designed and sewn myself—to The Elegant Lady."

Gavin's smooth forehead suddenly acquired several deep lines. "Are you telling me you've been at the top of your class in medical school for the past two years while you've been secretly working as a fashion designer?"

She hugged her knees more tightly, more protectively, to her chest. "I'll make a good pediatrician."

"I never said you wouldn't."

"Designing is a hobby. I do it for fun."

Gavin eyed her appraisingly. "It sounds to me like you'd rather be doing it for a living."

Rolleen stared at Gavin. He was amazingly perceptive. That wasn't so odd, she realized, when you considered what he planned to do with his life. His work depended on reading faces, finding the hidden context in what people said and did. She still found it a bit disconcerting. In the three months she and Jim had been together, her professor had never once intuited that she wasn't perfectly happy in medical school.

"I wouldn't have gone to medical school if I didn't think I would like being a doctor," she said.

"But you *love* designing fashions," Gavin guessed.

Rolleen sighed, unable to keep the wistfulness from her voice. "Yes. I do."

"Can you really make a living at it?"

"Not with as few designs as I've done over the past two years. But yes, with The Elegant Lady committed to buy as much as I can design, I could make a very comfortable living. And I'd be able to work at home, so I could be with the baby."

"Why didn't you ever tell your parents you'd rather be a fashion designer and just quit medical school?" Gavin asked.

She smiled mischievously. "I'm about to do that, aren't I?"

"But you aren't being honest with them," Gavin said. "They'll think you're giving up something you really want to do because of the baby. If you're so worried about their feelings, why not admit you prefer designing?"

"Because then they'd know I've been lying to them for a very long time," Rolleen admitted.

"I can't imagine Zach and Rebecca not supporting whatever profession you chose. Why lie in the first place?"

"It's hard to explain to someone who's not adopted," Rolleen said.

"Try."

"You have to imagine what it feels like to be abandoned, totally alone in the world, knowing there's no one who really cares if you live or die. Along comes this man and woman who say, 'We'll love you. We'll take care of you. You're precious to us.'" She lifted her eyes and met Gavin's intent, dark-eyed gaze. "You'd want to please those people because they've given you their love. And because if you didn't, they might take it back."

"Zach and Rebecca would never—"

"I know they wouldn't stop loving me," Rolleen interrupted. "That is, intellectually I know it. But inside—" She tapped her heart with a forefinger. "Inside is a frightened six-year-old girl, already forsaken once by parents who said every day they loved her—and then abandoned her one morning at a convenience store."

Gavin remained silent, giving Rolleen too much time to think…to remember. Her heart was racing, clutching, as it did every time she relived that awful morning.

She had frantically searched the store several times before she got up the courage to approach the clerk and ask, "Have you seen my mommy and daddy?"

The clerk had taken one look at her, barefoot and dressed in a calico shift with a torn sleeve and the hem half-down and said, "We don't allow kids in here alone."

"I came with my mommy and daddy. She's wearing a dress with flowers on it and he's tall and he's got a mustache."

The clerk had looked out the window for a run-down truck that wasn't there, said a word she knew she wasn't ever supposed to say and then called the police. Rolleen didn't remember much about the rest of what had happened that day. Mercifully she'd been in shock.

As an adult, Rolleen understood that her birth parents had believed they were doing the right thing leaving her to the state welfare system, because she needed clothes and shoes to go to school and food to grow up healthy, and they were too poor to afford them. She still woke up every morning wondering what had happened to them. She still wondered what she could have done differently to keep them from abandoning her.

It had taken a long time to learn to trust again. It had taken a great deal of courage to let herself fall in love. She told herself she had done nothing wrong as a child…or now…except to fall in love with a shallow man. But she had finally learned her lesson. She wasn't going out on that limb again anytime soon.

"Your turn to talk," she said to Gavin. "Why do you need a fiancée over Christmas?"

Gavin had known this moment was coming, and he'd practiced what he was going to say. When he opened his mouth to speak, nothing came out. He shoved both hands agitatedly through his sun-streaked, tobacco-brown hair, then let them fall onto his thighs. He took a deep breath and said, "My wife died—" He cut himself off, swallowed hard and corrected, "— My wife killed herself in January, and this is the first Christmas…" *That I will spend without her.*

Gavin could not understand the lump in his throat. He shouldn't be missing Susan, shouldn't be feeling pain at the thought of Christmas without her. She had betrayed him. But it wasn't only Susan he was grieving, he conceded, it was what they had been together with Beth—a husband and a wife and child—a loving family.

He shifted his glance to the stuffed kangaroo sitting on the sofa with the tiny baby in her pouch and thought how much Beth would love to have such a toy.

*Don't you see?* he felt like shouting. *I can't face a little girl I used to love…a little girl who wants me to love her still…when I can't anymore.*

His throat had swollen completely closed, making it impossible to explain anything. His nose stung and his eyes watered and he felt dangerously close to crying.

Telling Rolleen anything about Beth would have to wait. There was plenty of time over the next ten days to tell the whole sordid story. Gavin swallowed back the worst of the misery in his throat and said, "It would be easier if my grandmother and I weren't alone at the ranch over the holidays."

"So I'm going to be a buffer between you and your grandmother?" Rolleen asked.

"Hester and I get along fine," he said brusquely. "It's... She worries about..." He hesitated, then admitted, "I don't want to be alone this Christmas."

Rolleen could only imagine how Gavin felt, losing a wife, but she had lost Jim, and that was close enough to the same thing for her to understand and feel his pain.

*Don't feel too much,* a voice warned. *Don't get too close.*

Rolleen made herself listen to the voice. If she wasn't careful, she could be hurt again. It was all right to like Gavin Talbot. It was even all right to feel sorry for him. It wasn't all right to get emotionally involved in his life. She had to protect herself. They were two strangers who were going to part company at the end of the holidays. It was not necessary for her to know more than the bare fact that she would be helping him if she came home posing as his fiancée.

"Where's your home?" she asked, tactfully changing the subject.

"The ranch is about an hour south of here."

"That's where we'll be spending Christmas together?"

Gavin's stomach growled loudly.

Rolleen glanced at her watch and realized it was nearly one o'clock. "Lunch!" She bounced up as though one of the ancient couch springs had sprung and said, "You must be starved. Come on into the kitchen. I planned tomato soup and grilled cheese sandwiches. I hope that's all right."

"Sounds great. What can I do to help?"

"You can fix us each a glass of iced tea while I warm up the soup and cook the sandwiches."

During lunch, Gavin kept her riveted—and laughing until her sides were sore—with stories about the kids he was working with at the hospital.

"How can they find so much to laugh about when their lives are so uncertain?" she asked.

"The same way you've been able to laugh today," Gavin said. "Life goes on. You make the best of it. And it beats the heck out of the alternative."

Rolleen started to laugh and yawned instead.

"Looks like you need your beauty rest," Gavin said, standing and collecting the dishes. He was halfway to the kitchen before Rolleen caught up to him with the iced tea glasses. "Thanks," she said. "I guess we're going to have to cut this short. I am feeling a little tired."

"The baby?" he questioned as he settled the dishes in the sink.

She nodded as she put the glasses down on the counter, then placed both hands on her abdomen. "This little darling takes a lot out of me."

"May I?" he asked, gesturing toward her hands.

Rolleen moved her hands aside, and Gavin's hands, large and warm, covered her rounded belly.

"It seems like it ought to be soft, but it's so firm," he said, his hands gently cradling her stomach.

Rolleen felt an ache in her throat. *If only...*

"Don't be sad," he murmured. "I'm here now, baby."

Rolleen started at the use of the endearment. Was it for her? Or was he speaking to the child inside her? The look Gavin directed at her was so concerned, so loving, that she almost believed he really cared. "You called me baby," she pointed out to him.

"I know. We have to practice being in love," he reminded her.

*Practice. Pretend.* But it felt so *real*. Rolleen couldn't take her eyes off Gavin. His head was lowering toward hers, but she couldn't believe he really meant to kiss her. They'd known each other only a few hours.

He stopped when his mouth was close enough that she could feel his warm, moist breath on her cheek. "May I?"

"Isn't it a little soon to be kissing?" she asked breathlessly.

"We only have ten days to convince some very astute people that we're in love," he said quietly. "That I've had my hands all over you. That I've been inside you."

Rolleen took a hitching breath. "Holy cow."

"Is that a yes?" he said, his lips curling with amusement.

Rolleen nodded and closed her eyes as he pressed his lips against her own. They were softer than she'd expected and slightly damp.

"You okay, baby?" he murmured.

Her heart pumped a little faster. "Mmm-hmm."

She felt a tingle as his tongue came out to trace her closed lips. "Oh," she whispered in pleasure.

He took advantage of her open mouth to slip his tongue inside, then withdrew before she could protest. He slowly straightened, his gaze focused on hers, so she could see his dark brown eyes were almost black, his lips rigid with desire.

Rolleen felt panicky without knowing why. She put her hand on Gavin's chest to make a space and eased past him. "I think that's enough for today."

He followed her into the living room. "When can you meet with me again?"

"Next week," she said immediately. Rolleen wanted the rest of the weekend to recover from his touch, from the loving addresses, from his surprisingly sensual kiss.

"How about tonight?" he countered.

"So soon?"

"We don't have much time," he reminded her. "And we both have busy schedules during the week. Why don't I take you out for dinner and dancing?"

"Dancing?"

"It'll be fun. Pick you up at eight." He leaned over and gave her a quick kiss on the mouth. "Think of me while you're napping,'' he whispered in her ear. A moment later he was out the door.

Rolleen felt like she'd been caught up in a tornado that had come and gone and left her not knowing which end was up. When Gavin had tasted her in the kitchen, she'd wanted to keep on kissing him. And just now she'd been thinking how nice it would be if Gavin laid down with her on the bed and held her while she napped.

*Snap out of it, R.J.*

Rolleen wasn't going to make the same mistake twice. She'd fallen for Jim Harkness in a hurry and look how that had turned out. What she felt for Gavin couldn't be love, but whatever it was, it was dangerous. When he took her dancing tonight—she *loved* dancing—she was going to have to be careful not to like it too much.

# Chapter 3

In the ten days since Gavin Talbot had met Rolleen White-law, he had run the gamut of romantic experiences with her. They had gone from a couple just meeting to a couple who had mated—or rather, who could pretend they had. It had been quite an adventure, and Gavin had enjoyed every minute of it. There was only one cloud on his horizon: Rolleen still didn't know about Beth.

He had meant to tell her, but the better he got to know Rolleen, the less willing he was to confess his feelings to-ward his daughter. Because he was pretty sure when he did, he was going to lose Rolleen's regard. And he wasn't ready for that to happen yet.

Gavin knew he was only postponing the inevitable, but there was always the chance his feelings toward Beth would miraculously change when he saw her again. At least, that was his excuse for keeping Rolleen in the dark about his daughter.

In a matter of hours they would be leaving to spend the holidays with Rolleen's family at her father's ranch in northwest Texas. Gavin couldn't quite believe they were really going through with it.

As he thought back over the previous ten days, Gavin realized that he and Rolleen had become such good friends, it wasn't going to take much acting to pose as someone who loved her. Especially since—if the circumstances hadn't been what they were—they might have become romantically involved.

He would never forget the stunned look in Rolleen's eyes after he'd kissed her that first time. In fact, touching her and tasting her that day at her apartment had been so arousing, he had felt like picking her up and carrying her straight to the bedroom. The hard part had been remembering he didn't have that right, that everything they did was make-believe, because she needed a make-believe father for her unborn child.

It didn't seem fair to let himself start imagining the two of them together. Rolleen had already been hurt by one man who'd loved her and left her. While he might have fallen for her if she'd been free and single, he couldn't very well ignore the fact she was pregnant with another man's child. That complication alone would make any permanent relationship between them difficult, if not impossible.

Yet over the past ten days, Gavin had learned to like Rolleen Whitelaw better than he had liked anyone—man or woman—in his entire life. It was the confounded sexual attraction between them that had him uptight and confused. It wasn't something that had grown gradually. It had been there right from the start.

Rolleen hadn't simply moved to the music that first evening when he had taken her dancing, she had reveled in it. During a slow jazz tune, she had put the back of her hand against his nape, urged his head down and whispered, "I love dancing with you, Gavin. I mean, darling. Darling sounds lovely, doesn't it? Thanks so much for bringing me here tonight, darling."

The mere sound of her voice, that soft, sexy purr, had made his blood roar in his ears. Gavin didn't know when he'd been so aroused by a woman out of bed. His flesh had come alive along every surface where her slim, feminine form molded itself against his, and because it was all supposedly pretend, he had said exactly what he was thinking. "I'm on fire for you, Rolleen."

She made a whimpering sound and shivered and clung even closer to him.

Instinct drove him to lift her so they would fit better, when what he really wanted was to have her prone. He knew it was way too soon for that—or even the pretense of it. Which was when it had dawned on him that nothing was ever going to happen between them, because this was all *pretend*. Even if it felt damned real.

At the end of the evening, he had kissed her chastely on the forehead at her door, refusing her invitation inside for a cup of coffee. He knew better. It was as difficult holding on to his objectivity as it was keeping his distance. But it would have spoiled everything if he'd started kissing her and touching her for real.

The next step in their "courtship" had been an evening of Christmas shopping two days later.

"Shopping?" he'd said, much aggrieved at the idea.

She'd given him a coaxing smile—which had sent his heartbeat up a notch—and said, "Have you done yours?"

He'd been forced to admit, "Not yet."

"Then we might as well do it together. I have lots of people to buy for, and I'm still not done."

She had taken him to a huge mall on the beltway with a parking lot the size of an airport runway. "People actually shop in this madhouse?" he'd asked.

"I come to see all the Christmas decorations," she replied. "And to shop," she conceded with a smile. "I love the excitement and bustle of the crowd and the look of awe and enchantment in the children's eyes when they meet

Santa Claus for the first time. And the carolers. I love Christmas music. It's so full of…of joy!''

She had looked up at him, her face as bright and shiny as one of the Christmas balls hanging from the rafters and said, "You may have noticed. I love *everything* about Christmas.''

Gavin hadn't recently made a point of admiring the sparkle and glow of Christmas decorations, but he had trouble taking his eyes off of Rolleen's face. He didn't notice the crowds, because he was too busy watching her.

He stopped with her to observe the children being put on Santa's lap to make their Christmas requests—some crying, some laughing, some adorable. Like the shy little girl with short black hair parted in the middle and bangs that fell into her eyes who reminded him of his daughter.

*I wonder if Hester has taken Beth to see Santa?*

He could easily have slipped Beth into the conversation—if he hadn't felt so guilty at that precise moment. It wasn't Beth's fault Susan had been unfaithful. It wasn't Beth's fault she wasn't his flesh and blood daughter.

Guilt was quickly followed by another, darker emotion. Seeing Beth's face in his mind's eye reminded him that none of her features were his. Thinking of her brought back the anguished feelings of betrayal he had experienced the night he'd read Susan's letter, and it forced him to acknowledge that he was afraid to see Beth this Christmas because his emotions were so close to the surface. He was terrified he might fall to pieces in front of her.

Which was why he found himself Christmas shopping at a mall with Rolleen Whitelaw. She was going to provide the buffer that would allow him to get through this Christmas season with his… He made himself think the words: *my daughter.*

In fact, Rolleen's attitude toward her unborn child, and the fact she was adopted herself, had Gavin reevaluating his behavior toward Beth. If he wanted to keep Rolleen's good opinion—and he did—he needed to treat his daughter in a loving way. But behavior and feelings were two different things. Gavin could change his behavior. He wasn't so sure about his feelings.

"Look, Gavin! Carolers!" Rolleen exclaimed, interrupting his thoughts.

On his own, Gavin wouldn't have paid any attention to the choir in the center of the mall, but he was so fascinated by the radiant look on Rolleen's face that he listened to see what it was she found so inspiring about the music—and was assailed with nostalgic memories.

God rest ye, Merry Gentlemen!
Let nothing you dismay...

Christmas in his home had always been a wonderful blend of the secular and the religious. They had popped popcorn in the fireplace and read Charles Dickens after they opened presents on Christmas Day. His grandmother had kept the traditions alive after his parents died, and Gavin had maintained them with his family.

This year he hadn't been able to think about any of the things that made Christmas a special time of year. That is, until a few days ago. Seeing Christmas through Rolleen's eyes, Gavin wanted to be a part of it again—the gift giving, the music, the decorations...and the spirit of love he seemed to have lost when his wife died.

Gavin vicariously experienced the pleasure Rolleen took in selecting a model airplane for Colt while she explained, "Colt thinks nobody's noticed, but he's crazy about flying."

"Really?" Gavin said. "He never said anything to me about it."

Her lips curved in what was becoming to him an endearingly familiar smile. "He thinks he's keeping it a secret."

"It's not?"

"Dad gave him a couple of books on the history of flying for his birthday this year, and I've given him a different model airplane every Christmas for the past five. There isn't much you can keep secret in a household as big as ours."

"Yet you think we can manage it?" Gavin asked, dividing the weight of the packages he carried more equally. "Do you really believe we're going to get away without somebody finding out the truth?"

Her smile disappeared for the first time since they'd stepped inside the mall. She settled a package carefully in the crook of his elbow and said, "For everyone's sake, I hope so." She looked up at him and said, "If we were a married couple, and you were madly in love with me, what would you do if I said I was feeling a little tired and needed to sit down?"

Instead of telling her, Gavin acted on impulse. He set all the packages beside a nearby fountain, lifted her into his arms and settled himself on the edge of the fountain with her in his lap. "Are you comfortable now?"

She was too busy laughing to answer him. She had her arms draped around his neck, and as she leaned against him her breasts pillowed against his chest.

"That was wonderful!" she said. "My family will be truly impressed if you make grand gestures like that."

He put his palm against her cheek, angled her face toward his and said, "I didn't do it to impress anybody. I did it for you."

The laughter stopped abruptly and tears misted her eyes. "Oh, Gavin," she whispered. "What a lovely, romantic thing to say. You're so wonderfully convincing. They'll never doubt you are what you say you are."

He tucked her head under his chin, finding it strangely difficult to speak.

Before they left the mall he purchased a selection of eucalyptus-scented bath accessories for his grandmother.

Rolleen had been delighted to help evaluate each and every bottle and jar in the store—until the odd mixture of odors had finally made her nauseated.

"Uh-oh," she'd suddenly said, swallowing furiously. "Uh-oh."

"What is it?"

"I think I'm going to be sick."

He'd looked around frantically but there wasn't a bathroom in sight. He urged her out the boutique door, where he remembered seeing a bench in the mall. To his chagrin, the bench was occupied by an elderly couple he wouldn't ordinarily have asked to get up. But he found himself saying to the white-haired woman, "She's pregnant," and looking at the elderly man for understanding.

"Get up, Harold," the woman said, getting up herself, "and let the little lady sit down."

Gavin dropped his load of packages on the floor beside the bench and knelt in front of Rolleen, watching her take deep breaths, praying for the color to come back into her pale, sweat-dotted face as an interested crowd gathered around them.

"She's expecting," the elderly woman informed anyone who would listen.

Gavin knew Rolleen was all right when she suddenly pointed at a little boy across the mall who was squatted down on his heels watching a shark chasing a diver around a bowl of water. She was on her feet and headed for the toy store before he could stop her.

"You take care of her, son," the elderly man said as Gavin grabbed their packages and followed after her. "Nothing is more important than family at Christmas."

The sudden constriction in Gavin's throat had plenty of time to relax while Rolleen bought presents for some kids at the hospital. When she wasn't looking, Gavin purchased a doll for Beth that talked and ate and wet and hid it at the bottom of his single shopping bag. The doll was something

Gavin knew Beth wanted, and he realized he was glad to buy it for her, even if she wasn't really his daughter.

He dropped the packages and Rolleen off that night without coming inside. And without mentioning Beth.

Since Rolleen had been the one to select shopping as a joint activity, their next excursion was Gavin's choice. "I vote for a picnic on the beach," he announced.

"It's winter!" she protested.

"This is South Texas. We don't have winter."

"I can't get off during the day."

"We'll go at night."

"All right. I give up," she conceded, throwing up her hands in defeat. "A picnic on the beach. But don't expect me to wear a swimsuit. What can I bring?"

"Yourself. I'll take care of everything else."

The picnic hadn't quite turned out as he'd planned.

Gavin had figured they'd drive down to a beach house he owned near Padre Island and make themselves comfortable on the rug in front of the stone fireplace, where he imagined the two of them kissing in the romantic light of a crackling fire.

Unfortunately, when they arrived, the key to the front door proved useless, because the house was sealed with a padlock.

"I knew the caretaker was having trouble with vandals, and I told him to handle it whatever way he thought best," Gavin muttered. "But I had no idea he'd padlock the place."

"Can you get the key from him?"

Gavin shook his head. "He lives in Houston. I usually call before I come down. I'm sorry, Rolleen." He was surprised at how disappointed he felt.

"Why don't we take our picnic down to the beach?" Rolleen suggested.

"It's full of sand crabs and sand fleas and...sand," he said disgustedly.

She laughed. "We'll put down a blanket. Come on!"

She grabbed his hand and headed back to the Jeep to pick up everything they would need. She took off her tennis shoes when they filled with sand and made him take off his Docksiders. Gavin had to admit the sand felt wonderfully cool between his toes, but the salty breeze off the gulf was downright chilly.

"You're going to catch a cold," he protested when she shivered despite the sweatshirt she was wearing over a pair of faded cutoffs. "This was a mistake."

"It was a fabulous idea," she countered, her arms spread wide, her head back as she turned circles staring up at the night sky. "I've never been to the beach before."

He hurried to keep up with her as she skipped over a sand dune and down onto the beach. "Never?"

She shook her head, her windblown hair catching in her mouth. "Not a lot of ocean in northwest Texas. And I've been too busy with school to get down here."

Rolleen had trouble spreading the blanket by herself with all the wind, and Gavin had to drop what he was carrying and help her. They put picnic items on the four corners of the blanket to keep it from flying. Rolleen finally settled onto the blanket cross-legged and grabbed his hand to pull him down beside her.

Gavin laughed as he settled on the center of the blanket. "The picnic basket's holding down the north corner of the blanket. We're going to starve unless we sit closer to it."

"Not yet," she said, squeezing his hand.

When he looked into her gleaming eyes she said, "Couldn't we just lie back and look at the stars for a little while?"

She held on to his hand as she lay back on the blanket, and Gavin laid himself down beside her. They said nothing for a very long time. Gavin looked at the stars and found the Big Dipper and the North Star, which was the extent of his knowledge of astronomy.

He was very much aware of the fact Rolleen was flat on her back and how little effort it would take to pull her into his arms. He kept waiting for her to make some overt move toward him, to give him some signal that she wanted to do more than hold hands. But it didn't come.

"Pretty moon," he said at last.

"Yes, it is."

"Not a cloud in the sky."

"No," she said softly. "Just billions of stars. Do you suppose the star that led everyone to Bethlehem is still up there somewhere?"

"I don't know why not," he said. "You see a particular star you think might be it?" he asked, glancing at her.

"The brightest one."

He searched the sky, but they all looked about the same to him. He made himself see the sky through Rolleen's eyes and found one faraway star that winked brighter than the rest. "I see it," he said.

She squeezed his hand again, and he felt connected to her and in some odd way to the sand and the sea and the sky as well.

"Rolleen?" He heard the yearning in his voice but by then was beyond feeling pride. He wanted to hold her. He wanted to touch her. "We've been seeing each other for a week."

He saw her swallow hard. "I know. A wonderful week."

He opened his mouth to suggest they should graduate from holding hands, maybe indulge in another kiss, but bit his tongue before he spoke. She was right. It had been a wonderful week without the kissing and touching. He didn't need to indulge in the acts to know he wanted her, to *pretend* for her parents' sake that he wanted her.

To his surprise, she rolled onto her side facing him. "Gavin, would you kiss me, please?"

He soughed out a breath he hadn't known he'd been holding, then rolled onto his side facing her. There wasn't much space between them, just enough so he didn't have to look cross-eyed at her. "I'd like very much to kiss you, Rolleen," he said. "That's why I'm not so sure it's such a good idea."

She thought about that a minute and said, "Neither of us wants this charade to lead to entanglements. But I think we'd better do this anyway."

"Why?"

"Because my sister Jewel is going to ask me when I knew I was in love with you, how it felt, what we did. And I want this to be that moment. I think you should kiss me, so I'll have a lovely memory I can share with her."

Gavin's heart was in his throat, making it impossible to speak. He eased Rolleen onto her back and shifted his body over hers, holding his weight on his elbows, settling his body into the warm, welcoming cradle of her thighs. "All right, Rolleen," he said quietly. "Let's make a memory together."

He threaded his hands into her hair and angled her beautiful, vulnerable face up to his in the moonlight before he lowered his mouth and touched his lips to hers.

"Gavin."

The reverent sound of his name on her lips made his chest ache. He wanted to be gentle, to be tender, to be soft and giving and all the things a woman wanted from a man at such a moment. But he found himself plundering her mouth, grasping her hair to keep her from escaping his rough, urgent kisses, desperately taking what he wanted, what he needed from her. His tongue broached her lips, mimicking the sex act, as he pressed his body against hers, claiming her, making her his—if only for this brief moment.

She was a willing captive. Her arms came around his shoulders and held him tight, her fingernails digging into his skin through his sweatshirt as her body arched up beneath him. Her tongue thrust into his mouth, surprising him and inflaming him. He became a feral animal, without thought or conscience, wanting only one thing.

Gavin suddenly made a sound like a cat caught in a ringer and came up off of Rolleen like he'd been popped from a toaster. "Yow!" he yelled, jackknifing and grabbing for his toe.

"What is it?" Rolleen cried.

"A crab bit my toe!"

Rolleen giggled.

Gavin got the crab off a second before Rolleen shrieked and flapped her hands and cried, "There's a crab in my *hair!*"

Gavin laughed and scooted over to help her. "Be still so I can find it!" he said, gripping both her trembling hands in one of his. He pulled the crab free with the other and threw it aside, then stood and helped her up. "I guess we'd better find another picnic spot." And then, "I'm sorry about that memory you wanted to make."

"Don't be!" she said with a soft laugh. "This was absolutely perfect. Especially the part where the crab bit your toe."

"What?"

"Don't you see? It's so *real.* Who could make up a story like that?"

Gavin chuckled. "I see what you mean."

Rolleen leaned over and opened the picnic basket. "What have you got in here that I could nibble on? I'm starving!"

Gavin gave her a fried chicken leg and helped himself to a couple of deviled eggs, while they stood in the center of the blanket watching for crabs. When they'd demolished the contents of the picnic basket, Gavin put his Docksiders back on and started putting things away. "I think we'd better get started back."

Rolleen yawned as she tied her tennis shoe. "I'm afraid

I won't be much company during the ride back. I'm pretty worn out.''

"The baby," they said together. They shared a look that made Gavin feel they had shared a whole lot more. He forced his gaze away and said, "We'd better get going.''

"Thank you, Gavin," she said. "I had a lovely time.''

"No thanks necessary,'' he replied.

Five minutes after they were on the road in his Jeep, she was sound asleep, her head nestled against his shoulder, her hand resting on his thigh. Gavin felt protective and possessive—both appropriate emotions for a prospective groom. Which he was...and he wasn't.

There had been other enjoyable evenings together in the last few days of their ''courtship''—studying together in the library, playing billiards in a yuppie game room, doing laundry, going through each other's medicine cabinets and kitchens, sitting down with Rolleen's photo albums and discussing all the intimate details of each other's friends and family.

Except for Beth. Somehow the subject of Beth just never came up.

Gavin had let himself fall in love with Rolleen. He figured it was silly to fight his feelings for her, at least until the game was played out with her family and with his. Until then, the more in love with her he could pretend to be, the better. But it was beginning to feel more real...and less pretend.

"Gavin? Are you all right?''

Gavin realized he must have been daydreaming for quite some time. "I'm fine, Rolleen. Are you all packed?''

She set down a small suitcase next to the shopping bags full of gifts she was taking home. "I think I have everything.'' She rubbed her hands together nervously as she looked around her living room.

He caught her hands between his and said, "Don't worry so much, sweetheart. Everything will be fine.''

She tried for a smile but couldn't quite make it. "I'm not even used to having you call me sweetheart."

Gavin put his arms around her and rocked her back and forth in a comforting hug. He kissed her forehead and her cheeks and her nose and finally planted a quick kiss on her mouth. "Just don't forget I love you."

She looked up into his eyes and said, "And I love you."

Gavin caught his breath as she rose on her tiptoes and kissed him softly on the mouth. She teased his lips until he opened for her and her tongue slid into his mouth, giving him a brief taste of her, before she ended the kiss.

"Breathe," she whispered, the familiar mischievous smile on her face.

Gavin gasped a breath of air, tucked her head under his chin and held her tight against his thudding heart.

*Don't forget she's playing a role.*

"One more thing before we go," he said, pushing her away. He reached into the sport coat he was wearing with a button-down shirt and jeans and retrieved a small black box. He opened it and held it out to her. "This is for you."

She gasped and her eyes went wide as she retrieved the one-carat marquise diamond engagement ring from its velvet bed. "It's exquisite," she said as she slipped it on.

"I hope it fits all right."

"It's perfect. In every way." She met his gaze and said, "Thank you, Gavin. Are you sure you'll be able to return it later?"

"It belonged to my mother," he said.

"Oh."

She started to pull it off, but he stopped her. "I'd like you to wear it. Susan didn't— Susan never— It hasn't been worn since my mother died."

Her eyes brimmed with tears, and she put her arms around his neck and hugged him tight. "It's beautiful, Gavin," she said, her voice ragged. "Thank you."

Gavin pulled her arms away, cleared his throat and said, "We'd better get moving. We don't want to keep your family waiting."

# Chapter 4

"It's good to be home," Rolleen said as Gavin drove their rental car under a black wrought-iron archway that spelled out HAWK'S PRIDE.

Hawk's Pride had originally been a part of her grandfather's ranch, Hawk's Way, which had been settled by Whitelaws more than a century before. The grassy plains stretched for miles, and the steep canyon walls were etched with primitive drawings left by those who had roamed the land before the white man had come to settle it. The several-thousand-acre parcel her father owned had been given to him on his twenty-first birthday to do with as he liked.

Zach Whitelaw had built a whitewashed, Spanish-style adobe ranch house in a square around an enormous, moss-laden live oak, creating a lovely central courtyard where Rolleen had spent hours in her youth dreaming up exotic fashions. She loved her home every bit as much for its rich heritage as she did for its majestic beauty.

"The house is lit up like a Christmas tree," Gavin said. "I guess they waited up for us."

"I told you they would." Although Rolleen almost wished they hadn't. She and Gavin had made the trip to northwest Texas in his private plane, so there hadn't been any flight connections to tire her out, but worry about what her family would say when they saw Gavin and found out she was pregnant had taken its toll.

She directed Gavin around to the kitchen door, since only strangers used the front entrance. When she and Gavin stepped inside, Rolleen found her family gathered around the central island in the kitchen drinking egg nog and eating Christmas ribbon cookies.

"Rolleen!" sixteen-year-old Frannie shrieked. "You're home!"

"Welcome home, honey," her mother said with a smile and a hug.

"Rolleen's home!" her brother Jake announced to anyone who was listening.

The cacophony of greetings was deafening, and Rolleen did her part to make a joyful noise. Still bundled up against the cold, her nose a frozen berry, she was hugged and kissed and kissed and hugged as she was passed from one family member to another.

"You remember Gavin," she said to her mother and father, staying close to Gavin with an effort as their coats and scarves were taken away by Avery and Jake and the shopping bags full of gifts were taken to be put under the tree by Colt and her sister Jewel's fiancé, Mac Macready.

Rolleen waited for someone to notice her bulging stomach beneath her waistless dark green velveteen dress, but they were all distracted by Gavin's presence. "I invited Gavin to spend Christmas with us." She held out her hand, displaying the ring, and said, "We're engaged."

"Wow!" Frannie said, grabbing her hand. "Look at the size of that diamond!"

"You're drooling, Frannie," her twenty-year-old brother Avery said, using a forefinger to tip her gaping mouth closed. "Welcome to the family," he added, shaking Gavin's hand.

"You play football?" nineteen-year-old Jake asked as he shook Gavin's hand, a football curved under his opposite arm.

"A little," Gavin said, surprising Rolleen, who had never thought to ask.

Jewel gave Gavin a hug and said, "What a marvelous surprise! I'm so glad for you both."

Mac buffeted Gavin on the shoulder, smiled shrewdly and said, "Congratulations."

"Hi there, Gavin. Nice to see you again," Colt said, gripping Gavin's hand and pumping it up and down. "I can hardly believe you're going to be my brother-in-law after all," he said with a wink.

Gavin laughed, squeezed Rolleen's waist and said, "I just had to find the right Whitelaw woman."

"What's that mean?" Frannie asked.

Colt proceeded to tell the whole family his version of one of the many stories Gavin had told Rolleen. How Gavin had been attracted to Jewel when he first met her at the beginning of his summer at Camp LittleHawk and how Mac Macready, who'd been at Hawk's Pride recovering from a pro football injury, had quickly staked his claim on Jewel, cutting him out.

"Mac just flat outmaneuvered you," Colt said with a laugh.

Rolleen shot a worried glance at Gavin, who seemed to be taking her family's jests with good humor. She had never considered how overwhelming a Whitelaw welcome might seem to him, compared with his smaller family gatherings. Her eyes never left his face as her family escorted them like a circus parade from the kitchen to the living room.

"It's good to see you again, Gavin," her father said as soon as Rolleen and Gavin were seated side by side on the worn saddle-brown leather couch. "I have to admit I'm curious, though. How did you and Rolleen meet?"

Rolleen exchanged an amused look with Gavin. He checked his watch, reached for his wallet and handed her a five-dollar bill.

"What was that all about?" her mother asked.

"I made a bet with Gavin that Daddy would start asking questions within sixty seconds after he sat down," Rolleen replied with a grin.

"So how long have you two known each other?" her mother asked.

Rolleen looked at her watch, held out her hand again and Gavin put another five dollars in it.

Her mother laughed. "Anyone else you'd like to have ask a question?" she asked Rolleen.

"Nope. I only bet on sure things." She wasn't willing to hazard a guess at what might transpire over the course of the next few days. She had her fingers crossed for luck, because she was going to need it.

Her entire family—except Cherry and her husband Billy, who were at the Stonecreek Ranch putting their three children to bed—arranged themselves around her and Gavin in the living room. Her mother had settled in the pine rocker by the warmth of the crackling fire in the stone fireplace. Her father stood right behind her mother, his hands resting on her shoulders.

Mac Macready sat in a brass-studded, wine-colored leather chair, with Jewel angled crosswise on his lap. Her brothers and sisters had found comfortable spots on the Navajo rug, leaning against each other and the furniture. Despite the fact there was room, no one joined them on the couch.

Someone was crooning, "Chestnuts roasting on an open fire," on the CD-player, and the house smelled of the pine boughs decorating the mantel. Rolleen took a deep breath and let it out. She was home.

Her gaze lingered on the ten-foot-tall spruce hung with all the homemade Santas and reindeer and angels that all of them had created in six years of elementary school. Festive colored lights winked from behind store-bought ornaments that had been selected, one by each child in the family, every Christmas since Jewel had been adopted seventeen years ago. Rolleen located the glittery star, lace angel and graceful, feathery swan that were among her favorites.

"To answer your question, Mr. and Mrs. Whitelaw—" Gavin began.

"You called me Zach last summer," her father reminded him.

Gavin cleared his throat. "I wasn't sure whether...I mean—"

"You're Rolleen's fiancé and our guest," her mother said with a welcoming smile. "Make yourself at home. And don't you dare call me Mrs. Whitelaw."

Gavin laughed, and Rolleen felt her heart swell with emotion. He was so good to be helping her this way. And she could have kissed her parents for making him so welcome.

"To answer your question," Gavin said to her father, "Rolleen and I have known each other since August, when I followed up on Jewel's suggestion that I call and introduce myself to her when I returned to Houston." Gavin gave Rolleen a look that made her toes curl and added, "It was the most important call I've ever made."

Rolleen heard the silence after Gavin's pronouncement and felt the blood creeping up her throat. Gavin didn't have to lay it on quite so thick, did he? She glanced up at him and completely lost her train of thought. He was looking at her like a man besotted, like he wanted to hold her forever, like he loved her with all his heart. When Zach cleared his throat, it broke the spell and Rolleen turned to her father, aware of the twin spots of heat on her cheeks that declared her guilty conscience…and her involuntary physical response to Gavin's intense, loving gaze.

"We…uh…we kind of hit it off," she said lamely.

"I guess so!" Avery said with a snicker.

"Avery," her mother reproved.

"When are you two getting married?" Frannie asked.

"He just got here, Frannie," Rabbit said, nudging her in the ribs. "Give him a chance to breathe."

Frannie glared at Rabbit, then turned to Rolleen and said, "Well, when?"

Rolleen watched in awe—along with her family—as Gavin lifted her palm to his lips and kissed it.

"We haven't set a date yet," he said, smiling into Rolleen's eyes.

Rolleen dared a glance around the room and saw that as far as her family was concerned, the deed was as good as done. She wondered if Gavin knew what he'd let himself in for. Now that he was nearly one of the family, he could expect to be treated like one of the family, which meant no question was too personal, no inquiry off-limits.

Without warning, Rolleen's stomach churned, and she tasted acid at the back of her throat. Oh, no. She couldn't be sick now! Morning sickness was supposed to come in the morning. She wanted time to let her parents see her and Gavin together before they discovered she was pregnant. She wanted time— But there wasn't time.

Rolleen shot a desperate look at Gavin, who had been through enough moments like this over the past ten days to recognize the problem. She needed a bathroom in a hurry. But how could they manage it and still keep her secret?

To her surprise, Gavin didn't even try. He rose, bringing Rolleen to her feet at the same time, and said, "You'll have to excuse Rolleen. She needs a bathroom. Now."

Her family stared at her bemused for perhaps two seconds before Jewel grabbed her hand and pulled her toward the bathroom down the hall. Rolleen stared helplessly over her shoulder at Gavin, who was left standing in the middle of her gape-mouthed family.

Rolleen didn't have much time to worry about Gavin's upcoming interrogation before she was leaning over the toilet bowl with Jewel's gentle hand on her shoulder. Jewel handed her a damp cloth to wipe her mouth, flushed and put the seat down so Rolleen could sit on it.

Jewel settled on the edge of the tub, her knee nearly touching Rolleen's, and said, "When's the baby due?"

"You haven't even asked if I'm pregnant!" Rolleen said.

"Is it food poisoning? Stomach flu? Indigestion?" Jewel shot back.

"No."

"When?" Jewel repeated.

"The end of May."

Jewel's lips curled in amusement. "It must have been love at first sight. You just met Gavin in August."

"We…we…"

"I can see he loves you," Jewel said. "Do you love him?"

"I…uh…"

Jewel put a hand on Rolleen's knee. "You do love him, don't you?"

Rolleen looked into Jewel's ordinary brown eyes and saw a wealth of compassion and caring. Tears sprang to Rolleen's eyes, and she tried to blink them away.

"Oh, Rolleen," Jewel said, going to her knees on the bath mat and taking Rolleen's hands in her own. "I feel like this is all my fault, since I was the one—"

"I *do* love him," Rolleen sobbed. "He's the most wonderful man in the world!"

"Then what's wrong?" Jewel asked, perplexed.

"I… He… We…" Rolleen was on the verge of blurting the truth, when she caught herself. Their charade had a purpose, which was preserving Christmas for her family. If she told Jewel the truth, she knew that before the holiday was over she'd end up telling everyone. As bad as lying made her feel, she was certain telling the truth would be infinitely worse.

What had made her cry was the realization that she was beginning to have dangerously loverlike feelings for Gavin Talbot. He was a wonderful man, and he'd played the role of doting husband-to-be to perfection. What frightened her was the strength of her feelings for him on such short acquaintance. She refused to become a victim of the same sort of infatuation she'd had for her professor. She was desperately fighting the feelings she had for Gavin that felt like love and miserable because of it.

She swallowed back the acid in her throat and said, "Gavin wanted to marry me right away, but I thought it would be better to wait and make sure we're right for each other first. I'm so confused. I don't know what to do."

"You always did think too much," Jewel chided. "What about the baby?" she asked. "Is Gavin happy about the baby?"

Rolleen realized she and Gavin had never discussed the baby. She'd avoided the subject, knowing it wasn't going to be Gavin's concern. But she needed an answer for her sister. "Gavin seems fascinated by the whole process," she extemporized, remembering how he had marveled at the firm roundness of her body where the baby was growing inside her.

"That's a good sign," Jewel said. "So tell me. When did you know you were in love?"

Rolleen smiled, relieved that she had a story to tell that would ring true. "We were at the beach," she began, "having a picnic."

"How romantic! I don't think I should be the only one to hear this," Jewel said. "Otherwise, you're just going to have to tell it again for everybody else. Do you feel well enough to rejoin the family?"

Rolleen nodded, and the two of them left the bathroom. Even from down the hall, she could hear Gavin discussing her pregnancy. She hurried toward the living room, wondering what he'd been asked and what, exactly, he'd told her family.

The moment Rolleen was gone from the room, Gavin had taken one look at her family's faces and known he was in trouble. "Rolleen's pregnant," he announced baldly. "She's still having a little morning sickness." He settled back onto the couch, crossed his ankle over his knee and pretended to be comfortable while he waited for the inquisition to begin.

"Why aren't you married?" Zach asked.

Gavin wasn't fooled by the calm voice. Zach's body was one giant knot of tension, and a muscle jerked in his cheek where he had his teeth clenched. His eyes bored into Gavin's, demanding an answer…the right answer.

Gavin and Rolleen had discussed in some depth exactly what to say to relieve her parents' concern. He gave the prepared response. "Rolleen decided she'd like a little more time to make sure we're right for each other before we marry."

"It's a little late for that, don't you think?" Zach said in a hard voice. "With a baby on the way?"

Gavin's foot came down, and he sat forward, his arms braced on his knees, his body taut in a visceral response to the threat Zach posed. "I wouldn't force any woman into a marriage she didn't want."

"You should have thought of that before—"

Rebecca put a hand on Zach's arm to cut him off. "We can see you love her," she said.

Gavin opened his mouth to confirm it and couldn't get the words out. He hated lying to these people. He looked around and saw frowns and confusion where a few moments before there had been smiles and realized that the lies were a temporary, necessary solution to a very difficult situation. "I assure you—all of you—that I have every intention of making sure Rolleen's taken care of in the future."

That was no lie. He liked Rolleen well enough to keep an eye out for her when this was all over. There were a few advantages to being filthy rich. He'd make certain Rolleen had whatever she needed to keep her and the baby comfortable until she was earning enough designing fashions to manage on her own.

Gavin heard an audible sigh of relief in the room, and the expressions of concern eased into curiosity.

"What about medical school?" Colt asked. "Is Rolleen going to be able to finish?"

"You'll have to ask Rolleen about that," Gavin hedged.

"I'm planning to quit," Rolleen announced as she stepped from the hall into the living room. "So I'll have more time for the baby."

Gavin rose and reached out a hand to Rolleen, who took it and let him reseat her on the couch beside him. He put a protective arm around her shoulder, knowing what was probably coming. This was the point at which Rolleen expected the most resistance from her parents.

He had argued she ought to tell them the truth—that she planned to replace medical school with designing fashions. She had pointed out that her parents would be more suspicious of her starting a brand-new career with a brand-new baby, than with the notion of her quitting medical school and being supported by her husband.

From the corner of his eye Gavin saw she was right. The look her parents exchanged was pure anxiety.

"If it's a matter of money—" Zach began.

"It isn't," Rolleen interrupted. "It's a choice I've made freely."

Gavin watched Zach's lips flatten, saw Rebecca's mouth purse. He could see what they were thinking. *How freely*

*could the decision be made when Rolleen so obviously
hadn't planned to become pregnant?* Which made him the
villain. The accusation *Why weren't you more careful?* was
plain on her father's face. And her mother's eyes clearly
revealed her regret that things hadn't turned out more perfectly for her daughter.

*Rolleen miscalculated,* Gavin thought. It wasn't enough
to have the father of her child on hand. Her parents weren't
going to be happy until the two of them were tied up good
and proper. Gavin shoved a restless hand through his hair.
He'd gone as far as he was willing. Her family would have
to make the best of the situation, and if it spoiled Christmas
for them...

He felt Rolleen's hand on his thigh and looked at her in
surprise at the intimate touch. Her gaze was focused on her
father as she said in a quiet, intense voice, "I love him,
Daddy." She turned to her mother and said, "Please, Mom,
I love him."

Gavin turned to see whether her declaration had made a
difference, and realized he had underestimated Rolleen's
understanding of her parents. He watched the tension ease
out of her father's shoulders and saw the loving smile ap-
pear on her mother's face. Those few words had turned the
tide.

"Welcome to the family, Gavin," Zach said.

Gavin was amazed and relieved at how quickly their charade had been accepted.

"Now, Rolleen," Jewel said, "tell us when and how you
fell in love with Gavin."

Gavin couldn't believe how personal the question was,
or that Jewel expected Rolleen to relate something so private in front of her entire family. But they all waited with
bated breath, their bodies angled forward expectantly, their
eyes focused on Rolleen.

He felt Rolleen's hand caress his thigh and realized his
body was reacting involuntarily to her touch. He flushed

and grabbed her hand, holding it in his. She looked up at him, then smiled mischievously when she realized the problem.

"Why don't you tell them when you first fell in love with me, Gavin?" she teased.

Gavin was flustered. He knew the story on the beach belonged to her. That was the moment *she* had fallen in love with *him.* But they'd never come up with a moment when he'd first known he was in love with her. Gavin felt the tension mount as her family waited for him to speak.

*When did I fall in love with her? When did I know she was someone special? When could I have given her my heart?*

He looked into Rolleen's soft gray eyes and feelings he had kept hidden deep inside came pouring out. "From the first moment I laid eyes on Rolleen—late one night at the hospital—I wanted to hold her in my arms. And when we kissed for the first time, I knew my life would never be the same." Saying the words, Gavin felt drawn to Rolleen, connected to her, and he obeyed the urge to lean down and touch her lips with his.

He had forgotten entirely about her family, about where they were, about pretense. His mouth molded itself to hers, and he tasted her sweetness, her gentleness.

"Hey, you two. Break it up!" Jewel said with a laugh. "I want to hear how Rolleen fell in love with you!"

Gavin looked up to find Rolleen's family smiling—grinning was more like it—at the two of them. Well, he'd done his part. They were convinced the romance was real. He leaned back on the couch, keeping Rolleen close with his arm around her shoulder and said, "Your turn, sweetheart."

He saw the panicked look in her eyes and whispered to her, "You can do it. I'm here if you need me."

"No secrets!" Rabbit said. "We want to hear everything!"

"I was just advising your sister to edit the story for innocent ears," Gavin said.

"Oh, yeah," Rabbit said, blushing to the roots of his hair.

"Tell us everything!" Frannie urged.

"The truth is, I fell in love with Gavin at the beach," Rolleen began.

Gavin listened to her story with as much rapt attention as her family. For the first time, he was hearing what she'd been feeling that night, or rather, the story she'd made up about what she'd been feeling that night.

She turned and looked deep into his eyes. "It's hard to describe the mood I was in exactly." She broke away and said, "But imagine the moon and a million stars overhead—one star a little brighter than all the others—and the smell of the sea and the sound of the waves crashing on the shore and..." She focused her gaze on him again. "And a pair of beautiful, dark brown eyes staring down at me with such love... How could I not love him back?"

"What happened then?" Frannie asked.

Jake elbowed her and said, "Can't you guess?"

"Did he kiss you?" Frannie guessed.

Rolleen turned to them, smiled and said, "Yes. And then—"

"Rolleen—" her mother warned.

"A crab bit Gavin's toe!"

The whole family broke into raucous laughter. Gavin pulled Rolleen close and gave her a quick kiss on the nose to reward her for getting through the story and ending it on just the right note. At that moment she yawned hugely and they both said "The baby!" and everyone laughed again.

"You need your rest," her mother said, coming forward to grab Rolleen's hand and pull her onto her feet. "Let's get you settled. We can all talk more in the morning."

While Gavin watched, Rolleen left the room with her mother, followed by Jewel and Frannie close on their heels.

Mac stretched and said, "Guess I'll be heading over to the counselor's cottage. I expect Jewel will be here a while yet. Tell her I'll wait up for her, will you, Zach?"

"Sure," Zach said. "Now, Gavin, where shall we put you?"

"I'd be glad to stay in the counselor's cottage where I spent the summer," Gavin said.

Zach shook his head. "We're remodeling, so the heat's off. I wouldn't feel comfortable having Rolleen stay out there."

Gavin worked hard not keep his mouth from gaping. Zach planned for him and Rolleen to spend the night together? When they weren't married? Rolleen had assured him her parents would separate them. He couldn't very well ask to be put in a different room from "the woman he loved" without arousing suspicion. But this was going to cause some problems he and Rolleen hadn't discussed.

Rebecca reappeared in the living room with Frannie and Jewel and said, "Jewel's volunteered to let Frannie stay in the second bedroom at the cottage, so Gavin and Rolleen can share Rolleen's old bedroom."

"Good. That's settled," Zach said. "We'd all better hit the sack. We have a lot of things planned for tomorrow."

Zach slapped Gavin on the back as he passed by, and Avery, Jake, Rabbit and Colt each said good night and headed down the two halls to their rooms. Jewel gave Gavin a quick hug before she ushered Frannie toward the kitchen door.

"Rolleen's room is on the back side of the square," Rebecca said. "Go down the hall, make a right hand turn, then make another right hand turn."

"I'll come by later and make sure you have everything you need and say good night to Rolleen," Zach said.

"Fine," Gavin said. But he avoided looking into Zach's eyes as he headed for Rolleen's bedroom.

# Chapter 5

Rolleen's first inkling that her parents planned to put Gavin in her bedroom occurred when Colt knocked at her door and set Gavin's suitcase next to hers.

"Mom said I should bring this in here."

"What?"

Colt hesitated. "Would you rather Gavin stayed somewhere else? I can tell Mom—"

"No," she interrupted, recovering her composure. "Of course I want him to stay with me," she fibbed. "I just never expected Mom and Dad—"

"To put you two in the same room when you aren't married yet," Colt finished for her.

She nodded.

"They already went through this once with Jewel and Mac," Colt explained, setting down the suitcase. "Dad told me the important thing was they loved each other, and they were committed to each other. I guess he figures that's true of you and Gavin, too. Especially with a baby on the way."

"Of course," Rolleen whispered, because that was all

the sound she could get past the knot of guilt in her throat. "Thanks, Colt. I'll see you in the morning."

Colt looked like he wanted to say more, but Rolleen already had her hand on the door to close it behind him. She hurried to get her clothes changed before Gavin showed up. She had taken her dress off but hadn't yet found her pajamas in her suitcase when she heard a soft knock at the door.

"It's me," Gavin said. "Let me in."

"Just a minute." She threw things out of her suitcase, hunting desperately for the black silk Chinese pajama set she had brought.

"I'm coming in, Rolleen. Otherwise somebody's going to catch me lurking in the hall and start asking questions."

"Gavin, don't—" She found the pajamas at the same instant she heard him open and shut the door. She whirled to face him in her plain white underwear and bra, holding the wadded up silk pajamas in front of her. "I'm sorry about this," she said. "I had no idea they'd put us together."

She felt flustered standing before Gavin in the bedroom she'd shared with Jewel growing up. Especially with him staring at her as though he'd never seen a half-dressed woman. "Would you mind turning around so I can finish getting changed?"

He cleared his throat, said "Sure" and turned his back. "I'll sleep on the floor," he volunteered.

"There's plenty of room for both of us on the bed."

She watched him turn to eye the brass-railed double bed over his shoulder and realized he'd also caught a glimpse of her bra coming off.

He quickly turned away, cleared his throat again and said, "I don't think it would be a good idea for us to sleep in the same bed."

"We're both grown-ups," Rolleen said, feeling more comfortable in the concealing black silk pajamas, which covered her from throat to ankle. She stuffed her bra and panties into her suitcase and slid it to the floor. "You can turn around now."

He turned slowly, his eyes lowered.

Rolleen had never felt more like a grown-up than she did as Gavin's gaze moved from her bare toes up her legs to her silk pajama shirt, which was slit up the front so that flesh showed at her midriff. She felt her nipples peak even before his gaze got to her breasts and quickly crossed her arms to hide her unexpected—and unwanted—reaction. His gaze caught at the Chinese-style frog closure at her throat, and she was breathing like she'd done a hundred sit-ups by the time his eyes finally met hers.

"That's some outfit," he said. "Did you design it?"

She nodded jerkily.

He took a step toward her, and she resisted the impulse to retreat.

He paused and said, "I just want to feel the material, if that's all right."

"Oh. Go ahead."

He took two more steps and reached out to caress the soft fabric at her waist. "I'd like to be these pajamas right now," he murmured.

Rolleen was entranced by the ardent look in his eyes, by the raspy sound of his voice. He began gathering the silk fabric in his hand, exposing more of her midriff and at the same time pulling her closer, erasing the distance between them. "Gavin…"

She could have stopped him at any time. He hadn't laid a hand on her—only the silk. She let him draw her near enough that she could see he had ridiculously long eyelashes for a man, close enough that his intent, dark brown eyes made her think of hot, melted chocolate. "Gavin, we shouldn't—"

His lips touched hers, and she felt her knees buckle. She made a helpless sound in her throat and felt his arm slide around her waist to pull her tight against him and hold her upright. He explored her lips with his, tasting, touching, testing.

*Soft. So very soft. And gentle. And teasing,* she thought. He made her want. He made her yearn. He made her regret.

Rolleen turned her face away and pressed her cheek hard against Gavin's chest, hoping he wouldn't notice how much she was trembling. "There's no one here to see us now," she reminded him.

"Your father said he'd be by to say good night," he said in a husky voice. "I thought you ought to look kissed."

"Oh."

She instinctively jerked her head away when the knock came on the door, but Gavin's hand around her waist kept her close to him.

"Come in," he said.

Rolleen expected to feel embarrassed when her father found her in Gavin's arms. But the look of relief on her father's face when he realized Gavin was making love to her made her grateful to him for being so perceptive. "Did you want something, Daddy?" she asked.

"Only to make sure you both have everything you need."

She felt Gavin's eyes on her and his grating reply, "I've got everything I could ever want or need right here in my arms."

Her father looked pleased, and she was sorry this was only an act. She made herself smile and say, "Good night, Daddy."

"Good night, honey. See you both at breakfast," he said as he pulled the door closed behind him.

Rolleen hid her face against Gavin's chest, feeling the awful weight of her deception.

"I know that was tough," he said. "But think of the alternative."

"Thank you, Gavin," she said, enjoying the way his hand smoothed over her hair.

"For what?"

"For doing this for me. For pretending—"

He kissed her again, cutting her off. The kiss didn't feel like pretend. It felt unbearably, unbelievably, oh, so achingly real.

He released her abruptly and took a step back. "Get in bed," he said.

She tried a step backward but grabbed at his arms and gave a shaky laugh. "My knees are so rubbery I can't walk."

He swept her up into his arms, took the couple of steps to the bed and dropped her the last foot onto it. The bed bounced, making the springs squeak.

"Shh! Colt and Jake are on the other side of that wall!"

Gavin sat on the edge of the bed and bounced up and down.

"Don't do that!" she whispered. "My brothers will hear and think we're…we're…"

"Doing it?" he whispered back with a teasing grin.

"Yes!" she hissed, mortified.

He stopped but the grin remained in place. Until his eyes slid down her body to where her rounded stomach was so obviously apparent beneath the clinging silk.

Rolleen watched the grin fade. Watched Gavin rise and take a step or two back from her.

"I'll change when the light's off," he said, "and sleep on the floor."

"We can share—"

"Don't argue with me, Rolleen," he said curtly. "This may be pretend, but you're a woman and I'm a man and I can't help how I react to you—pregnant or not. Now get under the damn covers and turn out the light!"

Rolleen did as she was told.

She heard the zipper come down on Gavin's jeans, and

the whispery hush of denim being dropped in a pile. She felt him pick up the extra blanket at her feet and edge away as he confiscated the pillow next to her head.

"You can still join me if you get cold," she offered.

"I won't."

She knew why. He was physically attracted to her. She'd felt it from the beginning. She could understand her attraction to him. He was tall, dark and handsome. She had never understood his apparent attraction to her. She was pretty— but pregnant! That hadn't deterred Gavin's interest in the least. If anything, he had seemed fascinated by her pregnant body. *If only…*

Rolleen made herself face the facts. Gavin Talbot was helping her through a difficult situation. It wasn't fair to either of them to let herself dream of happily ever after.

"Good night, Gavin." She heard him shuffling around on the floor, spreading out the blanket and pounding the pillow and turning himself over several times, until at last he was quiet.

She wanted to stay awake and talk, but it had been such a long day she could hardly keep her eyes open. She was home. Her parents believed their ruse. This Christmas would be as happy as all the others. And Gavin's presence—and his pretense—had made it all possible. She owed him so much.

"Gavin?" Halfway through the word she yawned.

"You're tired. Go to sleep."

"It was perfect, Gavin," she said dreamily. "Everyone around the fire. Everyone smiling and laughing and happy. Just like Christmas should be. Thank you."

"It isn't over yet," he said.

"Only two days until Christmas Eve," she said. "We'll make it."

"Maybe you will," he muttered.

"What?"

"Nothing."

Rolleen laid her hand protectively over the baby, closed her eyes and moments later was sound asleep.

Gavin couldn't remember when he'd spent a more miserable night. His body had been a furnace of desire when he'd lain down on the floor, but during the night, the cold had seeped up through the rug from the Mexican-tiled floor. The blanket had been too short to reach his feet and his shoulders at the same time, and it had taken a great deal of fortitude not to join Rolleen in bed.

To make matters worse, the feather pillow had been too soft and the pillowcase had smelled of honeysuckle, a scent Rolleen sometimes wore. Gavin had spent the night aching for her. If he got involved—really involved—with Rolleen Whitelaw, it meant accepting another man's child as his own. But if he hadn't been able to accept Beth, whom he had adored the first four years of her life, how could he ever hope to love some stranger's child?

He had to make himself stop touching Rolleen. Stop wanting her. Stop thinking about her.

That was easier said than done.

Gavin had awakened at the crack of dawn and retreated to the bathroom across the hall to shower and shave before Rolleen and her family got up. He hadn't wanted to see her all warm and tousled in bed. And he had wanted all the time he could get to gather his courage before he had to face Zach and Rebecca again.

Last night, when Zach had come to the bedroom door, Gavin imagined how he would have felt if some guy had come to his home "pretending" to love his daughter—who was pregnant—and then abandoned her a couple of months later. No matter when Zach and Rebecca found out the truth, they were going to be angry and hurt.

But he also could understand Rolleen wanting to preserve the joy of Christmas for her family. No matter how hard he was finding it, Gavin owed it to her to try to keep his part of the bargain.

He simply had to stop kissing her like he had last night. Because it was too hard to keep from feeling things he would rather not feel.

Knuckles rapped hard on the bathroom door, and he heard Rabbit call out, "Hey! You done in there?"

He opened the door a crack, shaved but wearing only a pair of half-buttoned jeans.

The fifteen-year-old shot him an aggrieved look and said, "I hope you didn't use all the hot water."

"Rabbit!" Colt said, cuffing his brother on the shoulder as he passed by. "Let the guy finish getting dressed!"

Gavin peered out and realized the hall was alive with Whitelaws coming in and out of bedroom doors in various states of dress and undress. He should have known they'd all keep rancher's hours.

"I'm finished in here," he said, dropping his towel into the hamper and stepping barefoot out into the hall along with a cloud of leftover steam. "I took a quick shower," he promised Rabbit as he headed across the hall to Rolleen's bedroom.

"You're last tomorrow if you didn't," Rabbit threatened as he stepped inside and closed the door behind him.

Gavin felt himself grinning. He'd certainly become one of the family.

The hall was suddenly empty, and Gavin wondered where everyone had gone. He hesitated on the threshold of Rolleen's bedroom, fascinated by what he saw.

Rolleen was sitting up in the big brass bed with both pillows stacked behind her, a saltine cracker poised at her lips, her gray eyes crinkled at the corners and her mouth split wide by laughter. The sound was so beautiful—like twinkling stars in a winter sky or snowfall stacked on the boughs of a mountain pine or children dressed as angels— it took his breath away.

He watched as Rebecca lovingly brushed Rolleen's blond hair away from her face and said, "I don't have any firsthand experience, but all your aunts have told me the first trimester is pretty exhausting. How are you feeling, really?"

Gavin was startled by Rebecca's reminder that none of her children had been born Whitelaws, that every one of them had been adopted. She had learned to love eight children who were not her own.

"I'm fine, Mom. Really," Rolleen said. "And the baby's fine."

Gavin watched as Rolleen took her mother's hand and laid it over her belly where the child was growing inside her. He saw the look of delight on Rebecca's face and the glow that lit Rolleen's and made her every bit as beautiful as her laughter.

"Were you ever sorry, Mom?" Rolleen asked. "I mean, that none of us were your own?"

Gavin listened raptly for Rebecca's answer, knowing he shouldn't be eavesdropping, but unable to move from where he stood.

"I have always wondered what it would be like to feel a child growing inside me," Rebecca admitted. "It must be wonderful to give such a gift to the man you love."

Gavin saw Rolleen's hesitation before she nodded.

"But your father and I have had the unique pleasure of finding each and every one of you children—never knowing when or from where the next would arrive. It's been a life filled with wonderful gifts I wouldn't have missed for anything."

Both women had tears in their eyes, and Gavin wished he could disappear into the wall. He didn't need this. Of course Rebecca could love someone else's children. There was no history of deception, no feelings of betrayal connected to them. His situation with Beth was different. It had been impossible to keep loving Beth once he'd learned his wife had betrayed him in creating her.

In the early days after he had learned the truth about his daughter his grandmother had been the first to say, "People can learn to love children who aren't their own."

"That isn't the point," he'd argued. The part of himself he'd always believed was a part of his daughter no longer existed. Before he'd even had a chance to grieve that loss, he was being asked to love the part of his daughter that was a stranger, along with the part of her that reminded him of a wife who had betrayed him with another man.

So far, he hadn't been able to do it.

"You can't keep ignoring her," his grandmother had admonished the last time he'd left the ranch to return to Houston. "Take her with you, Gavin. Be her father. Love her. Beth loves you so much! She doesn't understand why you avoid her. She doesn't understand—"

"Please, Hester, no more," he'd said. "I can't face Beth right now and pretend everything is the way it was. I can't."

"You're breaking my heart," Hester had said.

He'd felt the ache in his throat and known he couldn't stay any longer. He had turned to leave the room and collided with Beth.

"Daddy, don't leave me!" she'd cried excitedly, holding her arms open wide to him. "Take me with you!"

His first instinct had been to pick her up, to hold her, to cherish her and protect her from the truth. He had dropped onto one knee and found himself looking into eyes that were not the shape or color of his—or Susan's. Beth's hands were already closing around his neck when he had caught her wrists and pulled himself free. "I can't, baby. I can't!"

She had stared at him confused, but not frightened, because he had always been so gentle with her. "Why not, Daddy?"

*I'm not your Daddy.*

Dark and dangerous rage. Huge and horrible grief. Aching, unbearable pain. He had felt all of it at once and jerked himself free of its source: his daughter...who was not his daughter.

Gavin had run. And been running for almost a year. At Hester's insistence, he was going home for Christmas. Home to face the blameless child he had abandoned and try to be a father to her.

"Gavin?"

Gavin realized Rebecca and Rolleen had noticed his presence while he'd been lost in thought. "I'm sorry. What did you say?"

Rebecca laughed as she rose from the bed. "I was just saying I ought to excuse myself so you two can finish dressing. We've got a hectic day ahead of us."

She was gone with a smile and a wave, closing him inside the bedroom with Rolleen.

Gavin took one look at Rolleen and felt his body draw up tight. He swore under his breath. He wanted her, but he knew better than to reach for her. The situation was just too damned complicated. He stayed where he was, restraining the hungry beast inside.

"Are you all right?" she asked.

"Why wouldn't I be?" he said, his voice hard and hoarse with desire.

"I know things aren't as private around here as you're used to," she said, putting her feet over the edge of the bed. She rose as though she had a book balanced on her head, and he suspected her stomach was unsteady.

*What kind of crazy man craves sex with a woman who has morning sickness?* He did. He wanted her something fierce, and she was totally oblivious!

"But we Whitelaws are a close-knit family who—"

"Why don't you tell them the truth?"

She froze, then turned to stare at him. "What?"

"I can see they all love you. They won't blame you for what happened. Why don't you just tell them the truth and get it over with?"

He watched the blood leech from her face and hurried over to sit her down on the bed and force her head between her knees. "Keep your head down," he said when she tried to raise it too soon.

"Please don't tell them," she begged. "Not now. Not yet."

He pulled her up and into his arms and hugged her. He felt bad for her and her parents. And helpless because there was nothing he could do to make things better.

Except keep playing the game.

Her hair felt silky in his hands as he tunneled his fingers up the back of her neck to rub at the knots of tension there.

"That feels good."

The sound of her voice resonated inside him, making his blood race.

"At least tell them you don't mind quitting medical school," he said, fighting the urge to crush her against him. "Will you do that for me?"

"I suppose I could say you're going to encourage me to work on some fashion designs at home," she said.

"It'll be the truth," he said.

She smiled up at him, and Gavin felt something tumble and shift inside. *It isn't just that I want her body. I want her. I need her.*

"You're a nice man, Gavin Talbot."

"And a hungry one," he said, watching the double entendre slide right over her head. *If only…* He forced himself to let go of her and asked, "When's breakfast?"

"You can eat anytime you want. I'm not having anything."

"Oh, yes you are," he countered. "I want you strong enough to keep up your end of the bargain."

"But I'll be sick if I eat," she protested.

"You can nibble on something."

Nibble was all she did, but he made sure she mentioned her plan to do some fashion designs for The Elegant Lady.

"What a wonderful idea," Rebecca said.

"You've always loved to sew," Jewel pointed out.

"And I've always wanted a sister who was a fashion designer," the irrepressible Frannie said.

"You would," Jake said. "So you can dress up in her clothes."

"What's wrong with that?" Frannie asked indignantly.

Everybody laughed.

Before Gavin knew it the whole family had tumbled out of the kitchen door like kittens out of a basket and were on their way to the stable to take a quick ride around Hawk's Pride.

When the ride became a race, Gavin excused himself and Rolleen, insisting she had promised to take him on a side trip down into the canyon where the stone walls were etched with primitive drawings.

"Thank you, Gavin," Rolleen said once they were on the narrow trail into the canyon.

"For what?"

"For helping me to have faith in my parents," she replied. "I should have known they would be supportive no matter what I chose to do. You'll make a good parent someday yourself."

Gavin stared at her, stricken. *But I'm not a good parent,* he wanted to shout. *I'm not even in the same class with Zach and Rebecca. They've opened their hearts to eight children who aren't their own flesh and blood. I can't even do it with one.* He glanced at her growing belly, visible in the jeans she wore to ride in, and realized it wasn't only one child he needed to love anymore. It was two.

He wanted to talk with Rolleen about Beth, to seek her advice, to seek solace, but once he had her alone at the bottom of the canyon, he couldn't help tasting her. And tasting led to touching.

He kissed the curls on her nape and the small birthmark he'd found beneath her ear, and he put his palms over her breasts and heard her moan as the nipples peaked.

"Gavin, please stop."

Through a haze of arousal he heard her plea. And did as she asked.

"Your brothers will expect you to look kissed," he said.

She was flushed, her cheeks rosy, her lips swollen from his kisses. But her gray eyes were troubled.

"We have to stop this, Gavin."

He didn't pretend to misunderstand her. "I like kissing you, Rolleen. And touching you." He brushed the back of his hand against her breast, and she hissed in a breath.

"I don't want to get hurt, Gavin. I'm starting to feel things…things I shouldn't feel for you. It doesn't feel like a game anymore," she said.

"Maybe it isn't," he murmured.

"What?"

"Maybe it doesn't have to be," he said, meeting her startled gaze. "What if we kept on seeing each other after the holidays?"

She stared up at him, her heart in her eyes for a brief moment before she turned away. "I…I don't know." She turned back to him and said, "I'll think about it."

Her brothers ribbed her unmercifully for her bright eyes and swollen lips and heated cheeks when they rejoined the rest of the party and Gavin made himself smile along with them, while inside it felt like someone had dumped the spoon drawer upside down, causing a great clatter and a great deal of confusion.

*I never told her about Beth,* he realized. *I have to tell her about Beth.*

After lunch they played flag football. The third time Rolleen got tackled by one of her brothers, Gavin picked her up and sat her in a chair on the stone patio behind the house and ordered in a very husbandly way, "Stay there and take care of our baby."

In the late afternoon Gavin volunteered to help chop more wood for the fire along with Rolleen's brothers. He almost cut his foot off when Rolleen cried out because a lizard had crawled across her boot. Her brothers razzed him unmercifully for not being able to take his eyes off of her.

He punished Rolleen for scaring him with a kiss in front of her brothers that left her cheeks pink. She got him back by threading her fingers into his hair and ravaging his mouth with her tongue until his jeans barely fit. He had to stand behind the woodpile until he was decent, while she smiled smugly and trotted off to the house with her sisters.

It was fun. The rambunctious activities went on for the next two days, with Rolleen notably absent for the rougher games and with the family joined by Rolleen's sister Cherry, her husband Billy, their twin ten-year-old daughters Rae Jean and Annie and the new baby Brett. Gavin didn't know when he'd enjoyed the Christmas holiday so much.

Rolleen laughed often and unselfconsciously. She teased and cajoled and got angry with her brothers and sisters and forgave them minutes later. She teased and cajoled and got angry with him, too. And forgave him with touches and kisses and looks that made his blood simmer beneath his skin.

His feelings felt like love. But he was always aware of the deception they carried out with her parents, always aware of the secret he kept from her that might make her turn away from him.

The more Gavin watched the loving play of the White-laws, the more time he spent with Rolleen, the more he dreaded the thought of leaving Hawk's Pride and heading for his home to play out the rest of their charade.

The moment came much sooner than he expected. And in a way that made it plain how much was at stake in the dangerous game they played.

# Chapter 6

Rolleen had let herself enjoy the days before Christmas without thinking about the future. But she was troubled by Gavin's offer to extend their make-believe relationship beyond the holidays. She was afraid to believe he loved her, afraid to believe she could be in love again so soon. She had made one mistake. She didn't want to make another.

"What are you doing hiding out here while everyone's inside?"

Rolleen scooted over in the wooden front porch swing that hung from the rafters and made room for her mother under the quilt she'd brought outside to keep herself warm. Then she started the swing moving again with her toe. "I wanted some peace and quiet to think before we leave for the Christmas Eve candlelight service," she said.

They both listened to the lonely sounds of the prairie. The screech of a windmill that always needed more oil. The soft lowing of cattle. The rustle of leaves in the giant live oak. The whisper of the wind through the buffalo grass.

"Gavin's a good man, Rolleen," her mother said.

"I know he is, Mom." Rolleen avoided meeting her mother's glance, afraid her mom would read the doubts there—or see the deception.

"Then why haven't you married him?"

"There are some things we need to work out," she hedged.

"Your father and I love you, darling, and we're behind you, no matter what course you choose. I know how hard it is for you to give your trust to anyone. But sometimes—"

"I'm afraid," Rolleen blurted.

She felt her mother's arm slide around her shoulder and laid her head against her mother's breast.

"What if I make the wrong choice, Mom? What if I mess up my life and the baby's?"

"Shh. Shh," her mother crooned. "Listen to your heart and believe in yourself and you'll know what to do."

Her mother hadn't offered a solution to Rolleen's dilemma, only love and trust and the belief that Rolleen could solve the problem herself. It was what she had always given. It was everything a child could want or need.

"Thank you, Mom," she said.

"Anytime, darling. Will you come inside now?"

"In a little while," she said as her mother stepped inside the house.

When Gavin showed up on the porch a few moments after her mother had gone inside, he said, "I've been looking everywhere for you. Rebecca said I'd find you out here. I was worried about you. Why aren't you inside with your family?"

He didn't wait for her to invite him under the blanket. He simply lifted it and her and sat himself down with her in his lap.

She laughed and rearranged the blanket over both of them. "You're getting good at that."

"It's going to get tougher as you get bigger with—"

"The baby," they both said together and laughed.

"Why can't it be like this the whole year long?" Rolleen said.

"Like what?"

"Everyone so happy, so generous and considerate and kind."

"I suppose there's no reason why it can't be like that," Gavin said, setting the hanging rocker in motion.

"I wish…"

"What do you wish?"

"I wish this were your baby."

His harsh intake of breath, the tension in his thighs beneath her and the stiffness in his shoulder under her hand all told a story much louder than words. She wished the baby were his. He obviously did not.

"Rolleen, I—"

She put her fingertips over his mouth to stop his denial. "You don't have to say anything, Gavin. It isn't your baby. It isn't your responsibility. I appreciate what you've done so far, and I won't expect anything from you once the holidays are over, I promise."

He grabbed her hand and pulled it away. "Rolleen, damn it, there's a lot you don't know about me. Things I haven't told you that are important—that make a difference!"

"It doesn't matter. None of it matters!" She was up and off his lap a second later, running for the front door. She pulled it open and found herself in the midst of a free-for-all in the living room.

She stopped stock-still in the doorway and stared at Jake and Colt and Frannie and Cherry and Mac and Billy. She and the baby would manage without Gavin. She might not be as happy, but she would be all right. She had her family to love—and to love her.

"Hey, Rolleen," Frannie shouted, pointing upward. "Look where you're standing!"

Rolleen saw the sprig of mistletoe at the same time Gavin slipped his arms around her from behind.

"You have to kiss Gavin!" Frannie said, her voice laced with adolescent relish for all things romantic.

The family began to laugh and clap, making it impossible for her to escape without making a scene. It should have been the simplest thing in the world to turn around and kiss Gavin. She had been kissing him for days in front of her family. But now she knew her dreams of happily-ever-after were nothing more than that. Now she knew this fairy tale was not going to have a happy ending.

She didn't want to pretend with Gavin anymore. When she hesitated, Gavin questioned, "Rolleen?"

"Kiss me, Gavin," she whispered. "Kiss me one last time."

Gavin heard the cheers as he leaned down to touch his lips to Rolleen's. His heart was thundering in his chest, and it hurt to breathe. He wanted her so much. *He loved her so much.*

Gavin ended the kiss and stared stunned at Rolleen for an instant. *I love her.* "Rolleen…"

The room was suddenly silent. Gavin could almost feel her family willing Rolleen to accept him and set a date for the wedding.

*I'm not acting, Rolleen. I do care for you.* But in this case, loving her was not enough. He must also be able to love her child. And his own.

The phone in the kitchen rang, but no one left the room to answer it.

Gavin saw the troubled look in Rolleen's eyes and knew what had put it there. She had wished her baby was his. She had offered him that precious gift—a child of hers— and he had not been able to accept it. What was wrong with him? Why couldn't he love them both?

Then Gavin realized the enormity of the harm he had done by wanting more than the game allowed. There was more in her eyes than regret. There was love.

*Oh, God, Rolleen. I'm so sorry. I never meant for this to happen.*

"I—I—think…" she stuttered. She turned and stared at the kitchen doorway. "Shouldn't someone answer that phone?"

"Set a date! Set a date!" Frannie chanted.

"Frannie," Rebecca chided lovingly. "Give Rolleen a chance to speak for herself. Get the phone please, Jewel."

"Don't say anything till I get back," Jewel shouted to Rolleen as she raced to the kitchen. "I don't want to miss this!"

Everyone groaned.

Jewel quickly returned from the kitchen and extended the portable phone to Gavin. "It's for you, a friend of your grandmother's named Ruby Jenkins. She says your grandmother's ill. She said you should come home right away and bring someone to take care of your daughter."

Gavin felt every pair of eyes in the room focus on him. He knew they were all wondering why he had never mentioned a daughter. He clutched Rolleen's hands to keep her from jerking away, turned to her family and said, "I'm sorry, Zach, Rebecca, everybody. I'm afraid Rolleen and I are going to have to cut our visit short. My daughter can be a handful."

Gavin held his breath. It was up to Rolleen now. She could either call everything off, or come along with him.

He looked into Rolleen's eyes and winced when he saw her pain and confusion. He should have told her sooner. He had thought he would have more time. Only, time had run out.

"I have to leave, Rolleen. Are you coming with me?"

*Are you going to keep your part of the bargain?*

Gavin didn't say those precise words, but Rolleen heard them. She felt like Alice, and she'd just fallen down the rabbit's hole into Wonderland, where nothing was as it seemed.

But she knew for sure now that Gavin hadn't really wanted her to set a date. Not when she knew nothing about the existence of his daughter. She realized how close she had let herself come to believing in happily ever after. She had to remember the rules of this game.

She felt both angry and hurt at Gavin's secretiveness. Realistically, there was no way she and Gavin could have learned everything about each other in two weeks. But a *daughter* was a pretty sizable omission.

Why hadn't he told her about the child? What was wrong with her? Was she sick? Dying? Was that why Gavin counseled dying children? Rolleen wanted answers, and the only way she was going to get them was to go with him.

She turned to her parents and said, "Momma, Daddy, I'm sorry to leave like this, but I need to go with Gavin. I should have told you sooner, but I'd planned all along to spend part of the holiday with his family. We'll just be leaving a little sooner than we'd planned."

"We'll miss having you here," her mother said.

The concern on her parents' faces made her want to confess everything, but so far Christmas had been wonderful. She wanted to leave her family with that lovely feeling.

Rolleen smiled, a look she hoped conveyed her gratefulness to her parents and her love for them. "I'll be fine, Mom. I'll call you when we get there. Merry Christmas, Daddy. Merry Christmas, everybody!"

Rolleen felt herself being moved through the room by Gavin's strong arm around her waist as her family reached out to wish her well, her brothers shouting, "Merry Christmas, Gavin!" and her sisters saying, "Call as soon as you can, Rolleen!" and "Let us know how your grandmother is, Gavin!"

Rolleen hugged her parents hard and watched from the

corner of her eye as Gavin shook her father's hand and said soberly, "Don't worry, sir. I'll take care of her."

Rolleen said nothing while she and Gavin packed their bags. She kept her silence as they drove to the airport and turned in the rental car. She waited patiently, biding her time until they were several thousand feet in the air where Gavin couldn't escape, before she began asking for answers.

"Tell me about your daughter."

He avoided her gaze. "What would you like to know?"

"How old is she? What's her name? Why have you kept her a secret?"

"She'll be five on January 22. Her name's Elizabeth Harriet Talbot, Beth for short. And I haven't mentioned her before because…she's the real reason I wanted you to come home with me this Christmas."

Rolleen brushed a nervous hand through her hair. "Well. That sounds like the truth, at least."

"I've never lied to you, Rolleen," he said.

"But you edited something pretty important out of your life, Gavin. What else have you kept a secret that I ought to know about?"

She heard the gusty sigh and knew there was more. "You don't have to worry that you're going to be obligated to me beyond the holidays," she said.

He turned sharply to look at her, then said, "When my wife died, she left a note telling me that Beth isn't my daughter."

Rolleen felt an ache in her chest at Gavin's revelation. She didn't know what to say. "I'm sorry," didn't seem like enough. "How awful!" sounded wrong. And any comment about his wife's behavior was too judgmental, when she knew nothing about their life together.

"You must have been devastated," she said at last.

"It hasn't been an easy year," he conceded. "I've gone home to visit Beth more this fall than I did in the spring, but I haven't been able to look at my daughter without..." He swallowed hard before continuing, "Without thinking about who her father might be. Without imagining... I've done my best not to let on to Beth how I feel. But it isn't easy when she wants me to hold her, and..." He swallowed hard again but said nothing more.

"I'm sorry," she said.

When Rolleen had been silent for several minutes, Gavin said, "Aren't you going to ask me anything else?"

"I don't want to cause you any more pain," she admitted.

He opened his mouth but closed it again without speaking.

She turned to look at him and waited.

"I can't..." He huffed out a breath and said, "I don't feel the same way toward Beth that I did before...before."

"I don't understand," she said. "Are you saying you blame Beth for what her mother did?"

"I don't love her anymore," he said flatly. "I can't bear to look at her. I don't want to be in the same room with her. Is that what you wanted to hear?"

He was breathing hard, as though he'd been running, but Gavin was still sitting in the same pilot's seat where he'd been when he'd started talking. He gave a ragged sigh. "I feel a tremendous responsibility toward Beth, but that's all. My grandmother can't seem to grasp the fact that my feelings have changed."

"What is my presence supposed to accomplish?" Rolleen asked.

"I figured if you were there Hester would understand why I'd rather be with you than with Beth and wouldn't be throwing me and Beth together so much."

"Is that what she does? Throw you and Beth together?"

Gavin scowled. "All the time!"

"From that phone call you got, it sounds like she'll likely be in bed sick and not bothering anybody."

"Hester's a sturdy old bird," he said. "Nothing keeps her down for very long. Believe me, she'll be back to her old, interfering self in no time."

"You could at least play with Beth while your grandmother's sick, couldn't you?"

He shook his head. "No. No, I couldn't."

Rolleen was trying to understand, and she was afraid she did. Her white knight's armor was beginning to look a little tarnished.

"I was adopted, Gavin, so I know adults can learn to love children who aren't their own. Couldn't you try that with Beth? Couldn't you pretend she's a child you found in an orphanage and learn to love her all over again?"

"But she isn't!" he snarled. "Every time she smiles I see my wife's smile. And every time I look into her eyes I see some stranger—some man who took my wife to bed—looking back at me!"

Gavin was shaking with anger. Rolleen had the feeling that if he'd been in a boxing ring he would happily have pulverized his opponent. If he'd been on the road, he might have rammed the nearest tree. Fortunately they were up in the air with nothing to run into but a bank of clouds and plenty of sky in which to maneuver.

Rolleen was trying to understand and appreciate and sympathize with Gavin's pain. Instead she found herself wearing Beth's shoes, because she'd worn them once herself and because she knew how much they hurt.

"Have you thought about what Beth must be feeling?" she asked.

"She's just a kid," Gavin said.

"Kids have feelings. At least I did."

She watched the frown burrow deep into Gavin's forehead. He didn't answer her, but she knew she'd made her point.

"You should have told me what you had in mind from

the beginning,'' she said. ''I could have told you then I couldn't be a part of it.''

He turned to stare at her in disbelief. ''What?''

''I couldn't possibly help you ignore your daughter just because she isn't your own flesh and blood, Gavin. I've been where she is. I've felt what she's feeling. Once we get on the ground, I'll find my own way back to Houston.''

''I helped you out,'' he said furiously. ''I gave you the Christmas you wanted. Now it's your turn. We made a bargain, Rolleen. And I'm not letting you out of it!''

''I won't go off with you and ignore Beth,'' she retorted, just as heatedly.

''Fine. Play games with her. Talk to her. Do anything you want with her. Just keep her away from me!''

Rolleen stared at Gavin, appalled at what he was saying. She had felt herself falling in love with him during the time they'd spent at Hawk's Pride, but she realized now what a good thing it was she hadn't said anything. He had let her down, but she wasn't going to let his daughter suffer as a consequence. That little girl was going to get the love she deserved at Christmas.

''All right,'' Rolleen said. ''I'll come home with you.''

''As my fiancée?'' Gavin asked.

''Is that really necessary? Couldn't I just be your friend?''

He hesitated and shook his head. ''I don't think so. I want the same thing for Hester that you wanted for your mom and dad. My grandmother doesn't have a lot of Christmases left, and I want this one to be happy for her.''

''And seeing you engaged will make her happy?''

''Having me married would make her a lot happier,'' Gavin said, ''but this is as far as I'm willing to go. Hester's afraid I won't be able to love another woman after what happened with Susan. You'll be proof that isn't the case.''

''What happens when we don't get married?''

''I could ask you the same question.''

They sat in silence thinking about what they'd done. Realizing what they'd wrought.

Rolleen wondered if Gavin could love another woman. Wondered if he could love his child. Wondered if he could love hers. She had to admit she still fantasized about a future with him. Foolish woman. That really was living in Wonderland.

"What were we thinking?" she muttered, shaking her head.

"We weren't," he said flatly.

Runway landing lights appeared in the distance. "Where are we?" she asked.

"That's a private air strip on my ranch," he said.

"This is your ranch?" she said, perusing the vast rolling hills studded with an occasional live oak that were visible in the pink light of Christmas morning.

"We've been flying over it for the past half hour."

Rolleen stared at him. "All that land was yours?"

He nodded. "The Lady Luck has been in the Talbot family for generations."

"I see," she murmured, realizing for the first time that if the Lady Luck went to Beth, it would be going to someone who was not a Talbot. "It's beautiful," she conceded.

"Yes," he said, his voice as soft and reverent as she had ever heard it. "It is."

The two-engine plane bounced and skidded as the wheels settled on terra firma, and an old army jeep began following them down the runway.

"Thanks, Rolleen," Gavin said as the plane slowed to a halt.

"Don't thank me yet," she said as a hired hand opened the plane door for her. "Let's wait until I meet your grandmother—and your daughter—and see if I can go through with this."

# Chapter 7

Rolleen was enchanted by the Lady Luck ranch house. "It's made of logs, like the ranch houses in the movies!"

Gavin grinned and said, "My great-great-grandfather came from Kentucky. He didn't want a Spanish hacienda or some southern plantation home. He wanted a simple log cabin, and that's what he built."

"Simple?" she said, cocking a brow in disbelief.

Maybe a primitive log cabin was what Gavin's ancestor had built, but generations of Talbots had obviously added to the place, making it a delightful hodgepodge of levels and sending it in several directions. The massive ranch house and rustic outbuildings sprawled across one of the rolling hills she'd seen from the sky, shaded by immense, tangled live oaks.

She and Gavin had stripped down to T-shirts and jeans to accommodate the warmer South Texas weather and left their coats and sweaters and suitcases in the jeep. But Rolleen had insisted Gavin bring in the shopping bag full of Christmas gifts, since her parents had added a few last-minute items for Beth from the gifts they'd intended for Cherry's twin girls.

"Your home is beautiful," Rolleen said to Gavin as they stepped onto the wooden covered porch in back.

"Thanks. Seeing it through your eyes, I can appreciate how unique it really is."

The back door was open, and in the early-morning quiet, Rolleen could hear someone humming, "She'll be Comin' Round the Mountain." It wasn't a Christmas tune, but it somehow fit the log cabin setting and made Rolleen smile. She sniffed, smelled yeast and said, "Someone's baking."

"That'll be Hester."

"But she's ill."

"Not too sick to bake, apparently. I'd recognize that smell anywhere. Hester makes the same breakfast every Christmas morning—the most delicious glazed pecan rolls you ever ate in your life. The pecans come from trees here on the Lady Luck planted by my grandfather, just so my grandmother would always be sure to have pecans on Christmas morning."

The screen door squealed as Gavin pulled it open, and Rolleen got her first look at his grandmother.

"Gavin! What a surprise!" she said, her face splitting wide with a smile as Gavin ushered Rolleen inside. "We didn't expect you before noon!"

Hester Talbot didn't look seventy-three—or the least bit sick. She was tall, slim and wiry, like some pioneer woman, her silver-gray hair in a bun at her crown, wisps of it escaping at her temples to frame a face given character by the lines etched on it. Her dark eyes were bright with interest, and her step—she was dressed in a Western plaid shirt, jeans and boots—was lively.

"Who's this?" Hester asked, her features curious but friendly as she examined Rolleen.

"Why aren't you in bed?" Gavin asked, giving his

grandmother a hug so warm he looked like a bear who'd found a honey pot. "You're supposed to be sick."

"Why would you think a fool thing like that?"

"Because Ruby Jenkins called and said you were."

"I'll dangle that woman from her own telephone pole some day, see if I don't!" Hester said, shaking her head. "I told her I had the *sniffles!* As you can see, I'm fit as a fiddle. Or will be, when you tell me who this is you've brought home for Christmas."

"I'll be glad to, as soon as I can get a word in edgewise," Gavin said with a laugh.

Hester apparently couldn't wait. "I'm Hester Talbot," she volunteered, holding out her hand in welcome.

"Rolleen Whitelaw," Rolleen said, surprised at the strength of Hester's grip and the hard calluses she felt against her palm. The shrewd appraisal in the older woman's eyes made her heart thump a little faster. It wasn't going to be easy deceiving this woman. Hester Talbot was nobody's fool.

For the first time, Rolleen realized how Gavin must have felt meeting her parents and knowing he was only playing a role. She opened her mouth to tell the truth, but Gavin spoke first.

"Rolleen and I are engaged," he said, slipping his arm around Rolleen's waist and giving her a playfully smacking but startlingly sensual kiss.

"Stop that right now, Gavin Talbot. You're embarrassing the poor girl!" Hester ordered. Only, it was plain from the heightened color on Hester's cheeks, she was the one who needed rescue. "I'm so pleased for both of you," she said, waiting until Gavin let go of Rolleen to give her a hug. "I see you're wearing the Talbot diamond."

"You don't mind, do you?"

Hester snorted. "Mind? That diamond only fits the women Talbot men are supposed to wed. It's sort of like Cinderella's slipper. Can't be sized, don't you know?

Didn't fit Susan,'' she said with a significant glance at Gavin. "Fits you fine, though.''

Rolleen stared at Gavin, wondering why he hadn't filled her in on that little bit of Talbot folklore. "I see,'' she said.

Gavin sniffed the air and said, "How long before those famous pecan rolls of yours come out of the oven?''

Rolleen saw the pleasure on Hester's face at Gavin's eagerness to sample her wares.

"No more than ten minutes, maybe less. Promised Beth she could have them with her bacon and eggs. Child could hardly sleep last night, knowing we'd be opening presents this morning. She's been fondling that package you sent her last week like it was a real baby and not a doll—and don't ask how I know you got her one. I expect having you here'll be all the present that girl really needs.''

Rolleen had been watching the byplay between grandmother and grandson, finding comfort in the evident love between them. So she saw the way Gavin tensed at the mention of his daughter. It was plain he wasn't looking forward to the meeting as much as Beth apparently was.

"Beth!'' Hester said. "How long have you been standing there, girl? Come and say hello to your daddy.''

Rolleen turned and saw a rail-thin little girl in the doorway staring at them from large, anxious wide-set eyes, one bare foot atop the other, wearing a puffy-sleeved, flower-patterned nightgown with a ruffle at the hem.

She held tight to the door frame with her right hand, while her left forefinger twined nervously around a strand of her short black hair, which was parted in the middle and came to her chin, framing her face. Her upturned nose held a spattering of freckles, and her eyes—an unusual gray-green color—looked warily back at Rolleen from beneath long black lashes.

"Come on over here, and give your father a hug,'' Hester encouraged the little girl.

To Rolleen's surprise, instead of running toward her fa-

ther, Beth scampered to her grandmother, hiding behind
Hester's Levi's and peering out at her father.

The yearning look on Beth's face was as heartbreaking
as the tight-lipped look on Gavin's. The thick lump in Rolleen's throat came without warning. Before it had eased
enough for her to speak, the oven timer buzzed.

"My pecan rolls are ready," Hester announced. "Why
don't you take Beth and get her dressed while I take them
out of the oven," Hester said to Gavin.

Rolleen was afraid Gavin was going to refuse, and she
couldn't bear to see the little girl hurt. "Would you mind
if I came along?" she said to Beth.

Beth looked anxiously from Rolleen to her father. "My
daddy says I'm not supposed to go with strangers."

Rolleen turned to Gavin. The next move was his. She
begged him with her eyes to make the right one.

"Rolleen's a friend of mine," he said to Beth. "If it's
all right with you, I'd like her to come along."

"Okay, Daddy. She can come." Beth held out her hand
to Rolleen and said, "Come with me, and I'll show you
where my bedroom is."

Rolleen looked over her shoulder and met Gavin's eyes
as Beth drew her down the hall. *All she wants is to be loved.
That isn't so hard, is it?*

Apparently, it was. Gavin followed them, but from the
sour look on his face he might have been the guest of honor
at a western necktie party—the kind where the guest was
left hanging when everybody else went home.

The furnishings in Gavin's home reflected as many different periods and styles as the outside of the house and
Rolleen was enchanted by the whimsical nature of the decorations. A 1920's era lady's cloche hat hung on an eight-
eenth-century mirrored hall tree, and a man's cherry-wood
humidor sat on a delicate marble armoire. The ranch house
was filled with museum pieces, but it had a lived-in look.

"I love your home, Gavin," Rolleen said. She stopped

at Beth's doorway and gasped in delight. "Your bed looks like a covered wagon!"

The twin bed had wheels at the four corners, and instead of a traditional canopy, the top was made of white canvas and was shaped in an oval like the top of a western covered wagon.

"This was my daddy's bed, too," Beth said proudly.

Rolleen watched as Gavin lovingly ran a hand over the carved wooden footboard and confessed, "My grandfather made it for me."

While Gavin was admiring the bed, Beth had gone straight to her chest of drawers. She took out a matching shorts set and a pair of socks and without further ado began tugging her nightgown off over her head.

"May I help?" Rolleen asked, crossing to her.

Beth's face appeared in the neck of the nightgown wearing a surprised expression. It was apparent the little girl was used to fending for herself. "Okay," she said.

Rolleen sat down on the edge of the bed and pulled the nightgown the rest of the way over Beth's head, then began helping her into the T-shirt. Once it was on, she helped pull on Beth's shorts over her underwear, then sat the child in her lap to put on her socks.

Rolleen was aware of Gavin standing by, his hands in his pockets, shifting his weight from foot to foot. He appeared ready to bolt at the first opportunity.

"You can put on Beth's left shoe while I get this other sock on," she suggested.

He made a quick face, but knelt in front of them with a pair of pink tennis shoes in hand.

"You have to untie two knots, Daddy," Beth said. "'Cause I tied them like you showed me."

"I see," he said, working on the knots without looking at his daughter.

Beth sat perfectly still and pointed her toe as her father slipped the first shoe on.

He tied the lace, double knotted it and asked, ''Is that too tight?''

''Nope.'' She pointed the other stockinged foot in his direction, and he slipped the other tennis shoe on.

It was obvious to Rolleen, when they both hesitated after Gavin had finished tying Beth's shoes, that there was some ritual they usually performed at this point. She waited to see if Gavin would follow through with it.

Hesitantly he held his arms out to Beth. As she leaped into his embrace, he lifted her high into the air and swung her around and said, ''She can leap tall buildings in a single bound!''

Beth shrieked with fear and delight. ''Superwoman!''

Rolleen laughed. ''Superwoman wears pink tennis shoes?''

''There used to be a pink towel that went with the outfit,'' Gavin said sheepishly as he set Beth back on the ground.

''Come on, Daddy! Let's eat breakfast, so we can open presents,'' Beth said, grabbing her father's hand and tugging him toward the door.

Rolleen gave Gavin a supporting look as she followed him out of the bedroom. *That wasn't so bad, was it?* she asked with her eyes.

But his gaze, when Rolleen managed to catch it at the breakfast table, was troubled as he watched his daughter chatter with her grandmother.

Rolleen couldn't have said why it was so important to her that Gavin accept his daughter, and not just accept her, but love her wholeheartedly again. Maybe it was because she had been rejected as a child herself and knew what it felt like to walk in those tiny shoes. And maybe it had something to do with the hope that refused to die inside her that she and Gavin might someday be more than good friends.

She might love Gavin, she was almost certain she already

did, but if he couldn't love her unborn child, there was no future for the two of them. However, if Gavin could learn to love Beth again, there was hope he could learn to love the child growing inside her.

Rolleen was putting her faith in the power of love. It could heal all wounds. It was the source of all joy. And if ever there was a time when love abounded, Christmas was the season for it.

Gavin's daughter had trouble sitting still at the breakfast table, she was so excited, and the instant Beth had taken the last bite of food on her plate she asked, "Can we open presents now?"

The little girl bounced her way into the living room, with Rolleen and Gavin and Hester following behind. She dropped to her knees on the rug beside the Christmas tree, her eyes going wide at the sight of the shopping bag full of presents Rolleen had brought along.

"Whose presents are those?" Beth asked, turning to her father.

Rolleen sat down cross-legged beside Beth and said, "I brought them." She reached into the bag and came out with a gaily wrapped present. She checked the tag and said, "This one's for your daddy."

She saw Gavin's startled look from the couch, where he had taken up residence. "I wasn't expecting anything."

"I know," she said with a smile as she handed it over to him. "But I had fun coming up with a present for you."

"Open it, Daddy!" Beth urged, bouncing up and down in place. "Open it!"

"Well, open it, boy!" Hester said, from her comfortable seat on a cushioned wooden rocker by the fireplace. "We want to see what it is."

Rolleen suddenly felt nervous. "I wasn't sure what to get for you so I—"

"Whatever it is will be—" Gavin stopped in mid-speech and stared at her gift.

"What is it, Daddy?" Beth asked, jumping up and crossing to him to get a better look.

Gavin was so absorbed by what he held, Rolleen realized he hadn't even noticed Beth was standing beside him, her hand on his knee. As close together as their faces were, Rolleen could see the child had none of her father's features. Apparently Susan hadn't been lying when she'd told Gavin the child wasn't his. But the longer Rolleen watched, the more similarities between the two she noticed.

Beth tilting her head as Gavin did when he was studying something intently. Beth pointing at the gift with two fingers, instead of one, the way Gavin had on occasion. Beth's brow furrowing with concentration, mirroring the look on her father's face.

Gavin stared at the small, oddly shaped, beribboned, cork-stoppered bottle, looked up at Rolleen and said, "What is it?"

Rolleen laughed and crossed to sit beside him on the couch, pulling Beth into her lap. "The bottle contains salt water and sand from the beach where we had our picnic at Padre Island. It can be a paperweight or—"

Gavin cut her off with a hard kiss on the mouth. "Thanks, Rolleen."

Beth was off her lap in the next instant and running for the shopping bag to pull out another gift, leaving Rolleen still staring at Gavin. "I thought you might like a memento—"

He kissed her again with enough passion to leave her breathless, then turned to his grandmother, held it up and said, "It's love in a bottle."

Rolleen's heart was in her throat. She had felt that way when she put the gift together for him. She hadn't realized it would be so obvious to him. She felt self-conscious having him make such a pronouncement to his grandmother, considering the circumstances.

"What a lovely gift," Hester said to her. "Just the sort of thing a prospective bride ought to give her husband."

Rolleen felt her stomach roll. *Not now. Please, not now.* She swallowed once, twice, then said, "Gavin!"

He took one look at her, bolted to his feet, grabbed her hand and raced for the closest bathroom.

"What's wrong with Rolleen?" Beth cried.

"She's going to have a baby!" Gavin said as he raced by.

"Right now?" Beth called after him.

Over Gavin's shoulder, Rolleen saw the worried look on Hester's face as she called Beth to her side and said, "No, not right now."

Rolleen felt better after she emptied her stomach, but as she lay on the bed in Gavin's bedroom with a cool, wet cloth over her forehead, she wondered what Gavin was telling his grandmother. Revealing her pregnancy to Hester had been no part of their plan, although she supposed they should have realized she might get sick—as she had.

Rolleen heard a soft knock on the door and Hester called, "May I come in?"

She sat up too quickly, saw spots and laid back down before she said, "Please do. I'm sorry to be such a bother," she apologized as Hester crossed the room.

"Are you feeling better?" the older woman said as she sat beside Rolleen on the bed.

"I sat up too quickly just now, but I'm almost as good as new," Rolleen said, as she tried again, sitting up slowly and carefully. She saw Hester glance at her stomach, gauging how far along she was, and said, "The baby's due in May."

"You two planning to get hitched before then?"

Rolleen felt the blood race to her head, heating her cheeks. "We haven't set a date yet."

"You couldn't do much better than that boy," Hester

said. "He's a good man. And a good father. Leastwise, he was before that woman he was married to broke his heart."

"You don't have to tell me Gavin's a wonderful man," Rolleen said. "I've seen it for myself."

"Then why haven't you been to see a preacher?"

Rolleen threaded her fingers together to keep herself from fidgeting and stared at them as though they held the answer she sought. She sighed, looked up at Hester and said, "This isn't Gavin's baby."

"And you're worried he won't be able to love it as much as a father ought to," Hester speculated.

Rolleen nodded.

"I can see where you might think that, seeing how that fool boy has been acting toward his own child."

"His own child?" Rolleen questioned.

"Same as," Hester said. "Might not be his blood running in that child's veins, but Beth's his all right. Take one look at the two of them together—I watched you do it—and a body can't doubt they're closer than a man and his shadow."

*Gavin doesn't think he can love Beth anymore. That's why he brought me along.* Rolleen thought it, but she couldn't bring herself to say it. She owed that much to Gavin. "Gavin doesn't seem very comfortable around Beth," she said instead.

Hester made a snorting sound. "That woman he was married to left him twisted up a bit inside. You trust that boy. He'll work it out." Hester rose and said, "You feel like joining us again?"

Rolleen swung her feet onto the floor and said, "Of course. I feel fine now."

Rolleen found Gavin sitting with Beth in his lap on the living room couch, reading her Charles Dickens's *A Christmas Carol* from a worn, leather-covered book.

"Tradition," Hester whispered in her ear.

The little girl was leaning back against Gavin's chest,

twirling a strand of black hair and listening intently as Gavin read the story of Bob Cratchit and Tiny Tim, of Ebenezer Scrooge and the ghosts of Christmases past, present and future. Beth held an oblong wrapped Christmas package curled in her arm as though it were a baby, and Rolleen realized it must be the doll that Gavin had sent to her for Christmas, still unopened.

Rolleen settled on the couch beside Gavin, while Hester sat down once more in the rocker beside the fire. They listened, with only an occasional snap and pop from the wood on the fire as Gavin read about the power of the Christmas spirit to turn selfishness to generosity.

"A Merry Christmas, uncle! God save you!" Gavin read. And then Scrooge's reply, "Bah! Humbug!"

Gavin made the chains rattle when the ghosts appeared to teach Scrooge a lesson and used a falsetto every time he became Tiny Tim.

"A Merry Christmas, Bob!" Gavin said at last, as a reformed Scrooge greeted Bob Cratchit. He finished the story, all except the last line, then stopped and waited while Beth chirped happily, "And God bless Us, Every One!"

Rolleen and Hester clapped. Rolleen smiled but her throat tightened with emotion as she watched Gavin brush Beth's bangs out of her eyes.

Beth looked up at her father and said, "Can I open my present now, Daddy?"

"Sure, pumpkin," he said.

"I'm not a—"

"Pumpkin," they said together with a laugh as he hugged her tight.

Rolleen met Gavin's eyes with tears in her own, and his face sobered. He hadn't needed her here, after all. It hadn't taken much more than the Christmas spirit to reunite Gavin with his daughter. He had never really stopped loving her.

The ribbon on Beth's present went flying, and she ripped the paper with both hands, exposing the colorful cardboard box beneath. There, staring through a cellophane covering, was a Baby Walks and Talks. Reverently Beth removed the doll from the box. It had blond hair and blue eyes and looked nothing at all like Beth. Yet Beth treated the doll as though she had borne it herself. There was a lesson there, Rolleen thought with an inward smile.

Beth pulled the ring that made the doll talk, and it said, "I love you, Mommy."

Beth beamed. She pulled the string again, and the doll said, "I'm hungry." Beth frowned and said, "Where's her bottle, Daddy? Mary's hungry."

"Bottle?" he asked, confused.

"Look in the box," Beth commanded.

Gavin searched the box and found the empty baby bottle and gave it to Beth.

"She needs some milk, Daddy."

"Let's go see what we can find in the kitchen," Hester said, rising and reaching out to take Beth's hand. "You two keep on opening presents. We'll be back in a minute."

"I have something for you, too," Gavin said to Rolleen, once his grandmother was gone.

"What is it?" Rolleen asked.

"Close your eyes."

Rolleen closed them, grinned and said, "I love surprises."

"I know," Gavin replied. His hands moved her hair aside, and she could feel his breath on her temple. "Be still, you're wiggling."

It was the shiver down her spine. What did he expect when he was touching her like that? "What are you doing?"

"Be still so I can finish. You can open them now."

Rolleen opened her eyes and felt around her neck. She lifted the slight gold chain and followed it to the end where a diamond lay in the center of a gold heart. "Oh, Gavin..."

"Do you like it?"

He looked so uncertain, she threw herself into his arms and hugged him hard around the neck. "It's beautiful. And so romantic!" she said with a laugh.

"I wanted to say thanks," he whispered in her ear. "I wanted to tell you how much I've enjoyed the past two weeks. How much your help has meant to me. I…"

He pulled her hands free and held them in his, rubbing her knuckles as he said, "I don't know what's happened to me since I came home this morning, but I can hold Beth and…and it's almost like it was before."

"Almost?" Rolleen whispered.

Gavin let out a soughing sigh and met Rolleen's gaze. "I love her, I think. But she isn't…something's missing."

Rolleen pulled her hands free. Gavin had given a part of himself back to his child. But he wasn't willing to risk everything. Until he was, there was no hope for the two of them.

"You have to love Beth with your whole heart, Gavin."

"But Beth is not—"

"Daddy?"

Rolleen turned to find Beth standing by the couch, a baby bottle in one hand and the doll in the crook of her arm.

"Daddy?" she repeated, her tiny brow furrowed.

She watched as Gavin met his daughter's confused, wide-eyed stare and then turned to look at her. His agonized expression asked *What should I do?*

*She only wants to be loved,* Rolleen said with her eyes. *Blood isn't the only thing that makes you her father. She needs you, Gavin. Love her. Just love her.*

Gavin turned back to Beth and held his arms open wide. "Come to Daddy, Beth," he said. "And let me give you a Christmas hug."

Beth shot a hesitant look at Rolleen, whose eyes had brimmed with tears of joy. She nodded to the little girl, who leaped into her father's arms and held him tight, crying, "Daddy, Daddy!"

Rolleen was happy for Gavin, but more than ever aware that she didn't belong in this picture. She had risen to leave them alone, when Gavin said, "I love you, Rolleen. Stay with us."

The love in Gavin's eyes was unmistakable. Rolleen's knees were threatening to buckle and it would have been easier to drop back onto the couch than it was to leave. But there was too much at stake to take the easy way out.

"It isn't just me you have to love, Gavin," she reminded him. "There's someone else who needs to be considered." She put her hand on her belly and felt a fluttery kick inside. She looked down and stared. "Oh."

"What's wrong?" Gavin asked.

"I felt something. The baby," she said. She lifted her eyes and met his gaze. "My baby needs a father as much as Beth does. Are you willing to take on that kind of responsibility?"

"I think I can."

Rolleen felt like she was going to throw up—and not because of the baby. *I think I can* just wasn't good enough. *I think I can* didn't come close to a lifetime commitment to love her and the child she carried inside her.

"It's not enough," she said. "Not nearly enough."

She turned and headed for Gavin's bedroom. She was running before she'd taken too many steps.

"Rolleen!" he called after her. She heard him tell Beth, "You play with Mary, and I'll see you in a little while." Then she heard his boots on the hardwood floor chasing after her.

She ran down the hall searching for the room where he'd taken her before. But she lost her way and found herself in a feminine bedroom with a lace canopy over the bed and a white lace bedspread. She turned to slam the door and found Gavin blocking the doorway.

"Wait, Rolleen," he said. "Don't run away."

She couldn't keep him out, but she couldn't face him,

either. Rolleen clambered onto the bed, grabbed a pillow and curled herself into a protective ball around it. "Go away!" she said. "As soon as I'm feeling better I want you to take me home."

She heard the door shut and Gavin's footsteps crossing slowly to the bed. She knew he was close when the steps became muffled by the rag rug beside it. She felt the bed sag as he lay down beside her, felt the heat of him as he scooted closer.

"I was wrong," he said, laying a soothing hand on her shoulder.

"What?"

He pulled her gently toward him, laying her flat so he was above her, looking down at her. "I said I was wrong. About myself. About my feelings."

"You don't have to say what you think I want to hear," Rolleen said.

"I'm not saying it because you want to hear it. I'm saying it because it's true. I love you, Rolleen. Which means I love everything that's a part of you. And this baby—" He laid his hand caressingly on her belly. "Is a part of you I'll always cherish—because it brought us together."

"Oh, Gavin." Rolleen couldn't see him clearly for the tears blurring her eyes. "I want to believe you."

He leaned down and kissed her belly. "Listen to me, you in there. This is your father speaking. I want you to stop making your mother sick, do you hear me? I want you to concentrate on growing so we can welcome you as part of the family." He met her gaze and said, "There. I'm already giving the kid 'what for.' Is that proof enough I'm ready to be his father?"

Rolleen gave a choked laugh. "You're ridiculous."

"I'm in love," Gavin said. "With you."

Rolleen met Gavin's gaze and saw nothing there but tenderness and yearning and desire. "I love you, too, Gavin."

"Will you marry me and have my baby?" he asked, his hand caressing her belly.

"Oh, Gavin," she said. "Oh, Gavin…"

"Will you be my wife, Rolleen? Will you be the mother of my children?"

Rolleen swallowed down the thickness in her throat and said. "Oh, yes, Gavin. Yes."

The door clicked open and Rolleen turned and saw a small face peeking in.

"What are you two doing?" Beth asked.

"Come here," Gavin said, extending a hand to her.

Moments later Beth and her doll were snuggled up between the two of them. "I like this," Beth said dreamily.

"Me, too," Gavin said. "How about if we ask Rolleen to hang around so we can do this all the time."

Beth eyed Rolleen and said, "Okay."

"I guess it's settled then," Gavin said as he gathered the two of them—the three of them, Rolleen mentally corrected—into his arms. "We're a family."

Rolleen met Gavin's eyes and smiled. "Merry Christmas, Gavin."

"Merry Christmas, Rolleen."

Beth snuggled close, gave a satisfied sigh and said, "And God bless Us, Every One!"

\*    \*    \*    \*    \*

# Taming the Lone Wolf

## by Joan Johnston

# Chapter One

STONY CARLTON took a bite of his hamburger and tried not to listen to the scene unfolding behind the counter of the Buttermilk Café between the waitress and a guy who seemed to be her boss. For a man used to solving other people's problems with his wits—and now and then a gun—it was impossible not to eavesdrop, given the agitation in the woman's voice.

He looked around the empty café. No one else was there to come to her rescue except him—and he wasn't exactly the knight-in-shining-armor type.

"Come on, Bud, I've told you I'm not interested," the woman said.

"Aw, Tess, just one little kiss."

"I said no."

"You oughta have a little more gratitude, seein' as how I let you leave so early in the day."

"You let me leave early because I come in two hours before everyone else," the woman replied with what Stony considered amazing composure.

"Yeah, well, you owe me for givin' you a job when you had no experience."

"I've got experience now, Bud, a whole year of it. I've got work to do, so if you'll just let me by—"

Stony heard muffled sounds suggesting a struggle. He set down his burger, wiped his hands on a paper napkin and threw it down as he left his booth headed for the counter. The man, Bud, had the woman, Tess, backed up against the wall beside the coffeemaker. She was fending off his attempts to kiss her, turning her head away and shoving vainly at his burly shoulders.

"Hey, Bud," Stony said.

Bud turned and glared, clearly irritated at being interrupted. "What?"

"Let the lady go."

"Butt out, mister."

"Afraid I can't do that," Stony said.

"Yeah? So what are you gonna do about it?" Bud snarled.

Stony was over the counter in an instant, as though it wasn't there. He grabbed Bud by the scruff of his food-stained T-shirt and slammed him against the wall, holding him there with his arm rigid, his palm pressed against the center of Bud's chest.

The waitress shot out of the way and stood at the kitchen door, hands clutched together, green eyes wide with fright.

Stony ignored Bud as though he were a bug on the wall and turned his attention to the woman. "You all right, ma'am?"

She nodded her head jerkily.

Stony had been in the Buttermilk Café probably once a month in the past year, yet he hadn't paid any attention to the waitress. Since he had sworn off women a couple of years ago, he had made it a point not to spend his time looking at the pretty ones, so he wouldn't be tempted to go back on his promise to himself.

Tess was definitely pretty.

In fact, she was the kind of woman it was hard to dismiss. Her auburn hair was pinned up off her neck, but it had that mussed-up look, with lazy curls at her temples and ears and throat, as though she had just gotten out of a man's bed. The green eyes that stared warily back at him from a heart-shaped face were curved at the outer edges, like a cat's. Her nose was small and straight, her chin dainty. She had an alabaster complexion, which suggested she didn't get outside much, because the Wyoming sun burned the hide off you summer and winter.

He had avoided looking at her figure because he found it so alluring. She had a bosom—about big enough to fit his hands—that drew a man's eye, a tiny waist and feminine hips. And she was small enough to incite a man's protective instincts. He was tall, over six feet, and he suspected her head would barely reach his shoulder.

"I'm all right," the woman said. "You can let Bud go."

Stony had completely forgotten about the man against the wall. He turned to Bud and said, "What is it going to take to convince you to leave the lady alone?"

"What I do in my own place of business is none of your concern," Bud retorted.

Stony glanced at the woman. "Do you welcome this gentleman's attentions, ma'am?"

He watched the dark flush start at the V neck of her peach-colored waitress uniform and skate up her throat to sit like two roses on those alabaster cheeks. Her green-eyed gaze flitted from him to Bud and back to him.

"I...uh...no," she said. "But—"

He cut her off by turning his attention to Bud. "The lady wants you to leave her alone."

"There's nothing you can do to stop me," Bud said smugly.

"I can testify in court when the lady files a harassment suit against you."

"Why, you— She won't have to file no suit, because she's fired!" Bud said heatedly.

"Bud, no!" Tess exclaimed.

Stony glanced at Tess and was surprised to see she was angry—with him!

"Now look what you've done!" Her fisted hands found a perch at her tiny waist. "I was handling things just fine on my own before you showed up."

His eyes narrowed. "The man was pawing you."

Her chin lifted mulishly. "I've been putting Bud off for a year, and—"

"This has been going on for a whole year?" Stony said incredulously. He turned back to Bud, who was still pinned against the wall. "You've been mauling this lady for a year?" He gathered up a bigger handful of Bud's T-shirt.

"Wasn't doin' nothin' she didn't want," Bud said. "Widow-woman needs a man more'n most."

"A widow?" Stony's glance darted to Tess.

"My husband was killed a year ago," Tess said in response to his cocked brow.

He saw from the flash of pain in her eyes that it was still a raw wound. Her boss hadn't done anything to help it heal. Far from it. Stony resisted the urge to slam Bud against the wall again. He forced himself to let go of Bud's T-shirt and take a step back, afraid he would hurt the man if he held on to him much longer.

Stony wasn't sure he had solved anything. Maybe he had made matters worse. He refused to ask Bud to keep the woman on, when it was clear if he did that Bud would continue to press unwanted attentions on his waitress. But Tess apparently wanted—maybe needed?—the job.

"What will you do now?" he asked Tess.

"Get my job back, if I can," she answered with asperity. She walked over and straightened Bud's rumpled T-shirt. "Come on, Bud. What do you say?"

She managed a crooked smile, but Stony saw her chin was trembling.

Bud shot a malicious look at Stony, then said to Tess, "You're fired, honey. You can pick up your check at the end of the week."

"But, Bud—"

Bud jerked his thumb toward the door. "Out." Bud turned to Stony and said, "Now get out from behind my counter."

Stony went back over the counter the way he had come. He glanced at the woman from the corner of his eye as he made his way back to his booth and sat down. He picked up his hamburger and took a bite, but it was cold, and he had trouble swallowing it.

He watched Tess argue in whispers with Bud and saw Bud vehemently shake his head. He watched her take off her apron and drape it over the counter before she headed for the kitchen. He waited for her to reappear. He wanted a chance to talk to her, to make sure she was going to be all right, to see if there was anything he could do to help. Although, with the kind of help he had offered so far, he wouldn't be surprised if she turned him down.

He waited maybe two minutes. When Tess didn't return, he threw some money on the table to cover his check, grabbed his shearling coat and Stetson off the antler coat-rack and hurried outside to the snow-covered sidewalk to see if he could find her.

Stony wasn't thinking about his vow to stay away from pretty women. He wasn't thinking about anything except his need to make sure Tess would be able to make ends meet until she got another job. That should have been his first warning. Not that he would have paid attention to it. Stony was the kind of man who would stand bare-assed in a nest of rattlers just for the fun of it.

He stopped dead once he was outside and looked both ways. The snow was still coming down in large, windblown flakes that made it difficult to see very far. She was nearly to the end of Main Street, which was only one block long in the tiny town of Pinedale, walking with her head bent against the wind and her winter parka pulled tight around her.

"Hey!" he called. "Wait for me!"

She took one look at him and started to run.

TESS WAS TRYING HARD not to cry. For the past year she had been deflecting Bud's attentions with flip humor. Only, last night her three-year-old daughter, Rose, had been sick, and Tess hadn't slept much. When Bud had approached her, nothing witty had come to her tired mind. Then that awful man had interfered and made everything worse!

She had been fired.

The desperate nature of her situation was just now sinking in. She had no savings. She had no job. In a town this small in the middle of the off-season there wasn't much likelihood of finding another. Especially if Bud kept his promise to make sure none of his friends in the restaurant business hired her. She didn't even have the money for a bus ticket to somewhere else.

*Damn you, Charlie Lowell! How could you lie to me? How could you be a thief when you knew what would happen to us if you got caught? How could you go and get yourself killed like that? And for rustling cattle! I hate you, Charlie! I hate you for dying and leaving me alone.*

She should have taken one of the marriage offers she had gotten over the past year from the cowboys who came into the Buttermilk Café. Or the Pinedale police chief, Harry DuBois, who had proposed to her for the second time only last week. At least then she and Rose would have been sure of having a roof over their heads.

She liked Harry, and he was good-looking in a rugged Harrison Ford sort of way, but she hadn't been able to feel anything—let alone love—for any man since Charlie had died. Besides, she wasn't sure she wanted to be married again, not after what had happened with Charlie. She had been deliriously in love when she had married at sixteen. She was barely twenty, but she felt much older and wiser. She no longer gave her trust so freely or completely.

But if she wasn't going to let a husband support her, she had to do a better job of it herself. She had barely been able to cope with her disillusionment and grief over Charlie's death during the past year. She hadn't done much planning for the future.

It seemed the moment was upon her. She was going to have to make some plans, and fast, or she and Rose were going to find themselves out on the street in the middle of a Wyoming winter.

"Hey! Wait for me!"

Tess glanced over her shoulder and saw it was that man from the café. He was coming after her! She wasn't sure what his intentions were, but she didn't plan to stick around and find out. She took off at a run, headed for Harry's office. He would protect her from the madman following behind.

Maybe she would have made it if the sidewalk hadn't been covered with a fresh dusting of snow that concealed the treacherous ice below. Or if she had been wearing a decent pair of snow boots instead of the cheap, leather-soled shoes she wore for work. Tess hadn't taken three steps when her feet skidded out from under her. She flailed her arms in a vain attempt to catch her balance and reached out with a hand to break her fall on the cement walk. It turned out to be a fatal error.

Tess heard the bone in her wrist crack as soon as her weight came down on her arm. She cried out in agony as her body settled on the cold, hard ground.

The interfering stranger was beside her a moment later, down on one knee, his dark brown eyes filled with concern.

"Now look what you did!" she accused.

"What I did?"

"If you hadn't been chasing me—"

"I wasn't chasing you. I was coming after you to—"

"This is all your fault!" she cried, hysterical with the realization that with a broken wrist she wouldn't be able to work for weeks. Not to mention the fact that she had no health insurance and no idea how she was going to pay a doctor to fix her up.

The tears she had so ably kept under control through her most recent disaster could no longer be contained. She fought the sob that threatened, but it broke free with a horrible wrenching sound. Then she was crying in earnest.

She felt the stranger pick her up, being very careful of her wrist, which he settled in her lap, and stand, cuddling her against his chest.

"It's all right, Tess. You're going to be fine. I'm going to take care of you."

She should have resisted. She should have told him in no uncertain terms that she could take very good care of herself. Instead she turned her face to his chest and surrendered to his strength, thinking how good it felt to give her burdens over to someone else, even if it was only for a few moments.

"I'm taking you to my Jeep," he explained as he began walking. "I'll drive you to the hospital, where someone will take care of your arm."

"I don't have money to pay the doctor," she mumbled against his coat.

"Don't worry. I'll take care of it."

They were such wonderful words. She had been in charge of so much lately, and the burdens had been so heavy. She was more than willing to hand everything over to someone else for a while.

"What's going on here?"

It was Harry. Harry must have seen what happened from the picture window in his office.

"She fell and broke her wrist," the man said. "I'm taking her to the hospital."

"Tess?" Harry said. "Do you want Stony to take you to the hospital?"

*Stony. So that was his name. And Harry knew him, so maybe he wasn't a madman, after all.*

It took too much energy to answer, or even to turn around and look at Harry. She nodded.

"All right, Stony," Harry said. "I'll follow you there."

"I can take care of it," Stony said, his voice rumbly against her ear.

"I said I'd follow you," Harry insisted. "My patrol car is parked down the street."

Stony didn't argue; he merely turned and headed for his Jeep.

Tess was feeling drowsy, which wasn't surprising, considering the amount of sleep she had gotten last night. She had also hit the back of her head against the pavement when she fell, but it was only beginning to hurt because all her attention had been focused on her throbbing wrist.

"Stony?" she murmured.

"What, Tess?"

"My head hurts."

"You must have hit it when you fell. I'll have the doctor check it out."

"Tess?" Harry said.

Answering took too much effort.

"Looks like she fainted," Harry said, hop-skipping on the dangerous surface to keep up with Stony's long stride.

"Knocked out by the fall, I think," Stony replied.

"I only closed my eyes," she mumbled. "I'm still awake."

"I'll be right behind you," Harry said, sprinting—insofar as that was possible considering the icy walks—for the police car parked nearby.

Stony set her in his Jeep and buckled her in. She heard

the engine rumble, and things got a little hazy. Behind her closed eyelids she was seeing a picture of the tall, lean, broad-shouldered man who had come to her rescue in the café, his dark brows lowered, his eyes feral and dangerous. And the man who had looked down at her as she lay hurt on the ground, concern etched in his granite features.

His face was weatherworn, with deep brackets around his mouth and a mesh of crow's feet around his eyes that evidenced a life lived out-of-doors. His straight black hair needed a cut. It hung at least an inch onto his collar, and a hank of it was forever falling onto his forehead.

When he looked at her, his dark brown eyes held her in thrall. They were lonely eyes. Or, at least, the eyes of a man used to being alone. They offered sympathy. They asked for nothing in return.

She had seen him in the café before, but not regularly, so he lived around here somewhere, but maybe not right in town. There were lots of cabins along the river in this isolated place where a lone wolf could find solace from the world of men.

She wondered what he did for a living. Judging by his Western shirt, jeans and boots, he could have been another cowboy. But a mere cowboy wouldn't have taken on Bud, who was big enough, and meaty-fisted enough, to be downright intimidating. Stony hadn't blinked an eye at confronting him. So he was probably a man used to being in charge, rather than one who took orders, a man who knew his own strength and used it when necessary.

But he wasn't a cruel man, or he really might have hurt Bud. She had seen how angry he was, but he had kept his rage on a tight leash. He was agile and strong and—

Stony jostled her broken wrist when he picked her up to take her inside the hospital, and the brief agony jolted her awake. But she couldn't seem to get her eyes open. Tears of pain seeped from her closed eyelids.

"Sorry, Tess," Stony said. "Hang on, and the doctor can give you something for the pain."

Tess drifted in and out of consciousness, aware of the murmur of voices, the sting of an injection, the buzz of the X-ray machine, the warm wetness of the cast being applied around her thumb, from the middle of her right hand half-way up her arm.

She heard the word "concussion" and realized that was probably why she felt so woozy. So it wasn't only the lack of sleep that made her feel so impossibly tired. She heard the doctor say she would have to stay overnight so she could be watched. But she couldn't stay, because she had to go pick up Rose from Mrs. Feeny.

"No," she muttered. "Can't stay. Have to go home."

"Be reasonable, Tess," Harry said. "You're in no condition to leave the hospital."

"Have to get Rose."

"Who's Rose?" she heard Stony ask.

"That's her daughter," Harry said.

"She has a daughter?"

The shock in Stony's voice made her smile. She wasn't sure if the expression got to her face.

"An elderly lady keeps the little girl for Tess while she works. Mrs. Feeny, I think," Harry explained.

Mrs. Feeny was very strict about Tess picking up Rose on time. Otherwise the old woman charged her triple. With all the extra she was going to have to dole out for the doctor, she needed every penny she had.

"Have to pick up Rose." She tried to get up, but a palm flattened her.

"I'll do it," Stony said.

"The kid doesn't know who you are," Harry said. "I'll do it."

"I said I'll do it," Stony countered. "After all, this is my fault."

Tess wanted to smile again. Stony sure had changed his

tune. Maybe he was feeling guilty. He ought to. This *was* all his fault!

She welcomed Stony's offer to pick up Rose. For some reason, Rose had taken an instant aversion to Harry. Her daughter had a way of making her feelings known. Tess licked her dry lips and said, "Okay, Stony. Pick up Rose."

"Tess, you don't know a thing about the man," Harry said. "He—"

"Don't interfere, Harry," Tess murmured.

"You heard the lady, Sheriff. She can make her own decisions without any help from you."

Tess realized she hadn't told Stony what to do with her daughter. "Take Rose home," she added.

"I'll do that," Stony said. "Don't worry, Tess. She'll be safe with me. I have lots of room at my place."

*His place?*

She had meant take Rose to her own home. Of course, he didn't have the key, and Mrs. Feeny, who was also Tess's landlady, was hardly likely to let a stranger into an upstairs apartment in her own home. So maybe it was better this way. Only, she had no idea where Stony lived. How would she find him when she wanted to reclaim her daughter?

She managed to force her eyes open a crack and sought out Stony's face. "Take me, too," she said. "Rose needs me."

"For heaven's sake, Tess," Harry said irritably. "You're in no condition to do anything but lie flat on your back in bed. Stay here in the hospital where you belong."

The situation was desperate. She reached out and grasped Stony's hand. It was big and warm and callused. His strength made her feel safe. "Rose needs me," she repeated. "Take me, too."

"All right," he said. "I'll take you both to my place."

"Promise?"

"I said I would."

He didn't sound too happy about the situation, Tess realized. But she wasn't about to let him out of his promise. "Thank you." Her eyes sank closed again.

If she could rest for a couple of hours, she would be fine. Stony could pick up Rose and come back for her. She would rescue her daughter from the clutches of the interfering stranger...as soon as she could get her eyes open again.

# *Chapter Two*

"WHERE AM I?"

"You're at my place, a cabin along the river about twenty miles from town. Don't you remember the ride here in my Jeep?"

"I...sort of. It's all kind of fuzzy."

Tess's gaze darted from the male face bathed in shadows beside the bed, to the natural pine log walls, to the wedding ring patterned quilt that covered her, and back to the face made even more attractive by a night's growth of beard. The faint mauve light filling the window across the room suggested it was nearly dawn. The snow had stopped, but it weighted down the branches of the Douglas firs outside the cabin, creating a real-life picture postcard.

She reached for her head with her right hand before a sharp pain and the weight of the cast reminded her that her wrist was broken. She switched to the left and gingerly touched the lump on the back of her head.

"Does it still hurt?" Stony asked.

"My scalp's a little tender, but my head doesn't ache

like it did.'' She realized what was missing and sat up with a jerk that made her dizzy. "Where's Rose?"

"Still asleep."

"Where?" she insisted, reaching out to clutch Stony's forearm. It was as hard as a rock. She realized what she was doing and let him go.

He gestured with his chin. "Right there beside you."

Tess realized why she hadn't seen the child. The bed was huge, and Rose was curled up in a pile of sheets and blankets on the other side. Tess took another look around at the heavy pine chest, the rocker with clothes thrown over the back, the man's wardrobe, and realized she must be in Stony's bedroom.

"I thought you said you had plenty of room," she accused. "Rose and I are in your bed, aren't we?"

"It was the only one in the house big enough for the both of you," he admitted with a crooked smile. "Rose refused to sleep by herself."

Tess turned back to her daughter and leaned over to brush a red curl from her daughter's cheek. "Did she give you a lot of trouble?"

"No more than two or three green-broke broncs."

"Oh, dear. I was a little afraid of that."

"We got along fine, once she figured out I wasn't going to give up or give in."

Tess flushed. "She is rather strong-willed. I suppose I let her have her own way too often."

"She's spoiled rotten," Stony said flatly. "And she has a temper."

Tess opened her mouth to defend her mothering tactics, then realized Stony hadn't been completely successful in controlling her daughter, either. After all, Rose had ended up sleeping in the same bed with her.

"Perhaps she is a little spoiled," Tess conceded, brushing at the stubborn curl that had found its way back to

Rose's cheek. "But she's had to cope with an awful lot over the past year."

Stony shifted from the chair beside the bed to a spot on the mattress near her hips. Tess tensed at the intrusion on her space. However helpful he had been, Stony was still a stranger. And she was in his bed wearing no more than— Good Lord—one of his T-shirts!

"I've been wanting to talk to you about that. I mean, about how you and Rose have been getting by," Stony said.

His voice had that rusty gate sound, as though he hadn't used it much lately. It rumbled over her, sending a shiver up her spine. She wasn't sure whether it was the threat he presented, or the temptation, that had her inching away from him.

"We've been just fine," Tess said.

"Don't bother lying."

"I—"

"I spoke with your landlady."

Tess sighed. "I'm only a month behind on the rent."

"You had to give up your phone two months ago. And I didn't see much in the cupboards to eat. How the hell you two have managed to make it this far, I'll never know."

Tess felt the anger rising and struggled to control it. Rose hadn't learned her redheaded temper; she had inherited it from her mother.

"I'd like to know what your plans are now that you've been fired," Stony said.

"I don't see how my future plans are any of your business," Tess retorted. "I'm sure I'll find something—"

"You can work for me." Stony interrupted her.

Tess was speechless. "Doing what?" she managed to say at last.

He made a broad gesture around the bedroom. "I could use a housekeeper, and I know you can cook. I couldn't pay much, but I could give you free room and board. It would give you somewhere to stay and food in your mouths, at least until your wrist is healed.''

Tess took a second look around the room. This time she noticed the layer of dust on the wardrobe, the stack of dirty, rumpled shirts on the rocker, the horse magazines strewn across the floor, the empty beer can on the chest. It was clear the man could use a housekeeper. But if he had really wanted one, he could have hired one long ago.

Her gaze shifted back to Stony's face. ''Why are you willing to do this for me?''

He frowned and rubbed his thumb along his lower lip. ''I don't have any designs on you, if that's what you're thinking.''

She flushed. Because the thought had occurred to her. ''I never—''

''Don't bother lying again. You've been itching to get out of here ever since you woke up.''

She heard the irritation in his voice. His thumb never stopped that lazy trail from one side of his mouth to the other. She felt a surprising curl of desire in her belly and jerked her gaze away from his mouth back to his eyes. That was no better. They were dark and fierce and feral. They made her feel hunted. She lowered her lashes to hide from him but felt her body quiver in anticipation of the need to fight or to flee.

''The way I figure it, I owe you a job,'' he continued, apparently unaware of her agitation. ''I'm the one who got you fired—even if you should have quit a long time ago.''

''And worked where?'' she demanded, incensed at the implied criticism. ''There aren't too many waitress jobs in Pinedale.''

''Couldn't you do something else?''

Her anger died, consumed by frustration at her lack of education. She had a high school equivalency degree, but she had believed that was all she would ever need. She had never considered the necessity of any further formal education because she had been perfectly happy being a wife and mother. She had been very good at her chosen profession.

"I had a job I was happy with, until it was taken away from me."

"Well, there you go. What was it?"

"Housewife."

She saw the stricken look on Stony's face and realized she shouldn't take out her bitterness over Charlie's death against him. "I'm sorry. Ever since Charlie got himself killed, I—" She took a shuddering breath. She wasn't used to speaking aloud about Charlie, and the sudden lump in her throat surprised her. She had believed she had come to terms with Charlie's untimely death. Apparently not.

"Was Charlie your husband?"

"Yes. Charles Lowell. He was a butcher at the local grocery store. Or so I thought. He was caught rustling cattle and was killed in the gunfight that followed."

She looked up and discovered Stony staring at her grim-lipped. His face had paled, and his eyes narrowed to slits. "It's not a pretty story," she admitted. "I was devastated, because I was caught off guard. I had no idea Charlie was involved in theft of any kind. I'm afraid I wasn't myself for a long time after that."

"Didn't you have any family who could have taken care of you?" he asked.

"I'm an orphan. And Charlie's parents are dead. It was—and is—just me and Rose. The sheriff's office collected some money for us. Looking back, I suppose it was strange for them to do such a thing—but it got us through the first few months. When I was myself again, I looked around and realized I would have to get a job. Bud was the only one who would hire me without experience.

"I think he did it because he thought he could pressure me into sleeping with him. I'm sure he had no idea I would resist his advances so long or so completely." Her lip curled up on one side. "I guess he finally ran out of patience."

Stony grunted in sardonic agreement. "Will you take the job I offered you, or not?"

She twisted the sheet in the fingers of her good hand. She didn't have any choice. It was take his job offer or starve. But she didn't like it. Stony made her nervous. He made her skin tingle. He made her feel things she didn't want to feel.

Nevertheless she said, "I'll take the job." And then qualified her acceptance. "But only until my wrist heals, and I can decide what to do with my life."

Or until the day came when it was no longer safe to remain with the lone wolf whose den she had invaded with her cub.

*HE HAD KILLED HER HUSBAND.*

Stony wished he had inquired about Tess's last name sooner. He had been shocked to hear her husband was Charles Lowell. He had been tracking that particular gang of rustlers for several months before he finally caught them in the act, and he had been forced into the gun battle that ensued. He had performed his job with the ruthless efficiency that had earned him his reputation, and Charles Lowell had died.

His identity as a range detective who hired out to large cattle spreads wasn't generally known, and Stony needed it to stay that way in order to infiltrate the roving bands of rustlers that plagued the vast Wyoming ranges. The police had cooperated and kept his name out of the local paper. For some reason, Tess Lowell had never asked the identity of the man who killed her husband, or she would have known who he was.

Stony knew he ought to confess immediately and give Tess the chance to spit in his face. But she didn't have anywhere else to go, and he was afraid she wouldn't stay if she knew the truth. At least he could give her a place to live until she was well again. She and the kid needed him, and he owed them something because he was personally responsible for the loss of both husband and father, even if the man was a felon.

But he resented the intrusion on his solitude.

He was thirty-three and had lived alone in this five-room cabin, which he had built with his own hands, for the past ten years. He liked the quiet. He had spent many a long winter night before a flickering fire with nothing to disturb his peace but the wind rustling in the pines or the buildup of snow sliding off the steep blue tin roof in thunderous clumps.

When he needed a woman, he sought out one who only wanted the same brief physical satisfaction he desired. Lately he had decided even that sort of relationship wasn't worth the risk it entailed. His isolation had become complete and comfortable.

Until this redheaded woman and her redheaded child had invaded it.

His attention was drawn to the child, who woke suddenly and popped upright in bed like a jack-in-the-box.

"Mama!"

"Don't be frightened, Rose. I'm right here," Tess said, holding out her good arm.

The little girl scuttled across the bed and flung herself across her mother's body as though she were being attacked by ravaging wolves. She peered up at Stony with green eyes a shade darker than her mother's and said very distinctly, "I want to go home."

"I know, sweetheart," Tess replied, brushing at the mass of bright red curls—shades lighter than her mother's deep auburn—that tumbled over her daughter's forehead. "I do, too. But we can't, not for a little while."

The child sat up abruptly. "Why not?"

"Because your mother's arm is broken. She needs to rest and recuperate," Stony said.

"What's reputerate?" the child said, her brows knitted in confusion.

"Get well," Stony amended, amused at the child's mangled effort to repeat the grown-up word.

The little girl's eyes widened, and her gaze slid to the cast covering her mother's arm. She reached out tentatively to touch it. "Mama's hurt bad?"

"The cast is there to protect the broken bone so it can heal," Tess explained.

Tears filled the child's green eyes and spilled over. Her lower lip stuck out, and her chin trembled. "Mama's hurt."

Stony was amazed at the instant transformation. How did the kid do it? He watched her mother fall for the act.

"Oh, sweetheart, I'll be fine," Tess said with a hitching sob as she gathered the child to her breast.

Stony snorted. He meant to convey disgust at the ridiculousness of sentimental tears over something that was done and over. He believed the little girl was simply manipulating her mother, for reasons he couldn't imagine and didn't care to figure out. Two sets of long-lashed, accusing green eyes settled on him, and the sound in his throat changed to something more contemplative.

"Is anybody hungry?" he asked.

"I am," Rose said.

Stony's lips twisted cynically when he saw how instantly the child's tears stopped. One clung to her lashes and skidded down her check when she gave him a wide-eyed blink.

"I'll make some breakfast," he said.

"I'll do it." Tess slipped her legs out from under the covers before she realized the T-shirt bared her all the way from her toes to her hips. She flushed and scooted back under the covers.

"Where are my clothes?" she asked.

"I had Mrs. Feeny put some things in a suitcase for you.

It's there in the corner. You can get the rest of your stuff from her later.''

Stony was still having trouble catching his breath after the eye-stopping exhibit he had just witnessed. The woman wasn't tall, but she had incredible legs, long and silky and perfectly formed. He fought off the image of those legs wrapped around him. His genitals drew up tight in response to such mental titillation.

''I'll go make breakfast while you get dressed,'' he said, backing his way out of the room. He felt perspiration dotting his forehead, even though the bedroom was far from hot. It disturbed him that his thoughts had taken such a decidedly lascivious turn. He had cast himself in the role of guardian. So long as Tess was under his roof, he had to resist any temptation to seduce her. He owed Charlie Lowell's widow that much consideration.

The whole wall of the house that encompassed the combined kitchen and living area contained French doors that opened onto a large elevated patio. The view included a forest of evergreen pines and fir interspersed with aspens that had lost their leaves earlier in the fall. The light and empty space immediately brought him comfort.

''Is this your house?''

Stony whirled from the refrigerator door and stared at the sprite who was standing barefoot not three feet away from him.

''You should be wearing slippers,'' he said to the child, aware of how parental he must sound, when the last thing he ever wanted to be was a parent.

She looked down as she wiggled her toes on the polished hardwood floor. She glanced coyly at him from beneath lowered lashes. ''Mama's getting me slippers for Christmas.''

Not without money, she wasn't, Stony thought grimly.

''Your feet must be cold,'' he said, scooping the child up and carting her back toward the bedroom. She didn't weigh as much as a case of beer. "You can wear a pair of socks."

"I'm not supposed to wear socks without shoes," she said soberly.

He met her gaze and frowned.

Her chin trembled. "Mama says so."

"I'm not going to bite you," he snapped.

Rose burst into tears. "Mama!"

"What's going on?" Tess said, hurrying from the bedroom.

Stony was dismayed to see she had left his T-shirt on and merely added a pair of worn jeans. It wouldn't take much to have her naked. She was barefoot, too.

"I told the kid she shouldn't be running around barefoot on this cold floor." He watched Tess's bare toes curl against the wooden floor. His gaze skipped back to her face, and he saw the blush was back in her cheeks.

"I don't have the money for slippers," she murmured.

"Put on a pair of socks."

"I think I'm capable of judging whether my feet are cold," she retorted.

He shifted Rose to one arm and bent down to touch Tess's bare feet. "Your toes are like ice," he said flatly. "Put on some socks."

"I don't wear socks without—"

"Shoes," he finished. "Then put on some socks and shoes."

"Is that an order?" she asked.

He wanted to say yes, but the mulish tilt of her chin advised against it. "A suggestion."

"Very well. I'll be right back."

"Bring some socks and shoes for Rose," he called after her. He looked down at the little girl who was peering at him wide-eyed.

"I don't like you," she announced.

"I don't like you, either," he said.

Rose didn't seem phased by the insult. "I'm hungry," she said.

"So am I," Stony muttered. "That's probably why I'm in such a foul mood." It couldn't have anything to do with the two females who had invaded his lair.

"I can help cook," Rose said.

"Can you now?" Stony set her on the counter beside the fridge so she would be off the floor while he rooted around for breakfast fixings. He set the eggs on the counter while he hunted out the bacon and English muffins.

A moment later he heard a tiny "Uh-oh," followed by the sound of eggs cracking on the floor.

He whipped his head up and caught it on the refrigerator shelf. He grabbed at the painful spot and turned to find the eggs spilled from the carton and creating a gooey puddle on his floor.

The little girl's eyes were wide with fright. "I'm sorry."

Stony fought down the urge to yell at her, remembering how quickly she could summon tears. Besides, accidents could happen to anyone. He was willing to give her the benefit of the doubt. This time.

"Are you going to spank me?" the little girl asked, her chin aquiver.

"I didn't think parents spanked their kids anymore," Stony said. "It's against the law, or something."

"Mama says she's going to spank me. But she never does."

"I'll bet," Stony said. That explained why the kid was spoiled rotten.

"Mama loves me," the little girl said solemnly.

Stony took in Rose's big green eyes, her unmanageable, curly head of hair, the chubby arms and legs, and felt an uncomfortable tug at his heart. Rose was lovable, all right. He had to give her that.

He looked down at the chaos she had created with a box of eggs. Lovable. And messy.

''Oh, no!''

Stony looked over his shoulder at Tess, who was eyeing the broken eggs on the floor with dismay. ''I'm so sorry.''

''No problem. We can have a bowl of cereal instead. No cooking. Saves on dishes.''

''I'll clean up that mess,'' Tess volunteered.

''I'll do it,'' Stony said, eyeing the arm she had arranged in the sling the doctor had given her. ''You're incapacitated.''

''What's 'pacitated?'' Rose inquired.

''Means she can't do anything with that broken arm,'' Stony explained to the child. He caught Rose around the waist and, stepping around the broken eggs, hauled her over to the far side of the breakfast bar, where he sat her on one of the two stools there. He grabbed a handful of paper towels and began sopping up the eggs and dropping the shells into the disposal in the sink.

''You must not get much company,'' Tess said, settling on the second stool.

''I can stand on this side of the bar,'' he said, rinsing his hands and drying them. He grabbed some bowls from the cupboard and dropped them with a clatter on the breakfast bar. He only had one box of cereal, a healthy wheat flake, and he began pouring it out into the three bowls.

''I don't like that kind,'' Rose said.

''It's all I've got,'' Stony replied.

''I want the kind with marshmallows,'' Rose insisted.

''Rose, darling—'' Tess said.

''Eat it or go hungry,'' Stony said.

Rose moved her bowl just as Stony began to pour milk, and it spilled across the counter.

Stony set down the milk carton as softly as he could, using his last bit of patience. ''It's time we had a talk, young lady,'' he said to Rose.

''I don't like you,'' Rose said, her chin tilted in a mulish imitation of her mother.

"I thought we settled that," Stony muttered, glaring back at the little girl. "I don't like you, either."

"Rose—"

"Stay out of this, Tess," Stony said.

"I will not," Tess said, rising from her bar stool, her green eyes flashing. "You seem to be forgetting who you are. And who we are."

"I'm an idiot," Stony muttered. "And you're interlopers."

"What's 'lopers?" Rose asked.

"Intruders," Stony snarled.

"What's 'truders?" Rose asked.

"Unwelcome guests," Tess answered before Stony could speak. "I think we can save you and ourselves a great deal of unpleasantness, Mr.—I don't even know your last name," Tess said, astonished at the realization. "I'm sorry we've intruded on your peace. If you'll allow me to use your phone, I'm sure Harry DuBois will be willing to come and get us."

Stony shoved a hand through his hair, catching the wayward curl on his forehead, which immediately tumbled back down again. "Look," he said. "I don't want you to leave. Besides, you have nowhere else to go."

Tess sighed. "Unfortunately, what you say is true. But I don't think this is going to work, Mr.— What is your last name, anyway?"

"It's Carlton, but call me Stony."

"Very well, Stony. As I said, I don't think this is going to work."

"I'm not used to having people around."

"Especially not children, it seems."

"I don't like kids," he said flatly.

"Why is that?" Tess challenged.

Stony thought of his father and his father's very young new wife and their new family that had excluded him. He had to admit his half brother had been cute. His father had been fascinated by his second son. That kid had gotten all the attention Stony had always craved from a father who had always been too busy working to play with him. Thirteen-year-old Stony had felt sick with guilt and shame at his uncontrollable envy and resentment of the time and attention his father gave his newborn son.

He couldn't tell Tess any of that. "Kids are a lot of bother," he said instead.

"I shall make certain Rose is not a bother," Tess said crisply. "Is there anything else?"

"Just keep her out of my way."

Tess looked around the small cabin. What Stony asked was unrealistic, considering the size of the place. "I'll do my best."

"I want to go home," Rose said to her mother.

Stony watched as Tess hugged the child. "I wish we could go home, too, Rose. We have to stay here."

"I don't like that man," Rose said.

Stony met Tess's gaze over the child's head. He wasn't proud of his behavior. But he couldn't help his feelings, either. However, there was something he could do to ease the situation for all of them.

"I've got another job up around Jackson Hole," he said. "I'll be leaving this afternoon, so you'll have the place to yourself. I have groceries delivered on a regular basis from town. If you need more, call the supermarket and give them a list."

He hadn't been meaning to take on more work right away, but it seemed best to put some distance between himself and Tess—for whom he felt too great an attraction, and the little girl—who didn't like him.

"What is it you do?" Tess asked.

"I find cattle rustlers. And bring them to justice."

Tess stared at him openmouthed.

He turned on his heel and left the room before she had a chance to ask if he knew the man who had apprehended and killed her husband.

# Chapter Three

STONY HAD SPENT most of the past six weeks on horseback or in his Jeep tracking a bunch of winter rustlers that had proved particularly elusive. He hadn't been home once since he had rescued Tess Lowell, spending his time instead at a place he kept in Jackson Hole within sight of the Grand Tetons. It was two days before Christmas, and he wanted to be in his own home for the holiday. Even if he had to share it with strangers.

He wondered if they had already left. Maybe Tess had figured out some other way to support herself, and she and the little girl were gone. Perversely, he found himself wishing they were still there.

Tess had been on his mind a great deal lately.

He figured it was simply that he hadn't had a woman in a long time, and he had found the sight of her green cat's eyes staring back at him from an alabaster face surrounded by wispy auburn curls especially attractive. He couldn't help remembering the look of her long legs slipping from under his covers. Or the soft weight of her breasts beneath one of his worn T-shirts.

He wanted her. There wasn't anything rational or reasonable about his desire. It was purely primitive. Like a male beast in rut. He had to have her.

He planned to have her.

His heart beat a little bit faster when he saw the smoke coming from the chimney of his cabin as he traversed the narrow, winding dirt road lined with ten-foot mounds of county-plowed snow that led up the mountain where he lived.

She was still there.

He left the Jeep outside rather than putting it in the garage and let himself in through the front door, anxious to see her again.

He was stunned when he stepped inside. His place didn't look the same. Not that it didn't look nice. The Western furniture had been rearranged to create a cozy sitting area around the wood stove in the fireplace and everything sparkled with cleanliness. She had brought evergreen boughs inside and strung them across the pine mantel, adding splashes of red with small velvet bows. And she had put up a Christmas tree with homemade decorations and lights. There were even presents beneath it.

It felt like a home. But not his home.

He hadn't celebrated Christmas since he had left his father's house at eighteen. It conjured too many memories of his father and the wife and child who had usurped what little place he had in his father's life. He had decided he didn't need anybody to love him. After college, instead of going into his father's lumber business, he had escaped to this mountain hideaway to be alone, renting a place in town until the house was done.

The Christmas tree brought back painful memories of being shut out, of feeling lonely and alone. Only he wasn't alone this Christmas. Not if the fire in the chimney meant what he thought it did.

His nose led him to the stove, where a savory stew was bubbling, apparently intended for supper later in the day. He used a wooden spoon to take a taste. It was delicious, tangy with sage and bay.

The house was quiet. Normally he liked the quiet. Now it irritated him. Where was she? Where was the little girl?

He went hunting for Tess and found her in the guest bedroom, sitting on the side of one of the twin pine beds, reading *The Three Little Pigs* to her daughter. He stood in the doorway, listening to their laughter as Tess huffed and puffed and blew the house down. It made his chest constrict for no good reason he could discern.

He knew when she felt his presence. Her shoulders tensed, and she stopped reading in midsentence. She could likely smell him, feel his heat. He felt hers.

"Why did you stop, Mama?" the child asked. "Did the big, bad wolf blow the brick house down?"

When Tess turned to look at him over her shoulder he felt a shiver of raw sexual hunger roll down his spine. The hairs stood up on his nape. His nostrils flared, and his body tautened.

She recognized the danger. He saw it in the way her pupils dilated, the way her mouth fell open to gasp a breath of air, the way her body readied itself to fight—or to flee.

She couldn't run from him. Not without the child. And the two of them hadn't a chance of escaping.

He saw the anxiety in her eyes, along with an unnaturally heightened awareness. She moved slowly, cautiously, standing and laying the children's book down on the bed.

He suddenly realized the cast was gone. Her arm was healed. But she was still here. He felt a surge of triumph, almost of euphoria. He had the oddest feeling she was going to walk right into his embrace.

He took a step, opened his arms to her, and found them filled seconds later as an exuberant little girl launched herself at him from the bed. He caught Rose only an instant before disaster.

"You came back!" Rose chirped, clinging to his neck like a limpet. "Mama said you would. Mama said you're a nice man. Mama said you're taking care of us."

He scowled. "I thought you didn't like me."

Her tiny brow furrowed uncertainly, and her worried glance skipped to her mother. "Mama?"

"I believe Rose is willing to give you a second chance," Tess said in a voice that shuddered over him.

He met her eyes. "Thanks to you, I suppose."

She smiled, and a spiral of desire drew his loins up tight.

"I might have had something to do with it."

Her smile faded as sexual awareness rose between them.

Rose grabbed his cheeks between her palms to turn his attention back to her. "I like it here," she said. "I can play in the snow, and chop limbs from trees and stuff. Mama said you might let us stay if I'm a good girl. I'm not supposed to say I don't like you anymore," she added naively.

Stony's glance shot to Tess and caught her blush of embarrassment. So that was how she had gotten the girl to change her mind about him.

"I promise to be good," Rose said. "Will you let us stay? Have you seen our Christmas tree? Mama made some presents for you. Do you want to see your presents?"

"Rose," Tess said, "give Stony a chance to catch his breath."

His breath was caught already—somewhere in his chest.

Rose wriggled to be let down, and he set her on her feet. She grabbed his hand and headed toward the living room as fast as her tiny legs could carry her. He glanced helplessly over his shoulder at Tess, who gave him a winsome smile as he was led away. He held out his hand to her at the last possible moment, and she laid her slight palm in his, allowing herself to be tugged after him.

Electricity shot up his arm as he made contact with her flesh. If it hadn't been for the hold the little girl had on him he would have taken Tess then and there. He flashed her a look that told her his intention and saw the trepidation rise again in her eyes. She recognized the trap too late. She had been caught, and he would not let her go until he had assuaged the powerful need in him to have her beneath him, to put himself inside her and make her his own.

TESS HAD REALIZED the danger too late. She had known Stony was attracted to her, felt it all those weeks ago when she had woken up in his bed. She had assumed he was civilized enough to control his impulses. She should have known better. No man was civilized where sex was concerned.

Harry had warned her. "He's dangerous. Stony Carlton is a lone wolf who doesn't live by anyone's rules. Watch yourself around him."

She had laughed at Harry and reassured him that after a year as a waitress at the Buttermilk Café she was perfectly capable of quelling the pretensions of a too-forward man.

She felt a frisson of excitement skate up her arm as Stony's hand tightened around hers. She had known she would have to deal with the attraction between them sometime. She just hadn't thought it would be this soon.

"Mama made you a—" Rose cut herself off, putting tiny hands in front of her mouth. Wide-eyed she confessed, "I'm not supposed to tell. It's supposed to be a surprise."

Stony led Tess to the sofa she had angled in front of the fireplace and drew her down on it. An instant later Rose was in his lap chattering again. Because her daughter asked a question she wanted answered herself, Tess didn't bother shushing her.

"Where have you been?" Rose asked. "What have you been doing?"

Stony's thumb caressed Tess's wrist. Her blood began to thrum, and goose bumps shot up on her arms. She stared at him, mesmerized, as he spoke.

"I've been chasing some bad men up near Jackson Hole."

"Did you catch them?" Rose asked.

"Not yet."

"Why did you come home?" Tess asked.

"For Christmas," he said simply.

Tess and Stony's gaze met over Rose's head. He might profess not to like children. He might have cut himself off from other people by living on this mountain. But Christmas was a time for families. And he had come back to spend it with them.

"I see you've been busy." Stony gestured with his free hand at the decorations and the tree. "Where did you get all this stuff?"

"The greenery I found on the mountain. The rest is ours," she said. "Harry DuBois brought it out here for us."

He frowned. It obviously hadn't yet occurred to him that she would have had to call someone to take her in to the doctor to have her cast removed. She saw the moment it did.

"I never thought about you needing a way to get around," he said. "I guess I should have."

"Harry was wonderful about helping me out when I needed to run errands. I could have called 911 in an emergency," she said.

His hand tightened on hers. It was an act of possession.

"You're hurting me," she said quietly.

His hold instantly loosened. But he didn't let her go.

"How soon before that stew is ready?" he asked.

"A couple of hours. I was just putting Rose down for a

quick nap before supper.'' She smiled ruefully. ''I'm afraid that's out of the question now.''

He arched a dark brow. ''What if I read to her? Do you think she'd lie down then?''

''You'd do that?''

He gave her a roguish grin. ''How long does it usually take Rose to fall asleep?''

She realized suddenly why he wanted Rose in bed. So he could take her to his.

''How would you like for me to read to you?'' he asked Rose.

''Will you be the big bad wolf?'' Rose asked.

''How's this?'' Stony growled menacingly in his throat.

Rose shrieked in mock fright and raced for the bedroom.

Stony winked at Tess and headed after the little girl. ''I'll see you in a few minutes.''

Tess suspected Stony's estimate was optimistic. As excited as Rose was, it would be a little longer than a few minutes before he returned. But she had better use whatever time she had to decide how she was going to handle the situation once she and Stony were alone.

She chewed on her thumbnail worriedly. She didn't believe Stony would force his attentions on her. Unfortunately he wouldn't have to use force. She had felt her body respond to his mere presence in the bedroom doorway, to the heat of him, the scent of him, the predatory look in his dark brown eyes.

To be honest, she had fantasized over the past weeks, as she had slept in the twin bed next to her daughter, what it would be like to spend the night in Stony's arms. If he beckoned, it would be difficult to refuse him.

But they would be two strangers having sex, not two lovers making love. It was tempting to imagine herself lying beneath Stony in his bed, but she wasn't sure she would be able to face herself in the morning. Her husband had been the only lover she had ever had. And though they hadn't been married when they made love for the first time, she had been deeply in love with him.

It had happened on a hot summer night, on a blanket laid out on the prairie grass with the sky and stars above them. She had been so frightened and so very excited, because she loved Charlie so much. She had trusted him not to hurt her. Only, it had hurt that first time, and it had never been as good for her as it was for him. But she had wanted to please Charlie, wanted him to love her as nobody else ever had. He had been a cowboy for one of the ranches in the area, much older than her—twenty-three—and, she had thought, much wiser.

But Charlie hadn't used any protection, not that first time, and not later. She was equally responsible for what had happened. She accepted that now. But her foster parents had been sorely disappointed in her when she told them she was pregnant and had kicked her out of their house. If Charlie hadn't married her, she didn't know what she would have done.

She understood the male need for sex because her husband had possessed it. She had not understood that a woman could feel the same…hunger. That was the only word that described what she was feeling—had been feeling over the past six weeks—for Stony Carlton. She was surprised because she knew she couldn't possibly be in love with him. She hardly knew him. But she was attracted to him in a way she had never been attracted to any other man, even her husband.

She had heard it said that for each person there was a perfect mate, that somewhere in the world the other half was wandering, waiting to be found. She felt that way about Stony, that he was her other half, and that she had to fit herself to him, make him a part of herself, or she would never be complete.

Yet she shied from joining herself with a man she didn't love. It seemed…ruthless, heartless, unfeeling.

Not unfeeling. She was feeling entirely too much. Her body sang with excitement. Her skin tingled. Her breasts felt achy. Her belly curled with desire.

She stood and paced the living room, like a mountain lion in a cage. She wanted him. But she would be damned if she would give in to such animal urges. She was a rational human being. She should be able to act in a cool and rational manner.

She would tell him no. And she would mean it.

She turned abruptly as Stony appeared in the hallway that led into the living room. He stopped where he was, and she had the sense of being prey, of being hunted. She looked around and realized there was no escape. She had to go through him to get to the front door of the house. Not that she could leave without Rose. And he knew it. Knew she was trapped. She saw it in the merciless smile that curled his lips.

"Hello, Tess," he said.

His rumbling voice skittered over her spine and made her shiver. "No," she said.

He quirked a dark brow. "I haven't asked for anything. Yet."

She shoved a wayward curl behind her ear and huffed out a breath of air. Her palms were damp, and she rubbed them down the sides of her jeans, then curled her arms around herself protectively.

"You feel it, don't you?" he said.

"No."

His eyes crinkled at the corners as his smile broadened. "I can hardly believe it myself," he confessed. "I swore off women a while back. You've made me rethink my decision."

"We're strangers," she said pointedly.

He shook his head slowly, the smile suddenly gone.

"We've never been strangers, Tess. We've known each other forever."

So he felt it, too. Whatever it was. That strange connection between them, urging their bodies together, promising a wholeness, a joining of souls.

Yet, she fought it. Because it couldn't possibly be right to have sex—it could only be sex—with this man she hardly knew.

"I want you," he said as he took a step toward her.

She held her ground.

"I haven't been able to think of anything but you." He took another step.

She searched for an escape route, a means of avoiding him. There wasn't any. Her body quivered as she stood still, waiting.

"I need you," he said, his voice guttural, animal. His eyes were lambent, lit by a fire that heated her inside. He took the last step that brought them into contact. "I have to have you."

She moaned as his arms slid around her and pulled their bodies together. She felt her breasts crushed against his hard chest even as his palm curved around her buttocks and lifted her until her hips fit into the cradle of his, against the hard, thick length of him.

Her hands rested on his shoulders, yet she couldn't summon the strength of will to push him away. It felt so good to be held by him, so impossibly right!

"This is crazy," she said at the same time she laid her head back so he could more easily kiss her throat. His lips and teeth and tongue feasted on her flesh, sending shivers of sensation shuddering through her body.

She grasped his hair, intending to free herself, but clung to him as his mouth captured hers, his tongue probing until she let him inside.

And then she was lost.

His hips thrust against her in time with the movement of

his tongue in and out of her mouth. She groaned and arched her body upward, needing to be closer, resenting the layers of denim and cotton that separated them. His hand slid between her legs, and he lifted her nearly off the ground. His thumb caressed her until she gasped, as he found the spot he had been seeking.

She reached for him with her mouth, needing to be closer, to be connected to him. Then her tongue was in his mouth, tasting him, teasing his inner lip, biting at his lower lip until he growled deep in his throat.

They began tearing the clothes off each other, couldn't get them off fast enough. Buttons popped, clattering across the hardwood floor, zippers came down, T-shirts were ripped off until they stood naked before each other.

His eyes were heavy-lidded, his gaze feral, the pupils huge, making his eyes dark black pools into which she might fall and never return. His body was surprisingly tanned, lean, but muscular, with sinews visible in his arms and shoulders. His belly was flat, his chest furred with black hair that became a narrow black line leading to the curly bush that surrounded his genitals.

Her gaze rose to his. She was panting, unable to catch her breath. Frightened. And exhilarated.

It was going to happen. He was going to claim her. He was going to make her his.

She felt her knees weaken, nature's way of making sure the female was prone, so the male seed could take root. He caught her before she fell and lifted her into his arms, holding her tight against his chest.

She hadn't given a thought to where they were, the fact that her daughter could waken and come upon them.

He carried her to his bedroom, to the king size bed that hadn't been slept in since he had left. He pulled down the covers and laid her on the cool sheets, following her down until he lay atop her. He nudged her legs apart with his knees and put his hand between her thighs to touch her.

She flinched at his touch, though it was gentle. It was almost embarrassing how wet and ready she was. His touch made her even more so.

She stared up at him, wondering what it was about this particular man that made her so vulnerable to him. He reached into the bedside table and found the protection she hadn't thought about.

*He really doesn't like children,* she thought.

But she was grateful he was taking the precautions that had been the farthest thing from her mind. She knew better. She knew the consequences of being foolish and in love.

Well, she was certainly foolish, anyway.

He spread her hair on the pillow around her face, playing with it, caressing it between his fingertips.

"It's softer than I thought it would be. Because of all those curls," he explained with a smile that made her heart beat faster.

She slid her hands through his hair. "Yours is soft, too." She tugged his head toward her, wanting his mouth on hers.

The kiss was long and slow and deep. Her body arched upward into his, an itch seeking to be scratched.

His hand curved around her breast, and she made an animal sound at the feel of his callused fingertips on her flesh. He cupped the soft mound and held it steady for his mouth. He sipped at her, licked and bit and licked again. Then he suckled her, drawing her nipple into his mouth.

She nearly came off the bed.

He spread her legs with his knees once more and placed himself at the entrance to her. She expected him to thrust quickly, but he took his time, entering her a little way and then backing off, only to return and probe a little deeper, until at last she reached up with her legs around him and urged him inside to the hilt.

He gave a satisfied sigh as he sank into her that was matched by a guttural sound of her own.

Then he turned her face up, so she would be looking into

his eyes and began to thrust, in and out, slow at first, and then faster, as his thumb played with her between their sweat-slick bodies.

She began to writhe beneath him, and her eyelids floated downward. She had never felt like this. She couldn't seem to control her body. It began to contract, to spasm in a way that was both frightening and immensely pleasurable. She fought the lack of control, fought the loss of self.

"Look at me, Tess," he commanded. "Come with me," he urged.

She opened her eyes and met his gaze, fierce and intense, deep and dark as a well. She began to slide into the darkness where there was nothing but joy, the two of them no longer separate but joined as one euphoric being.

"You belong to me," he said triumphantly. "You'll always be mine."

It was the last thing she heard before the darkness consumed her.

# *Chapter Four*

THE LOVEMAKING Stony had just experienced far surpassed anything he had ever known with a woman. But he had no idea what had possessed him to utter those unbelievable words at the moment of climax.

*"You belong to me. You'll always be mine."*

He had to be out of his mind. For years he had been a loner who didn't need anyone. He had no reason to marry, because he never intended to have children. What had made him stake his claim on Tess Lowell—a woman who came packaged with a three-year-old imp?

He hardly knew the woman.

He felt like he had known her all his life.

It had to be lust that had prompted his behavior. He had desired her, so he had taken her to bed. Now that his need was slaked he would be fine.

Only, he wanted her again already, and they had just finished a bout of lovemaking that was indescribably satisfying. He couldn't imagine not wanting her tomorrow and the day after that. So maybe it was something more than lust. But what?

He raised himself on his elbow so he could watch Tess while she slept. The curls around her face were damp with sweat, and her lips were swollen, pouty from his kisses. He had left a love bruise on her throat. He slowly trailed the sheet away, so he could look at all of her.

It was, after all, only another female body. He had seen his share of them. Why did he find this one so exquisite? Nipples the pink of prairie roses. Breasts full and exactly the right size for him. A slightly rounded stomach. The deep russet curls between her legs. And, oh, those legs! He liked the way she had wrapped them around him, her heels digging into his buttocks, demanding to have him inside her.

He was aroused again merely looking at her.

He wasn't sure what he should do about the situation. He had never wanted anyone to love him because he had no intention of giving love in return. Loving left you vulnerable. He had vowed when his father abandoned him never to give anyone the chance to hurt him that way again. It was safer not to ask for love. It was safer to be alone. Even if it was occasionally lonely.

Good Lord! Did he want her to love him?

No, of course not. Though she didn't yet know it, he was the one responsible for making her a widow. Better not to let his thoughts wander in a hopeless direction.

But he had no intention of letting Tess go anytime soon. Even though he could never let himself love her. Even if all they could ever have together was fantastic sex.

Her eyelids fluttered open, and he watched her eyes fill with tears. He kissed away the first salty drop before it could reach the pillow. "What's wrong?"

"I...I don't understand what compelled me to do such a thing. I hardly know you." She suddenly realized she was naked before him and scrambled to cover herself.

"Don't," he said, catching her wrist and preventing her from drawing the sheet back over her. "I like looking at you. You're beautiful."

"I'm not. I have stretch marks. And my legs—"

"Are perfect." He smiled. "All of you is perfect." He hadn't noticed the stretch marks. He searched for them and found them along her hips, silvery lines where her flesh had stretched to accommodate a baby. He had a fleeting picture of her grown huge with his child and brushed it away.

"We have to get dressed," she said. "Rose will be waking soon."

"Don't worry. I locked the door. She can't get in."

A rueful smile appeared before she said, "You don't know Rose. She'll stand at the door and yell until we let her in."

"All right. We'll get up. Soon."

She started to rise, but he levered himself over her and kissed her deep and hard. It only took a moment before he was protected and inside her again. He saw her flush and realized she had been wet and hot and ready for him.

She had wanted him again, too.

He threaded his fingers through hers and held her hands prisoner above her head as he slowly thrust into her. He stared into her eyes, willing her to accept his claim. Her chin trembled, and her eyes grew liquid with feeling.

"This was meant to be," he said. "The two of us together. Don't fight it, Tess."

She groaned and arched upward, raising her breasts to him, an offering fit for the gods. He supped, drinking the heady wine she offered him.

"Please," she begged. "Please."

He knew what she wanted. He gave it to her.

Himself. All of himself, enough to make two halves into one whole. Enough to fill them both full. Enough to take them to paradise again.

* * *

*I NEED HIM. I want him. I never want to leave him.*

They were the first thoughts Tess had when she surfaced from a deep well of pleasure for the second time in as many hours. They frightened her.

All she had ever wanted her whole life was to be loved, to belong to someone who would need her as much as she needed him. She had needed and loved each set of foster parents who had taken her in. But the most she had ever received in return was adequate care. She had never been mistreated; but she had never been loved, either.

She thought she had learned her lesson: not to give her love where it wasn't wanted, not to lay herself open to the pain that came inevitably when she had to acknowledge she wasn't loved in return. Even with Charlie—heaven forgive him—she had known her love was not returned.

He had wanted her body, and he had been honorable enough to marry her when she had gotten pregnant. But Charlie had never loved her. He had been incapable of the emotion.

Here she was making the same mistake again. She didn't want to feel what she was feeling. But she didn't know how to stop. She turned and stared at Stony, who was sleeping beside her. She had to get out of here before she let this man sneak past her guard and into her heart.

He didn't like children. He liked living alone. He had no room in his life for her and her child. She would be a fool to trust another man, to give her heart to him. Especially this one.

She had asked Harry about Stony Carlton and gotten few answers. Stony wasn't a lawman, yet he hunted outlaws—rustlers—for a living. She wondered if he knew all about her husband's activities. Her thoughts shied away from contemplating such a possibility. It was better not to know.

Theirs was clearly a relationship doomed at the start. Yet she had let it start. Better to end it now, before she got hurt. Although, there would be hurt, even now. Because, though she wouldn't have wished it, would never have dreamed it, this lonely man already possessed a part of her soul...the part that had been missing all her life.

Tess dressed quickly and left quietly, closing Stony's bedroom door behind her. She was relieved that Rose wasn't yet awake and took advantage of the slight respite to spend some time alone in the living room.

She sat cross-legged on the comfortable sofa in front of the wood stove and watched the flames flickering inside the glass door.

She should leave.

Only, where would she go? Her situation hadn't changed one iota since she had accepted Stony's charitable job offer. She didn't want to continue imposing on him now that she was well. But she had tried to find a job in town once the cast was off her arm and discovered there was no job to be had until the season began. She was stuck here until spring.

She felt Stony's presence before she heard him. She supposed a man used to sneaking up on rustlers had to be able to move quietly. It irritated her nonetheless that she hadn't heard him coming. Although, when all was said and done, there was nowhere she could run.

She turned and found him standing right behind her dressed in nothing more than a pair of jeans. He had left the top button undone, and it was plain he wasn't wearing anything beneath them. The aged denim hugged his body like a glove, revealing the vivid outline of his arousal.

She wrenched her gaze away and turned to stare at the fire.

"We have to talk," he said, vaulting over the couch and settling softly beside her, his legs crossed Indian style.

She was aware of him, the heat of him, the musky male scent of him. "I have nowhere to go—"

"—or you'd leave," he finished for her.

"Yes, I would," she said, her chin jutting. "This... thing...between us is...disturbing."

"What if I said I understand what you're feeling?"

She glanced at him quizzically. "You do?"

"Something...unusual...has happened—is happening—between us."

"Something magical," she said quietly, almost wistfully.

His gaze softened as he met her eyes. "You felt it, too?"

She nodded, then ruffled her hair with her hands. "It doesn't make sense."

"All I know is I don't want you to leave right now," he said.

Her lips twisted cynically. "Lucky for you, I can't get another job until the season begins in the spring."

He smiled. "That settles it, then. You'll stay."

"But this...thing...between us... What are we going to do about it?"

"If this is something we both want, I don't see why we can't enjoy each other—take physical pleasure from each other—without letting it go any further than that. I don't want a wife."

"Or kids," she reminded him.

"Or kids," he agreed. "But I do want you."

"And I want you," she admitted. "So we merely take what physical pleasure we can from each other for a few weeks or months without any other commitment between us?"

"I don't see why not," Stony said.

Tess saw more than a few pitfalls in his plan, but she looked at him and realized she wanted to feel again the wholeness she experienced when he held her in his arms. "All right," she said. "Until spring. Agreed?"

"Agreed."

She held out her hand, and he took it. Electricity arced up her arm. She tugged her hand free and stood, needing to put some distance between them before they ended up in bed again.

"When's supper?" he asked. "I'm hungry."

"I'm hungry, too," Rose said, appearing in the doorway to the kitchen.

"You're barefoot again, young lady," Stony admonished.

Rose yelped and raced back toward the bedroom.

"Where's she going?" Stony asked.

"To get socks, I imagine," Tess said with a smile.

"Can she get them on by herself?"

"I'll have to help her. The sock drawer's too high for her to reach."

"You're busy," Stony said, rising from the sofa. "I'll do it."

Tess arched a disbelieving brow. "You don't like kids," she reminded him.

"Yeah, well, I'd like it even less if she got sick. Besides, I'm hungry, and you're putting supper on the table." He winked, a charming gesture that made her heart flutter. "I think I can handle it."

It was impossible not to smile back at him. "Be my guest," she said.

Stony didn't hurry down the hall because he knew Rose would be there waiting for him. He hadn't counted on the little girl's resourcefulness. She had pulled out the bottom drawer of the chest and was standing on it in order to reach the top drawer of the chest, which she had managed to open. The whole chest was in danger of tipping over onto her.

"Rose!" he said, his voice harsh with fear.

She leaned back, startled. Her weight, added to that of the open drawers, was all it took for the chest to begin its tumble.

He snatched her off her precarious perch and caught the falling chest with his hip. He grunted in pain as everything on top came thumping down onto the braided rug.

"What's going on in there?" Tess called from the kitchen. "Is everything all right?"

"Everything's fine," Stony called. "Hunky dory," he muttered under his breath. He clutched Rose tight while he gave his adrenaline-laced heart a chance to slow down. His hip throbbed where the chest had caught on the bone. He leaned his weight back to force the chest upright.

"What's hunk-dory?" Rose asked, apparently oblivious to the danger she had been in.

"It means you nearly got killed, but you didn't," Stony retorted as he shoved in the bottom drawer of the chest with his bare foot. He shifted her onto his arm so he could look her in the eye. "You should've asked for help. You could've been hurt."

"I was getting socks," she said in a small voice, "like you said."

Which made the whole thing his fault, he supposed. It surprised him to realize he cared enough about her to be worried that something might happen when he wasn't around to keep an eye on her.

She pointed to the mess on the floor. "Everything fell down," she said, her chin trembling.

"Yeah, well, nothing's broken," he said gruffly. "We can put it all back again." He knew he was an idiot to be trying to placate a three-year-old, but there wasn't anyone around to catch him at it, so he could do as he pleased.

She wriggled, her sign to be let down, picked up a pewter bookend and handed it to him. "Here," she said. "I can help put it all back."

They worked together over the next several minutes. He picked Rose up at her insistence so she could rearrange everything to her liking on top of the chest. By the time they were done, she was smiling again. Seeing that smile made him feel ten feet tall. It was ridiculous to let her under his skin. Especially when she wasn't going to be hanging around very long. But he didn't call Tess to come get her kid. Hell, he was enjoying himself.

"You still need socks, young lady," he said, folding his free hand around her ice cold toes.

She giggled. "Can you do piggies?"

"Do what?"

"You know. Piggies."

He was afraid he did know. It sounded like fun. But he wasn't going to let her make a substitute father out of him. "You need socks," he repeated.

He opened the top drawer and pulled out a pair of pink socks.

"Not those," she said firmly.

"What's wrong with these?"

"I want the ones with Mickey Mouse."

Stony started to argue with her, saw the mulish cast of her mouth and changed his mind. Tess would be wondering what had happened to them. He searched through the whole drawer and came up empty. "There are no socks in here with Mickey Mouse on them."

"Where are they?" she demanded.

"How should I know?" Frantic to avoid the tantrum he could see coming, he grabbed a pair of socks with white lace and pink bows along the edge. "How about these?"

Her eyes widened, and she said with three-year-old reverence, "Those are only for Sunday school." And then, "They're my very favorite."

"You want 'em, you got 'em, kid." He sat down on the bed and tugged the socks on, despite the resistance of her curling toes.

Rose looked first at the lacy socks and then up at him with something akin to awe. He felt absurdly delighted to have pleased her so well. He took her hand and headed back down the hall. "Come on. Let's go see your mom."

The first words out of Tess's mouth when she saw the two of them was, "Those are her Sunday school socks. She'll ruin them if she walks around in them without shoes."

"I'll buy her another pair," Stony said, exchanging a glance with Rose, who beamed back at him.

"I don't want you spending your money on us," Tess countered.

"It's only a pair of socks," he argued.

"Maybe to you it's only a pair of socks," Tess said, meeting his gaze. "To me it's an hour of work behind a counter." She turned to Rose and said, "Go put on a pair of shoes. Now."

Rose turned to Stony. "Do I have to?"

Stony saw the alarm on Tess's face at this clear sign of rebellion in the ranks. His own mother had died when he was very young, so his father's word had always been law. Now he saw what might have happened if his mother had lived. When there were two adults in a child's life, there was room for appeal. Only, Rose wasn't his daughter, and he had no right to be making decisions that affected her life.

"Do as your mother says, Rose. She's the boss."

To his surprise, Rose didn't argue, just stomped her way back to the bedroom.

He let Rose go, then had an awful thought. "Where do you keep her shoes?"

"On the floor of the closet," Tess replied.

He heaved a sigh of relief. At least she couldn't knock anything over. He realized he was worrying about her—as if she was his responsibility or something. Which she wasn't. And never would be.

But he was plagued with guilt at the thought of how dire Tess's circumstances must be if she had to be careful not to ruin a pair of child's socks. It was small solace that her husband would probably be in jail now, if he weren't dead. Perhaps a good lawyer might have gotten Charlie Lowell off with a short sentence. Perhaps he would already have been out of prison and back helping his family.

They needed help from someone. For a while, so long as Tess and Rose stayed, it might as well be him.

IN THE MONTHS that followed, whenever he went out hunting the ever-elusive rustlers, Stony wore the navy blue mittens and scarf Tess had knitted and given him for Christmas. When he was home, he spent his days playing in the snow with Rose, and his nights loving Tess.

If he let himself think about it at all, Stony had supposed Tess would have less time for him because of the child. It had been that way with his father. Time and attention given to his new family had taken away from time and attention given to him.

Somehow, Tess managed to make him feel a part of the time the three of them spent together. Her warmth and joy enfolded both him and the child. The jealousy he had expected to feel toward Rose—akin to the shameful resentment he had felt toward his halfbrother—never materialized. He wondered if it was because he didn't want or need Tess's attention as much as he had wanted or needed his father's love.

Actually the opposite was true. What he needed from Tess far exceeded the care and respect he had wanted from his father. It dawned on him as he lay in bed with her spooned against his groin, his arm under her breasts, that he wanted her love.

The thought terrified him.

What if Tess was like his father? Would he always come second behind the child? Would he always end up with whatever love—and time—was left over after she had given to Rose first. It was selfish to want Tess's love all to himself. But he did.

He was unaware he had made a disgusted sound in his throat.

"What's wrong?" Tess whispered into the darkness. She

turned in his arms and pressed herself against him. His body instantly hardened.

"Don't, Tess." He didn't want to need her any more than he already did.

"What's wrong?" she asked.

He heard the caring in her voice. She had plenty of time for him now. Rose was sound asleep. "I don't want to talk about it."

She sat up. "You've been moping around for the past three days. You might as well tell me what's troubling you. Neither of us is going to get any sleep until you do."

"It's nothing," he insisted.

"Fine," she said turning her back on him. "Keep it to yourself."

When he tried to put his arm around her, she shoved him away and said, "Leave me alone."

Here at last was the rejection he had expected from her all along. He refused to accept it.

"Don't turn away from me, Tess."

Tess heard the longing in his voice and recognized the need for what it was.

"Oh, Stony." She turned back into his waiting arms, pressing herself against him. And felt the fire ignite between them as it always did.

She tried not to let her love show, tried not to give too much of herself. When Stony thrust inside her she arched into him. When his mouth captured hers, she surrendered to his passion. When their bodies joined at last, she knew her soul was lost. To a man who didn't want to love her, a lone wolf who couldn't be caged.

# Chapter Five

STONY HAD REALIZED over the course of the winter that he couldn't live without Tess. He resented the time he had to spend away from her hunting down rustlers. He was ready to admit he needed her in his life. However, he had some daunting hurdles to get over before that was possible.

He had to tell Tess that he was the man who had killed her husband. And he had to come to terms with the fact that he would always have to share her with Rose, in the same way he had been forced to share his father with a half brother. Both obstacles loomed, seemingly insurmountable, before him. The need to resolve them consumed his waking moments and haunted his dreams.

He knew Tess was aware of his distraction, yet she didn't confront him about it. He was glad, because he had no idea how he could explain why he had kept his part in her husband's death a secret from her all these months. He was living a lie. Unfortunately he knew exactly how Tess felt about lies.

The second time he had returned to his cabin, having left

it to return to Jackson following his brief Christmas holiday
with Tess and Rose, he had found things achingly familiar,
even to the savory stew bubbling on the stove.

At supper he had said, "I don't know when my house
has ever seemed so much like a home. Thank you, Tess."

She had blushed, those marvelous roses appearing in her
cheeks. "Do you mean it, Stony? Really?"

"I don't lie. Especially about important things."

"That means a lot to me," she said, her eyes downcast.
He thought she wasn't going to explain herself, but the rest
of it came tumbling out. "I was devastated when I found
out that Charlie had been lying to me—about the rustling,
I mean. To this day, it's the one thing I can't forgive him."

He had felt a pang of remorse at the lie of omission he
was perpetrating. *Tess, there's something I have to tell you.
I killed your husband.* The words were on the tip of his
tongue. He could hear himself saying them. They remained
unspoken.

Surely, when the time came to tell Tess everything, he
would find a way to make her understand why he had kept
the truth from her. Fear of what she might say and do when
she learned his part in her husband's death upset his stomach. He had laid down his fork, the pleasant meal abruptly
ended.

During the past four months, the right time had never
come to confess. The longer the lie lay between them, the
more difficult it became to tell her the truth.

He was running out of time. The snow was melting off
the mountain. It was already gone in town. Soon the tourists
would begin to arrive, and Tess would leave him to return
to her life in town.

Unless he could make things right about what had happened with her husband. Unless he could offer love, even
when it meant accepting second place to someone else in
her life.

Stony turned on his side in bed and stared at Tess in the

early golden light of morning. She was more beautiful to him than ever. And infinitely precious. He should wake her up and confess the truth.

Now was not the right time, either. He had gotten a call last night, a lead on the rustlers who had proved so elusive all winter. He was closing in on them. He had to leave this morning and return to Jackson. He didn't know how long he would be gone.

He lay back down and folded his hands behind his head, staring at the ceiling. He was going to lose her. Deep in his gut he knew it, and he was bone-deep scared.

One second the room was silent. The next, a tornado of energy came whirling in. Rose's pajama-clad behind plopped down on his stomach, and her hands landed flat against his bare chest. He gave a *"woof"* as the air in his diaphragm was pushed out by the weight of her. She rubbed her nose against his and said, "Good morning, Stony."

Her visits had become a morning ritual. After the first nearly embarrassing episode several months ago, he had stopped sleeping naked. It was a small enough sacrifice to enjoy the light she brought with her each morning.

"Hi there, little bit," he said. "What's up?"

"Is it spring yet?" she asked, glancing out the window.

Snow from an early March storm was melting from the tin roof, dripping off the eaves. "Almost," he said.

"You promised to let me ride a pony when spring comes."

"So I did." He rubbed his morning beard. There was no putting it off. "I have to leave for a while, Rose. I have to go chase the bad men again."

She frowned, a ferocious glare worthy of the vilest villain in a penny dreadful. "I don't want you to go."

A sudden lump formed in his throat. He didn't want to go, either. How had Rose become so dear to him when he harbored such resentment against her for the place in her mother's heart she stole from him? It was hard not to be enchanted by Rose, who gave love freely and demanded nothing in return.

She bounced up and down on his stomach. "Don't go. Don't go. Don't go," she chanted.

He grabbed her hips to save his solar plexus. "I won't be gone long. And when I come back, it will be spring."

"Promise? And I can ride a pony?"

"I promise. And you can ride a pony."

"Yippee!" The bouncing started again, as though she were already on the horse, a wild bucking bronc.

"Whoa, there, cowgirl! Wait until you have the horse under you." He slid Rose onto the bed between them, tickling her once he had her down. She giggled delightedly. It was all part of the game between them.

Rose turned to Tess, who by now was always awake and leaning on her elbow with a grin on her face, watching their antics.

"I'm hungry, Mama," Rose said.

"Breakfast will be ready as soon as you put on the clothes I left at the foot of your bed last night," Tess said.

Rose hugged her mother and got a kiss on both cheeks and the tip of her nose before she disappeared into her own bedroom to dress.

Stony proceeded with the next part of the ritual, which involved him and Tess and a few drugging early-morning kisses that occasionally turned into hard, fast and unbelievably satisfying sex. But not this morning.

Tess leaned back and searched his face, looking for something.

"What is it?" he asked.

"Remind me what it is, precisely, that you don't like about kids," she said.

His eyes shuttered immediately. This was forbidden territory, and she knew it.

"Don't shut me out, Stony. Talk to me."

"What is it you want me to say?"

"Explain why you profess not to like kids when I can see with my own eyes how good you are with Rose."

He sat up against the headboard and shoved an irritated hand through his hair. He couldn't tell her about the lie. Maybe he could tell her about this. "It's not something I'm proud of," he admitted, hoping that would be enough to placate her.

"Can you tell me what it is? Will you?" she persisted.

It came out in a rush, before he could stop himself. "My mom died when I was little, and it was just my dad and me. He must have missed my mom a lot, because after she was gone, he lost himself in his work. He never had any time to spend with me. So I spent my time alone.

"When I was thirteen, my dad remarried and started a second family. He changed his priorities. My half brother, Todd, suddenly got all the attention I'd been yearning for ever since my mother's death." He shrugged. "That's it."

He was amazed at her perception when she said, "I see. Oh, I see. Why you profess you don't like children, I mean. You resented sharing your father's love with a baby."

"I don't want to share you," he said, the words torn from him almost against his will.

"Oh, Stony." Tess slipped her arms around Stony's waist and laid her head against his chest, where she could hear his heart madly thumping.

"Don't you know love is boundless?" she said quietly. "It doesn't have limits. I can love Rose and still have more than enough left over for you."

It was an admission of love, of sorts. Even that was more than Tess had intended to say. Yet, she knew Stony had needed to hear her say it.

"Leftovers," he grumbled, pulling her tightly, possessively, against him.

She hesitated only a second before plunging even farther into dangerous waters. "No. Not leftovers. I love you differently than Rose. She's my own flesh and blood. I feel responsibility and delight and devotion when I look at her.

"But you, Stony. You're the other half of me. I've been looking for you all my life. I love you with every particle of my being."

His arms tightened until she thought her ribs would crack. She waited to hear the words from him, needed to hear them. She silently begged the wary wolf to take the few steps necessary to reach the hand she had held out to him.

"God, I love you, Tess."

She felt her nose burn and tears sting her eyes. She clutched at him, a sob of joy clogging her throat. "Oh, Stony. I love you so much."

"What about me?" Rose demanded. She stood beside the bed fully dressed, her shirt on inside out, tugging at the sheet that covered them.

Tess looked at Stony, and they grinned at each other. He reached down and scooped Rose up in one arm and pulled her close to include her in their hug.

"I love you, too, Rose," he said, his dark eyes focused on Tess.

Tess knew what it meant for him to make such an admission. Knew it was only the beginning for them all. There would be no need for her and Rose to leave now. The future loomed before them, bright and shining.

"Are you going to be my daddy?" Rose said.

Tess looked to Stony for his answer, her heart in her eyes. *Say yes,* she willed him. *We come together as a package. It won't mean leftovers. I have plenty of love for both of you.*

He cleared his throat before he spoke, prolonging the moment, a wary wolf until the very end. Then he surprised her, because she had really thought he was going to say yes.

He said maybe.

"We'll see, Rose," Stony said. "We'll have to see."

Tess was startled—almost alarmed—at how quickly Stony extricated himself from their cozy cuddle. "What's the hurry?" she asked.

"I've got to get going," he said. "I have to be in Jackson by noon."

Since it was early morning and Jackson Hole only an hour's drive away, his excuse didn't make much sense. Maybe everything was moving too fast. Maybe he didn't trust her not to give him leftover love. Or maybe he was being forced into a commitment he didn't really want to make. Whatever it was, she felt the lone wolf retreating from her.

"Why don't you go into the kitchen and get out the orange juice," she said to Rose. "Then wait for me, and I'll help you pour it into the glasses."

"Okay, Mama," Rose said.

Tess heard her trotting down the hall. "Can you drop me off in town before you leave?" she asked Stony. "I have some errands to run. I can get a ride back from Harry."

"Why is Harry so willing to give you all these rides?" he said, stepping out of bed and yanking on a pair of jeans.

"Because he's my friend," she said. "Why else?" She got out of bed herself, because that was no place to argue with a man.

"I don't know," he said, plainly irritated as he buttoned up his fly. "Why don't you tell me?"

"Are you trying to start an argument?" she asked, fisted hands perched on her hips. "Because if you are, I'll be more than happy to give you one."

"Am I about to see that famous redheaded temper of yours?" he snarled. "I've been waiting four months for it to erupt. I knew it was only a matter of time."

He was purposely provoking her, but she couldn't seem to stop herself. "I suppose you don't have any foibles."

"My foibles never bothered anybody when I lived alone."

"That can easily be arranged again!" She shot the words back. She was heartsick, listening to herself. She didn't want to leave him. She loved him. But he must want her to leave. Otherwise, he would never have started this argument. Unless there was something else.

"What's wrong, Stony? What is it you aren't telling me?"

*Tell her now! Dammit, tell her.*

He couldn't. He was too scared. Happiness of a kind he had never imagined was in his grasp. He couldn't take the chance of losing it.

"Dammit, what do you want from me?" he raged.

"I want an answer!" she retorted, easily as infuriated as he was.

He grabbed her arms and pulled her to him, capturing her mouth with his, his tongue thrusting possessively between her teeth. His palms cupped her buttocks, and he dragged her up the front of him until his hard length was pressed against her. She wasn't nearly close enough. He jerked her panties down, tore open the buttons of his jeans and shoved down his underwear until he was free.

He lifted her legs around his hips and thrust inside her, deep and tight. He gripped her buttocks as he drove into her, hard and fast, reaching a climax only seconds later.

He felt the weight of her as his senses returned. She was trembling in his arms. Her breathing was as ragged as his, and he could see the rapid pulse pounding in her throat.

He eased her legs away from his sides and disengaged them, because his knees were threatening to buckle.

It was only then he realized he hadn't used a condom.

He always used a condom. Because he didn't want kids, didn't like kids. Only, Tess had made him realize that was another lie. One he had told himself for years.

"Tess, I..."

"Don't say anything."

"I'm sorry," he said anyway.

Her eyes slid closed, and she clung to him. It took him a moment to realize her knees were threatening to buckle, too.

"Sit down before you fall down," he said, urging her onto the bed. He rearranged his clothing and picked up her silky underwear from the floor where it had fallen and handed it to her. When she didn't take it, he dropped it on the bed beside her.

She sat unmoving. Silent.

He didn't know what had come over him to make him take her like that, without warning. Her continued silence scared him even worse than her anger. "Tess, we'll talk about this when I get back, all right?"

She didn't answer him.

He gripped her chin and forced her to look at him. "You'll be here when I get back." It was an order. One he was afraid she would defy.

She remained mute.

He let go of her chin, and paced before her like an animal in a cage. "Look, I couldn't stand the thought of Harry DuBois pawing you like your boss."

She looked up at him, her brow deeply furrowed. "Harry is nothing like Bud. He's my friend. That's all we are to each other."

"Then you'll come back here and wait for me after you've finished your errands in town?" he asked anxiously.

"You'll have to give me a ride into town first," she said with the beginning of a smile.

"About...about what happened," he said, his hand plowing its way through his hair. "I...I don't know what came over me."

She glanced up at him coyly. "If I didn't know better, I'd think you were jealous of Harry DuBois."

He grabbed at the excuse she had given him for his behavior and managed a sheepish grin. Maybe he had been a little jealous. "You belong to me," he said. "Be here, Tess."

"I'll be here when you get back," she promised.

TESS HAD fully intended to keep her promise to Stony when she made it. She hadn't counted on finding out the dreadful secret he had kept from her for more than four months.

*Stony had killed Charlie.*

She had gone to Harry's office to ask for a ride home, and he had seen the love bruise on her throat that Stony had put there during their tempestuous lovemaking that morning.

"Why do you stay with him, Tess?" Harry demanded. "I've told you time and again the man's dangerous."

"Not to me," she replied with a smug smile. "Come on, Harry," she said, slipping her arm through his. "Have a piece of pie with me at the Buttermilk Café before I pick up Rose from Mrs. Feeny. Then you can drive us home."

"All right, Tess. Against my better judgment, I'll give you a ride back up to his place."

They were settled in a booth with a slice of the buttermilk pie for which the café was famous in front of them when Harry said, "How soon do you think you'll be coming back to town? There's an apartment coming available in the complex over by the hospital next week."

"I don't think I'll be coming back to town," Tess said.

"You'll have to, once you get a job."

"I don't think I'll be looking for a job in Pinedale."

"What are you talking about?" Harry asked. "What's going on, Tess?"

"I think I'll be staying at Stony's cabin. With him."

"You'd actually consider living with him indefinitely? When you won't even consider a marriage proposal from me. Explain that to me, Tess."

Tess flushed. "He loves me, Harry. And I love him."

"You know nothing about the man!" Harry snarled, keeping his voice down to avoid being overheard by the growing lunch crowd in the café.

"I know everything that's important to know about him."

"Like the fact he killed your husband?" Harry snapped.

Tess's heart actually stopped beating for an instant. "That's…" She started to say impossible, but she had known for months that Stony hunted rustlers for a living. She settled instead for, "Unbelievable."

"Believe it," Harry said. "I don't understand why he never told you himself. I didn't think he had, or you wouldn't be in love with the man."

"He…he was only doing his job." She hated herself for defending Stony, when what she wanted to do was rage at him. She closed her eyes and gritted her teeth to try to stop her chin from trembling.

Why hadn't Stony told her? He couldn't care for her feelings very much, or he would have confessed his part in Charlie's death long ago. He had said he loved her. Had he stretched the truth about that, too? More likely, he just liked sleeping with her, making love to her.

"Stay in town with me, Tess. Don't go back to him. I'll take care of you. You won't have to worry about anything. You can stay at my place and keep house for me."

"Rose doesn't like you, Harry."

Harry snorted. "Rose is stingy with her favors, Tess. Tell me, does she like Stony?"

She hadn't, at first. She loved him now. The thought of how disappointed, how utterly heartbroken her daughter would be if she never saw Stony again, made Tess's throat constrict. It was painful to swallow the bite of pie in her mouth, but somehow she managed it. A tear scalded her cheek as it slid free. She brushed it angrily away. She wasn't about to cry over any man who could so callously lie to her.

She had been a fool again and given her trust to yet another untrustworthy man. Only this time it was infinitely worse. This time the man who had betrayed her held more than her heart. He possessed the other half of her soul.

"Tess, let me comfort you," Harry urged. "Let me take care of you."

"No!" she snarled across the table at him. "The last thing I'd ever do is put my life in another man's keeping. Take me back to Stony's cabin, Harry."

"What for?"

"I want to pack mine and Rose's things."

"Then what?"

"I have a little money saved—my salary for the past four months," she said with a cynical twist of her mouth. "I plan to use it to buy us tickets on the first bus that passes through town."

"Where will you go, Tess?"

"Anywhere that takes me away from here."

## Chapter Six

HARRY WAS INCENSED at the way things were turning out. Not only had he lost his chance of getting Tess Lowell into his bed, but it was likely Stony Carlton was going to show up in the wrong place at the wrong time and spoil a real sweet thing. Damn Charlie Lowell for getting himself killed. The replacement Harry had been forced to hire to run his rustling operation wasn't nearly as reliable or as accessible. Every time he had to make contact with the man it increased the danger of getting caught himself.

It had been damn handy over the past four months having a spy in the enemy camp. Not that Tess had known the role she played. But every time she called on him for a ride into town he had known for sure that Stony was out in the field. He had promptly gotten his band of rustlers out of harm's way.

Only, this time, Stony had left home the very day Harry had scheduled a tractor trailer pickup of stolen beef. Harry wasn't sure he could get in touch with his henchman in time to warn him. He had tried phoning his contact in Jack-

son, but there hadn't been an answer, and he refused to
leave an incriminating message on an answering machine.

Harry had no choice except to drive to the rendezvous
point himself and warn his man off before it was too late.
He didn't want things spoiled too soon. A few more good
runs, and he would have all the money he needed to buy
himself a ranch someplace nice and warm, like Arizona.

When Harry arrived at the rendezvous, he saw the trailer
was already there being loaded. He watched for a long time
from seclusion, making sure there was no sign of the range
detective before he drove down into the valley.

"Hey, boss," his contact said. "What are you doing
here?"

"There's trouble," Harry said. "Stony Carlton is on the
prowl. Take what you've got, and you and your men get
out of here."

"There's only a dozen more head to load, boss. Then
we'll go."

"I said now, and I meant now."

The man opened his mouth to argue before he caught
sight of Harry's hand resting on the butt of his police re-
volver. "Sure, boss. Whatever you say."

It wasn't as simple as it should have been for the truck
to make its escape. The rear wheels had stuck in the mud
caused by melting snow. Harry had only stayed to make
sure the men didn't disobey him, and he was furious when
he realized they were going to have to unload the cattle
already in the truck in order to break it free.

"Get the damn chute back in place," he shouted into the
truck window. "And get those cattle out of there!"

"Not so fast."

Harry whirled and uttered a string of foul expletives.

Stony arched a brow. "Very inventive. Too bad you
couldn't have used a little bit of that intelligence to avoid
getting yourself into this situation in the first place."

Harry started to reach for his gun.

"I wouldn't do that if I were you," Stony said. "I've already had to kill one man in the past year. I'd hate like hell to make it two."

Stony had to keep an eye on the men in the truck, which caused his gaze to waver from Harry for an instant.

"Don't, Harry!" Stony said as Harry reached for his gun.

"I'm not going to jail," Harry said as he drew.

Stony shot to kill. It was what he had been taught. A wounded man with a gun could still shoot back. Harry grabbed his chest as he fell backward, the gun flying from his hand. Harry's bullet caught Stony's sleeve and ripped through a quarter inch of his arm.

Stony ran up to Harry, to kick the gun out of his reach and to see if there was anything he could do for the man. From the corner of his eye he saw the two men in the truck take advantage of his distraction to shove open their doors and run. They wouldn't get far. Help was already on the way.

"Damn you to hell," Harry muttered, clutching at his chest.

Stony knew the wound was serious. He did what he could to staunch the bleeding, but it didn't look good. He saw from the resignation in Harry's eyes that he knew he wasn't going to make it.

"There's an ambulance standing by," Stony said. "The police will call it in as soon as they get here."

"How did you find us out?" Harry asked.

"I've been hunting you for months, watching your patterns. I took a guess where you would hit next." He shrugged. "I was right."

"How did you know to wait for me?" Harry insisted.

Stony's eyes narrowed. "I didn't. If you hadn't shown up when you did, we would never have known about you. Unless your men gave you up."

"Charlie threatened to do that if I didn't give him a bigger share," Harry said. "That's why I had to kill him."

"What?"

"Shot him with a rifle from the hill behind you."

"But I—"

"Your bullet only wounded him. Mine killed him."

"I don't believe you," Stony said.

"Why would I lie?"

"Why would you tell me the truth now?"

"Because I'm dying. Because I owe Charlie Lowell something. Because I like Tess. Ask the coroner, if you need proof. He'll tell you what kind of bullet killed Charlie Lowell."

Stony's eyes narrowed. "You think this will make a difference to Tess?"

Harry tried to laugh, but coughed blood instead. His voice was weaker, and he had to pause often to catch his breath. "I told her you killed Charlie. She hates your guts. Good luck."

"Damn. Oh, damn."

"She leaving you, Stony. She's taking the next bus out of town."

They could hear police sirens in the distance. But the light was already dimming in Harry's eyes.

"Tell Tess I'm sorry," he gasped.

They were the last words Harry said. Stony closed Harry's eyes and stood to wait for the Jackson police to arrive.

It took an interminably long time to point out which way the two rustlers had gone on foot, get his arm bandaged and explain the circumstances of Harry's death. He excused himself as quickly as he could, pleading a family emergency.

It was an emergency. If he didn't hurry, he wasn't going to have any family. He drove like a crazy man along the treacherous curving roads that followed the Hoback River through the mountains from Jackson south to Pinedale.

Stony was glad he hadn't turned out to be the one responsible for Charlie Lowell's death. It would make it easier in later years when Rose was old enough to be told how her father had died. But he had a feeling his innocence wasn't going to help much where Tess was concerned. He had lied to her. Even though he hadn't known it at the time.

He skidded his Jeep to a stop in front of the Buttermilk Café, where the bus that was headed north from Rock Springs along U.S. Route 191 would stop.

She wasn't there.

For a panicked moment he thought the bus had already come and gone. Then he saw a couple of people with traveling bags drinking coffee and realized he had arrived in time.

Except, if she wasn't here, where was she?

He tried several other restaurants within sight of the Buttermilk Café, figuring maybe Tess hadn't wanted to wait there because of Bud. She wasn't in any of them. He thought of Mrs. Feeny's place, but the elderly woman said Tess had picked up Rose around noon. She had no idea where Tess had gone from there.

Stony was getting frantic. Maybe Tess had hitchhiked, caught a ride with some tourist passing through town. Didn't she realize how dangerous that was? Surely she would have rejected such an idea, in consideration of Rose. He felt like going from door to door through town looking for her, but he knew the futility of that.

He realized there was one other place she might be.

As he made the last turn up the winding road to his cabin he saw the smoke coming from the chimney and felt his heart begin to pound.

*Let her be there. Let her be waiting to hear my explanation. Let her be understanding.*

There was no one in the living room when Stony stepped

inside. There was a stew bubbling on the stove with the familiar scents of sage and bay filling the room—and making his senses soar.

He followed the hallway to Rose's room, where he found Tess reading *Little Red Riding Hood*. He saw the moment she realized he was there. Her body tensed, and she hesitated ever so slightly before she continued reading.

"What big teeth you have, Grandma," Tess said.

"The better to eat you with," Stony finished in his best big-bad-wolf voice.

"Stony!" Rose cried.

He opened his arms, and she threw herself into them.

"You're home! You're home! I want to go ride a pony. You promised."

"Yes, I did," Stony said. "As soon as you wake up from your nap, we'll go." He paused and added, "If that's all right with your mother."

"Please, Mama. Oh, please," Rose begged.

Tess kept her back to Stony as she put the book between the pewter bookends on top of the chest. She turned to him at last, and he saw the damage his lies had done.

"Stony and I have to talk, Rose. You take a nap, and we'll decide later whether there's still time for a ride before…dark."

Before…they left?

So she hadn't forgiven him. This was only a respite. His work was still ahead of him, convincing her that she belonged with him. That she could trust him with her life.

And with her love.

Rose started to whine. "I want to ride now."

"Do what your mother said, Rose. Lie down and go to sleep," Stony ordered in a voice the little girl immediately obeyed. He couldn't promise her the ride would come later. He had no idea what Tess would do or say. He had no idea whether the two people he loved most in all the world would still be here at the end of the day.

He followed Tess into the living room and sat with her on the couch. The wood stove was lit to take the chill from the room. They watched the flames through the glass door in silence.

"How can I make you believe you can trust me?" Stony asked at last.

"Why, Stony? Why did you lie?"

He took a breath and let it out. "I was afraid of losing you."

She turned to stare at him. "Did you really kill him, then?"

He shook his head, unsure what to say. "I thought I did. It turns out Harry DuBois actually killed him."

"What?"

"I caught the rustlers I've been hunting since the fall. It turns out Harry was the brains of the outfit. Charlie worked for him. He killed Charlie because Charlie asked for a bigger piece of the action."

"Oh, Charlie. Oh, no," Tess moaned.

He reached for her but she jerked herself out of his way. "Please, don't touch me. Not yet."

He had the terrifying feeling she wasn't going to let him back in, that she was going to shut him out. He kept talking. So long as they were talking nothing was settled.

"The rustlers were so successful eluding me because Harry was informing them every time I came hunting for them. Harry knew what I was doing because whenever I was working you asked him to give you a ride back and forth from town."

"Oh, no!"

"Pretty nifty work on his part, I have to admit."

"I'm sorry if I was responsible—"

"If he hadn't been using you, he would have figured out some other way to keep tabs on me. It's harder to catch the bad guys when the good guys are the bad guys."

She shook her head. "I think I know what you mean."

"About us—"

Tess interrupted him. "I want to believe you lied to me because you were afraid of losing me. I want to forgive you."

"But…"

"But I'm afraid, Stony. I gave you my trust, and you let me down. Just like Charlie."

"I'm not at all like Charlie," Stony countered. "I would never purposely do anything to hurt you. I love you, Tess. I want to marry you."

She gasped and turned wide eyes toward him.

He hadn't known he was going to propose until the words were out of his mouth.

"You must be desperate," she said, the hint of a smile teasing at her lips.

His features remained grim. He wouldn't believe she belonged to him until she said yes. "Will you marry me, Tess?"

"I have a daughter, Stony."

"I know that. I love her, too, Tess. Will you marry me?"

Tess had done a great deal of thinking in the hours since Harry had given her and Tess a ride to Stony's cabin. It was a known fact you could never really tame a wolf. Stony Carlton had been a lone wolf for a very long time.

Still, he had come a long way in the months she had known him, from the man who wanted no commitments, the man who wanted no children, who had rescued her in the Buttermilk Café, to the man who had proposed to her and waited now for her answer.

The truth was, there was a great deal of risk involved in loving any man. She had to choose between loving Stony, and spending her life without him. Given those two choices, she knew what her answer had to be.

"I love you, Stony."

Stony let out a whooshing breath and scooped Tess into

his lap. "Lord, woman, don't ever leave me in suspense like that again!"

Tess tunneled her fingers into the hair at his nape and pulled his face down for her kiss. "Love me, Stony."

"I do, Tess. More than life."

His mouth came down hard on hers, and Tess willingly surrendered to his strength.

"Are you going to marry me?"

"Anytime you want," she said with a grin.

A small head popped up behind the sofa. "Are you going to be my daddy?" Rose asked.

"Rose!" they both exclaimed together.

Rose stood her ground. "Does it?" she demanded.

They looked at each other and grinned. She was a proper wolf's cub, all right—all spit and fight.

Stony grabbed Rose by the arms and dragged her over the top of the sofa into Tess's lap, so he was holding both of them. "Yes," he said. "I'm going to be your daddy. Is that all right?"

"Do I still get to ride a pony?" she asked.

Stony laughed. "Yep. You might even get one of your own."

"Yippee," she said, bouncing up and down. "I'm gonna have a daddy *and* a pony!"

"You have a nap to finish first, young lady," Stony admonished. "And where are your slippers?" he asked, catching her bare feet in his hands.

Rose slipped out of Tess's lap. "I'm gonna go take a nap," she said. "So I don't need any slippers."

She was gone an instant later.

"Good Lord," Stony said. "Do you suppose they'll all be like that?"

"All? How many did you have in mind?" Tess asked.

"At least one more," he said. "If that's all right with you."

"I'd love to have your baby—as many babies as you'd like."

"Come here, Tess. I want you."

His eyes were feral, dangerous. The predatory beast was back, wanting her, loving her, a lone wolf who had finally found his mate. Some other woman might have tried to tame him, but Tess was perfectly satisfied with the wily rogue who had claimed her for his own.

\*   \*   \*   \*   \*

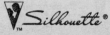

In December 1999
three spectacular authors invite you to share the
romance of the season as three special gifts are

# Delivered by Christmas

## A heartwarming holiday anthology featuring

### BLUEBIRD WINTER
by *New York Times* bestselling author
# Linda Howard

*A baby* is about to be born on the side of the road. The single
mother's only hope rests in the strong arms of a dashing doctor....

### And two brand-new stories:

### THE GIFT OF JOY
by national bestselling author **Joan Hohl**

*A bride* was not what a Texas-Ranger-turned-rancher was
expecting for the holidays. Will his quest for a home lead to love?

### A CHRISTMAS TO TREASURE
by award-winning author **Sandra Steffen**

*A daddy* is all two children want for Christmas. And the
handsome man upstairs may be just the hero their mommy needs!

*Give yourself the gift of romance in
this special holiday collection!*

*Available at your favorite retail outlet.*

## THE FORTUNES OF TEXAS

*Membership in this family has
its privileges...and its price.
But what a fortune can't buy,
a true-bred Texas love is sure to bring!*

**Coming in December 1999...**

# A Willing Wife by

# JACKIE MERRITT

Dallas Fortune lived alone and liked it that way. So he
was shocked by the deep emotions single mother
Maggie Perez and her young son awakened within him.
But would the eligible rancher's wounded heart allow
him to join this ready-made family?

**In January 2000
THE FORTUNES OF TEXAS continues with
CORPORATE DADDY by Arlene James.**

Available at your favorite retail outlet.

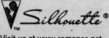

Silhouette®

Visit us at www.romance.net

PSFOT4

# LINDSAY McKENNA
## continues her heart-stopping series:

### Coming in October 1999:
### HUNTER'S PRIDE
Special Edition #1274

Devlin Hunter had a way with the ladies, but when it
came to his job as a mercenary, the brooding bachelor
worked alone. Then his latest assignment paired him up
with Kulani Dawson, a feisty beauty whose tender
vulnerabilities brought out his every protective instinct—
and chipped away at his proud vow never to fall in love....

### Coming in January 2000:
### THE UNTAMED HUNTER
Silhouette Desire #1262

Rock-solid Shep Hunter was unconquerable—until his
mission brought him face-to-face with Dr. Maggie Harper,
the woman who'd walked away from him years ago.
Now Shep struggled to keep strong-willed Maggie under
his command without giving up the steel-clad grip on
his heart....

Look for Inca's story when Lindsay McKenna continues
the MORGAN'S MERCENARIES series with a brand-new,
longer-length single title—coming in 2000!

*Available at your favorite retail outlet.*

Start celebrating Silhouette's 20th anniversary
with these 4 special titles by
*New York Times* bestselling authors

*Fire and Rain*
**by Elizabeth Lowell**

*King of the Castle*
**by Heather Graham Pozzessere**

*State Secrets*
**by Linda Lael Miller**

*Paint Me Rainbows*
**by Fern Michaels**

On sale in December 1999

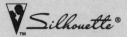